COLLECTION

VOLUME
—9—

THE Regency COLLECTION

VOLUME
—9—

A Biddable Girl?
by
Paula Marshall

The Wolf's Promise
by
Alice Thornton

*MILLS & BOON and MILLS & BOON with the Rose Device
are registered trademarks of the publisher.*

*First published in Great Britain 1999 by
Harlequin Mills & Boon Limited,
Eton House, 18–24 Paradise Road,
Richmond, Surrey, TW9 1SR.*

The Regency Collection © by Harlequin Enterprises II B.V. 1999

The publisher acknowledges the copyright holders of the
individual work as follows:

A Biddable Girl? © Paula Marshall 1996
The Wolf's Promise © Alice Thornton 1996

ISBN 0 263 82353 9
106-0001

*Printed and bound in Spain
by Litografía Rosés S.A., Barcelona*

A BIDDABLE GIRL?

by

Paula Marshall

Dear Reader

When I began to write historical romances for Mills &
Boon®, I chose the Regency period for several reasons.
I had always enjoyed Georgette Heyer's novels—still
among the best—and had spent part of my youth
working at Newstead Abbey, the home of Lord Byron,
one of the Regency's most colourful characters. It
involved me in reading many of the original letters and
papers of a dynamic era in English history.

Later on when I researched even further into the
period I discovered that nothing I could invent was
more exciting—or outrageous—than what had actually
happened! What more natural, then, than to write a
Regency romance and send it to Mills & Boon—who
accepted it and started me on a new career.

Like Georgette Heyer I try to create fiction out of
and around fact for the enjoyment and entertainment
of myself and my readers. It is often forgotten that the
Regency men had equally powerful wives, mothers and
sisters—even if they had no public role—so I make my
heroines able to match my heroes in their wit and
courage.

Paula Marshall

Paula Marshall, married with three children, has had a varied and interesting life. She began her career in a large library and ended it as a senior academic in charge of history teaching in a polytechnic. She has travelled widely, has been a swimming coach, embroiders, paints pictures and has appeared on *University Challenge* and *Mastermind*. She has always wanted to write, and likes her novels to be full of adventure and humour.

Other titles by the same author:

CHAPTER ONE

'MY DEAR Constantia, how like Papa. Inconsiderate in life, how should we expect him to be any different in death? To leave his estate in trust at the lawyers, and the will only to be read at the end of six months to give a chance for Jack to be traced. Now the six months is up, the will is to be read today, and all is still at sixes and sevens. I suppose there is no news of Jack? Useless to expect that, too. I am astonished that Papa wished him to be found after what happened twelve years ago.'

The Lady Constantia Maxwell, the speaker's sister—they were the daughters of the late Earl Devereux—who was always a little timid in the presence of her dominant elder twin, Amelia, Lady Thaxted, answered her as placatingly as she could.

'No need to worry, I am sure. My dear Edward says it is highly unlikely that Jack is still in the land of the living. Gone to the devil long ago, most likely. The estates not being entailed, Papa is sure to have left everything away from him. And since Jack was the very last male heir, if he is dead, the title will die with him.'

Lady Amelia preened herself a little as she listened to these reassuring words. As the wife of an inordinately rich peer who was only a baron, she was certain that her father would have left things so that she, and not Constantia, would inherit the lion's share of the well-endowed Devereux estates. If so, it would almost certainly mean that when the next round of new peers was created, the Devereux title would be resurrected so as to raise her husband to it.

'I am sure that we cannot wish that Jack is dead,'
she said, holding a handkerchief to a dry eye, for it
would not be proper openly to rejoice that a brother's
death was needed to bring about such a desired outcome, 'but seeing that no one has seen hide nor hair
of him since Papa turned him out and disinherited
him, and Thaxted says that so far the lawyers have
been unable to trace him, we must assume the worst, I
fear. Which brings me to another matter,' she finished
meaningfully.

Constantia, well aware of what her sister was thinking, mused sadly on the bright little boy that Jack had
been, so unlike his serious and censorious elder
brother Philip, dead these three years after a riding
accident. Such a pity that Jack had become so wild
that their father had seen fit to turn him out so
summarily after that mysterious business at the time
of their mother's sudden death.

She and Amelia had been nearly ten years older
than Philip, and fifteen years had separated them from
Jack. Their mother had been only eighteen when they
were born. And what was this 'other matter' of which
Amelia was hinting?

'Which matter?' she asked plaintively.

'The Scrap, of course.'

'The Scrap?'

Lady Thaxted was impatient with her echo.
'Cassandra Merton, of course. It is what Thaxted calls
her. Such a scrap of a thing. If Papa has made no
provision for her, what in the world are we to do with
her? I am sure that I do not wish for a plain stick to
be hung around my neck, to be found a dowry and
hawked about. I am equally sure that you and Edward
will not wish to be saddled with her, either.' She
sighed. 'I wonder why Papa chose to bring her into his
household. He never took the slightest notice of her,
and no wonder.'

'Papa never took the slightest notice of anyone but himself,' said Constantia, a trifle mutinously. 'But you are wrong, Amelia. He did take notice of her during the last six months of his life.'

'Well, that doesn't help us now. Nearly nineteen, is she not? And still has old Strood to wait on her, even though she no longer needs a governess. A fine waste of money. Turn Strood away, I say, and send the Scrap to be companion to old Cousin Flora. She was complaining in her last letter to me that her companion needed pensioning off—she is growing deaf and foolish.'

Since Cousin Flora could also be called deaf and foolish, this suggestion seemed a trifle harsh on the companion, and even harsher on the Scrap.

'No hope of marrying her off, then?' Constantia ventured. She was never as hard-hearted as her sister.

But Amelia was not listening to her. She was looking around the library. 'The first thing I shall do when we take over,' she announced firmly, 'is improve Devereux House. This room, for instance, has grown most shabby. Papa had become too much the recluse, Thaxted says. We have plans for the estates, as well. They sadly need improvement. Papa's agents are living in the Dark Ages—they will have to go too, and soon.'

She smiled complacently as she uttered these cruel words and added, 'That's all settled, then. I shall write to Cousin Flora as soon as the will is read. The child ought to be grateful that we have settled matters so well for her.'

Out of sight of the two women so callously arranging her future, and that of other helpless subordinates, the Scrap, Cassandra Merton, sat up indignantly, her colour coming and going, her dark eyes—her best feature—glowing with anger.

She shouldn't, of course, have been in the library

to hear what was being said by the great ones of her world. She should have been sitting in the small drawing-room, primly doing her canvaswork—a singularly boring thing showing improbably huge cabbage roses on a dull beige ground. Instead, Cass had borrowed Lady Thaxted's copy of *Sophia*, that delightful novel By a Lady which she was not supposed to read—but was, avidly, every forbidden word. . .and wondering why they were forbidden!

The best place to hide herself, she had discovered long ago, was on the wide window-ledge in the library behind the thick damask curtains, where the light was good and she had a splendid view of the gardens of Devereux House, just off Piccadilly. She was so well concealed that anyone who cared to look for her inevitably gave up, and assumed that she had retired to her poky room on the fourth floor, just below the attics where the servants were housed, next door to the old schoolroom.

Which, Cassandra always told herself severely, was her just and proper place, since she was that unconsidered, in-between thing, a poor relation of no consequence given a home by the late Earl Devereux. He had felt a duty towards the only remaining sprig of a branch of the family which had broken away from the main trunk over a hundred years ago.

'Call me cousin, my dear Cassandra,' he had told her on the first occasion on which they had met, even though their cousinship was such a distant thing.

Just twelve years old and shaking a little in her shabby shoes, she had gulped a 'Yes, sir' back at him, and that had been that. He had hardly spoken to her again until his last illness, when he had surprisingly sought her company, asking her to read to him because his sight was rapidly failing.

But, in those early years, for her to call so cold and grand a person 'cousin' would have been beyond her.

So, all in all, it was fortunate that their paths had seldom crossed, since until the end of it she had always lived in the background of his busy life.

And now he was dead of apoplexy, or of disappointment that he had never achieved office in Lord Liverpool's government which had so recently consigned the late Emperor Napoleon to exile on St Helena. Lord Devereux's place of exile had been the backbenches of the House of Lords.

Cass had been reading *Sophia* partly so as not to think what would become of her now that her protector was dead. His married daughters, the Ladies Amelia and Constantia, both disapproved of her, she was sure, and had never shown her the slightest affection. The only source of *that* was her one-time governess, now her companion, Miss Emma Strood, who would doubtless soon be fussing around, trying to discover where she had vanished to.

The sisters had launched into their conversation so briskly that Cass had had no time to emerge from her hiding place and inform them of her presence. And once they had begun to speak of such confidential matters as their father's will and her own abrupt disposal it was too late. It would be highly embarrassing to all parties if she were to reveal that she had overheard their plans for her.

And such plans! How unkind of them to speak of her so! And if Lord Devereux had not shown her much affection, at least he had been willing to give her a home—which was more than either of his daughters was apparently prepared to do.

And Jack, the Earl's missing son. Where was he? In all the six years during which she had lived in Devereux House and at the Earl's big country mansion at Coverham on the Yorkshire moors, no one had ever mentioned the name of Jack Devereux to her,

other than to hint that he had mortally offended his
father.

She had known the Honourable Philip Devereux,
the heir, who had, like his sisters, disapproved of her
as she had disapproved of him. He had never called
her the Scrap, though. That piece of cruelty had been
left for Lady Thaxted and her husband to commit.
They had been constant visitors to Devereux House
and Coverham, and the nickname had hurt her more
than she could have believed possible.

She had seen much less of Lady Constantia and her
husband, Edward Maxwell, since they were settled on
Mr Edward Maxwell's estates in Westmorland. They
had rapidly travelled south when the news arrived that
Lord Devereux, who had turned into a fretful hypo-
chondriac, was dead.

The vultures, thought Cass unkindly, always gathered about a corpse and, from what she had overheard
both the Thaxteds and the Maxwells were certainly
vultures. If Jack, who would be the new Earl
Devereux, was still alive and had not immediately
arrived to claim his supposed dues when his father had
died, then that must be counted in his favour.

Cass wondered exactly what it was that Jack had
done which was so terrible that it had resulted in
banishment. As she pondered on this she heard the
door close. The sisters had gone—leaving her to her
book. But, alas, the realities of her own life and those
of the Devereux family now had more claim on Cass's
interest than the fiction which was *Sophia*.

She would ask Miss Strood about Jack Devereux.

But Miss Strood was nowhere to be found. Like
Cass, she was undoubtedly dodging the two Ugly
Sisters, as Cassandra had irreverently dubbed Lady
Thaxted and Lady Constantia Maxwell since she had
overheard them in the library. She had probably

sought refuge in the housekeeper's room, and was taking tea there, leaving Cass to her own devices.

Cass made her way to the beautiful front hall where stood the small fountain brought from Bologna by the third Earl, the late Earl's father. The paintings by Tintoretto which adorned the walls had been acquired by the second Earl on his Grand Tour. If Jack—or was it John?—Devereux brought anything back with him, when and if he was found, it was to be hoped that they would not be Tintorettos. He was far from being Cass's favourite painter.

What foolish things to think of! She had no more idea than the man in the moon what the missing Jack Devereux might be doing or what he might be like. It would be much more sensible to visit the housekeeper's room and see if Mrs James would consent to give her a cup of tea. Her room had been a refuge for Cass when she had first come to Devereux House, but since she had reached the the ripe old age of almost nineteen Miss Strood had gently suggested that it was not proper for Miss Merton to hobnob with servants, even superior ones like Mrs James herself.

Well, pooh to that today! She much preferred Mrs James, even if she were only the housekeeper, to either of the two great ladies who had disposed of her so callously. She was to walk poodles, was she? Or read religious tracts to a deaf old woman—for she knew that Cousin Flora was of the Methodistical persuasion, adhering to the Countess of Huntingdon's connexion. 'A most genteel mode of worship', she had told Cass some years ago, on her one visit to Devereux House.

Mrs James welcomed her warmly. She thought that Miss Merton looked a trifle wan and, ignoring the slight disapproval on Miss Strood's face, she immediately put her big copper kettle on the fire to make a fresh pot of China tea. She also set out her most delicate porcelain cup and saucer, produced a plate of biscuits baked only that afternoon, and sat Cass down in her most comfortable armchair.

'Miss Strood, why does no one ever speak of Jack Devereux?' questioned Cass, after she had drunk her tea.

The reaction of the two women was interesting. Mrs James shook her head and Miss Strood primmed her mouth. 'My dear child. . .' Miss Strood's diction was even more formal than usual as she answered Cass. 'He was Lord Devereux's younger son, who was disinherited and turned out without a penny twelve years ago for being wild. Something to do with stolen money or property, I believe. It happened before my time here. I do know that m'lord ordered that his name should never be mentioned again by anyone, either servant or family, on pain of dismissal or banishment.'

'I gathered that,' interjected Cass inelegantly, her mouth full of biscuit. 'But what exactly did he do?'

It soon became apparent that neither the housekeeper nor Miss Strood really knew why the Earl's younger son had been turned away. 'He was reputed to be a very wild young man,' admitted Miss Strood at last, 'not at all like Mr Philip. *He* was very steady.'

'Too steady.' Mrs James, who was normally a comfortable soul, was acid. 'I liked Master Jack; he always had a friendly word for us all. Mr Philip, now, he took everything we did for him for granted.'

'There's not so much as a picture of him anywhere,' Cass commented.

'Oh, m'lord had them all taken down. I remember that there was one splendid portrait of him as a very young man, done before he and m'lord were at outs. It was taken up to the attic. He had his pet hawk on his arm. He always loved animals, did Master Jack. Mr Philip, now, he couldn't abide them.'

'Oh, *that* portrait,' offered Cass, without thinking.

She had gone up to the attics beyond the servants' rooms one day when she was bored. She had looked out of the small windows across London and then had explored among the broken boxes and old furniture and the paintings propped against the walls.

Curious, she had turned some of them around. They had been mostly brown with age, as though good gravy had been poured over them, but she had come to one which had held her entranced. She had been fourteen at the time and had fallen in love with the unknown and handsome young man pictured inside the ornate gilt frame. She had thought that he resembled every hero in the Minerva Press novels which Miss Strood had recently and reluctantly allowed her to read.

He was tall and shapely, with long legs, russet-coloured hair and curious greeny-yellow eyes. He wore a fashionable version of country clothing: his jacket was green and his pantaloons, descending into highly polished boots, were a deep cream. But it was his smile and his rapt attention to the hawk on his outstretched wrist which had held Cass in thrall.

She could believe that the pictured young man had been wild, for she had thought that he resembled his hawk, but she could not believe that he would do anything wicked enough to deserve being turned away for ever from his home and family. She couldn't believe that he was dead, either, whatever Lord Thaxted had said. He had seemed so alive and kicking—a favourite saying of Geordie, the groom who had looked after her pony when she had been a little girl before she had lost her parents and been taken in by the Earl.

There had been some enchantment in the portrait which had wrought its magic on Cass, so that whenever she had been bored or lonely she had gone up to the attic, had turned the painting around and had sat before it so that she could imagine that the hero in the novel she had been reading looked exactly like him.

Miss Strood said coolly, 'So, Cass, you found it when you were exploring in the attics?'

Cass, surprised into a reversion to her childhood—which was not, after all, so far off—put her hand before her mouth and then, taking it away with a rueful grin, said, 'You knew, dear Stroody?'

'Of course, but it seemed a harmless enough way for you to pass a dull afternoon, and I could have a nap in peace.'

Fellow conspirators against the dull and proper regime laid down for Cass by the late Earl, they grinned at one another.

'I feel let down and cheated,' announced Cass dramatically, reaching for yet another biscuit. 'There I was, thinking that I was rebelling against you and the Earl, and you knew all the time what I was up to.'

'And about the window-seat in the library too,' Miss Strood agreed, taking a biscuit in her turn. 'Mr Hunt told me about that.'

Mr Hunt was the Earl's librarian. He and Miss Strood had arranged a course of reading for her; having improved the schoolgirl French which Miss Strood had taught her, Mr Hunt had recently been introducing her to Latin.

She was aware of Miss Strood and the housekeeper smiling kindly at her; Cass knew that without them and Mr Hunt her life would have been barren indeed. And, shortly, she would be losing them all for good. Poor plain Scrap, to be disposed of like an unwanted picture: not turned towards the wall, but sent to be companion to a cross-grained old woman. The only wish that she had left before she was retired from life forever was that she might meet Jack Devereux, to find out what he looked like twelve years after his portrait had been painted. If he were alive, that was.

Cass was just about to take another biscuit, despite Stroody's disapproving eye—she always asserted that if Cass indulged her overlarge appetite she would become fat, despite Cass remaining obstinately and painfully thin whatever she ate—when there was a knock on the door and Mr Greene the butler, came in.

'Beg pardon, ladies—' he bowed, '—but Miss Strood and Miss Merton are required to attend on Lord and Lady Thaxted, and Lady Constantia and Mr Edward Maxwell in the library. It seems that the reading of the late Earl's will is to take place this afternoon. Lord Thaxted was most particular that all the members of the late lord's household should be present. That, of course, means you, Mrs James.'

What a to-do followed! Mrs James and Miss Strood at once declared that they were not properly attired to be present at such an important occasion. Cass, dressed in a drab grey high-waisted poplin gown of indeterminate style, with a small Quakerish linen collar, could not have cared less what she was wearing.

Miss Strood wailed at Mr Greene, 'Is there no time for Miss Merton and myself to change into something more *comme il faut*?'

A shaking head from Mr Greene stifled Miss Strood's complaints—to Cass's relief. Nothing was more calculated to induce boredom in her than to be constantly changing one's clothes—particularly when one had a wardrobe as limited as Cass's. To change from drab grey to dull brown, and both outdated, was hardly her notion of passing an exciting afternoon.

So, at least one person following Mr Greene to the big withdrawing room was happy. Further happiness for Cass would consist of being in the library with Mr Hunt, spending a pleasant afternoon with him and his book learning.

Once they reached the library they found that Lord Thaxted was thoroughly in charge of everything. Quite why this was so Cass was at a loss to understand. True, he was the husband of Amelia, the late Earl's elder daughter, but until the will was read no one could know whether that entitled him to give orders so grandly around Devereux House.

She said as much to Miss Strood, who replied in a shocked tone, 'It is not for very young ladies to question such things, Cassandra. You grow above yourself.' She only called Cass Cassandra when she was really cross with her, so Cass said no more, simply contented herself with thinking all the things which she was apparently not to say, but which so obviously needed to be said. No need to distress poor Stroody overmuch—particularly when they were so shortly to lose one another.

It was plain that she was unable to please anyone since, when they reached the library, Lord Thaxted, who was already there with a small covey of legal gentlemen standing deferentially by him, glared impatiently at her late arrival. But was it Cass's imagination or was there a gleam in the most import- ant legal gentleman's eye which had a touch of the satiric in it? Cass had discovered some time ago that she could, if not exactly read minds, understand or feel what people were actually thinking rather than what they ought to be thinking.

Chairs had been set out, and they were all directed to sit in them by Mr Greene. Cass was at the back, almost out of sight behind the senior servants and the Thaxteds and Maxwells. She thought that the gleam in the chief lawyer's eye grew brighter when, once they were all seated, Lord Thaxted, a portly man with a rubicund face, announced brusquely, 'Get on with it, man, what are you waiting for? After all, you have had six months to prepare for this day!'

The chief lawyer, a Mr Herriot as Cass was later to discover, bowed, a little too humbly, she thought— more secret satire from him, perhaps? In as neutral a voice as he could manage, he murmured, 'With all due deference, m'lord. . .' a phrase which Cass, despite her youth, knew really meant the exact opposite of what was being said.

'With all due deference, my lord,' he repeated, 'we must wait a moment before the remaining member of the party arrives.'

'Now who the devil can that be?' roared Lord Thaxted, whilst his wife looked daggers at both the lawyers and the company. 'Are we not all assembled here?'

'Not quite,' riposted Mr Herriot with a smirk; as though on cue, the door at the far end of the library opened—the secret door between two tiers of book-shelves which gave access to the late Lord Devereux's study—and two men entered by it.

At the sight of them Lord Thaxted almost bellowed, 'By God, no. I refuse to countenance this.'

No wonder, thought Cass, for the first man who came in resembled no one whom Cass had ever met before, either in appearance or in his clothing.

He was very tall, broad-shouldered, slim-hipped and long-legged. His clothing was shabby in the extreme. He wore a pair of elderly bottle-green trousers, not pantaloons, above heavily scuffed black half-boots. His jacket, also shabby, was a long wide-skirted navy blue one, with large brass buttons of the kind which sailors on shore wore. His shirt was clean—had once been white, but much washing had frayed it and had turned it cream. His cravat was simply a black silk scarf, loosely knotted so that the ends hung down in front of his disastrous shirt.

But it was his face which drew everyone's attention. It was the hardest and coldest which Cass had ever seen. So hard and cold and harsh, indeed, that it made the appearance of every other man whom she had ever met seem soft and womanish. His hair was a deep browny-red, long, and tied back in the manner of the late eighteenth century. His nose was as aquiline as a hawk's or an eagle's, and his mouth was a grim straight line, frightening in its severity.

But it was his eyes which told the fascinated Cass at whom she was staring. They were a feral greeny-yellow beneath straight black brows—they were those of the handsome young man in the portrait in the attic! Here was Jack Devereux at last! So shocked was she by him and by his changed appearance that Cass did not even see the large square man who followed him like his shadow.

For a moment after Lord Thaxted's bellow there was a deathly silence. Then the grim man before them spoke. 'Who the devil are all of you?' he demanded in a parade-ground voice. 'What are you doing in my house? I want the whole pack of you, except the servants, out of here in the hour.'

CHAPTER TWO

ANOTHER deathly silence followed before there was a clamour of raised voices. Lord Thaxted jumped to his feet, bawling, 'And who are you, I should like to know, to give orders here? And you, sir,' he now roared at the lawyer, who was doubtless, Cass thought, grinning behind his impassive mask. 'Why have you brought this. . .creature here to insult us all?'

Mr Herriot replied, his voice sounding as though he occupied an island of calm in an ocean of storm, 'No creature, m'lord, but the proven and undoubted John Augustus, fifth Earl Devereux, present because, on the instructions of the late Earl, he was traced and found, and the will was read to him, as the late Earl so ordered, in my office earlier this morning. He has, as his words to you have indicated, inherited all, with one proviso of which I am instructed to inform you, as well as some details concerning his bequests to a number of old servants.'

Further clamour ensued. Amelia announced that she had no intention of being left high and dry by her father, who must have been in his dotage to do such a thing as disinherit her, whilst Constantia staged an elegant swoon, falling half across her husband. Lord Thaxted, his face turning even more purple than usual, announced loudly, 'Have you run mad, man? You have said nothing to me of this either before or after my late father-in-law's death. No word that my wife and her sister were to inherit nothing.'

Jack Devereux's thick brows rose. He was lounging against one of the pillars which upheld the painted library ceiling, a sardonic expression on his face, apparently content to let his lawyer speak once he had thrown his thunderbolt at them.

Nothing loath, Mr Herriot began again, after giving a short apologetic cough. 'M'lord, I did try to warn you to take nothing for granted about the disposition of the late Earl Devereux's estate, but you chose to ignore me. I could not make myself completely plain because to have done so would have been to go against his instructions—which I was legally bound to follow—to divulge nothing until the will had been read to the new Earl.'

The company thought that he had paused, but he had not. He gave another apologetic little cough and said no more.

Edward Maxwell, that mild and lethargic man, spoke at last. Since the late Earl's death he had been content to let his more dominant brother-in-law take the lead. Lord Thaxted having been reduced to help-less splutterings, he now chose to comment.

'And that is all?' he asked. 'We are to learn no more?'

Jack Devereux, still lounging against the pillar, said in his harsh, commanding voice,'Have you grown deaf, sir? My man here plainly said that there was a little more to it than that I had, surprisingly, I agree, inherited everything. Were you to cease badgering him he might inform you of the rest. He might also read to you what my late father had to say of you, but I would advise that you did not ask him to do so. You might not like what you heard.'

'I like nothing about this,' bellowed Thaxted, stand-ing up now, his chair thrust behind him. 'Particularly you, yourself. Where the devil have you been for the last twelve years? Are you, sir—' and he addressed the lawyer now '—completely certain that this... rogue. . .is truly Jack Devereux?'

'The fact that you consider me a rogue,' Jack said

coolly, his feral eyes glowing, 'would doubtless seem to confirm that I am the unwanted Jack, wouldn't you say? You undoubtedly thought me a rogue years ago, when I was more conventionally attired and bespoke—did you imagine that I might have changed?'

Whatever Cass had thought Jack Devereux might be like, she could not have imagined the man who stood before them. If everyone else was behaving exactly as she would have expected them to—including Miss Strood, who was whimpering into her handkerchief, 'Oh, Cass, if he turns us out, wherever shall we go?'— then he, at least, was proving a surprise. Hardly a pleasant one, perhaps, but none the less a surprise. As troubled as Miss Strood about her possible future, Cass was, nevertheless, finding the whole scene as good as a play.

And one which she was having the pleasure of appreciating without the chief character in it even being aware that she was present. Seated at the back behind the large chef and the equally large Mr Greene, she was sure that Jack Devereux and his silent shadow—and who was he?—did not even know that she existed.

What he would do when he learned that the late Earl had taken her into his home and kept her for the last six years, she couldn't imagine. Presumably he had not seen fit to mention her in his will. Unless, of course, he had counted her as one of the servants— but she didn't think that he had.

And, in their disappointment, how merciful to her would Amelia and Constantia be? Suddenly, the banishment to Cousin Flora, which had seemed so terrible, might now be viewed as some sort of a lifeline! To this had she been reduced in a few short minutes.

She would have to collect her wandering thoughts; Lord Thaxted had been persuaded to sit down, although Jack was still lounging against his pillar, and Mr Herriot had taken the will from its parchment envelope and was reading from it that the late Earl had left everything to his supposedly lost heir, John Augustus Devereux. . .

At this point the lawyer paused dramatically. Oh, yes, Cass decided, suppressing a nervous giggle, he was undoubtedly enjoying himself, with all his recent tormentors at his mercy.

He resumed, '. . .with one condition, that, since I have decided that I do not wish the name and title of Devereux to become extinct, my son John shall have conditional charge of all that I die possessed of for the duration of three months only, during which time he must immediately take to himself a wife. From that moment on, he shall inherit unconditionally all of which I die possessed. If, however, he chooses not to marry, then everything will revert to the Crown, for I have no desire to enrich those whose sole interest in me has been to inherit that which I may leave, and who could scarcely wait for me to die to do so.

'It is my last dying wish that my son John will do as I beg of him, and thus ensure the continuation of the Devereux line.'

'He was mad,' announced Amelia dramatically, 'quite mad. He must have been to recall and reward after such a fashion the son whom he once threw off. . . And why should he have thought that Jack would oblige him. . .? He had never done so before.

Jack took his hands out his pockets, abandoned his lounging position and walked to stand beside the lawyer. 'Oh, but I am determined to do so,' he announced pleasantly, his grin as feral as his eyes. 'It is, you must all agree, worth saddling one's self with a wife in order to inherit such a prize. Certainly you all thought it worth while to spend the best part of your lives dancing attendance on him in order to inherit, so you can't criticise me for snapping up what is mine by right.

'I have already decided that I shall ask the first marriageable woman whom I meet to become my wife. I don't doubt that she, too, will think that being the Countess Devereux will be worth the pains of having me for a husband!'

This came out with such sincere and good-natured savagery that Cass felt like applauding—or would have done if her own position had not been so precarious.

'And in the meantime,' Jack continued, still in the same pleasantly savage tone, 'I meant what I said. I want the pack of you out of here. I've changed my mind and will give you until tomorrow morning. To insist on you going on the instant would discommode your servants more than you, and they don't deserve that of me, even though the rest of you do. And, speaking of the servants, Mr Herriot, let us hear the rest of the will.'

It was read in silence. M'lord had been more than generous to those who had been his retainers for so long, but, as Cass had half expected, there was no mention of her.

As he finished, Mr Herriot folded the will and laid it on the desk before him. 'Has anyone any questions of me, before I take my leave?' he asked. 'If so, pray put them now. We shall save a deal of time.'

Beside Cass, Miss Strood, who had also not been mentioned, was quietly sobbing. For where would she and poor Cassandra go now? Cast to the winds, first by the old Earl and now by the new—for like Cass she was bitterly aware that they could expect no help from the passed-over Ugly Sisters now.

No one said a word. Cass, suddenly aware that were she to say nothing, nothing might be what she gained, stood up before she had time to be afraid of being unladylike and drawing attention to herself.

'Mr Herriot,' she asked, 'am I to understand that
the late Earl Devereux made no provision for my
companion, Miss Strood, and myself, Miss Cassandra
Merton, in his will? And, if so, pray will you tell us
where we may be expected to go, if we are to leave by
tomorrow morning, as the new Lord Devereux
wishes?'

She had the pleasure of seeing Jack Devereux's
head swing sharply to where she had appeared
between the twin bulks of the chef and Greene—both
of whom m'lord had remembered, whilst forgetting
her. She had not wished to beg, but Jack Devereux
had been so plain-spoken that he could hardly complain if such an insignificant creature as herself should
also make her position as clear as he was making his.
Oh, yes, such a mannerless lout of a fellow deserved
nothing more than that those who had to suffer him
should be as brusque as he was.

The heads of Amelia, Constantia and their spouses
also swung round. Amelia began angrily, 'Well,
really—' before Jack Devereux rudely interrupted her.

'Now, who the devil have we here?' he demanded
of the lawyer, in the parade-ground voice which he
had used earlier. 'Who is neither relative, nor servant,
and of whom I have no knowledge?'

Mr Herriot took him by the sleeve and whispered
quickly and urgently into his ear; Jack Devereux nodded as he spoke. Then he began to speak equally
quickly and urgently to the lawer, one hand outstretched, the other ticking off points on his fingers, as
though he were issuing instructions.

Mr Herriot looked across to where Cass was still
standing, although Miss Strood had tried to pull her
back into her seat by tugging at her gown. Cass had
resolutely refused to oblige her. With no one to defend
her she must defend herself, or go homeless into the
street. To do—what? It did not bear thinking of.

She watched whilst, under his breath, Mr Herriot began to remonstrate with Jack, but nothing he was saying seemed to register with him, for he was shaking his head and smiling. He pushed the lawyer away and said aloud, 'Enough! I have made up my mind. Miss Merton, I wonder if you would do me the honour of joining me here?'

Uproar followed again. None of it touched Cass. She had begun to live in a world gone mad as everything that had underpinned her life collapsed about her. If that was what the monster before her wanted, then she would do as he wished. She pushed her way along the row of curious servants to emerge into the aisle and walk coolly up it towards where Jack, his lawyer and his shadow stood.

She thought that Jack's shadow gave her a shrewd and a pitying stare, but she had no time for that. She gave the new Earl a bow, not a deferential one, but as from one equal to another for, however much he intimidated others, she would not allow him to intimidate her.

Now that she was near to him she could see the returned prodigal more clearly. He had, she noted, shaved very carefully, even if the rest of him was farouche. Though he was shabby, he was spotlessly clean, as was the hand he had placed over his heart when he had bowed to her. It was square and strong; his fingers were spatulate and his nails were cut short, but had been carefully trimmed. There was a deep wave in the reddy-brown hair, and that, too, was clean.

Some intuition, some knowledge of the truth rather than what others wished to be considered the truth, told Cass several things. First and foremost, what Jack Devereux was wearing was not necessarily the clothing he usually wore. Secondly, she also knew that whatever Jack Devereux was now, he had once been a soldier.

He resembled nothing so much as the portrait of the *condottiere*, an Italian mercenary captain of the early fifteenth century, which hung in the library. There was the same expression in his feral cat's eyes, in the set of his body, in the uncompromising thrust of his stern mouth. He was ready for instant action. Worse, the instant action he was ready for now was to do with her.

But she must not flinch as his eyes took her in: her slightness, her smallness, her plainish face, her undistinguished brown hair, the whole aura of permanent poor relation which she and her clothing gave off. Cass thought that she hated him as she watched him so ruthlessly catalogue what she was, the predatory eyes roving over her. He began to speak, and his first remark surprised her, for it was a question.

'Exactly how old are you, Miss Merton?'

'I shall be nineteen in a month, m'lord.'

He shook his head at her. 'Not, m'lord, Miss Merton, Jack.'

Cass nodded. Oh, yes, he was a bully, as she had realised from the first moment he had walked into the room. When he said 'Jump' in that gravel voice, he expected people to jump. But she would not jump for him.

Something in her attitude must have reached him, for he said softly, 'I do not intend to hurt you—quite the contrary. . .' His voice tailed off and he was cataloguing her again. 'I have another question for you, Miss Merton. Think carefully before you answer me. You heard the will read just now?'

Why should that need a careful answer?

Nevertheless, she paused a moment before replying, 'Yes, Jack.'

'And you understood what the will said? That I must marry before three months are up?'

Cass said, 'Yes, Jack,' again. What could he be getting at?

'And you have no home, now that you have lost this one. My father saw fit virtually to adopt you, but did not see fit to leave you the means of living after his death?'

Cass repeated, 'Yes, Jack,' again, but her face said quite plainly, why should you be asking me questions to which you already know the answer? She was aware that behind her the assembled family and servants of the late Earl were hanging on his words, as baffled as she was.

'I should like to offer you a home, Miss Merton.'

Salvation, surely. But Cass did not like the gleam in his strange eyes.

'Have you nothing to say, Miss Merton, to my kind offer?'

He was mocking her now. But she was equal to him. She was resolved always to be equal to him if she were to be a dependant of the new Earl as of the old, since being unequal with the old Earl had left her abandoned to the world.

'I suppose, Jack, from the manner in which you speak to me that there is a condition attached to this offer. I should like to know what it is.'

She would also have liked to know what he was thinking, although the knowledge would not have pleased her. Miss Skin and Bones is a shrewd piece, being his silent verdict on Miss Cassandra Merton.

'You are right, Miss Merton, and it is clever of you to guess. You heard me say that I would ask the first marriageable woman whom I met after I became Earl to marry me, so you may have a roof over your head if you will become my wife.'

He had made the declaration before the whole room. And if there had been uproar before, it was as nothing to what followed now.

Miss Strood let out a loud and anguished cry. Almost as loud as the one which came from the Thaxteds. Jack's silent shadow was smiling ruefully, as though it was all he expected from his companion. Mr Herriot was shaking his head. The only unmoved persons in the whole room were Jack himself and Miss Cassandra Merton, who had put her head on one side to examine him as solemnly as though he were a rare species of insect. Or so it seemed to the amused Jack.

'Do you expect an answer now, Jack?' she asked him as the noise died down. Miss Strood had risen from her chair and was rushing up the aisle towards them. To protect her, no doubt. Cass did not need protecting.

'I would like an answer as soon as possible,' he said, as though he were saying the most natural thing in the world, and was not behaving so preposterously that his audience could hardly believe what he had done, was doing, in making a public proposal to a penniless young woman whom he had only just met. 'Seeing that it will save me three months' tiresome chasing of marriageable women if you accept me. You are a lady, you appear to be healthy and have enough spirit to endure me as a husband. A man could hardly ask for more.'

Something inside Cass shrieked, A woman might ask for love, but I suppose persons of our class cannot demand that.

Instead she said, as cool as he was, 'Then, Jack, I suppose I must accept you. I am, I collect, as big a bonus to you at this moment as you are to me—seeing that by marrying one another, we shall each acquire a roof over our heads which we might not otherwise possess!'

Jack threw his head back and let out a crack of laughter. Behind Cass, a disbelieving Miss Strood, her hands over her eyes, let out a low moan at these appalling goings-on which defied all the careful etiquette by which her life had been ruled up to this moment.

Jack stopped laughing, to say, 'Bravo,' and then, to the dismayed watching spectators, 'You heard that, I trust. Miss Merton has agreed to marry me. The conditions of my father's will are to be fulfilled. I give you all, sisters and brothers-in-law, leave to remain here so that you may see us legally married as soon as a special licence has been obtained.'

He bowed to Cass, who stood silent, swaying slightly, as the enormity of what she had just agreed to struck home.

But it was too late to retreat or to deny what she had done. She had, without any real pressure being put upon her, publicly and formally said that she would become the monster's Countess. Through a haze of sudden fright at her daring she could hear Jack telling her that he wished to speak to her alone, about their marriage, the legal and other arrangements for it, and the organisation of their life after it.

He had taken her small hand in his large one and had begun to lead her from the library into his late father's study. He signalled to his shadow to follow them, and was about to order Mr Herriot remain in the library until he halted as its big double doors were thrown open.

The excitements of the afternoon were not yet over!

CHAPTER THREE

An EAGER-FACED young man of flyaway appearance, in his very early twenties, pleasant-looking rather than handsome, rushed into the library to stare at the company which was about to process solemnly out of it, the day's business plainly being over.

'Oh, I say!' he exclaimed. 'I'm late, aren't I? Didn't get your message, sir,' he went on, addressing a grim-faced Edward Maxwell, 'until an hour ago when I arrived at my rooms after travelling up from Brighton. Had to change, don't you know. My presence wasn't needed, I trust?'

'Not really, Fred.' Frederick Maxwell's usually lethargic father was both short and acid. 'But it would have been all the same if it had. In any case, it has been a fool's errand for all of us.'

'How so, sir?' Fred was still eager. His happy stare found Jack, Cass standing beside him, and he opened his mouth to ask his father who the devil was the commoner who had poor Scrap in tow.

Cass was acutely aware that, like the great cat whom she thought he resembled, Jack's whole body had immediately tensed when Fred Maxwell had burst in. She knew this because he was still holding her hand. And that was the oddest thing too. For, from the moment he had taken it, it was though pins and needles had invaded it, had run up her arm and had travelled down her body to her toes. She had never, in her whole short life, been so conscious of the presence of another person. It was an almost hurtful sensation, but delightfully exhilarating.

'Who's he?' Jack rasped at Cass out of the side of

his mouth, meaning Fred. Well, perhaps it wasn't surprising that he hadn't recognised Fred, who had still been a boy when Jack had been thrown out of the nest.

'Your nephew Frederick Maxwell,' Cass whispered back. She didn't add, He's rather wild, like you were, but there's no malice in him—in fact he's rather silly. For some reason, she thought that there might be quite a lot of malice in Jack Devereux. He was watching his brother-in-law explain who he was to a bewildered Fred.

'My uncle Jack? The new Earl? Never! You're bamming me, sir. He looks like a longshoreman touting for work.'

This came out so loudly and so incredulously that Jack heard it and began to laugh.

'*He's* truthful, at least,' he remarked to Cass, his face one grin. He dropped her hand and walked over to where Fred was now staring at him. 'Hello, Fred. Yes, I am your uncle. I didn't recognise you, either. Not surprising, since you were little more than a howling babe when I last saw you. You've come on a lot since then.'

Fred remembered his manners at last. He gave the new Earl a low bow, said cheerfully, 'Sorry I wasn't as respectful just now as I ought to have been. But you must admit that I couldn't really have guessed who you are. You don't look a bit like Grandfather, or Uncle Philip, that's for sure.'

'We must meet again soon,' offered Jack, more friendly towards young Fred than he had been to any of his elders, 'but not today. I have an engagement—' and he pulled out of his coat pocket a battered watch to check the time '—shortly, I see, so I must leave when Miss Merton and I have had a comfortable chat about our coming marriage.'

Fred turned scarlet and then white. He had a *tendre*

for Cass which he had never confessed to anyone, and certainly not to her. 'You're going to marry Cass? How long have you known her?'

Jack consulted his watch again. 'About fifteen minutes, I should say. Your papa will inform you why I am marrying her, if you are curious to know.'

'Well, it's the oddest thing I have ever heard of,' returned Fred. 'I suppose there is a reasonable explanation for it,' he offered doubtfully.

'Well, I haven't time to give you one now.' Jack wasn't doubtful at all, Cass noticed, only amused by what was happening.

'Nor have I time to listen to you now,' said Fred eagerly. Amiable and eager were his middle names. 'I am due at Fronsac's Fencing Academy later this afternoon, for a lesson with their new master, Jacques Duroy.'

For some reason this seemed to amuse Jack Devereux mightily. He began to laugh, pulled out a tattered piece of clean linen which served him as a handkerchief and wiped his eyes with it. All his relatives, scandalised, watched this performance with stony faces.

They were even more scandalised when Jack remarked, as coolly as though he were discussing matters of the most supreme gravity, 'Well, that's an odd coincidence, Fred, my lad, seeing that you're coming to have a lesson with me. I'm Louis Fronsac's new instructor. I should scarcely call myself a master.'

'You're an instructor! In a fencing academy! You can't be! Besides, your name's not Duroy. You're a Devereux.' Fred was only uttering the thoughts of all those in the library, masters and servants, who were listening, fascinated, to this exchange. For the moment no one had any wish to leave.

'I'm Duroy at the Academy because the customers like to think that all fencing masters are French. And

I teach there because, until this morning, if I hadn't worked for my living I'd have starved.'

'Well, you needn't work now,' remarked Fred incontrovertibly.

'On the contrary.' For the first time Jack was grave. 'I have a duty to work for Louis until he finds a replacement for me. He gave me employment when no one else would. I owe him a debt of gratitude, and that's the biggest debt of all—as you may find out if you live long enough.'

This last dour remark broke the strange interlude in which Fred had held the floor on his own. Jack turned away to rejoin Cass, and the noise of angry voices rose again behind him. Lord Thaxted pushed Fred on one side and caught Jack roughly by the arm to detain him.

Cass watched Jack freeze. He stood quite still, his back to Thaxted, resisting his pulling arm. And then, his face an Aztec mask, so expressionless was it, he half turned, removed the offending hand and said conversationally, 'I'll thank you not to manhandle me, Thaxted. I've killed for less. Say what you have to without touching me again.'

'Damn you, Jack Devereux,' Thaxted roared, 'you're as ill-conditioned as you were when your father turned you away. But even you must see that the Earl Devereux cannot continue to be a so-called fencing master in a low dive where blackballed gamesters and pigeons to be plucked, like Fred here, congregate.'

This pretty speech had the disadvantage of setting Jack laughing and causing Fred's father, Edward Maxwell to exclaim, 'Now, see here, Thaxted, you wrong Fred, indeed you do. There's no real harm in him—and why should he not learn to fence? Louis Fronsac's as respectable a house as any.'

Thaxted had gone beyond reason. 'Not with Jack Devereux in it, it isn't. The sooner he mends his manners and takes his proper place in the world, the better. What will society think. . .?'

He got no further. Jack turned back again, thrust his face into his brother-in-law's and said between his teeth, 'I don't give a damn what society thinks, or you either. And if you weren't Amelia's husband I'd teach you a lesson in manners.'

He drew back as Thaxted recoiled from the feral mask presented to him, and said cheerfully to Fred, 'See you later, my boy. Don't take any notice of Thaxted here. He never had any sense when I first knew him, and he seems to have lost what wits he had whilst I've been away!'

'Oh, I won't,' exclaimed Fred happily and tactlessly.

In the meantime, Amelia shrilled at her husband, 'You aren't going to let him get away with speaking of you like that, Thaxted, surely?'

The large man, Jack's companion, spoke at last, to Amelia, of all people, in a commiserating voice, pitched somewhere midway between educated speech and that of the commonalty. 'Oh, I shouldn't advise you to make him provoke Jack too much, missis, if I were you. Jack's even more of a devil with pistols and sabres than he is with a rapier, and that's saying something. He's got a short fuse, too.'

Missis, indeed! As though she were the cook or the housekeeper! Amelia clapped her hands over her ears and made for the doors. Cass was hard put to it to contain her amusement. This was wrong. This was not seemly. They were here because a great man and a relative of them all had died; since Jack Devereux had arrived, he had turned the place into a bear garden. The joke was that he was the bear who ought to have been baited, and instead he was doing the baiting.

She was certain that every word he had uttered had been designed to strike home. There was nothing impulsive in him, only cold calculation. If he had been humiliated, turned out into the world to fend for himself, unloved and ignored by all, he was paying them all back in coin of his own choosing, not theirs.

But whatever was she marrying? Why in the world had she decided to live with this cold-hearted brute with a vicious tongue? Cass almost wavered in her resolve, but then Jack took her gently by the arm and led her into the study, shutting the door behind them, and she was changing her mind again. For was he not offering her a kind of freedom—the freedom not to starve?

'It's true what I said to Fred,' he told her. 'I haven't much time to talk to you, and I am needed at the Academy. But I wanted to reassure you. I meant it when I said that I had no desire to hurt you. It's quite plain from what Herriot said to me briefly just now that you are one of their victims. You and your companion, who were about to be turned into the street. I wanted to secure your future, and as you so accurately pointed out, I can do so by benefiting both of us. You understand me?'

Cass nodded. She didn't know whether he frightened her more when he was speaking to her so coolly and reasonably than when he was in his savage mode. Which was the true man? Did she want to find out? Well, one thing was certain. Life with him was never going to be dull. And what had he been doing before he had become a fencing teacher? Fred had said that he was a new instructor. Had he always been one? She had thought him to have been a soldier, but perhaps she was wrong.

He was speaking gravely and seriously to her. 'Before you marry me, I must make one thing plain. I intend this marriage to be one in name only. I shall not touch you—other than in friendship, that is. That is partly why I have chosen you to be my wife. I have no desire to have a family, and every desire to thwart my late father by marrying to secure the estates and then not providing the Devereux line with the heir he so dearly desired. Damn the line, I say. I will see that you have a rich and comfortable life, and in return you will be faithful to me. You look the faithful sort.'

He means that I am plain and biddable, thought Cass numbly. But let him wait until after he has married me! He says that he is giving me freedom, and I mean to enjoy myself as I have never been allowed to do before. I shall keep my word if he wishes me to be faithful—but that is all.

But she said nothing, bowing her head meekly. And with a quizzical expression on his harsh face, he began to speak again.

'If this bargain is not to your liking, say so now, and I shall go outside and tell them that you have changed your mind, and I must start looking for a bride again. I don't think that I shall have much difficulty in finding one, do you?'

'No,' said Cass simply, 'I'm sure that half the mamas in society would throw their daughters at you, and you would be spoilt for choice. So why me? You could have rank or beauty, or rank and beauty. You know I have little rank, and it is plain by the way in which you speak to me that you don't think that I have beauty either. So again, why me?'

'For that very reason,' drawled Jack carelessly. 'I don't want some spoiled and pouting miss, who would expect me to dance attendance on her and would cry at and to Mama if I wish to go my own way. Now, according to Mr Herriot you are a sensible girl, who will do your duty, as you have been doing since my father brought you into his house, and will spare me all missishness I might otherwise acquire. Still haven't changed your mind?'

A mute shake of the head was Cass's response to this.

'Good. Now, before I go, have you any questions to ask me? Not long ones, I beg.'

'Yes.' Cass, putting her hands behind her back, said demurely, 'One question. Who is your shadow? What is his name? And will he be part of our household?' She rather liked the 'our household' bit. It told him how determined she was to see him as her soon-to-be husband—no missishness there.

If Jack was surprised by this unexpected request, he did not show it.

'He is Dickie Dickson. He is my great friend, and we owe each other our lives—which creates a bond between man and man, you understand. And yes, he will be part of our household. He will be my general factotum and still my friend—not really a servant at all. We have been Dev and Dickie far too long for that.'

Dev and Dickie. There was one other question she must ask him, even if she could guess by his manner that he was anxious to be away.

'Dev and Dickie. He knew your true name, then?'

Jack shook his head. 'Until today he and the world—or that part of it in which I have lived for the past twelve years—has known me as Jack Devlin.'

Cass thought that it would not be wise to ask him exactly in what part of the world he had been living and what he had been doing in it. If he wanted her— or anyone else—to know, he would tell her or them. Patently he did not. She didn't think that Dickie possessed a looser tongue than his master. It was also patent that they were a good pair.

'Enough. You have no more questions for me?' he asked, raising those strong eyebrows and giving her his feral stare.

Cass had none for the present, but there was one thing which she couldn't resist saying—even if one ought not to twist the tiger's tail.

'He won't like it, you know,' she offered him ellip-tically. But, surprisingly, he knew what she meant.

'Lord Thaxted, you mean? That Dickie and I will be friends and not master and servant?'

Cass nodded.

'Then he may go to the devil. I take it that you don't. Mind Dickie and me, I mean.'

'Oh, no,' Cass said. 'That is your mystery, as Mr Hunt, our librarian, once told me when we were discussing some ancient manners and customs. Each age and person has their own, he said.'

'Did he, indeed?' Jack was grave again. Perhaps she *had* surprised him a little. And now he was bowing over her hand, as elegant as Lord Thaxted would have liked him to be with everyone, and not just with her, in private. Before he straightened up he kissed the back of it, leaving behind such an odd but pleasant burning sensation that long after he had gone, 'to do his duty' as he had said, she could still feel it, as though he had put a brand upon her.

Which must be a sort of wizardry he was practising on her, must it not? And did everyone feel like that when he touched them, or was she the only victim?— if victim was the right word.

And now she must go to see dear Stroody and tell her that she was safe. And there was another qualifi-cation she must make—if anyone could be counted safe who was to live in Jack Devereux's shadow.

'Child,' said Miss Strood sorrowfully, 'do you know what you are doing?'

'No,' said Cass. 'Of course not. Not at all. But I need a home. And so do you. He is giving us one. It's as simple as that.'

'Oh, yes, child, but at what a price! To marry him, such an ogre. Does he not frighten you?'

'Yes,' said Cass, 'of course.' There was no point in

denying the truth. Anyone who was not frightened of him must be a fool. As Lord Thaxted had been, downstairs in the library. But he excited her too, and she couldn't say *that* to poor Stroody.

'He is using you.' Miss Strood's voice had become a wail. She plainly saw Cass laid out on Jack's bed as on a sacrificial altar, her body the price for security. A joke, really, seeing that he had decided not to touch her.

'True.' Cass nodded. 'But then, I am using him, so we are quits. Would you rather that we walked the streets? Whatever the Ugly Sisters might have decided to do with us, once Jack arrived they were ready to abandon us. To spite him—and the late Earl.'

Now this was a piece of shrewdness which until today Cass had scarcely known she possessed. Was it Jack Devereux, or being in a tight corner which had brought it on?

Miss Strood had no answer to Cass's last statement. Her thin hands worked convulsively together, plucking at one another. She had lived on the verge of ruin for so long that she could not believe that she had been saved. She did not like to think that Cass had been sacrificed to save her.

More than that, in all their previous dealings she had been the dominant one, Cass her pupil. Now their positions were reversed. Cass had gone beyond her and she would never catch up with her again. Cass would be Lady Devereux, the mistress of a grand establishment, a personage in her own right—as Jack would be in his.

Hesitantly she asked, 'Do you wish me to remain with you, or would you rather I looked for another post?' She knew that Cass would 'see her right' as they said, but there was a plea in her voice that she should not be left to go, friendless, into the world.

Cass spoke as lovingly and gently as she could. 'Of

course I shall want you to stay with me, Stroody. I shall need a friend.'

She was surprised at her own calm—no more surprised than Miss Strood was, perhaps. But then poor Stroody did not know the truth: that Jack Devereux did not want her, would not touch her—at least not yet, for Cass was hard-headed, and thought that he might change his mind when he had been Earl for a little while and found that he wanted a child after all.

'Damn the line', he had said earlier, but would he always mean it? No time to think of that now. For the present, he meant it, and that must be enough.

And she was not sacrificing herself as poor Miss Strood believed—or was she? Queen Elizabeth, Good Queen Bess, had cried aloud when she had heard that her cousin and rival, Mary, Queen of Scots, had borne a child, 'And I am but of a barren stock!' She, Cass, would be of a barren stock. Unless Jack changed his mind, that would be her sacrifice.

Might it not have been better to have been turned out, to have taken her chance of ruin, the ruin which awaited those of genteel birth thrown upon the street? She had no illusions as to what her destiny would have been... She doubted very much that the Lord would have provided her with anything better than the opportunity to sell her body; after all, He had provided her with very little in her short life so far.

But that was being ungrateful to Him—for had He not provided her with Jack Devereux?—and Jack Devereux she would have to be content with.

Miss Strood was watching the changing emotions chase themselves across Cass's face. It was as though she were growing up before her.

'Don't do this, child,' she said, and put her arms around Cass as though to protect her. 'Somehow we shall survive without you becoming Lord Devereux's prey.'

Cass comforted her by patting her on her back. She wished that she could tell poor Stroody the truth. But that would not be wise. She had survived so far in her life by telling very little of anything to anyone.

'There, there, there,' she crooned. 'No need to repine. He will play fair with me, I am sure.' But she mentally crossed her fingers as she spoke. For what did she really know of him?

Comforting Miss Strood was a tiring occupation— for both of them. Finally, Cass sent her companion to rest in her own small room, a few doors away from Cass's, leaving Cass to do the same thing in hers.

But she had hardly sat down on her hard and narrow bed, little better than that of a servant, when her much-needed solitude was broken by a peremptory knock on the door. Without waiting for Cass to reply, the door was flung open wide, and Amelia Thaxted, wearing the face of a tragedy queen, advanced upon her.

'My poor dear child,' she exclaimed, her tone suggesting that she and Cass had been bosom bows until Jack's sudden reappearance, and that she was renewing that friendship on the instant in order to help Cass in her time of need. 'This marriage is quite impossible. Most unfair to you at your young age to be saddled with such a violent rogue as Jack Devereux appears to be. Thaxted and I are in agreement, as is dear Constantia, that we shall find you a home between us, so that you do not feel the need to sacrifice yourself to him in order to gain a roof over your head!' She paused dramatically.

Sacrifice! Was everyone obsessed with the word where she and Jack were concerned? No one, apparently, had thought that she was being sacrificed when it had been agreed that she should be sent as companion to a bad-tempered old woman in the far North, and that poor Stroody should be turned out on the street. Cass decided to find out what new fate, if any, had been decided on for her companion.

'And Miss Strood?' she asked pleasantly, as though falling in with Amelia's wishes.

Oh, this was better—it showed that the child knew her proper place—which was not that of the Countess Devereux.

'Naturally, we should also offer a home to Miss Strood until she finds a new post. It won't be for long, of course, as I am sure that you understand.'

'I see,' said Cass, and then fell silent.

Silence was rapidly taken as consent.

'I am to tell Thaxted, then, that you will give up this ridiculous notion of marrying Jack, and be taken under our wing?'

Their wing? Where had that refuge been before Jack's sudden and unwanted arrival, when she and Constantia and the rest of them had been so willing to turn her away? It was plain that in their desire to thwart Jack, to make it difficult for him to fulfil the conditions of his father's will, his sisters and their husbands were prepared to do anything to stop his marriage to Cass.

Cass's swift agreement had solved his problem for him on the instant, so anything which delayed his acquiring a countess would please them mightily. If they were not to inherit their father's estates, then they would try to prevent Jack from doing so. 'Wing' was the wrong word for Amelia to use. 'Dog in the manger' were the right ones, that was sure.

'Cass? Cass?' Heavens above! Amelia was pleading with her! And what a delightful turn-up that was, given that Cass's conversation with her had always taken the form of bullying roars from Amelia directed at the poor dependant on Devereux charity! Cass would give her an answer, and as plain a one as she could.

'Oh, no.' She smiled sweetly. 'Much though I would like to accept your kind offer, I have given my word to Earl Devereux—' she would not say Jack '—and I must keep it. Now, had you made it earlier then I should have been bound by my word to you. But as it is. . .' And she shrugged her shoulders eloquently.

Was not this the most delightful revenge for the selfish way in which her disposition had been arranged? The only flaw was that she could not let Amelia know that she was aware of the somersaults which Jack's offer had caused them all to turn. That would be most unwise.

Amelia turned purple again at this demure answer. She could almost have sworn that the child was laughing at her as she made it. Desperate, she tried again. She had told the others that she would bring Cass round, and she would not give up without a fight.

'You can hardly wish to go through this pantomime of a marriage simply to become Countess Devereux? What use would a title be against the unhappiness that a union with such a ne'er-do-well as Jack would bring you?'

'True,' sighed Cass, 'but I gave my word—a trifle hastily, perhaps—and I must now live with it. We even shook hands.' She pulled her handkerchief out of her small reticule and wondered whether to dab her eyes with it, but thought that that might be going too far.

She had already gone too far. Amelia could see that the case was hopeless. She clenched her fists and hid them in the skirts of her gown—a maroon one, which did nothing for her complexion. 'I have to say that I consider that you are being most unwise, and when in a few months you come running to us for help, life with such a one as Jack being unsupportable, then do not think that Thaxted and I, or dear Constantia and Edward will be willing to help you. I have given you

your opportunity to retract—and you have refused it.
Mark that!'

She finished with an exclamation of such violence
that Cass shrank from it. 'You have made your bed,
my girl, and you must lie on it—with him!'

Which was not quite the threat that she thought it
was.

CHAPTER FOUR

Two men were fencing when Fred Maxwell walked into the big hall of Louis Fronsac's Academy, which was situated in an old house in an alley off the Haymarket. Fronsac had been a protégé of Henry Angelo and was widely regarded as one of the supreme modern masters of the small sword.

The room was lit with long windows that were curtained, when Fred arrived, to prevent the sun from blazing into the duellists' eyes. Light came from several chandeliers beneath a high roof. A small audience was watching the two men, who were both dressed in the formal court clothing of the late eighteenth century: white silk shirts, black silk knee-breeches, and light black silver-buckled shoes. To complete the illusion of the past they both wore their hair long, carefully tied back with black grosgrain ribbon.

They were fencing with light buttoned foils, masks over their faces. To watch them was as good as watching a play, or a ballet danced without music, so excellent was their performance. There seemed to be little to choose between them in skill.

A page or flunky, a large watch in his hand which he constantly consulted, suddenly rang a bell. Immediately, as though they were automata, both men stood back, pulled off their masks, raised their foils before their faces, and kissed them as though they had been involved in a duel to the death instead of a demonstration of the beauty and elegance of fencing for the benefit of the group of watching novices who had just finished their own lessons.

It was only when the two men, nothing between

them in height and grace, walked towards him, panting and sweating slightly, that Fred realised that one of them was his new-found uncle Jack Devereux, so different was he in appearance and manner from the 'longshoreman' which Fred had dubbed him earlier that day.

Jack had seen Fred walk in as he had swung away from his employer, Louis Fronsac, to dodge that gentleman's attack in *tierce*. They usually worked out together at some point in each day to keep their competitive edge. Too much time spent in teaching novices and incompetents was likely to destroy their fine control.

Dickie Dickson, who sat watching them, a sabre across his knee, was a good performer with that weapon, but had to acknowledge that he was not in the same class as Louis and Jack with a small sword, however much they tried to help him to improve his performance.

'Thought that you might give your lesson a miss after this afternoon's *brouhaha*, sir,' remarked Jack as he towelled his face and watched Fred's man help him to prepare for his lesson. He had seen Fred's surprise at his changed appearance, and was happy to have wrong-footed him. He had made a specialism of wrong-footing people from the day on which he had been turned away from his home, had been thrown down the steps of Devereux House by three sturdy footmen and told never to come back.

Now he was watching his nephew, and presently began his lesson as impersonally as though he had never met him before, calling him 'sir' most respectfully, which only served to embarrass Fred mightily. Especially since it soon became plain to Jack that whatever Fred might excel at he was never going to become a master of the small sword, however hard he tried. And try he did; Jack had to grant him that.

After half an hour's gruelling work Jack led Fred to a mirror, and made him lunge at it, pointing out that, while he did so, Fred could see for himself that his body was at quite the wrong angle for his thrusts to be successful. By the end of the lesson Jack was still perspiring lightly, whilst Fred's shirt and breeches were wet through: he was soaked to the skin.

The lesson over, Jack led Fred to a small table at the rear of the big hall where drink was set out—ale, wine, port and several large pitchers of lemonade. Jack picked up a glass and poured himself lemonade whilst Fred, feeling a bigger fool than ever after his inept display, downed a giant tankard of ale.

Jack surveyed Fred's stocky body, not at all that of a master fencer—he was too short for one thing, and his reach was ineffectual—and asked conversationally, 'Tried boxing, have you, sir?' Nothing in his voice or manner betrayed that he thought that he and Fred were relatives and social equals.

Rendered uncomfortable by Jack's professionalism and servant-like impersonality, Fred muttered, 'Come off it, Uncle. You *are* my uncle, goddamit, and that ass Thaxted is right. You shouldn't be capering here, calling your inferiors "sir".'

The reaction he got surprised him, but would not have surprised anyone who had known Jack Devereux for the last twelve years. He seized Fred by the throat and pinned him, spluttering and turning purple, against the wall.

'You damned young puppy, has no one taught you sense or manners? A few months as a seaman on a Navy ship or a private in the infantry would do wonders for you. I do an honest job for an honest day's pay, which is more than you have ever done, and I demean neither myself nor my clients by calling them sir. They paid for that, as you have done. And in here I'm not your uncle, remember that. I'm Louis

Fronsac's man. Besides, out of here I'll have you call me Jack, or nothing at all. Understood?'

Jack could not understand why he was so angry. For most of the last twelve years he had kept his hot temper under firm control. But ever since he had walked into Devereux House and seen that pack of parasites who called themselves his relatives battening on the work and labour of others, he had felt the red rage building in him, and poor silly Fred was getting the benefit of it!

He released Fred and stood back. 'Shouldn't have done that, sir,' he said, conversational again. 'Most unprofessional, but you did ask for it, sir. Now, answer my question, sir. Do you box?'

Fred felt his bruised throat, then replied with as much dignity as a man could whose voice was hoarse and whose eyes were watering after such a vigorous manhandling, 'A little, Duroy. A little.'

He was pleased that he had remembered Jack's professional name, and Jack was pleased, too. There was hope for the boy yet. All he needed was a little discipline.

'Had any lessons from Jackson?' He cast a cold eye over Fred. 'You're a trifle overweight, sir. I recommend less ale. Try the lemonade—or water.'

'Last year. He said that he thought that I was promising, but I fancied myself with a small sword. That's why I'm here.'

'A mistake, sir, I think.' Jack was polite without being servile. 'I don't think you've much talent for it, to be honest. My advice is, go back to Jackson and let him work on you.'

Fred was suddenly resentful. He had wanted to cut a dash with the foils, not sweat and grunt like a bruiser. He decided that attack was the best form of defence, and damn his uncle. . . Jack. . .if he attacked him again.

'Really mean to marry Cass, do you?'

'Not here,' riposted Jack grimly. He had no wish to discuss Cass or any of his affairs with this half-fledged boy. 'I don't want to discuss Miss Merton here.'

'Here,' returned Fred robustly. 'Here, because I'm the gent, ain't I? So you must obey me. Do you mean to marry her?' He felt briefly and exhilaratingly in charge of the tiger before him.

'Yes, sir.' Jack suddenly grinned and pulled an imaginary forelock. And who am I mocking, he thought, myself or poor Fred?

'Right,' said Fred, 'and now let *me* tell *you* something. If you do anything to hurt Cass you'll have me to reckon with—understood?'

Jack was hard put to it not to laugh at him, but for Fred's sake kept his face straight. Which was more than Dickie, who had been eavesdropping on their conversation, could do. He was openly smiling at the mere notion of young Fred being able to force any kind of reckoning on a man who could, if he were so minded, kill him in a dozen different ways, choose how. Nevertheless, he was pleased to see that Jack did not mock at his nephew, but nodded as gravely as though he were Fred and Fred were him, in terms of age and experience.

'Trust me,' Jack said, adding as an afterthought, 'sir.'

Fred thought that he did. There was something about Jack Devereux which compelled respect, whatever his father and his mother, or his uncle and his aunt had said of him. He possessed a strength, a sternness which belonged to no one else whom he knew. He felt it necessary to add, 'Cass hasn't anyone else to defend her—no father, no brother. So it's up to me, you see.'

Jack saw. He saw that Fred was sweet on Cass, to put it at its mildest. He also saw that he would never

have been allowed to marry her, so he was not doing
Fred out of anything. Whether he was doing Cass out
of anything was a different matter. He thought not.
That he was exploiting her, he had no doubt. But it
was an odd form of exploitation, one had to admit,
which ended up in a penniless girl of plain face and
mere skin and bones becoming a countess.

Even if she did have to take Jack Devereux with the
title.

Jack continued to wrong-foot everyone by deciding to
live at Devereux House whilst he continued working
for Louis Fronsac, a decision which infuriated all his
relatives and raised the eyebrows of everyone who
lived in the polite world. Louis had told him that he
would release him from his agreement to work on
until he found a replacement, but had met Jack's cold
stare and Dickie's asmued one.

'On no account.' Jack's voice had been even frostier
than it usually was. 'You are only suggesting it because
I am Earl Devereux. If I were still plain Jack Devlin
you would not even have considered making me such
an offer. Besides, your offer is foolish after another
fashion—think of the extra money you are earning
because so many curious fools are coming here in
order to boast that they have been taught by the Earl
Devereux.'

Louis had given in, as Dev and Dickie had both
known that he would. He redoubled his efforts to find
another fencing master as soon as possible—it was
neither right nor proper that the owner of a great
name and great possessions should be 'capering round
a fencing hall', as Fred had to tactlessly put it.

The only person beside Dickie Dickson who
approved of Jack's decision was Cass. She was compelled to listen to his relatives bemoaning it—for their
own reasons they had all stayed on at Devereux House

for the wedding, which was to take place ten days after the will-reading. Even Miss Strood hinted that she thought his behaviour barely proper. Great men, with great names, it seemed to Cass, need not honour their contracts—if made with their inferiors, that was.

She had said nothing to Jack of her reaction to his conduct, because after his proposal she had not seen him. He left Devereux House early in the morning and only returned long after she had retired for the night. It was plain that not only did he not wish or expect her to share his bed, he did not expect her to share his life. She knew this because, shamefully again, on the one afternoon which he had spent at Devereux House, she had overheard him and Dickie talking about her in the library.

She had been sitting in her favourite place behind the curtain, and he and Dickie had come in and started to talk before she had had time to let them know that she was there. And then it had been too late. . .

'Why are you doing this, Dev?' Dickie had asked him.

'Doing which particular thing, Dickie?'

'You know what I mean,' Dickie had grunted.

'Oh, marrying Miss Skin and Bones,' Jack had said carelessly.

Now, this was worse than being called the Scrap, and no wonder he didn't want to go to bed with her. Cass shivered, almost put her hands over her ears, but the instinct to survive was now so strong in her that she listened on. Knowledge was power, Mr Hunt had so often said, and she wished to know Jack. Though how that might give her power over him, she had at the moment no idea.

'I would have thought it was obvious.' Jack's voice was still careless. 'She is a woman whom I can marry quickly, without wasting time on some dam'd fine lady who won't accept me, however much she might want my lands and title, without me dancing a monstrous quadrille around her. I've no stomach for that. Besides, this one will be grateful—be a biddable girl, I shouldn't wonder. Plain is better than pretty. I doubt whether she will be betraying me with every handome young fellow she sets eyes on.'

At these callous words Cass clenched her small fists. Damn him—she would betray him with every handsome young fellow she met, if she were so minded.

'She's not the usual sort of woman, Dev,' his horrid friend was saying.

'I have no "usual sort of woman", Dickie, only the common sort. They're all much of a muchness, you know. Most women have no character at all, as the poet said. I doubt me that this one's different.'

He was so indifferent, so dismissive, that Cass's toes curled. Well at least he was affording her the privilege of hating him. Just let him wait until she was his Countess! She would show him what was what. Gratitude to him for her salvation was flying out the window. She would demand the biggest jointure she could get, an establishment to rival a crown princess's. The Devereux estate could afford it. She would sleep on satin, dine on lark's tongues and strawberries out of season, buy Miss Strood, as well as herself, some decent bonnets. . .

This descent into bathos almost had Cass laughing out loud at herself. She clapped her hands over her mouth. It would not do to be discovered.

He was talking about her again. She wondered if he would mention their bargain to his friend, but so far he had not. He had said that it was their secret and he was keeping it so.

'Why worry at this bone, Dickie? You have never troubled yourself about my women before.'

'This one's to be your wife, and she's so young. . . almost a child.'

'But a shrewd one, you must admit. Did you not mark the speed with which she jumped to be my Countess?'

Damn being your Countess, Cass thought inelegantly. It was the opportunity not to starve which I was jumping at!

Dickie changed the subject, asking anxiously, 'You're sure that you want me to stay with you now that you're Earl, Dev? This kind of splendour ain't my line, you know. We allus did the bowing and scraping to others. We was never bowed and scraped at.'

Jack was laughing. 'Much bowing and scraping we did, Dickie, but I take your point. This way round is better, you'll find. And why should it not be Dev and Dickie in good times as well as in bad? Even if I don't wish to be Earl Devereux.'

'Will the good times be as good as the bad ones were?'

For a second there was silence, and then Jack spoke, his voice slow and serious, the carelessness gone from it.

'I take your point, Dickie. We always stood between authority and those authority ruled. The fun lay in reconciling the two things and outwitting them both. Who do we outwit now that *we* are authority? The answer's simple. All of them. All of the dam'd mealymouthed canting crew who've always known where their next meal was coming from. The men who have never waited for their death at dawn, the women who have never had to sell themselves for necessity, only for pleasure. We always had fun in the past, Dickie, now let's have fun in the present. We've both got scores to settle with life—let's settle them together.'

There was silence after that. Dickie's reply was so low she could not hear it, and then they were gone. Cass tried to make sense of what she had overheard.

Miss Skin and Bones was easy enough to understand,

if hurtful. That was what he thought of her, and there was nothing that she could do about it. Except make him pay a little after they were married.

But for the rest—what was she to make of that? What had he and Dickie been doing? Conspiring together, of course, but about what?

Cass had given up the puzzle after a little time, and when she had been sure that they were safely away, had pulled back the curtain and made for her room.

Miss Skin and Bones. Yes, he would pay for that or her name wasn't Cassandra Merton!

'No!' she had announced furiously to her mirror on the fourth night, when he had still not had the decency to come near her. 'This is not good enough. He owes me something, after all. If he is saving me, I am saving him.'

She had finally gone to bed with a complaining and tired Miss Strood toiling at her rear at twelve, midnight. She had pleaded that she wished to finish the book she was reading, in the hope that Jack and Dickie—she knew that Dickie would be with him—would arrive home before she would be compelled to retire for sheer propriety's sake.

One thing was true. She was having a great deal of trouble sleeping. And the reason for that was Jack Devereux. No sooner did she lie down than he was in her mind whilst she was awake, and in her dreams when she was asleep. Which was really stupid, seeing that she did not think that he had given her another thought after he had walked out of the library on the day in which she had heard him talking so carelessly of her with Dickie Dickson. Miss Skin and Bones, indeed!

So it was quite shameful of her to be so obsessed by him—but there seemed to be nothing that she could do about it. And it was those feral greeny-yellow eyes which were doing the most damage to her hard-won composure.

Once in her room, she refused to dress for the night, and scowled first at the mirror and then at the clock. She gave Miss Strood time to undress and go to sleep, before she crept onto the landing and made her way silently down four flights of stairs. The first one of them was uncarpeted, because it led to the servants' quarters, except for the rooms occupied by Stroody and herself. It was to be hoped that the Thaxteds and the Maxwells, including Fred, were all snoring peacefully.

Descending into the hall, she could hear male voices coming from the drawing room. One of the voices was Jack's—and it struck her that she had only met him once and overheard him once, and yet everything about him was indelibly engraved on her memory. His looks, his voice, his clothes...she would know his voice anywhere.

Her hand on the doorknob, she hesitated at the very last moment, overcome by the enormity of what she was doing. Suppose the other male members of the household were there? It wouldn't matter, if it were merely Fred, but to endure the stares of the Lord Thaxted and Edward Maxwell...they had made their opinion of her plain: from being a rejected poor relation she was now dubbed an outrageous fortune-hunter, and was so being described to the rest of society. Well, pooh to the rest of society. But she was still made a little unhappy at the prospect of the displeasure of those under whose thumb she had lived for so long.

She finally turned the doorknob and walked in, a face-saving lie ready at the end of her tongue to justify her presence if it were necessary.

It wasn't. Jack Devereux stood facing the door, talking to the only other person in the room. Dickie

Dickson, of course. Jack was propped up against the beautiful marble fireplace which his grandfather had brought from Italy. He no longer looked like the longshoreman that Fred had called him.

Not that he looked like an ordinary gentleman either. He was wearing black silk knee-breeches, an open-necked white silk shirt and a longish black coat trimmed with silver. His hair was tied back by a large grosgrain bow. His face hadn't changed; it was as stern and harsh as ever. Cass was not to know that he was still wearing the clothes in which he fenced.

He bowed to her on her entry. It was so low that she thought he was mocking her slightly. She couldn't be sure. Well, two could play at that game.

'Miss Merton, may I assist you in any way?'

Yes, he *was* mocking her. Had he guessed that she had come down determined to speak to him? And now that she had, what on earth was she to say?

'I was a trifle restless on retiring. I decided to read, but I found that I had left my book behind.' Which was true, because she had left it in the drawing room deliberately.

'This?' he enquired, picking it up from the chair in which she had been sitting. He looked at it curiously. 'Young's *Night Thoughts*, hmm. A strange choice for a young woman.'

'Mr Hunt recommended it,' Cass returned primly. She had not really come down to discuss her taste in reading with him. But what had she come down for? Dickie Dickson was standing up. She thought he looked tired. He was not dressed like Jack. He was wearing a scarlet jacket and blue trousers. He had spent the day teaching young gentlemen to use a sabre, though Cass was not to know that. After that, he and Jack had visited an inn near Fronsac's Academy and they had drunk rather heavily, though neither of them was overset.

He rose, bowed to Cass, though not as low as Jack had done, and more deferentially.

'I will leave you,' he said. 'You doubtless have much to say to one another.'

Cass thought that Jack's expression announced that he had nothing to say, so indifferent was it. Anger ran through her. It was shameful that he should occupy both her thoughts and her dreams, that she was about to become his wife, and that he should hardly know that she existed.

'You needn't leave if you don't want to, Dickie,' he drawled. 'I'm sure that Miss Merton would not object if you wished to stay.'

The look Dickie gave him was a reproachful one. He raised his shaggy brows and was gone.

Jack indicated an armchair to Cass.

She shook her head, said, still prim, 'I didn't come down in order to stay.'

'Yes, I know,' murmured Jack. 'You came to collect the delectably fascinating Young. Pray, excuse me if I don't believe you. Were you the innocent young creature which Dickie thinks you, you would not be here at all. Alone with me in the middle of the night. You really ought to be more wary of me. All your relatives and that governess of yours would tell you to avoid wild Jack Devereux until the marital knot was well and truly tied.'

'But then, they don't know what I do, do they?' Cass's voice was as steady as she could make it. He was really hateful. He was hardly seeing her, and plainly regarded her as little more than someone who was a thing which he was using.

Mr Hunt had told her about Immanuel Kant, and that he had said that the worst thing that you could do to another human being was to treat them as a thing, and not as a human being at all.

'That is,' she added, 'if you really meant what you

said. We shook hands on the bargain. Have you already decided to go back on it? Because if so I shall withdraw, and you may look for another young woman to be your untouched Countess.'

The feral eyes lit up. 'Oh, it bites, does it? I must remember that. No, I mean to keep to our bargain, and when I said that you weren't innocent I merely meant that you *understood* quite well what you were doing when you accepted me, not that you were in any way experienced. Persuade me that you didn't come down quite deliberately in order to speak to me.'

'No, because that is exactly what I did do.' Cass was defiant. 'You should have the grace to talk to me occasionally. No one else does.'

She had not meant to say that—it reeked of self-pity. She was near enough to him to know that he had been drinking, and that he was not quite in the perfect control of himself which he had been on the day of the will-reading—and in the library.

'Nobody.' He said the word slowly and deliberately. 'You mean besides your companion?'

'Miss Strood. Her name is Miss Strood. And yes, she talks to me. She deserves to have a name as well as I do—and you.'

'Oh, I have so many names that I have difficulty in remembering which one I am using at any given time,' he told her, laughter in his voice now. 'But you are right to rebuke me. So, you are being ostracised for marrying me.'

Indifference had fled from his voice. He was angry. And when he was angry he would be formidable, Cass knew. Thank God that he was not angry with her.

'Oh, I don't mind,' she assured him, quite truthfully. 'But it would be pleasant if you spoke to me occasionally. Even my faithful Stroody does not like it that you are ignoring me.'

'I am not ignoring you. I have a life to live which

has nothing to do with Devereux House—or you. You might more truthfully say that I am ignoring everyone because I haven't time to do anything else at the moment but pay my debt to Louis Fronsac.'

Near to him as she was, Cass found his eyes more fascinating than ever. She could also see that he needed to shave. His beard was dark on his chin. This, strangely enough, she found exciting. She was not yet experienced enough in life and love to know that what attracted her to Jack was his uncompromising masculinity, his power. She shivered a little. Her skin seemed alive, crawling. Suppose he were to touch her? What would she feel then? If the very idea was frightening, it was also exhilarating.

'You owe a debt to me as well as to Louis Fronsac,' she announced sturdily. 'You ought to acknowledge that.'

'Bitten again.' Now he was laughing openly. 'I chose you because I thought you were a biddable girl. Are you?'

'Perhaps. If I am treated properly, that is. Will you treat me properly, Lord Devereux?'

'Perhaps,' he mocked, echoing her. 'If you'll call me Jack.'

'Oh, you are not treating me seriously,' she raged. 'It's nothing but a joke to you. Are you never serious?'

Oddly, this seemed to touch him. He moved nearer to her. Cass held her ground. She would not let him intimidate her, even if she were alone with him.

'Oh, you wrong me,' he told her softly, 'I am always serious. Even though I may not sound as if I am. I find it an absolute necessity that you call me Jack. Earl Devereux is someone I don't know yet.'

'But you must know him soon.' Cass spoke with great urgency. 'For that is what you are. You are no longer Jack Devlin, or any other of the names of which you spoke. *That* is being serious, being Earl Devereux.'

'Thrice bitten,' he announced humbly, and Cass thought that this time he was being serious. 'But you must understand I have been for twelve years now someone quite different. And I liked being that man. Would you believe me if I told you that I don't want to be Earl Devereux?'

She remembered that he had said as much to Dickie, that day when she had been hidden on the window seat.

'Yes, I believe you. You spoke of a duty to Louis Fronsac, and I think that you are right to fulfil it. But surely you also have a duty to your name, and to the people who depend on you because of that name?'

'"A Daniel come to judgment! O, wise young judge".'

Cass's eyes widened at that. Wild Jack Devereux quoting Shakespeare! What next?

Jack saw her surprise and laughed again at her confusion. Cass only knew that he was constantly surprising her. Well, she hoped to surprise him, and then they would be quits. She gave a little sigh and looked at the clock—to be surprised at the time it told her.

He read her face correctly. 'Bedtime for little girls,' he murmured. 'And before you go, yes, I will find time to speak to you, and to. . . Miss Strood.'

He had surprised her again. 'Thank you,' she said simply. 'That is very good of you.' She bowed. 'Good-night, Jack.'

He had yet another surprise for her. He leaned forward and kissed her passionlessly on the cheek. 'Sleep well, my soon-to-be Countess. Reflect that after we have married no one will wish to do other than please you. Whether that *will* please you is another matter!'

CHAPTER FIVE

FIVE days before the wedding Louis Fronsac found another instructor and Jack was freed from his obligation to him. That same afternoon the lawyers arrived and Cass was sent for—and Stroody and Lord Thaxted. Thaxted was there because Jack and the lawyers wanted him to witness that Cass was being fairly dealt with in the settlement made for her on marriage.

Fairly dealt with! Jack was being munificent. Her jointure, her future as the Dowager if he should suddenly die, were all arranged so that she should be richer than any past Countess Devereux had ever been. Whether it was because of what she had said to him at dead of night, Cass would never know. Certainly since then he had made it his business to seek her out every day and spend some little time with her. 'Getting to know you,' he had told her.

Well, she ought to be getting to know him, but the more she saw of him the less she knew of him.

She had sought out Mr Hunt on the day after her midnight conversation, and had tried to find out what he thought of the new Earl. Discreetly, of course, and obliquely. It would not have been proper to talk vulgarly and openly about her future husband with one of his dependants, and a youngish one at that!

Cass was well aware that Mr Hunt, fortyish and a little prim, had a *tendre* for her, but whether that would ever have gone beyond merely yearning after her, she now would never know.

She could see that life was going to be difficult—she had been able to talk freely with Mr Hunt, Mrs James and some of the senior servants before her elevation to the status of a great Lady.

She had read about chameleons and how they could change colour according to their circumstances; Jack could be a chameleon, no doubt about it.

On this afternoon, to be spent with Thaxted and the lawyers, he arrived very simply dressed—like a cit, Thaxted complained to Amelia. Cass thought that neither of them could talk about Jack without whining. He was wearing a very plain, inexpensive pair of black trousers, a white cotton shirt, a short jacket and an almost non-existent cravat. His manner was quiet, and it was obvious that he wanted the whole thing over as soon as possible.

All the same Cass could not help wishing that he had arrived in his fencer's uniform. Hate him she might, but she had to admit that he had looked splendid in it. In his cit's turn-out he still looked the hard man he was, but not at all romantic. In his black silks he had looked just like one of Lord Byron's heroes—*The Corsair*, perhaps; 'there was a laughing devil in his sneer' seemed an apt description of Jack at his naughtiest.

But he wasn't being naughty that afternoon, though the afternoon did contain some odd overtones, all the same. After the dull but exciting business about money was over, most of it relating to Cass, Mr Herriot turned to Jack and said, 'I take it that you would wish me to remove the Devereux heirlooms from our strong room, where they have been kept since your mother died, and hand them over to your Countess once you are married?'

'Of course.' Jack seemed faintly bored by the whole business.

Cass wasn't. 'Heirlooms?' she asked, voice tentative. 'May I enquire what these heirlooms consist of?'

'Of course, Miss Merton. It is only proper that you

should know. The Devereux family possess a splendid collection of jewels, all designed for the reigning Countess to wear.'

'The reigning Countess'! So that was what she would be in less than a week.

'I could itemise them for you, Miss Merton.' And without waiting Mr Herriot picked up a piece of paper and began to read from it. It appeared to Cass, as he informed her of parures, tiaras and suites of jewellery, all of them consisting of every precious stone of which she had ever heard, and some of which she hadn't, that the Devereux family were the owners of an absolute Golconda—an Aladdin's cave of such magnificence that her mind reeled at the prospect of wearing any of it, let alone all of it.

Mr Herriot paused when he reached the end, then said smoothly, 'Of course, in the event of your husband's death—which we hope will be long delayed—you would, of course, return them to us to hold until the heir marries.'

'Of course!' echoed Cass, as though disposing of thousands of pounds' worth of jewellery was a commonplace thing for her.

'You will note, my lord,' continued the lawyer, still smooth, 'that I have not listed the Star of Rizapore. That valuable piece is still missing.' He hesitated meaningfully—why meaningfully? thought Cass—before adding, 'As I am sure that you are aware.'

Jack's grin was malevolent. 'Yes, I am aware, thank you. It has never turned up, then?'

'No, my lord,' he replied, and then added, 'But that does not surprise you, I am sure.' The look which Jack gave the lawyer had Cass shuddering. She thought that if Jack resembled anything at that moment it was a leopard about to strike. He controlled himself visibly, remarking in a voice which would have cut steel, 'One more innuendo of that nature, man, and I will take

Devereux business elsewhere, and see that no one else
ever hires you. You understand me?'

They locked eyes for a moment before Mr Herriot
replied, his voice, remarkably, still as smooth as
before, 'Completely, my lord.'

Lord Thaxted, who had remained a silent witness of
the proceedings so far, gave an admonitory cough,
although exactly who he was admonishing was a mystery to Cass.

She gabbled hastily, before anyone said anything
which they might regret later, 'May I enquire what the
Star of Rizapore is?'

Mr Herriot bowed in her direction to show, presumably, that she still had his approval. 'Certainly, Miss
Merton. It is a diamond of the first water, the largest
which ever left India. My lord's grandfather fought
with Clive and brought it back with him. He had it
mounted for the then Countess Devereux to wear as a
pendant at the end of a chain embellished with sapphires, rubies and pearls assembled as small flowers. It
has been a Devereux heirloom ever since.'

He hesitated, half glanced at Jack, who looked
grimmer than ever, then said, 'The Star disappeared
about twelve years ago, and has never been traced.'

Lord Thaxted gave another cough, and Miss Strood
looked distressed—a common expression for her.

Cass thought that the Star sounded vulgar, but
decided that it would be tactless to say so. Instead she
faltered, as girlishly as she could—for Jack and the
lawyer were still staring bleakly at one another—'It
must be immensely valuable as well as beautiful,' as
though her one aim in life was to wear it immediately,
if not sooner.

'Yes, it *was*, Miss Merton.' His use of the past tense
seemed to please Mr Herriot, for he smiled as he
spoke. Cass's remark, however, spurred Jack into a
comment which was as acid as it was terse.

'My mother hated the dam'd thing,' he offered. '"Too heavy, too much of everything", was how she described it.'

'Indeed.' Mr Herriot bowed. 'That is all, Miss Merton. That completes the list.'

'And quite enough,' Cass returned briskly. 'I calculate that I shall be middle-aged before I have time to wear all of them once. Perhaps it is just as well that the Star has disappeared.'

This frivolous remark had Mr Herriot, Lord Thaxted and Miss Strood frowning—and Jack smiling. 'That's the spirit,' he said approvingly. 'Although I must say that they will do better adorning my Countess than locked away in a safe.'

'Exactly.' Mr Herriot bowed again. 'That concludes this afternoon's business, my lord. Unless you or Miss Merton have any further questions to ask me, that is. I shall bring all the papers for you and Miss Merton to sign tomorrow, if that pleases you.'

Jack shrugged. 'Nothing about being Earl Devereux pleases me, but, yes, bring everything tomorrow—and the jewels. I should like personally to hand one of the pieces to Miss Merton immediately after we are married.'

Oh, so we are to adorn Miss Skin and Bones after she has been translated into a countess, are we? Cass had a sudden delightful vision of herself, gems on every finger, around her neck and wrists, in her hair and her ears, stuck on her inadequate bosom, and she looking plainer and thinner than ever in consequence. She saw Miss Strood's agonised grimace as she contemplated saying something to that effect, and decided to spare Stroody's feelings.

But the satiric curl of her mouth had been registered by Jack, who immediately decided that there might be depths to plain and retiring Miss Merton which he had not yet plumbed. He offered her his arm, after bowing punctiliously to Miss Strood.

Cass had been pleased to note that since she had reproached him for his carelessness towards her he had been irreproachably courteous to Miss Strood. So much so that she had informed Cass that she thought that Lord Devereux was a much misunderstood man. 'His manners to me are perfect,' she had concluded, 'even if he is a trifle brusque towards everyone else.'

Well, calling him 'a trifle brusque' was doing him a favour! Yet it was true that he was kindness itself to all the Devereux dependants, however short he was with his relatives and the few people in society who had called upon him to acknowledge his return to the ranks of the respectable.

So, that was that. Jack exchanged a few innocuous words with her and Stroody. 'I hope, Miss Strood,' he ended, 'that you are seeing that your charge will be propertly attired for the wedding.'

This had Miss Strood all of a-twitter. 'Oh, we shall be off to a fitting tomorrow morning,' she told him, thinking again that handsome was good, but that strength and character in the face were better. 'My only worry is that the dear child is far more interested in visiting bookshops and libraries, and consequently does not value being dressed à la mode as much as she ought!'

'Oh, we can't have that, can we, Miss Strood?' Jack was all helpful gallantry. 'Not when my dear Miss Merton is about to become my bride. She will have plenty of time to study once we are married. For now, my dear—' and he turned to address Cass directly '—you must bend all your efforts towards being as *comme il faut* as possible. Take heed of everything Miss Strood tells you and all will be well.' The feral eyes were mocking her, telling her that this was his small revenge for twitting him over his manner towards her poor companion.

But he made up for that by kissing both their hands before he left, announcing cheerfully, 'And I am setting you both a good example by visiting my tailor, so that I shall be a veritable tulip of fashion, I dare swear, before the bishop who is to tie the knot.'

'Bishop!' exclaimed Cass and Miss Strood together, Miss Strood reverently regarding the back of her hand which Jack had favoured.

'Oh, did I not inform you?' he asked them airily. 'Yes, the Bishop of Bath and Wells is by way of being one of my late mother's cousins and, having arrived in town for the Season, has promised to officiate. So, you see, Miss Strood, you must look as magnificent as possible yourself. Spare no expense, I beg of you. I shan't. My hair is being cropped tomorrow. We can only pray that, unlike Samson, losing it will not deprive me of all my strength on my wedding day, when I shall surely need it.'

Cass could not help it. He had given her the merriest grin as he came out with this last piece of impudent double meaning, and she exploded into helpless and vulgar mirth. Turning scarlet, she crammed her hands over her mouth to stop the giggles whilst Mr Herriot and Lord Thaxted, who had been talking together, as well as poor Stroody, gazed at her in wonder.

Only Jack, delighted to have provoked Miss Cassandra Merton into revealing a little of her true self, was enjoying himself. 'Glad to see you so happy, my dear. I shall tell Dickie that you are on your highest ropes at the prospect of marrying me. The dear fellow was a little exercised at the notion that you might find both myself, and the whole *brouhaha*, too much for you. I shall be delighted to inform him of your good spirits. He will enjoy the ceremony so much more if he thinks that you are doing so.'

Lord Thaxted's heavy eyebrows rose. Who cared

what that vulgar fellow who followed in Jack's shadow thought about anything? It was not for him to worry about the state of mind of the future Countess Devereux. He had softened a little towards Cass over the last few days, since she seemed to be bearing up so splendidly, and was behaving herself so well—until her recent outburst, that was.

Yes, she knew that Jack was twitting her, but she could not prevent herself from saying, 'Must you cut your hair? I like it as it is.'

'Yes, I must.' He put on the most mournful expression. 'Dickie tells me that I shall be regarded as irredeemably eccentric if I continue to wear the style of nearly thirty years ago. I am assured that a Brutus cut, suitably windblown, will transform me into someone either fit to be in Court, before the Lord Chancellor, or at Court, before the Regent. Where Dickie ordains, I must obey. He ordains so seldom.'

'Where is he this afternoon?'

'Drinking with some friends from—' Jack checked himself, ended smoothly, '—from I don't know where. He also ordained that I should not join him. He wants me sober for the wedding.'

Cass had not enjoyed herself so much in years. The evident disapproval of everyone in the room of Jack's light-minded conversation was a bonus. Marriage, even if it were not quite what she had expected it to be, was evidently not going to be dull.

'Yes,' she informed him gravely, 'sobriety would be better.'

'I shall be as grave as the Bishop,' Jack assured her. 'I am told that that is the correct thing to be on one's wedding day, and I am always determined to do the correct thing, as I am sure that you are aware.'

She was not aware of any such thing, seeing that so far he had not done the correct thing once!

* * *

That lively pair, Dev and Dickie, disappeared for the last three days before the wedding, after Mr Herriot had brought the documents round for Jack and Cass to sign; Miss Strood and Dickie being their witnesses.

Disappointed because he had seemed to revert to his earlier careless ways once the legal formalities which preceded the wedding were over, Cass, on the day before the wedding, sought refuge in the usual place—the library's window-seat—a new novel in her hand.

She supposed that it would be the last time that she would hide there, away from an unkind world. In twenty-four hours—if Jack turned up for the ceremony, that was—she would become the Countess Devereux, and the Countess Devereux would not need to hide herself away. The Countess Devereux could indulge in every whim and fancy she cared to, and Cass was going to make sure that she had a good supply of whims and fancies to indulge in.

Meantime, she was still simple Miss Cassandra Merton who was not allowed to have any—except that of anticipating the wedding, which she had already begun! She was supposed to be attending the dress-makers and milliners for a final fitting of her wedding finery. Her wedding finery! The plain white dress, with sweetly pretty silk snowdrops arranged at its high neck, did nothing for her, merely accentuating the fact that Jack was marrying Miss Skin and Bones. And its colour, or rather lack of it, only served to emphasise her pallor.

Once she was married, she would make sure that she only wore clothes which flattered her instead of clothes designed to flatter a plump, blue-eyed, blonde beauty. She wasn't sure that she knew what they would be, only sure that she would be able to find a dress-maker who would supply them.

Thinking about this, and other delights which she

had begun to plan to make her life interesting and to provoke Jack Devereux either into wishing that he had not married her or into taking a little more interest in her, Cass found herself unable to read her book—a new experience for her, and a strange one. She had always been able to lose herself in a book, any book: her taste ranging from the latest Minerva Press novel to the more erudite volumes in the Devereux library, which only she and Mr Hunt had ever read.

A sleepless night didn't help matters—especially since it was Jack Devereux's fault again. He had a nasty habit of crawling into the nooks and crannies of her mind, so that when she was sure that she had forgotten him he popped up again to plague her, particularly in the midnight hours when she could not sleep, and when the most improper notions invaded her tired brain.

She was just about to fall into an exhausted doze when the curtain was drawn back and Mr Hunt stood there.

'You are not feeling unwell, I trust, Miss Merton?'

'Oh, no,' said Cass, and then apologetically, 'I wanted to be alone. How did you know that I was here?'

Mr Hunt inclined his head deferentially. Best to do so when he was talking to the future Countess Devereux. 'When the sun is in this direction, Miss Merton, it throws your shadow onto the curtain. I have known for some time that this place was your refuge. I have only disturbed you because Miss Strood is distressed by your disappearance.'

'Remiss of me to hide,' sighed Cass. Astonishingly she realised that tears were not far away. She steadied herself. She must not cry in Mr Hunt's presence. Not on the day before her wedding. Perhaps it was his kind and concerned manner and expression which were undoing here. Something certainly was.

There was, however, one mystery he might solve for her. She had asked Miss Strood more about the missing Star of Rizapore, but she had told Cass that it must have disappeared before she had come to Devereux House, and that no one had ever spoken to her of it. Perhaps Mr Hunt would be able to help her—he had been librarian to the late Earl for the last fifteen years. So she put her question to him.

'The Star of Rizapore,' he echoed, as though he had never heard of it before, his manner a trifle constrained. 'One of the Devereux heirlooms as I understand. Why do you ask?' And then, smiling a little, he went on, 'Of course, the lawyers came: it would be natural for you to want to know what happened to what would have been the most remarkable gem in your collection. I understand that it disappeared in mysterious circumstances about twelve years ago, just after the late Countess's death, and that is all that I can tell you. The late Earl was a close-mouthed gentleman, as I am sure that you are aware.'

And that was that. It was no more, perhaps a little less, than Mr Herriot had hinted. What was certain was that it had disappeared at about the time that Jack had been exiled. Were the two things connected?

It was not a mystery that she could solve, nor did she wish the Star to be found. It was not at all the sort of thing which she would want to wear.

'Will there be anything further, Miss Merton?' Mr Hunt was speaking to her as though she had already passed beyond his ken. Apparently, in marrying Jack she was losing his friendship: the happy afternoons which they had spent together in the past were to be considered things of the past. She was Miss Merton now, soon to be Lady Devereux, no longer Cassandra. Cass felt desolate.

'We shall, I hope...' she was surprised to find
herself on the verge of stammering '...be able to
continue our course of study after my wedding, Mr
Hunt?'

He seemed to think before he answered. 'I expect
that you may find that your new duties will take up
most of your time.'

This sounded so final that the tears threatened
again. What new duties could he mean? Not going to
bed and getting a new heir for the Devereux line—
that had been denied her. Oh, dear—was that what
was wrong with her, that she wanted Jack to be her
true husband? Could disappointment be eating her
up? She didn't like him, so she couldn't be wanting to
climb into his bed—particularly when he had made it
so plain that he didn't want her in it.

Mr Hunt was waiting for her to answer him, and,
since she was struck dumb by what she had discovered
about herself, he was turning away, no doubt thinking
that their conversation was over.

Not so. Cass was suddenly aware that she wanted to
retain Mr Hunt's friendship and the library as a place
of refuge, if not behind the curtain then before the big
table, where he laid out what he thought that she
ought to be reading.

'Oh,' she told him, as lightly as she could, for he
must not think her overset by what was about to
happen on the morrow, 'I hope that I shall still find
time to improve myself. I am sure that Lord Devereux
would expect it of me, seeing how young I am.'

Mr Hunt's expression told her that he thought such
a supposition most unlikely, but politeness kept him
quiet. Cass thought it unlikely too. Did Jack Devereux
really wish to have a blue-stocking for a wife? She was
sure that he had had no mistresses who were blue-
stockings in his previous life—wherever it had been
lived.

If Stroody was distressed, then she must go to reassure her, to try on the unsuitable dress, the equally unsuitable bonnet, and acquire the bouquet which she must carry but which would do nothing for her. Lilies of the valley, snowdrops and harebells in silk were scarcely the symbols of Cass Merton's character.

Mr Hunt, who had turned away, was now turning back again. It was plain that he was screwing himself up to say something. He hemmed and hawed for moment, turned red then pale before he muttered, a little hoarsely, 'Miss Merton, I respect your mind. For a female's it is a good one. You possess a power of logical thought rare in your sex. If, in the future, you should ever need a friend be sure that you will find one in the person of Edward Hunt.'

He held out his hand to her, in token of what he had just said. He did not say that he wished that he had offered for her hand before Jack Devereux had risen from the dead, but it was in his mind, and had been since he had heard of her coming marriage.

How like him to speak of himself so humbly in the third person, and how unlike he was to that selfish and arrogant monster Jack Devereux, thought Cass dazedly.

She said gravely, rewarding him with her hand to shake, 'That is very kind of you, Mr Hunt. I shall remember what you have just said to me.'

He held onto her hand for a moment, then said, the words wrenched from him, 'I only wish that I might have been able to introduce you to my mother. She has a good mind, too. You would like her.' He fell silent. This time he had finished.

And what a turn-up that was. Nothing in Cass's short life had prepared her for such a thing. Every day seemed to be bringing her new shocks. Surely there could be no more.

But there were. After she had endured her fittings

and Miss Strood's cooings as to how sweetly pretty she looked, which brought her an acid answer from Cass—'You mean my clothes look sweetly pretty. I don't.'—she returned to Devereux House to find Jack and Dickie still missing, but Fred in the drawing room, looking *distrait*.

He had been waiting for her, he said. He looked pointedly at Miss Strood, who absented herself, for Cass, so soon to be married, was now considered fit to speak to young gentlemen on her own. Besides, Fred hardly qualified as a man. Stroody simply saw him as an overgrown boy who could be no threat to Cass.

'Yes, what is it, Fred?' Cass was short. She was tired, what with no sleep and being pulled in and out of a series of unbecoming gowns, stockings and shoes.

Fred took no note of that. He was dragging at his cravat in the oddest fashion, as though it were strangling him. Like Mr Hunt he turned first red and then white, which should have warned Cass of what was coming, but didn't.

'Look here, Cass,' he burst out suddenly, after one final tug at his cravat, which rendered it completely undone, 'do you really want to marry such a fellow as my Uncle Jack is?'

'Well, I must, musn't I?' said Cass employing her famous powers of logic for which Mr Hunt had praised her. 'Seeing that I have agreed to be his wife.'

'But only under a kind of duress, surely,' exclaimed Fred. 'You thought that you had nowhere to go, seeing that my father and mother and uncle and aunt had not the decency to offer you a home. I mean, that was why you accepted his offer, wasn't it?'

Something seemed to have improved Fred's powers of logic, thought Cass numbly, but she still didn't know where they were taking him. She was soon to find out.

'Perhaps,' she answered him, as obliquely as she could, 'we shouldn't be having this conversation, Fred.'

'Oh, but we should,' he told her passioantely, and went down on his knees before her to prove it. 'Oh, Cass, if I had arrived earlier, and had known the truth, I would have offered for you. It's not too late, you know. Say yes to me, and we can be off to Gretna Green. We can take Stroody as a chaperon and be married as soon as we get there. I can't sleep for thinking of you married to Jack! Do say yes, please.'

He was clutching at the skirts of a woman who had just discovered that, rogue and trickster though he might be, she was so attracted by Jack Devereux that her one regret was that once they were married he wasn't going to take her to bed.

Cass hadn't the slightest wish to get into bed with either Edward Hunt or Fred, and surely that was what the whole business of being married was about.

With my body I thee worship. She didn't want to be worshipped by the poor infatuated young man on his knees before her. She could only be sorry for him and let him down as gently as she could. She would try to do so without hurting him too much.

'Oh, Fred, I can't. First of all, think what your mama and papa would say if I were to agree. We would both be ruined if I consented to such a thing. Besides, I have given my word to Jack, both publicly and privately, that I will marry him tomorrow, and I can't go back on it.'

Fred stood up, muttering mournfully, 'I knew that you would say that. You are a good girl, Cass, whatever Pa and Ma say. You're not marrying him just for the title, as they keep hinting, are you? Say you're not.'

'My reasons for marrying Lord Devereux are for me to know,' returned Cass, still trying to be kind. 'But no, I'm not marrying him for his title; you may be sure of that.'

'So that's that,' said Fred, suddenly prosaic. 'But I

had to try to change your mind, feeling as I do about you—you do see that. And if you ever need a friend in the future, be sure that you can count on me. I've already told Jack he will have to answer to me if he makes you unhappy. I can't say fairer than that.'

So Jack would have Mr Hunt and Fred after him if he made her unhappy. The idea of such an unlikely pair being able to intimidate the hard man he was should have made Cass laugh, but instead her throat closed and she could not speak.

Suppose either of them had offered for her before Jack's arrival, what then?

There was no doubt in her mind that her answer to them would still have been 'No'. Because much though she valued Mr Hunt as a friend she could not see him as a husband; and for her to have accepted Fred would have ruined him, as she had already told him—his parents would never have consented to the match. . .

What had been unforeseen, though, was that she should acquire two admirers, as well as a future husband, in the last few days—something which Cassandra Merton would not have considered possible at the beginning of that time.

If life had begun to surprise her, and was continuing to do so, could it be possible that her future might be equally as remarkable as her past and present were proving to be?

Apparently calm—Miss Strood had already complimented her on her *savoir-faire*—Cass was actually living in a stew of fear. By evening Jack had still not returned to Devereux House, and she was contemplating the frightful possibility that he had changed his mind about marrying her, and was about to resume his unknown life again. No one seemed to be curious about what that life had been and what he had been doing for the last twelve years. Frightened to find out what exactly he had been getting up to, no doubt, or too frightened of him to enquire. There was no doubt that he had thoroughly intimidated all of his relatives except Fred.

Cass was on her way down to supper—a lonely one, for she had missed dinner on the grounds that she preferred to rest after the strain of enduring so many fittings in one afternoon—and had reached the entrance hall when Jack and Dickie finally arrived home. Miss Strood might miss the signs of strain which Cass was trying to suppress, but Jack obviously had the power to detect them. Or was it the little sigh of relief which she gave at the sight of him which told its story?

He bowed to her and said, in that gravel voice which had the power to entrance as well as frighten her, 'My dear Miss Merton, were you a little worried that I might have disappeared again? If so, I must say that you flatter me—or is it that you are merely worried that you might not become Countess Devereux tomorrow, not that you might regret losing a husband?'

He *was* a beast, but an intelligent one. No one but Cass seemed to think that he was clever, but she had already decided that he was too astute for his own good—as Stroody had once said of the politician, George Canning.

Cass, putting her nose in the air, replied loftily, 'Not at all. If I am a little *distraite* it is because I wish to be absolutely *comme il faut* tomorrow, and not let either of us down. That would please all your relatives mightily, and I have no wish to oblige them any more than I need.'

She knew at once that she had given something of herself away to the subtle man opposite to her. His feral eyes danced. Yellow sparks almost shot from them.

'Oh, bravo,' he murmured. 'So pleased to hear it—my sentiments exactly. I see that my life with you will not be dull. I owe you an explanation for my absence. I have been clearing up the remnants of my life before I became Earl. Among other things I owed a debt of gratitude to my landlady and I have been busy paying it...something which I am sure you would approve of.'

His landlady! Probably his mistress, or his woman. A man who looked and sounded like Jack would be certain to have had more than his share of both. She had decided that he was, or had been, a soldier, but apart from her own instincts she had no evidence which might lead her to believe that her assumption was correct.

She inclined her head graciously, practising at being Countess. 'Oh, I believe that, as you said the other day, you would always wish to be correct. That assurance will sustain me through the ceremony tomorrow.'

Jack gave a crack of laughter. Miss Skin and Bones had guts, no doubt about it. There was more to her than met the eye. She was twitting him, telling him that she knew that he was deceiving her. Dickie had warned him, as Fred had done, that he must treat her properly, not hurt her, and he had growled at him, 'Whenever did I treat a woman badly, Dickie, tell me that?'

Dickie had growled back, 'You have to remember that she's not the kind of woman you've been dealing with lately, Jack. She may be shrewd, but she's still little more than a child and can easily be hurt. I'll be watching you, so mind your manners.'

Jack had been piqued. 'Well, one thing, Dickie, she certainly possesses the power to make men want to protect her. First that ass Fred Maxwell threatened to have my guts for garters if I mistreated her, that middle-aged librarian I've inherited looks wounded every time he sees me with her, and now I've to endure you behaving like an old woman on her behalf. What mysterious power does she possess, and why can't I see it?'

'None so blind as those who will not see,' Dickie had murmured cryptically. 'Just remember what I said. And remember that I'm neither a silly boy, nor a womanish book-reading cleric.'

Jack had shrugged.

Now, looking at Cass, he was still a little puzzled that she had the ability to make so many of those around her wish to protect her. He thought that she was well able to protect herself, but perhaps he was wrong. He shrugged again.

'You have everything you need for tomorrow? Wedding gowns and all that?' he enquired a little tentatively, well aware that he was not good at this kind of small talk, but, dammit, he had to placate Dickie a little. He was almost sure that Miss Casssandra Merton would prefer him to be more plain-spoken—it was, ridiculously, Dickie and the rest whose sensibilities he was protecting, not hers!

Amazingly, she seemed aware of this. 'I'm not good at this kind of thing,' Cass offered apologetically. 'I mean, talking without saying anything. Stroody says that I throw facts at people, and most people don't want to catch them.'

'After tomorrow you may throw a few at me,' returned Jack, grinning now, 'and I promise to catch as many as of them as I can.'

Did he know how much his smile transformed his face? The uncompromising sternness that it possessed in repose disappeared. He was almost the young man with the falcon again. Did he know that when he did that to a woman she would want to do anything he wished of her without question? Was he even aware how much plain Cassandra Merton, Miss Skin and Bones, was coming to lust after him?

'That's what you say now,' riposted Cass, her smile transforming her thin face, 'but is that truly what you will say after we are married? Husbands are said to take their wives for granted.'

Jack winced internally at this. It seemed that Cass might speak plainly to him, but he was not to do so to her—or so everyone was telling him. Whose sensibilities were being offended? He had none to offend, or so it was supposed. Now he had become a gentleman, nay, a nobleman, again, was he about to acquire some? He had spent twelve years turning himself into such a hard man that in the world in which he had lived his cold self-control, his lack of care for his own and other people's feelings had become a byword.

'My dear infant,' he said, remembering that Dickie had called her a child, 'you may be sure that since we shall not be an orthodox husband and wife, we may make up our own rules. I cannot say fairer than that.'

Cass's smile was radiant again. She dipped him a modest curtsy. 'Oh, Lord Devereux, I am delighted to hear you say so. And I shall hold you to your word once we are married. I shall call on Dickie here to be a witness to what you have said.'

She had called him Dickie without thinking, because they were Dev and Dickie in her thoughts. She did not know it, but nothing she could have said would have pleased Dickie Dickson more. He was one of the unconsidered in the new world to which Dev had introduced him, and at a stroke Cass had shown that she thought of him as a human being, like herself, and her future husband's friend.

Everyone else in Devereux House allowed their eyes to rove over him contemptuously, mutely suggesting that the new Earl was demeaning himself by calling a nobody from the gutter his friend. Yes, Miss

Cassandra Merton deserved to be protected, so she did, and no mistake.

What Cass also didn't know was how many allies she was collecting around her. Jack was not yet one of them, even though he was the person who filled her world the most. Changed, damaged by his past, both known and unknown, the young man with the falcon had stepped down from his picture frame and she was to marry him on the morrow.

Cass held this thought to her all the way to her bed, and to her surprise she slept soundly and dreamlessly that night, to greet her wedding day with a smile as a peacock's shrill scream woke her from sleep.

CHAPTER SIX

HER wedding day! It was fine, which was something to be grateful for. Miss Strood arrived early, twittering, and immediately behind her Lady Constantia Maxwell swam in, already dressed *à l'outrance*, even though she had not yet breakfasted and the ceremony was some hours away.

She rudely dismissed poor Stroody, who was babbling about what Cass should wear before she changed into her wedding finery, and Cass made an immediate note that this was the last occasion on which Lady Constantia would ever be rude to herself and her poor companion.

It was stupid of her to forget that after the wedding Cass, as Countess, would take precedence over her everywhere: at court, in the ballroom, at the races and in every house which they visited. She would, in the strict terms which governed their lives, have to 'yield the *pas*' to Cass, and Cass was determined that yield it she would—and Amelia Thaxted, too. It might be a small revenge and a petty one, but she had years of slights to make up for.

Meantime, she endured Lady Constantia's contemptuous patronage of the wedding dress of which Stroody was so proud, and which was laid out piece by piece, including the bonnet which Cass was to wear when she and Jack drove to Roehampton, not far from where the Bessboroughs lived. The late Earl's father had built a small and elegant villa there for a ballet dancer whom he had brought over from Paris, and whom he had dismissed when, arriving early one day, he had found her in bed with the gardener.

It was small enough to be human, Jack had told her—to Dickie he had said that he had chosen it because it held no memories for him, either good or bad. He had never told Dickie why he had been disowned by his father, and Dickie, like Cass, knew better than to ask.

Lately, since Jack had christened her Miss Skin and Bones, Cass had taken to eating more than usual, but that morning, waiting to become Jack's wife, she found that she could neither eat nor drink. Food stuck in her throat, and she could not swallow liquid. Miss Strood came in again with a tray of food, after Lady Constantia had left her—not before reeling off a list of admonitions as to Cass's behaviour before, during and after the ceremony.

Cass waved it away. The sight of food made her feel ill. Miss Strood quavered at her, 'Are you well, my dear? You don't look well. You might feel better if you ate or drank something.'

'No, I shouldn't. I should feel worse. Don't ask me to go downstairs, Stroody. Let me stay in my room. I need only to change once, into my wedding dress—if I do that. You know how much I hate pulling clothes on and off.'

'You may be sure,' said Miss Strood briskly, 'that after today you will have your own lady's maid. I am surprised that Lord Devereux has not made arrangements for you before. Or that his sisters didn't insist on it.'

'Oh, I don't think that Jack has lived the sort of life in which wives and ladies' maids figured much,' remarked Cass with a wry smile. 'And Amelia and Constantia can't wait for the ceremony to be over. I believe that they all intend to leave as soon after the wedding breakfast as is decently possible. Why do they call it a breakfast when we shall be eating it this afternoon?'

'I'm sure I don't know. Mr Hunt might be able to tell you, but I don't think that it would be proper of you to consult him today. You are sure that you won't come downstairs? You might find that you wish to eat when you are in company.'

'Oh, I'm sure that I shall not.' And that was that. Cass realised that to Miss Strood she was already Countess, and that the days of Cass's tutelage were over.

She wondered what Jack was doing. Dressing, presumably. The ceremony was to be held in the biggest salon in Devereux House, the Chinese Room. It was rarely used, being reserved for great occasions, like entertaining the King or the Prince Regent. It was called the Chinese Room because it was hung with the most exquisite Chinese paper and contained a fabulous collection of Chinese porcelain and furniture. Cass had thought that she might like to have a Chinese-style dress made, in delicate yellows, pinks, greens and blues to match the paper, but Miss Strood, and the Ladies Amelia and Constantia, had thrown fits at the mere idea.

But she had already decided that once she was married she would order the dress to be made, and a fan to match—a big one—and some lemon and blue and pink feathers for her hair—tall ones—and little turned-up slippers like the Chinese ladies were supposed to wear.

This delightful notion, together with some others, equally eccentric, entertained her so much that she forgot to be frightened, and managed to eat some of the food which Miss Strood had brought her. Shortly afterwards, Amelia Thaxted's maid arrived, and told her that her mistress had sent her to help Miss Merton dress herself. It would not be proper for her to do it herself, nor for Miss Strood to assist her now that she was to be Countess.

So Stroody sat in a chair and directed matters and made suggestions whilst Cass was pulled about, and finally she and the maid pronounced her to look 'sweetly pretty', and a bigger misjudgement than that Cass could not think of! She hoped that Jack would not laugh when he saw her.

After that Miss Strood was dressed, and Cass told her that she looked so well in her new leaf-green gown with its pretty saffron trimmings that it was a pity that Jack was not a little older so that she could be Countess.

Miss Strood blushed becomingly at this unlikely compliment, and, with the maid holding up the small train of the light coat which Cass wore over her dress, they processed downstairs into the Chinese Room, where all the company was assembled.

Cass knew hardly any of them: they included the Bishop of Bath and Wells and some other grandees, friends of Amelia's and Constantia's families, to whom Cass was introduced before she took up her stance against one of the double doors which led into the room. Jack, she was informed, would enter through the other, come over to her, and escort her to where the Bishop stood, before a giant Chinese vase which had snorting dragons climbing all over it.

Lord Thaxted, to give the whole business a semblance of decency, or so he had informed his wife, was to stand by Cass until Jack arrived. Cass would much have preferred Mr Hunt, Fred or even Dickie to have performed this office for her, but could not say so. She supposed that Dickie would be supporting Jack. Not that that gentleman needed any supporting.

She could see Fred and Mr Hunt among the spectators. They were both gazing at her with the same slightly mournful expression, as though she were going to her execution. The senior servants sat to the immediate rear of the family, and the more important of the junior ones were behind a rope at the far end of the room. She found out afterwards that Jack had insisted on their presence.

Opposite to Cass was a French clock—a piece of make-believe chinoiserie, seeing that the Chinese had no clocks. Time seemed to go so slowly that Lord Thaxted, grunting, pulled out his watch to check whether or not Jack was late. He was due to arrive at half past eleven of the clock, and surely it must be that now!

But no. Just as the clock sweetly chimed the half-hour the door at the far end of the room opened and Jack came in, Dickie in attendance. Cass could hardly recognise them, particularly Jack—he looked so splendid. The servants thought so too. A buzz of excited exclamations ran round the back of the room until Edward Maxwell, seated at the front, rose and turned to glare at them all, so that they fell silent.

Jack's russet-coloured hair had been cut short, and had fallen into light waves, artfully arranged à la Brutus. His dress rivalled that of the most à la mode dandy. His cravat was a snowy vision, his black jacket, skin-tight black pantaloons, silk stockings and light black shoes showed off his strong face and superbly athletic body to perfection.

He wore no jewellery of any kind. An earl usually had some sort of star or decoration to pin on his coat or hang around his neck: Jack had nothing. But the lack of such baubles did him no disservice, for there was nothing about him to diminish his natural splendour. . .or his natural air of authority. . .

Behind him, Dickie, loose-boned and stolid, was tricked out in a plain black suit of a more orthodox cut than Jack's, and his black silk stock—he had refused to wear a white one—sat uneasily round a neck unaccustomed to such finery. 'Just for today, Dev,' he had said, 'and in *her* honour.'

'Not mine, then?' Jack had grinned at him. He knew Dickie well enough to be aware that, friend though he might be, Dickie had no illusions about Jack or any of his doings.

His arrival was the signal for the ceremony to begin. Afterwards, Cass could remember little of it. She moved through it as though she were in a dream. She knew that she said the right thing at all times, held out her finger for Jack to put the ring on it, smiled until her face ached, caught sight of herself looking composed and thoroughly in charge of herself in one of the great mirrors with which the room was adorned, however odd and strange she felt.

After the wedding and before the breakfast, Jack took her by the hand and led her downstairs to the huge kitchen where, among the copper pans and on the long oak table before the giant hearth, a meal was laid out for the servants to eat after they had finished serving their masters upstairs. There were bottles of good wine too, and glasses. Jack took one of the glasses, filled it, handed it to Cass, and then ordered her to toast with him, 'Those who have made this day possible for us by their hard work.'

Behind them she heard Dickie, who had also been handed a glass mutter 'Amen'. Mr Greene called for three cheers for m'lord and his lady, and the cheers were so heartfelt and enthusiastic that they were heard by the guests upstairs, who were waiting impatiently for Jack and his bride to favour *them*.

Before they left, Mrs James came over to her and kissed Cass on the cheek. 'Be happy, my dear. You have married a good man. He has given me a cottage at Coverham and a little pension so that I may retire at last, in comfort. He says he remembers the sugar buns I used to bake for him when he was a lad and came to the kitchens for comfort.'

After that, the reception upstairs was all anti-climax.

There was no one there to wish Cass happiness, and even though everyone said all that was proper it came from cold hearts and not from warm ones. Perhaps the Bishop was a little kinder than most of the others, but she did not really know him. Perhaps he beamed like that at everyone.

Jack had told her that he would behave correctly, and so he did. Occasionally, his large warm hand was there to hold her small cold one, and give her comfort as the eyes of the quality silently quizzed and questioned the upstart who had married the ne'er-do-well Earl. And then she was led upstairs, where a girl whom she had never seen before was waiting in her room, and who told her that m'lord had chosen her to be m'lady's maid, and that she was to dress her for the journey to Roehampton—so she had been wrong to believe that Jack would not think of such things as a lady's maid for his new Countess.

But a shock awaited her when she reached the big entrance hall where Jack stood waiting for her, a living statue to rival the marble ones of long-dead Greek and Roman heroes that stood in every niche in Devereux House. The shock was that Miss Strood was evidently not accompanying her. She was still wearing her leaf-green dress, and was holding a small lace handkerchief to her eyes.

Cass forgot herself. She was no longer that self-possessed person the Countess Devereux. She was the small Cassandra Merton, who had possessed but one friend in Devereux House, and that friend Stroody. They had never been parted since Jack's father had introduced them on the day she had arrived from her northern home.

A small cry was wrenched from her. 'Stroody! Are you not to come with me?' She suddenly sounded her real age.

Jack, who had ordered their parting, put an arm

around her shoulders, to reassure her, saying, 'Never fear. Miss Strood will be waiting for you when we return after the honeymoon.'

It was as though, at last, Cass realised the enormity of what she had done. In a trice her whole world had turned upside down. No Stroody! It was like saying no God, or no sun, moon and stars. Her companion took her handkerchief away from her eyes, moving forward to kiss her on her cheek and to say bravely, 'You have a husband, now, my dear. He must come first. I shall be waiting for you, you may be sure.'

'Promise,' said Cass fervently, kissing Stroody back, and not looking at Jack, who must be thinking what a cry-baby he was marrying—for although she had shed no tears she knew that her very real distress was patent.

I must behave with dignity, she thought. I am a married lady now. Stroody's position has changed, as mine has.

She handed Stroody her bouquet, which she was still clutching. For some reason she had picked it up after her maid had eased her into her new coat and fastened the strings of her bonnet for her. She let Stroody go, saying gently, 'You knew that you weren't coming with me, didn't you? Why didn't you tell me?' There was no reproach in her voice, only a sad dignity.

Miss Strood stood back. 'Time for you to grow up, child. You will not always have me.'

Jack pressed her arm. 'Come, my dear. The carriage is waiting, and the servants are outside to cheer us on our way to Roehampton. We must not keep them waiting.'

He was still being correct. And she must be correct. The Earl and Countess Devereux were about to take their first journey together. The first of many, perhaps? And horses must never be kept waiting. Cass knew that. She had heard the late Earl say it often enough,

and for the first time in Jack's severe gravel voice she
could hear an echo of the inflections of his father's
softer, gentler one.

She was handed in. He was beside her. He had
changed into something looser than his tight, fashionable clothes. He was wearing new-fangled loose
trousers and a soft shirt with an open collar, such as
Lord Byron often wore, with a thin black silk scarf
knotted loosely around it, the ends dangling down in
careless elegance.

He didn't look much like Lord Byron, though,
whom Cass had seen on several occasions when she
had been in society. He was much taller, and broader,
and his face was so much sterner than Lord Byron's
soft one. Cass thought that now that the ceremony was
over and they were alone together he looked sterner
than ever. She shivered.

Jack felt the shiver and exclaimed, 'How can you be
cold, Cass, on such a hot day?' For the late afternoon
sun was filling the coach, and gilding them with its
orange rays. And then he laughed and said ruefully,
'For the same reason, I suppose, that soldiers in Spain
felt cold when waiting for the battle to begin on the
hottest day of Spain's hottest summer. You are not to
be to frightened of me, Cass. I may be a swine in many
ways, but I always keep my word.'

Soldiers in Spain! Did he know that he had given
himself away? Or did he think her unable to add two
and two together? She had suspected ever since she
had met them that he and Dickie had been soldiers
together, and he would not have said what he had if
he had not been speaking from knowledge, surely.
Had he been with the Duke's Army in the Peninsula?
And, if so, in what capacity?

Jack put a gentle arm around her. He had no idea
what to say to his bride. So far he had teased her, paid
her the compliment of assuming that she had a good

mind, and spoken to her more frankly than he would have spoken to most young things. But what did he really know of her? He had watched her from beneath hooded eyes during the wedding ceremony and afterwards—she had behaved with a natural dignity which put both of his sisters to shame.

Dickie and Fred had warned him not to hurt her, and he would try not to. But he had had so little to do with innocent young girls since he had left home. The women he had known were frank, generous and mostly unchaste. His mouth twisted, and he looked more dour than ever. There had been one woman who had been different, but she was long dead, and he thought that he might not meet her like again.

Well, he had married this particular young woman partly as a joke and partly to spit in the faces of the respectable, by defying the usual rules of polite society. But in order to spare her feelings he had ended up by behaving as correctly as a newly breeched parson, when his natural inclination had been to make them all go on paying for what had been done to him twelve years ago.

How silent she was! He had already learned that she knew when to speak and when to be silent, and she had impressed him by her *savoir-faire* and her composure on this difficult day. Except for that one heartbreaking moment when she had discovered that her companion was not to accompany them, she had behaved like a woman years older than she was.

She deserved more from him than cold silence and indifference.

'You do understand why I ordered Miss Strood not to come with us?' he said abruptly.

Cass nodded. She had been thinking about this very thing for the last few minutes. 'Because I must grow up,' she told him simply, 'become a real Countess and not a pretend one, dependant on others. And that is why you did not tell me beforehand.'

She had surprised him again. She was making a habit of it. He must not underestimate her, for to do so might also be a cause of inflicting pain.

He nodded. 'Exactly. It's a cruel world out there, and you must learn to survive in it.'

'Did you learn to survive in it?' She did not know how to address him. Should she say 'Devereux', as Amelia called her husband Lord Thaxted 'Thaxted', or should she call him Jack?

As though he had read her thoughts, he turned towards her and smiled, a flash of superb white teeth. 'Call me Jack,' he told her. 'I asked you to do that when we met, and I haven't changed my mind.'

'Jack,' said Cass thoughtfully. 'It suits you.'

'It's the only part of my name which has remained constant,' he said lazily. 'And, yes, I learned to survive in the cruel world. Just.'

Cass waited for him to continue. He wasn't going to tell her anything about his old life. That disappointed her a little. Was it that he did not trust her, or was it because his life had been shameful? Looking at his hawklike profile, she didn't think that could be true. Besides, Dickie Dickson would not be the friend of a bad man. Now, how did she know that?

'Has Dickie come with us?' she ventured.

Jack shook his head. 'No. Fair's fair. If I took Stroody away from you, then it was only fair that I lost Dickie. He's gone to stay with some friends in Shoreditch. He will return when we're back at Devereux House.'

'Did you live at Shoreditch?' Cass was sorry that she appeared to be quizzing him so desperately, but she had a not unnatural desire to know all about him, to find out what had changed him from a pretty boy to a stern and striking-looking man.

Jack's smile was an odd one. Dickie had called her shrewd. 'You have a mind for a life at the Bar?' he asked her. 'Such questions, and all of them so ruthlessly probing.'

'You know everything about me,' Cass said simply, 'and I know nothing about you.'

'Well then, yes, I had lodgings in Shoreditch. And that is all I shall tell you. Better so.'

Cass didn't think so. She gave a small sigh and sank back into the cushions. She felt weariness claim her. She shut her eyes. The motion of the carriage, the warmth which surrounded her, even the sensations which being so close to Jack were rousing in her were all combining to lull her, to drive her to the brink of sleep. Why was it that she felt safe with him when, in some off way he was constantly warning her against knowing too much of him? For so she interpreted his wariness, his refusal to commit himself, his determination that most of him should remain a secret to her. . . and to everyone else.

Sleep took her. And because she was asleep Jack's arm crept around her. He did not want to feel anything for him but a distant friendship. Safer so, for he felt nothing for her but a kind of pity for one who had been so unconsidered.

Nevertheless, when they reached Roehampton and the coach stopped, and footmen ran about opening doors, unloading luggage and pulling down steps for them to descend from the coach and enter the waiting villa, why was it that he waved them away and carried her, still sleeping sweetly against his heart, across the threshold of their first home?

CHAPTER SEVEN

'M'LADY.'

Someone was shaking her gently. Wherever could she be? Cass opened her eyes to stare at a delicately flowered canopy over her head. She was lying on a large four-poster bed, still in the clothes in which she had left Devereux House.

Memory returned. She had been in the carriage talking to Jack and now she was here, in a strange bedroom, and her new maid, Betty Aston, was rousing her gently. She was Lady Devereux, Jack's wife; everything which she had known for the last six years had vanished. She was in unknown territory.

Cass swung her legs over the side of the bed. Jack—or one of the footmen, perhaps—must have carried her in. Betty was removing her light coat, urging her to allow her to remove her new dress, to wash herself, and was leading Cass, still feeling a trifle dazed, into a large room off the bedroom where there was a washstand with a china bowl on it, and a free-standing bath. There were jugs of warm water waiting for Betty to pour into the china bowl so that Cass might wash her face and hands.

It was odd to be so waited on, for until today she had looked after herself. 'The child must not get ideas above her station,' Miss Strood had been frequently told by the Ladies Amelia and Constantia.

Well, her station was above theirs now... Cass yawned as Betty eased her into a nightdress of the finest pink silk trimmed with the most delicate lace. It did not at all resemble any of the sensible cotton ones which Miss Strood had thought fit for her trousseau.

Betty saw her surprised look at it and offered as respectfully as she could, 'M'lord ordered this for you, m'lady.'

'But it is surely not time to retire yet,' protested Cass, a little frightened, and yet a little expectant. He had said that she would not be his true wife, so why had he given her this sinful-looking nightwear?

'It is past ten of the clock at night, m'lady. You have been sound asleep ever since m'lord carried you up. See!' And Betty drew back the heavy brocade curtains which covered the windows, to show her the dying May moon of 1818 in its last quarter. So Jack had carried her to bed. Did that mean anything—or nothing?

Food was waiting for her on a tray placed on the small table opposite to her bed, and wine in a tall bottle with a crystal glass to drink from. Betty poured some for her, and for the first time that day she ate the delicate sandwiches, the tiny cakes, and drank the fizzy white wine with real enjoyment.

'M'lord said that he would come to you when he has eaten supper. He thought that you would prefer not to be woken in order to take it downwstairs with him. So he ordered me to bring your supper up and prepare you for the night.'

Oh, Jack intended to come to her room, did he? Was he about to break their bargain despite all he had said? And would she object if he did? The wine was delightful, and the fizzy bubbles seemed to be bursting in Cass's head, making everything which was happening to her seem unreal. After she had eaten, Betty helped her into the bed again. It was so high, and was set on a dais as well, so that a small pair of steps was needed at its side to enable her to climb into it.

On the nightstand, besides a candlestick, was a small pile of novels. On the top was the latest from the author of *Sophia*, entitled *Anna Gentry*. Betty saw her pick it up, and said quietly as she unpacked Cass's bags and hung up her clothes, 'M'lord chose those for you, the housekeeper said. He told her that you would be sure to enjoy them.'

By her speech and manner Betty obviously thought that Earl Devereux was a most considerate husband. Cass smiled a little sadly and tried to read *Anna Gentry*, but whether it was because of the situation in which she found herself, or the wine she had drunk, she could make little of it. Betty curtsied and retired, leaving Cass alone in the vast bedchamber.

But not for long.

There was a knock on the door, and when she called 'Enter' in as firm a voice as she could, although she was quaking inside, Jack came in.

He was carrying a bottle of red wine and a wine glass. He was not fully dressed; he had shed his coat and had pulled off the black silk scarf which he had worn earlier. The top buttons of his shirt were undone, so that Cass could see the thick dark hairs curling on his chest. The sight made her mouth dry and her stomach contract. That he had rolled up his shirt-sleeves, revealing strongly muscled arms also dusted with a sprinkling of fine reddy-brown hair, didn't do much for her composure either.

'Good evening, my dear,' he said, putting the wine and his glass down on the tray which held the remains of her supper. 'I see that you have eaten well, and that Betty has looked after you.'

He walked towards the bed and sat down on its side, near to her. 'Had you been awake I would have told you that tonight, at least, I must spend in your room if the servants—some of whom are undoubtedly in the pay of one or both of my sisters—are to be deceived as to the truth of our relationship. Any hint of our bargain and my sisters will be crying foul, and challenging my father's will. Now, I have come to the conclusion that over the past twelve years I have more than earned my inheritance, so I want no one to question the validity of our marriage.'

He picked up Cass's hand, which was lying lax on the splendidly embroidered counterpane, and said gently, 'You are not to be afraid of me. I have no intention of doing anything to hurt you, no intention of breaking my word.'

Cass did not know whether to be glad or sorry at what he was telling her. He was so near to her, so masculine in his light clothes, which concealed very little of the superb athlete that he was, that her heart beat faster than ever. He mistook her pallor, lifted her hand and kissed it gently before replacing it on the bed. 'You are a brave child, my dear, and you will make me a worthy Countess, I am sure.'

Every time that he touched her, however lightly, Cass's whole body seemed to throb and quiver. It was only with the greatest difficulty that she prevented herself from putting out her own hand to stroke not only his smooth cheek, but the strong jaw with its light dusting of dark stubble. She had noticed some days ago that by evening he needed to shave again if he were to preserve the smoothness which he had achieved in the morning. She wondered what it would be like to feel the rough strong hairs against the soft palm of her hand. . .

Jack continued to mistake her silence for fear. He rose, turned away, and Cass's heart resumed its normal rate. Over his shoulder he said, in the gentlest voice which she had yet heard from him, 'We shall have to provide some evidence that we shared a bed. Betty brought my nightclothes up; to spare your feelings I shall change in the dressing room.' And he picked up a valise before he left her.

She could not help it. Cass had a sudden vision of him with absolutely nothing on. She was sure that he was as muscular all over as his bare arms suggested. As for the parts of him which made him male, as opposed to those which made her female, she knew roughly what to expect, having seen the statues which adorned Devereux House. But the notion of seeing in warm reality what she had only seen in cold stone was simply adding to the dizziness which was afflicting her. She closed her eyes, but that only seemed to excite her the more.

Jack's return in a nightshirt which showed little of him should have reassured Cass, but didn't. In it he seemed larger than ever, and more formidable. He sat down in the chair on the other side of the bed from the nightstand. He was carrying two glasses of wine— a white one for her and a red one for him.

He raised his glass to her and Cass replied in kind. He drank his wine in one swallow, and said wryly, 'Nothing in my life has prepared me for this night...'

Cass interjected rapidly, 'Nor mine either.'

'Nors yours either,' he replied. For the first time since she had seen him that morning his face was full of its usual sardonic humour. 'It is not exactly the kind of situation which *Sophia* is wont to describe, I do admit. I must apologise to you. I was wrong to marry you—wrong, having done so, to afflict you with strange bargains. But, alas, the deed is done and we are stuck with one another. I shall try to be kind to you, but I am a man of strong temper, as Dickie is so fond of reminding me.'

'Yes, I *had* noticed that,' responded Cass dreamily. She calculated that she had probably disposed of almost the whole of a bottle of white wine on top of having eaten very little.

Jack's crack of laughter at her reply was a genuine one. 'Well, at least I chose a girl of spirit to play my tricks on. Dickie and the rest are afraid I shall overwhelm you, one way or another. Shall I, Lady Devereux?'

'Well, you haven't, so far.'

'No, indeed. But you haven't seen me at my worst.'

Drink made Cass bold. 'Why do you always set yourself down, Jack? So far you have not said or done anything to disturb me, and when you have lost your temper it has usually been with good reason. Now, Philip. . .' She fell silent. Even a drink-loosened tongue ought not to betray her into indiscreet comments about a man's dead brother.

'Now, Philip. . .?' Jack was mocking her slightly. 'What about Philip? Am I not to know?'

Cass shook her head. 'No, indeed. Only. . .' She hesitated a little '. . .for all your brusqueness there is a kindness in you which was not in Philip, or your father. Don't make me say any more.'

Jack was silent. Then he gave way to an impulse which descended on him out of the blue. He leaned forward, put out a strong hand, pulled her face towards him and kissed her. At first it was a chaste kiss on the cheek, and then his mouth, controlled by itself and not by him, sought out and found her tender lips.

So sweet! So sweet! Cass had never been kissed before, and his mouth so soft on hers, so gentle, touched off tremors which ran down her body to her very toes, taking in parts on the way which no lady should confess to owning. It was like the effect touching his hand had on her, only infinitely more exciting.

Oh, God! Cannon were going off in Jack's head. He was becoming roused. Roused by this impudent child, whose innocence he had vowed not to subvert, even if he was using it for his own purposes. His inclination was to throw up both their nightgowns, climb into bed and finish what he had so mistakenly started. He had meant to reward Cass with a brotherly kiss, comfort her a little for being a brave girl, and here he was feeling as he had not felt for years.

He was a bee sucking at her lips. He was a boy, kissing his first girl. The lost years which had taken away his true youth almost before he had enjoyed it vanished. He was innocence kissing innocence. . .

Memory returned. He was Jack Devereux, ruthless Jack Devlin, whose way with women had been notorious, who had spared no one, not even himself, in his drive towards self-fulfilment in everything that he had cared to undertake, towards asserting that, whatever he had lost all those years ago, what he had gained since in self-worth and character was of greater value.

Where he found the self-control to pull away from Cass he never knew. Her eyes on him were like stars. She clung to him, murmuring, 'Oh, Jack. Oh, Jack.' She was his for the taking. Honour screamed No, and whatever else he had sacrificed he had never sacrificed *that*—and he must not start doing so now.

'I shouldn't have done that,' he said hoarsely. 'Forgive me.'

'Forgive you?' Cass's expression was dazed, drugged, as though she had drunk laudanum. 'Why should I forgive you? It was. . .wonderful. I never knew that kissing could be like that.'

Oh, damn, damn, damn. He had breached her innocence.

Cass wanted to say, Why did you stop? But reason told her that young ladies, even newly married young countesses, probably ought not to ask such a question. It was for men to lead and women to follow, in marriage as in life. No one had ever said such a thing to her bluntly, but the inference had always been there. But were not inferences there to be challenged?

Jack sprang up. He walked over to where he had left the bottle of wine. He poured himself another glass, drank it down, picked up the half-empty bottle and came over to where Cass sat, numbly believing that in some way she had done something wrong.

Of course, he must have thought that she was trying to break their bargain. She must go carefully or he would think that *she* was trying to trap *him* in some way. Yes, that was it. And yet it was he who had started the kiss, not she. Oh, being grown up and married was damnably difficult. Saying and doing the right thing was no easier now than when she was a child. Once she had thought that when she was grown up everything would become simple: she would always know what to say and do.

Oh, what a wrong thing to think! Being grown up was harder, not easier. Being Cassandra Merton was child's play compared with being Cassandra, the Countess Devereux.

'My dear,' Jack said—wine didn't seem to be affecting *him*. 'We must give the servants something to think about. In the morning I shall empty the remains of this bottle on the sheets, so that when the servants come to make the bed they will find a cause for gossip.'

Cass nodded. By his manner he was pretending that what had just happened between them had not happened.

For the first time she felt anger. He had no right. She was his wife. She was not a child, even though he might think her one. And if he had a temper, so had she. But she would not show it now.

'How are we to sleep, then?' she asked him, a little timidly. 'Are we to share the bed?'

He nodded. 'You between the sheets. Me on top of the counterpane,' he told her briskly. Jack thought that he would be able to withstand temptation if he didn't actually touch her. He had discovered that, astonishingly, his child bride presented a very real threat to his self-control. And not quite the way which Dickie and the rest thought.

That seemed to be that. Jack blew out the candles. Cass settled herself between the sheets. He lay down on top of them, trying not to let the delicate scent of woman, lilac perfume and clean clothes, which wafted to him from where Cass lay, affect him too much.

He was not aware that Cass, before she drifted off into a sleep which came surprisingly soon, was trying not to allow the masculine scent which Jack gave off disturb her over much. Philip Devereux had smelled of soap, Fred Maxwell of horse, Mr Hunt of dust and books, whilst Jack Devereux gave off the aura of a strong and roused man.

Waking, Cass might have wondered how she knew that, but sleeping, she did no such thing.

Waking was yet another thing. Cass, sleepy but happy, rolled over to put her face into the pillow on which Jack's head had rested all night. His scent, masculine and disturbing, was there, but he was not.

He had left her. Disappointment ran through Cass until she heard masculine sighs and exclamations coming from behind the closed doors of her dressing room cum bathroom. By the sound of it, Jack was having a bath or an extended wash. Further disturbing visions of Jack in the bath began to plague Cass.

There must be something wrong with her—every time she thought of him it was in this forbidden way. Miss Strood had always rushed her by naked statues and certain pictures in the galleries which they had visited, and perhaps she had been right . . .

The dressing room door opened, and there was Jack. His reddish hair, wetly plastered against his skull, had turned black, making his stern face sterner. He was wearing the light clothing in which he had arrived the night before, and was plainly not going to get back into bed with her.

Without thinking, Cass smiled and stretched herself

luxuriously, like a little cat enjoying life. It occurred to her that, as Countess, one of her privileges might be that of not leaping out of bed early, but of enjoying it a little longer.

Jack saw Cass's imitation of a cat and looked away. He had woken up earlier to find that during the night she had somehow insinuated herself into the crook of his left arm and was lying against his chest. The sight and feel of her had done nothing for his self-control. He had jumped out of bed, made for the bathroom, ripped of his nightgown and begun to pour over himself the stone-cold water from the pitchers left there the night before.

If that didn't make his treacherous body behave, nothing would. And then the artful little minx—or the complete innocent, and he couldn't decide which—went and tortured him by giving him such a dazzling smile that it transformed her plain face, and it had shown off her body into the bargain.

Well, to be fair, she hadn't shown him her body so much as reminded him that she possessed one. He had to either rush to the Haymarket to find a woman, or try to control that part of him which was telling him, Dammit, she is your wife, and last night virtually offered herself to you, so why are you hanging back?

Because I don't want to hurt her. Later, perhaps—when she's grown up a little, and we know where we stand.

Meantime, he smiled back and said, 'Would you like to breakfast in bed? I usually go for a ride, first thing. And then we can decide on a programme for the day.'

Cass nodded. She didn't want him to leave her, but he was apparently anxious to be off, and breakfast in bed seemed an excellent idea. While she was waiting for it she threw a robe about herself and went over to the window, to discover that it looked down on a paved courtyard where Jack, now wearing riding clothes, was walking a black horse up and down—a horse as magnificently male as he was.

She had seen all the Devereux men on horseback, but she soon grasped that none of them could ride like Jack. He and the horse were one. There were grooms standing by, and Jack began to put his horse through a series of manoeuvres which had one of the younger grooms crying, 'Bravo, m'lord!' He was reprimanded by one of his elders, who nevertheless murmured something admiring to Jack as he dismounted. Next, he mounted one of the late Earl's big greys and mastered him.

Only the arrival of her breakfast took Cass from the window; when she looked out again, horses and men had all gone, and the courtyard was empty.

She didn't see Jack again until the late afternoon, when he walked into the pretty drawing-room with its portrait of his mother by Romney over the hearth. She was wearing the Star of Rizapore. He was carrying a pile of official-looking papers, which he put down on a small desk which stood in an alcove. He was dressed in his fashionable finery, and asked her gravely whether he might sit with her while he worked.

Cass, who was busily engaged on her canvaswork, a kneeler for the Devereux chapel at Coverham, murmured, 'Of course,' before she rang a bell which brought in a pretty young maid.

'Tea for m'lord and me,' she ordered, as coolly as though she had been doing it all her life. Jack sat himself down at the desk and began to read his papers as though his life depended on it. When the tea-board arrived, he moved to the big armchair facing Cass, on the other side of the hearth. There was no fire in it, but someone had placed before the empty grate a large Chinese vase containing early summer flowers.

They sat there as comfortably as though they had been married for years before Jack spoke.

'You have not been too lonely, I trust. I am sorry to seem to neglect you, but Herriot has forwarded the accounts from Coverham and I started to look at them before I realised what a task I had set myself. Sadly, my sisters appear to be correct in their condemnation of the agent there. He has been robbing the estate blind. It looks as though I shall need to appoint a new agent for Coverham as well as a new secretary for myself. My father's secretary, Sedgeby, has grown too old and careless, but he can stay on for a little time to break his successor in.'

Cass sighed. She agreed with him over Sedgeby, but she had rather liked the courteous old man who had grown grey in the service of the Devereux family.

'And Sedgeby? What will happen to him?'

'A pension and a cottage at Coverham, if he wishes it. He can use the library there. I understand that he has in mind a great work on Anglo-Saxon Yorkshire. He will now have time to write it before he grows too old.'

He saw Cass's relieved expression and frowned. 'You surely did not expect me to turn the old man out into the world?'

Everyone had said how heartless Jack was, but it seemed that they were wrong. She remembered some years ago that his brother Philip had urged his father to turn Sedgeby away because he was growing incompetent, and the late Earl had said, 'I have a mind for us to grow old together.'

Jack was watching her, his face dour. Cass thought that she might have hurt him by appearing to believe that he would throw Sedgeby out into the world. To change the topic completely she exclaimed as artlessly as she could, 'Now that I am Countess, may I have lessons from someone who can teach me the harp?'

'The harp!' This diverting suggestion certainly took Jack's mind away from the revelation of the low opinion which his relatives had of him. 'Why the harp?'

Cass had attended several concerts where a mistress of the instrument had played some hauntingly lovely tunes. But it was not only that which had entranced her. The sight of her long elegant arms and hands plucking at the strings had also attracted. Fred had once told Cass that she had beautiful arms—perhaps, she had thought sadly at the time, because she didn't possess a beautiful anything else. If they *were* beautiful, then playing the harp would be the best way to display them.

'Yes, the harp. There are harps at both Coverham and Devereux House, I believe.'

There was silence for a moment and then Jack said, his voice colourless, 'Yes, they were my mother's.'

It occurred to Cass that he had spoken several times of his father, but never of his mother. She had been a beautiful woman, if the Romney portrait was anything to go by, but none of her children had resembled her—except Philip, a little.

'Do you play any other instrument?' he asked her. 'I believe that to do so would be helpful to you if you wish to master the harp. When we return to Devereux House I shall make a point of finding you a teacher.'

Being Countess had its pleasant side, then. There were other things which she wished to do, but she had no intention of telling Jack of them. She thought that he deserved to be surprised a little. So far he had been the scene-setter in all their encounters and she had, so to speak, always run behind him. It would not hurt for him to run a little after her.

Apparently inconsequentially, after informing him that she could play the pianoforte, Cass asked him if he had enjoyed his ride.

'Ah, you did see me, then,' he said, and Cass wondered, a little annoyed, if there was anything that he missed. 'I thought that I caught a glimpse of you at the window. Yes, I did. My father's horses have been well-schooled. You must come riding with me tomorrow. No reason why we should not go out together each day. You do ride, I trust? If not, I will teach you.'

Why, when he was being so perfectly correct and serious with her, did Cass regret that he was no longer teasing and quizzing her as he had done in their earlier encounters? Perhaps it was Dickie's absence, or was it because she was now Countess, and he must be punctilious with her? Whatever the reason, she preferred the former Jack to the present more sober one.

They chattered about nothing whilst they drank their tea, until Jack excused himself and went back to his papers. He studied them with the same fierce concentration with which she had seen him control his horse—and Dickie—and herself! It occurred to her that she still knew little of him, and hoped that his brief interlude which they were spending alone might bring them together.

But at the end of it he remained as much of a mystery as ever.

He was perfectly courteous to her. After the first night, he came to her room for a short time before retiring to his own, which, she had discovered on her first day up, was joined to hers by a connecting door.

He was always scrupulous about not surprising her; came to her after her maid had put her to bed, always knocked on her door, and talked to her gently on a variety of subjects. They spoke of everything and nothing. He was well-informed, she found, and surprisingly well-read. She quizzed him a little more penetratingly than usual over this.

'I can see,' he told her, lying back in his armchair,

and watching her as she sat up in bed, the candlelight painting shadows on her face, as it did on his, 'that I must satisfy your curiosity. There were *longueurs* in my life, and I soon found that boredom was relieved if I read. I had liked to read as a child, neglected it as a very young man, and found it again when I grew older—and lonely.

'I had a friend—not Dickie—who possessed a small library, and we used to talk of what we read, until—' He shrugged, his face growing sombre. 'But no more of that. I am self-educated—I had only one year at Oxford before the world fell in—and after that I had to organise my own course of reading.'

He fell silent again, the candlelight telling her how he would look when he was old, with his face all severe planes, angles and hollows. 'Hunt told me that you liked reading, and were an apt scholar,' he said abruptly.

'It was kind of him to say so.'

Jack was suddenly the blunt man she had first met. 'Not kind,' he rasped, 'if he was tellng the truth. Kindness would be if he lied about you. He wasn't lying, was he?'

'No, and I would like to go on studying when we return to Devereux House, if being Countess will allow me to do so.'

'Time will be found for you. I promise you that.'

He stood up. His eyes were hooded. He always had the power to surprise her, for on this last night of her honeymoon, after having refrained from touching her at all since his kiss on the first night had sent them up in flames, he came over to the bed, dropped his hands on either side of her as she sat looking at him wide-eyed, and kissed her again.

Cass shuddered under it. She saw that the pupils of his eyes were dilated, and that he was controlling himself with difficulty.

He stood up, towering over her. His face as inscrutable as one of the Central American masks which a Devereux ancestor had brought back from a visit there.

'If you are ever unhappy, you must tell me so. I do not intend to make you unhappy. Within reason, whatever you want you may have. Only if what you want seems excessive to you need you come to me for permission. You understand me?'

Cass nodded. She could not speak. She wondered if the emotion she was feeling was affecting him too.

Surely not! For was he not older, experienced, and could he not have any woman he wanted—so why should he want his undistinguished wife? Some demon which ruled her occasionally, and which had got her into trouble with Stroody on more than one occasion, made her ask, her own voice slightly mocking, 'Am I legally your wife, Jack?'

Now, as she must have intended, she had shocked him.

Jack tensed. His big body became quite still. His hands clenched into fists. She had, after some fashion she could not understand, touched a nerve.

'Why are you asking me this—at this late date?'

'Why should I not, Jack? For all I—and the world knows—you already have a wife and child somewhere. Have you?'

His eyes were suddenly cruel. He took a step towards her. His hands clenched and unclenched. His voice was as harsh as he could make it.

'No wife, or child. I had a whore once, for several years. And a child. They are both dead. Cruelly so. They are no concern of yours.'

The demon had driven Cass to do something that she had not intended and that she now regretted. She had hurt him, and now, for all his promises, if she were not careful, he would hurt her. What to say to him: I had to know something of you, for you tell me so little?

No, that would not do. Instead, keeping her own voice steady, which was difficult for his passionless mask was frightening her, she said, 'Everything that concerns you concerns me, Jack. I am sorry if I hurt you.'

The tension leaked out of him. His young wife had neither cringed, cajoled nor been cravenly apologetic in reply to his own brutal plain speaking. 'Yes, I think you are. I am sorry to be so secretive, but that has been my way for so long I cannot gainsay it. I can only say that you must accept that I am a blank page so far as you are concerned, but that I shall always deal fairly with you.'

That had to be enough. The demon sank back into the cave from which he occasionally emerged. Fortunately only occasionally, for Cass usually had herself, and him, under as much control as Jack was wont to display in keeping his own demons in order.

But Cass knew that to live with someone as strong and as dominant as Jack was would take all her strength and all her resolution if she were not to be overwhelmed.

When they returned to Devereux House, Stroody came to meet them in the entrance hall. She held Cass off for a moment and exclaimed, 'You look well, child!' As though, Cass thought amusedly, she had been for a cure at a spa, instead of on her honeymoon.

Jack looked around him, presumably for Dickie, who was not there to greet him. Cass removed her new bonnet, and allowed Stroody to lead her into the drawing room where tea awaited her. Now Stroody was behaving as though she had been to the North Pole and back.

Jack said when they reached the door, 'You will

forgive me for a moment—I shall be back immediately,' and strode away in the direction, Cass thought, of the stables. Ever since their conversation last night he, too, had been treating her as though she were some sort of invalid.

Stroody, looking significant, rather like a Papal Nuncio about to pass on some bad news, leaned forward confidentially once Cass had sat down and been handed a cup of tea. 'He will not find him, I fear. That man of his left Devereux House the day after you were married and has not been seen since.'

It was not like Stroody to gossip, but this was perhaps too big a tit-bit not to pass on. Cass said nothing, merely raised her eyebrows, a trick of Lady Constantia's to signify that she had heard what had been said but would not comment on it; it was a trick which she was beginning to find useful, and one which nonplussed Stroody a little. She was used to Cass making forthright answers, not playing the fine lady.

Jack returned. He took the tea which Miss Strood offered, made polite noises about the weather, the state of the gardens at Devereux House as compared with those at the Roehampton villa, and was altogether as politely null as Cass was being. Stroody was probably privately wondering what their honeymoon had done to them both to quieten them down so much, but if so she wasn't speaking of it.

Later, when Cass had gone upstairs to her room to be manoeuvred out of her travelling clothes by Betty and into a modish semi-evening gown, and was seated on a sofa before the window which looked out across the lawns where the peacocks were displaying themselves, Jack came in, already wearing his loose informal clothes. He had driven her from Roehampton in his curricle, behind four of the greys which she had seen him with on the morning after their wedding.

'Dickie has gone,' he said abruptly. There was something forlorn in his manner.

'Yes, I know. Miss Strood told me.'

Jack walked to the window to stare out of it at one particular peacock whose splendour was greater than that of his fellows. 'He had no need to,' he exclaimed. 'There is a place for him here; he knows that.'

Cass contemplated a painting by Wright of Derby, showing a woman and a child admiring a sickle moon through a window. 'Perhaps he did not think that there was.'

If they had been soldiers, what relationship had there been between them? She had thought long and hard on the matter and had decided that Jack could not have been an officer, and neither could Dickie. They had been comrades, that was plain, and each trusted the other. Equally plainly Jack was used to command, far more than Dickie was, and consequently she thought that he had possessed some rank which Dickie had not, but which still allowed them to be friends.

Jack broke into her thoughts. 'Oh, no! He must be aware that wherever I am, whatever I am, I should never desert him.'

Cass was logical. 'But you have not—other than by becoming Earl, which he may see as a form of desertion.' She did not say, You have not deserted him, *he* has deserted *you*, for it did not need saying, and it was that which was troubling Jack.

He came over, sat beside her, took the book she was reading from her hands and said, almost with violence, 'Where did you acquire such wisdom, Cass? Doesn't it trouble you, to be so young and so composed? When I was your age I was an impulsive savage, and most of the young ladies I have met have been frivolous fools. Why are you different?'

She met his hard stare with a serenity which shamed

him. 'I don't know. The only thing I can say is that I have never, until you married me, possessed any kind of stability, any real assurance that tomorrow I might have a home, or even another meal. I have been a dependant with no claims on anyone, and that has served to make me think carefully about myself and those about me.' She hesitated, gave a small smile. 'I don't think that I'm wise. On the contrary, I'm aware of my ignorance.'

He took up her hand and kissed it.

'And that,' he told her, 'makes you wise. Be wise about our marriage, Cass, and you will survive it and me. You know that I shall have to find Dickie. I owe him my life, and to some extent my sanity. I know I ought to let him go free—except that I also know that he has nowhere to go—and I need him here. If that makes me selfish where he is concerned, then so be it. But at the least I can offer him a home and something to do worthy of his talents. If I cannot, what is the worth of my being Earl?'

Later, when he had gone, after telling her that he would try to trace Dickie in the morning, Cass thought of what he had said to her about being wise.

Wise? Was she wise? She thought not, for had she not already decided to play the Countess to the utmost, to make him know that he possessed a wife whose spirit matched his own? Was that wise? For she had no idea of what the outcome would be.

CHAPTER EIGHT

'THERE is a person arrived who says that she had come to teach you the harp,' Stroody announced agitatedly. Cass, who had discovered that Jack had been correct in saying that his mother's harp was at Devereux House, had now to discover that he had arranged for Signora Corelli to come to teach her to play it.

'I never knew that you wished to learn to play the harp,' Stroody twittered at her as they walked into the music room, where the harp had been taken out of its bag and Signora Corelli and her tall male acolyte were examining it. Or rather the *signora* was examining the harp and the acolyte—Silvio, Cass was to discover— was examining the pianoforte.

Nor did I, thought Cass, until I became Countess. There were a lot of other things which I did not know about myself, and which I am determined to discover!

'A secret passion,' Cass lied coolly. 'Oh, and Stroody, dear, tomorrow afternoon Madame Rosina the dressmaker is calling. I am determined to show the world that Lady Devereux's taste in dress is worth a second look. I am tired of sweetly pretty gowns which make me look like little Miss Muffet wondering where her tuffet has disappeared to!'

Whether it was Jack's influence, or whether she had always possessed such a talent but had never before found it wise to use it she wasn't sure, but Cass was also discovering in herself a bent towards the lively in conversation, which had poor Stroody exclaiming, 'Oh dear, Cass,' every few minutes or so.

She suppressed it whilst the *signora*, with Silvio performing on the pianoforte, gave her her first lesson.

'It appears,' Cass remarked irrepressibly at the end of it, 'that mastering the harp is rather more than the ability to wave one's arms gracefully around it!'

'M'lady is pleased to jest,' smiled the *signora*. 'You 'ave a talent for ze 'arp, no doubt of zat.'

Cass, who thought that the *signora* probably hailed from somewhere within the sound of Bow Bells rather than from Milan or Rome, also thought that she was not above flattering great ladies, even if they were not yet twenty.

In this she wronged her teacher and herself, as the following weeks were soon to show, and she began to master the instrument. But the hard-headedness that poverty and neglect had bred in her did not disappear with her changed circumstances.

But certain of her other attributes were already beginning to change. That afternoon she sat in the drawing-room with Stroody, looking at the fashion plates in *The Ladies Magazine* and shaking her head over them, when Fred Maxwell called. If he had hoped to see Jack he was to be disappointed, for as Cass told him, he had an engagement elsewhere. She did not tell Fred that he had gone once more in search of Dickie — for that was Jack's business, not Fred's.

Fred was carrying a small posy of carnations which he handed over to Cass before sitting down and saying to her in his frank and eager fashion, so different from Jack's cool self-control, 'I say, Cass, you look prettier than ever. Bein' married must suit you, eh!'

He had no sooner come out with this than he blushed scarlet, for surely this was not quite the thing to be saying to a young girl, even if she had recently been introduced to the delights of the marriage bed.

'I'm sure you know what I mean,' he added, a little glumly. 'No harm intended, I assure you.'

Cass pretended not to have heard him by the simple

expedient of exclaiming excessively over the flowers he had brought and asking Stroody to arrange for them to be put in water immediately.

No sooner had Stroody gone than Fred leaned forward to say earnestly, 'You *are* happy, Cass, I hope. Jack's treatin' you properly, and all that?' And what a *double entendre* that was!

'Oh, yes,' responded Cass. To her own secret amusement she found herself fluttering her eyelashes at him—and where had that trick come from? 'I'm as happy as could possibly be expected.'

She also secretly wondered what Fred's response would be if he were to discover that Jack had not touched his bride other than in friendship. Would Fred think that that came under the heading of 'treatin'' Cass properly?

This interesting conundrum occupied the back of Cass's mind whilst Fred continued his interest in her welfare. 'Mama thought you might be bored when you became Countess,' he finally offered. 'Are you bored, Cass?'

'Oh, not at all, Fred. Nothing could be more delightful, I assure you. Why, I am at present engaged in planning a whole new wardrobe, and I spent this morning learning the harp.' Her descent into brainless frivolity was amusing Cass as much as it was exciting Fred.

'The harp, Cass!' Fred was enchanted by this news. 'I say, Cass, you will play us some tunes when you're ready?' And then he added doubtfully—he must have been talking to Stroody—'I never knew that you were interested in playing the harp!'

'It is, of all things, the one thing I have always wanted to do,' carolled Cass untruthfully. 'And, Fred, there *is* something you can do for me. I know that you are most knowledgeable about dogs—are quite famous for it, in fact—and I am determined to have a dog of my own. I have always wanted one—' another lie, but no matter '—and I thought of you when I made up my mind that I could wait no longer!'

A dog! This was even better than discovering that Cass was learning to play the harp. 'But shouldn't you speak to Jack about buying one?'

Cass shook her head. 'He said that I was to do exactly what I wished, now that I am Countess, and only ask him for advice if what I wanted to do was enormously extravagant. Buying a dog doesn't come under that heading, I'm sure. No, Fred, you must advise me.'

'A poodle,' offered Fred, 'or one of those dear little creatures you can put in your lap.'

'Oh, no.' Cass was at her most incisive. 'Not at all. I don't want a *little* dog. I rather fancied a wolfhound. A really big one. Just imagine walking in the Park with such a noble animal by my side!'

Fred threw caution to the winds. He had been about to ask, Would Jack approve? when the notion of walking or driving Cass in the Park, with a wolfhound of all beasts with them, became suddenly entrancing.

'Right, a wolfhound it shall be, if that's what you wish. I say, Cass, I can see you intend to go the pace a bit. Wolfhounds and harps! Is there anything else you fancy that I could help you with?'

Cass considered. This was going to be more fun than she had thought. Fred obviously wished to be treated as some kind of *cavaliere servente*, as the Italians called a young man who existed simply to escort a respectable married woman.

'Not at the moment, Fred. As I said I do intend to improve my wardrobe by ordering some unusual toilettes, but it's hardly the thing for me to ask you for advice on *that*.'

Fred was in complete agreement. 'Mama wants to give a dinner party for you and Jack. She says that we must not appear to be at outs with him now that he has inherited—even if we didn't expect him to. I shall look forward to it no end, now I know that you intend to let the world know that the Devereux have a Countess at last. You won't be able to bring the dog along to dinner, though. Not quite the thing.'

Cass contemplated with wicked delight strolling into the Maxwells' drawing-room with her new pet and seeing how they coped with having to respect the whims of the poor relation whom they had so constantly snubbed. But she feared that Fred was right. Wolfhounds and little dinners to celebrate the inheritance of the new heir did not really go together.

'You're sure Jack won't object to all this?' he enquired a little anxiously.

'Of course not,' Cass told him, not having the slightest idea of what Jack might object to. 'After all, he was most enthusiastic about me learning the harp.'

'Then that's settled.' Fred smiled, and Miss Strood's return had them all talking most decorously on a number of topics, none of them concerned with wolfhounds, harps or daring toilettes.

'Sorry to have missed Jack,' he told them as he left, and spoke no less than the truth. The slightly feather-headed Fred found Jack's forcefulness something to admire, he possessing so little of it himself.

Jack arrived at Louis Fronsac's rooms. He had finally driven to their old lodgings at Shoreditch to be told that Dickie was working for Louis. He waited patiently while Dickie instructed a young sprig of nobility in the art of using the sabre. Dickie was concentrating so hard that he did not see Dev until the lesson had ended. He tucked his sabre under his arm, pulled off his mask, and walked over to where Jack was leaning against the wall.

'Thought you might track me here,' he offered quietly.

Dev was equally quiet. A dangerous sign.

'Then why the devil did you make me follow you? You know that there is always a place for you, wherever I choose to live.'

Dickie shook his head. 'No, Dev. We're not equals any more. You're Earl now.'

'Damn that,' snorted Jack, raising his voice a little. 'We've been equals since we met, Dev and Dickie.'

'Were,' said Dickie equably. 'Were!'

'Dickie.' Jack's voice was almost desperate. 'I haven't a friend in the world apart from you. None of my damned relatives gives tuppence for me. All of the friends I made as a boy are long gone. I doubt if they'd know me or I them if we met. Except for you the friends I made in the past twelve years are lost to me. There will always be work for you—I'm not asking you to live off me for nothing. You're one of the best men with horses and carriages I've ever known. Come and be my best man.'

'You have your wife,' was Dickie's answer to that.

'Cass? She's a child.'

'She could be your friend. If you treat her right, that is.'

'Treat her right? Of course I'll treat her right.'

'You could hurt her—easily.'

How did they come to be talking about Cass, for God's sake? Was Dickie in love with her?

'I won't hurt her. She's so young. Good God, I've not so much as touched her.' Which was not quite true, but would serve.

'I know,' remarked Dickie cryptically.

'So, come back.'

For an agonising space of time Dickie considered. He had pulled his sabre from under his arm and was gazing at it.

'Remember that Frenchman who nearly did for me at Salamanca, Dev?'

Jack nodded, wondering what was coming next.

'You did for him, instead. I'll come back—for a time anyway. I pay my dues.'

Exasperated, Jack suddenly roared, 'Damn you, Dickie, that was in return for what you did for me. We're quits—equals. That's why I want you back.'

'I have my pride, Jack. Acknowledge it. As you must acknowledge your wife's.'

Cass again. 'Very well, Dickie.'

'But I'll have to keep my word to Louis, as you did. I'll work mornings for you until then.'

'And live at Devereux House. A bargain, Dickie.'

'A bargain, Dev. But remember, at Devereux House I'll speak to you as Earl in public. Better so.'

Thus is was arranged.

And all the way home Jack pondered on what Dickie had said to him of Cass.

He walked into the drawing-room shortly after Fred had left, to find Miss Strood moaning gently, 'Oh, dear, Cass, no,' over Cass, who was drawing little fashion plates of her own—*The Ladies Magazine* cast aside. He flung himself down in an armchair, booted legs stretched in front of him, the very picture of masculine ease. Cass knew at once, without being told, that he had found Dickie and that all was well.

'What is it, Stroody?' he asked. 'What naughtiness is my bride committing now? Is my strong husbandly hand needed to bring her into line?'

Jack was laughing gently at them both. Imitating Cass, he had taken to calling Miss Strood 'Stroody', and far from resenting this she loved him the more for it. Her delight showed itself in one vast blush.

'Cass wishes to dress herself in the most *outré* fashion,' she wailed, 'instead of wearing the pretty toilettes we chose for her before she was married.'

Jack looked at Cass, who was trying not to look pleadingly at him. He must not side with Stroody, he must not! Not only did she wish to make her mark on the world in her own way, but she wanted to be independent at last of the restraints which she had endured for so long. But he was her husband; what he might decree concerning her actions was law.

He was laughing openly now. 'Oh, no, Stroody. You have inspired in me the most intense curiosity to find out what my wife considers *outré*. Let her have her head, even if it means that she rejects the pretty toilettes.' The greeny-yellow eyes were testing them both. He was happy, and was trying to share his happiness with them.

The strangest thing happened to Cass. On their honeymoon she had experienced the most intense physical desire for him that first night, when he had kissed her. But what she was feeling for him now was quite different. Her pleasure at his pleasure was mixed with the tenderest sensation, which demanded that his feelings, his desires, must be satisifed or she would feel miserable herself.

It was as though she were part of him and felt his pleasure over regaining Dickie, his happiness at coming home to find Stroody and herself bickering gently and each turning to him for support. Here was a side of him which she had never seen before, and she wanted to hold him, to stroke his warm cheek and his smiling mouth. . .in friendship, as well as in love.

Love! That was it! She loved him. Not only that, but she was in love with him—and when in the world had *that* happened? Cass was so shocked by this discovery that she fell silent, the world about her disappearing. She surfaced to hear Jack saying, his tone kind but mocking, 'Silent, Cass? Here is a turn-up to be celebrated.'

'Wha. . .what. . .' she stammered at him, her senses

whirling, for how was she going to live with this knowledge?

'I was asking you when you proposed to launch your refitted self upon the world?'

'Soon, soon,' she mouthed idiotically at him. He must never know, never—for had he not married her so that he should not have to take a wife for love and children, as well as to acquire his father's estates? And he could not love Miss Skin and Bones. But why should she not make him come to love her? And now her campaign for him to take notice of her took on a different and deeper meaning.

Jack stood up energetically. 'Soon? Good. Now I must change. Oh, by the by, how did your lesson with the *signora* go?'

'Famously,' Cass told him, having discovered her composure. 'She assured me that I shall be giving recitals soon, but I think she says that to all the Countesses she teaches! Oh, and Fred called. He says that his mama will be giving a small dinner party for us. To launch us into society.'

'Will she, indeed? So I am to be forgiven for inheriting. May I enquire when we shall be so signally honoured?'

'Fred said before he left that your sister will be calling tomorrow to hand us a formal invitation. She will be asking the Duke of Wellington to be one of the guests. She met him when she was in Paris with her husband last year, after Waterloo, and Fred says she got on famously with him.'

'Wellington!' Jack gave a snort of laughter. 'He gets on famously with all women—particularly married ones who are still pretty, like Constantia. Do you get on famously with Fred?' he asked her a trifle abruptly.

'He was always kind to me,' parried Cass. 'He likes talking to me.' Seeing that Jack had no interest in her other than as a convenience to him, then why should he not be aware that other men found her attractive, even if not for the usual reasons for which men chased women? She had not told him of Fred's proposal to her, for she knew instinctively that he would not like to hear of it.

The invitation was duly made, and Cass attended the little dinner party and met the Duke. Unfortunately, her *outré* gowns were not yet ready for her to wear, but the Duke seemed to like the little Countess, despite her schoolgirl's turn-out.

The Duke frowned when he was introduced to Jack, who was himself turned out in the splendid rig that he had worn for their wedding and was wearing a semi-military cravat, called the Napoleon, and an expression of ineffable goodwill quite unlike his usually stern one.

'Devereux,' he acknowledged formally as Jack bowed to him. 'I knew your father.' And then, 'I seem to fancy that *we* have met before—though I can't think where. Have we?'

This came out in a commander-in-chief's bark, but Jack, nothing daunted, bowed again, replying smoothly and lying as he did so. 'I think not, Duke, for I am sure that I should have remembered such an occasion.'

The lie was because he had met the Duke before, for the briefest of moments, one man among many, and had said wryly to Dickie just before he had left for the Maxwells' dinner party, 'His memory is said to be remarkable. Will it be remarkable enough to remember me? I hope not.'

Dickie had shrugged. 'Well, you didn't look then how you look now. You're clean, to begin with. . .'

They had both laughed at that, but all the same it worried Jack a little to catch the Duke staring thoughtfully at him, and for him to say before they left, 'I do have the oddest feeling of familiarity, Devereux. You're sure?'

Jack didn't care to have to lie again, particularly with Cass's shrewd eye upon him, and when they were riding home in their carriage, to divert her from the topic of Wellington's curiosity, he asked her, 'What was all that about a dog? Fred was quite excited when he was talking to you, but I couldn't catch why.'

'Oh, he's choosing a dog for me. I asked him to advise me on buying one. What with all your work on the Devereux estates taking up so much of your time, I thought you might prefer me to give Fred something to do.'

'What sort of dog? A poodle?'

Now it was Cass's turn to lie. 'Oh, I'm not sure. I haven't quite made up my mind.' And then she went hot all over, for she was sure that he must know that she wasn't telling him the truth. But Jack was too busy with his own worries to detect that Cass had hers. The devil was in it if the Duke should remember him. He had no wish for his past to surface. Not that he was ashamed of it, but it was dead and gone, as he and Dickie were agreed.

Dickie was waiting to see to the putting away of the horses and the carriage when they arrived home. If it wasn't quite like the Dev and Dickie of old, it was still better than nothing, as they were both coming to acknowledge.

Society was agreed after the Maxwells' small dinner-party, which was really a very grand occasion, and not small at all, that the new Lady Devereux was a taking little thing, quiet and modest, and that Jack was something of a shock. No one had expected him to be such an impressive figure of a man. The Duke had added to the interest in him, with his patent obsession with having met Jack before.

'Memory going at last,' he remarked irritably to his

crony—some thought his mistress—Mrs Arbuthnot, when he next met her. 'Bit early on, surely. Ain't as old as that yet.'

Consequently, invitations showered in on them. The mirror on the drawing-room mantelpiece was stuck full of visiting and invitation cards, and, if Cass had valued such a thing, her mirror took the *pas* in such matters by being by far the most crowded in the whole of society.

Which meant, as she wailed at Stroody, that she and Jack would be having to give dinner parties and thrashes of their own. But the wail was a pretence, for Cass was coming to find that she enjoyed the *brouhaha* which surrounded her being Countess.

Fred delivered her new dog, a giant wolfhound already trained for her, during a week when Jack was away on business at Roehampton, having taken his new secretary, Mr Peters, with him. Fred had found for her quite the most impressive animal that Cass had ever seen. She had named him Caesar because he had such a proud and haughty look.

The following afternoon she asked Dickie, who was now in charge of the stables—the old man who had served the late Earl having been pensioned off—to take her, Stroody and Caesar to Hyde Park in the Devereux landaulet. This impressive carriage had painted on its side an Earl's coronet above a shield with the Wild man of the Woods holding a bough on it. One of Jack's jokes was that he was the only true descendant of the original of the Wild Man, who dated back to the fourteenth century and was supposed to be the first Baron whose reputation was, to say the least, notorious for its violence.

Cass and Dickie had struck up an odd friendship, in which Cass talked to Dickie, and Dickie listened. She often tried to pump him about Jack and their joint past, but at this point, in Cass's opinion, Dickie's silences turned from golden to lead.

He looked doubtfully at Caesar, and even more doubtfully at Cass, who was wearing a female version of the uniform of an officer in the Rifle Brigade, even her hat and boots being exact replicas of the originals. Thus accoutred, she was sure to draw all eyes, and so poor Stroody was moaning, not hesitating to call on Dickie to agree that it was most improper for Cass to venture out, so dressed—'and with this giant of a dog, too'.

'Caesar needs a walk, and I shall take him for one when we reach the Park,' announced Cass firmly.

'Does Dev, I mean, m'lord, know about Caesar, and. . .?' Dickie waved a helpless hand at Cass's military finery.

'Of course,' retorted Cass. 'He said that I was to use my own judgement about what I wore, and he knew that I was buying a dog.' Which was an answer calculated to deceive, as Cass was well aware.

There was nothing to be said after that. Dev's word was law, and so they set off for the Park. Cass had already arranged to meet Fred there, and Dickie had hardly drawn up the landaulet beneath some trees before Fred arrived on horseback, and behind him a bevy of society ladies and gentlemen whose acquaintances Cass had made in the previous week.

'I say, Cass,' said Fred eagerly, leaning over the side of the landaulet, 'you look quite famous. I do declare you grow prettier by the day.' He heard Stroody's quiet moan, but took no note of it. 'I have brought along some of the fellows to meet you.'

He proceeded to introduce her to a group of young men as idle as himself, all of whom were entranced by Cass, her daring outfit and Caesar. They were even more entranced when Fred dismounted and, holding his horse, helped her and Caesar out of the landaulet, poor Stroody declining to come, so that they might process along one of the walks.

It was a glorious day. The sun shone; all society was present, including the Duke of Wellington, and all society was exclaiming over the little Countess, whose outfit was so exactly designed to flatter her, enrage all other women and enchant the men.

Fred was as delighted by the sensation which they caused as Cass was. Let Jack think of her as a quiet appendage who was helping him to cheat his late papa whilst he enjoyed himself with bits of muslin, barques of frailty and ladies of the town! He would soon discover how wrong he was.

The Duke drove towards the crowd around Fred and Cass in his curricle, an elegant equipage, bright yellow, with a silver curricle bar and silver-mounted harness. On reaching them, he swept off his black bicorne—as much as part of his mystique as his hooked nose, his distinctive carriage and his splendid well-matched horses.

He dismounted, threw the reins to his tiger and bent to pat Caesar, who growled at him but, being well-trained, did no more, and then, in passing, he offered Fred a 'Hello, there, Maxwell. Devereux not with you, hey?'

Next it was Cass's turn. 'So you have joined the Rifle Brigade, my dear Lady Devereux! When may I expect you to present me with your first despatch?' And his shrewd eyes were admiring her for, of all things, the Duke loved pretty women, and after that women, even if not so pretty.

'My first despatch shall be presented, Duke, when you win your next battle,' was Cass's piece of impudence in reply to his question, which had him laughing. 'And my husband is on estate business at Roehampton,' She added, 'so my nephew Fred kindly offered to arrange a walk for me in the Park with my new dog, Caesar.'

The Duke liked the impudence of 'my nephew Fred', whilst Fred mournfully and privately deplored it. 'Devereux's nephew, she means, sir,' he explained.

The Duke continued his conversation with Cass by saying, a frown on his handsome face, 'I shall remember where I met your husband, you may be sure, for I am also sure that my memory is better than his. Remember me to him.'

Cass's place in society was thus assured. The Duke approved of her and the Maxwells approved of both her and Jack, when many had thought that they might reject Jack.

One haughty blonde beauty in her late twenties, on the arm of her husband and also leading a dog—a black poodle—walked over to the group now dominated by the Duke. She did the pretty to them all before speaking to Cass.

'My dear Lady Devereux, you will forgive me for speaking to you when we have not been introduced, but Fred here may do the honours. I used to know your husband well, when we were children together.'

Her mouth was smiling but her eyes told Cass that she thought her an upstart who had managed to net Jack by some remarkable piece of luck.

'Lady Luxcombe and Sir Chalres,' intoned Fred obediently. He was enjoying the sensation Cass was creating, and felt that he was partly responsible for it, having supplied Cass with Caesar.

'Delighted,' responded Cass with a low bow. 'I am sure that Jack will be sorry to have missed meeting you.' She was not sure of any such thing, but thought she ought to say so.

'Oh, I am sure he will,' drawled the beauty. 'We were bosom bows once. Childish bosom bows,' she amended, lest anyone misunderstood her. 'You have known him long?'

'Long enough—' Cass's drawl matched her interlocutor's in insolence '—but not so long as you, I collect—those bosom-bow days of yours being long gone, of course.'

The beauty wasn't sure whether she was being quizzed or not, and Fred grinned at this elegant putdown of a woman who had put down so many others. Unlike Lady Luxcombe, he was aware that Cass's barb regarding her age had been a deliberate one.

'But he is not with you? Most surprising, seeing that your marriage was so recent. Doubtless he has affairs of great moment which take him from you.'

'Doubtless.' Cass was easy, put up a hand to stifle a yawn. 'Walking in the Park being an affair of such little moment he may be thought to have overlooked it, but no,' she added, looking beyond the beauty, 'I do believe that he has arrived, after all. His affairs of great moment must be over.'

Cass was right. Jack's business at Roehampton had finished earlier than he had expected, and he had driven Mr Peters and himself in his new curricle, also an elegant equipage picked out in blue and scarlet, to Devereux House after a light luncheon. At the back of his mind had been the rather pleasant notion that he would surprise his wife by walking in on her unexpectedly.

Unfortunately, when he walked into the drawing-room he found it was empty, and was informed that m'lady and Miss Strood had gone for an outing in the Park. 'I believe that Dickson was driving them, m'lord.'

'Then I shall go to join them there.' And Jack strode into the stables, calling for his first four—a quartet of elegant chestnuts—to be harnessed to the curricle to

replace the greys which had done their duty by him by
pulling him home.

As he had expected, the Park was full. He saw the
Duke of Wellington—a small crowd around him, as
usual—before he saw Dickie and the landaulet containing Miss Strood beneath a tree. Miss Strood was
talking to the inhabitants of another landaulet drawn
up beside them, his sister Thaxted aboard, behaving in
her most bullying dominant manner.

'What are you doin' here, Strood? Where's the
Scrap? Surely she is with you? You cannot be taking
the air on your own. Oh, gone for a walk, has she?'

'She is with the Duke, over there.' Miss Strood was
less accomodating to the great lady than she usually
was, being the attendant of an ever greater lady so far
as status was concerned.

Lady Amelia swivelled to see Cass in her new-found
glory, walking towards them surrounded by an interested crowd, the Duke of Wellington prominent
among them.

She put up her lorgnettes, displayed for effect—her
sight was excellent without them. '*That's* the Scrap?
Whatever have you been doin' to her, Strood?' She
was obviously nonplussed.

'*I*? I have done nothing to her,' bridled Miss Strood,
belligerent for once. 'She is Countess now, and Jack
lets her do as she pleases.'

The incriminatingly familiar 'Jack' did not escape
Lady Thaxted. So the poor attendant was allowed to
call him 'Jack' was she? It was plain that Devereux
was still as loose a fish as he had been before Papa
had had him thrown out of Devereux House.

'*Lord Devereux*,' she announced, awefully, 'should
have the good sense to consider his wife's reputation
before allowing her to gad about London dressed like
a man. Ah, there you are, Devereux. I was just advis-
ing Strood here as to how your wife should conduct

herself now that she has the good fortune to be surnamed Devereux. It seems that she is badly in need of guidance as to her conduct.'

Jack pulled gently on the reins before dismounting and telling his tiger to hold them. The tiger, known to the Devereux stables simply as the Imp, since he was even smaller than usual for a tiger, was unconventionally dressed—not in black and yellow stripes, but in red and blue ones. Jack walked over to take off his hat to Miss Strood and to address his sister, now purple in the face with disapproval and the effort of bellowing at him at a distance.

'Cass misbehaving herself, Amelia? Surely not. Where is she, Stroody?'

'Over there, m'lord, with the Duke.'

'*Jack*, Stroody. No "m'lords".' He swung round to look more closely at the crowd around the Duke, his sister's baleful stare searing his back.

The crowd had thinned off a little, so that now he saw Cass in her green uniform leading something which looked like an aggressive black and white calf. She was talking animatedly to Wellington whilst a respectful and amused Fred followed her. *That* was Cass? By the stares and bows directed towards her, she had been creating something of a minor sensation.

The Duke bowed to Jack, a slightly puzzled look on his hawklike face as he tried again to remember where he had encountered him before. Jack bowed back. 'Your wife is well informed on the war in the Peninsula, Devereux. It seems that she had the duty of reading my despatches to your later father. I congratulate you.'

Jack, for once, murmured all the correct platitudes which society demanded of him. He tried not to look too hard at his wife, who was the picture of youthful innocence. He hoped that the Duke was respecting it, but which of the two was manipulating the other he was not sure: he was too busy staring at Caesar, who had begun to strain at the leash. Jack knew the feeling—it was one which Cass was beginning to induce in him, too.

Nevertheless, he acquitted himself well before the Duke dismissed him and he began to walk her—after a curt nod to Fred, who thought that it might be discreet to disappear—towards the landaulet, where Dickie was also enjoying the fun at a suitable distance.

'I thought,' he told her as they walked along, 'that you might like to drive home with me.'

'Oh, famous,' replied Cass eagerly. It was the first time that Jack had made such an offer. 'You finished your business early, I collect.'

'Indeed, and arrived in time to find that my wife is the sensation of the Park. And what, may I ask, is that cross between a calf and a wolf?' And he pointed at Caesar, whose long pink tongue was now lolling out in the heat.

'That? Oh, that is Caesar—the dog I told you that I was buying.'

'That? You bought that monster? Why, I distinctly remember you saying that you were buying a poodle!'

'It was you, Jack, who said I was buying a poodle,' retorted Cass truthfully. '*I* said nothing on the subject.'

'Most unlike you—to say nothing on that subject, or any other,' said Jack wickedly. 'You were bamming me, were you not?'

This rapid and shrewd assessment of the mild naughtiness she had been engaged in had Cass giggling. She stopped dead, primmed her face and remarked severely, 'You were bamming yourself, Jack.'

She was delighted to see that he was not really cross with her, that he was teasing her—and under the nose of Lady Thaxted, who was glaring down at her from the landaulet where she was doubtless engaged in annoying poor Stroody.

Jack's oddly coloured eyes were dancing. 'Yes, I see that I shall have to listen a little more closely to what my wife is saying to me. I do believe that I had the right of it when I said that you would have made an excellent lawyer. Now, Lady Devereux, be ready to be driven about the Park and then home by the husband whom you have successfully bammed. But you must hand the hound to Stroody to look after; I'm not having him in the curricle. Only a poodle would suffice in such a confined space. Up with you.'

Caesar disposed of in the landaulet—to Stroody's dismay—and his sister coolly informed that he was taking his wife off to ensure that she did not disgrace the noble name of Devereux, Jack manoeuvred his curricle through the Park. Cass bowed graciously from her high seat to the many new friends whom she had made during the past few weeks.

She took off her tall rifleman's shako and allowed her curls to swing free.

Another surprise for Jack! His eyes homed in on the curls. 'You have had your hair cut, Cass,' he announced accusingly.

'Yes,' said Cass, giving her curls, which had appeared when her hair had been shorn, another complacent shake—she liked the feel of them about her ears. 'Stroody says I look just like Lady Caroline Lamb with my hair off.'

'Not exactly the best person to imitate, one might think!' Jack's tone was glacial.

Oh, dear, this time she had really annoyed him. Cass decided that innocence was the best ploy. 'You don't like my new curls, then?'

Jack looked harder at her, a trifle nonplussed by his wife's cheerful goodwill in the face of his disapproval. He had not really looked at her properly since their honeymoon. It had to be admitted that she did look rather charming. Her complexion was losing its sallow tinge, her cheeks were flushed and her eyes were shining.

'It's not that I don't like it, but. . .' And he stopped, having nowhere to go.

'But it was a bit of a shock,' offered Cass helpfully.

'Yes. . . No. . . I'm never shocked—you should know that.' To his astonishment, Jack found himself forced on the defensive—a position he usually forced on others.

'You did say that I didn't need to ask your permission over the unimportant things I wished to do. I didn't think that having my hair cut short was important.'

But it was, for, stealing a glance at her as he turned out of the Park and made for home, Jack saw that a new Cass was slowly emerging from the chrysalis which had been unkindly nicknamed the Scrap and Miss Skin and Bones.

CHAPTER NINE

THE SCRAP to be the rage of the Season! What a turn-up. The only person not in a tizz about her unwonted success was Cass herself—she took it all in her stride. And as if this were not enough, Cass's campaign to make Jack take notice of her continued apace.

She had persuaded him to allow Dickie to teach her to drive a lady's perch-phaeton after she had cajoled Jack into buying one for her. Jack had argued with her, before Dickie, that she was biting off more than she could chew by wanting to become a lady driver, but Dickie had taken Cass's side.

He had been improving her riding skills—Cass had been taught to ride as a child, but since arriving at Devereux House she had rarely had the opportunity to sit on a horse—and Dickie had told Jack what a good and willing pupil she was, how eager she was to learn.

He even had the nerve to tell Jack that she would have made a good jockey if she had been a boy. 'She's a natural, Dev,' he said one evening, when they were pretending that nothing between them had changed and that they were still the Dev and Dickie of old.

They were sitting at the far end of the garden behind Devereux House, on the veranda of a small wooden summerhouse, and Dickie was enjoying a pipe and Jack was smoking a cigar—something he rarely did.

'A real natural. She's brave and skilful. Too brave, if anything—even though she does look as if butter wouldn't melt in her mouth. She'll make a good driver, I'm sure.'

He fell silent. He couldn't tell Dev how he really

felt about Dev's innocent young wife. It wouldn't be proper. He could only watch out for her and make sure that Dev did the right thing by her. Dev had always done the right thing by women before, but those women had been quite different from Cass. Beneath her bravery and her fun she was a sensitive little thing. . .

Unaware that she had a watchdog-cum-guardian, Cass went her merry way. She even had a scarlet and blue dragoon's outfit made for her to wear when Jack took her driving—to match his tiger, she said. The one she wore when she was on her own was a variant of her green rifleman's uniform.

Jack and Dickie took one look at her scarlet and blue outfit the first time that she wore it, and they both laughed together. Even the Imp's solemn face cracked a little.

'You don't like it?' she asked sadly.

'We're not laughing at you, it's just. . .' And Jack began to laugh again.

It was a pity that they couldn't tell her how charming she looked as a parody of a cavalryman from the Heavy Division.

'I'll change it,' she said, still sad.

'No,' said Jack, and impulsively he did something which he had never done before, other than on the first night of their so-called honeymoon. He kissed her on the cheek—a friendly kiss, even though they were both a little shocked by what it did to them.

In search of lost treasures suitable for a countess to deck herself in, Cass went up to the attics one day. She found there chests of old silks, and a covered basket which was stuffed with fans. Some the moths had eaten, others, wrapped in silk, were still as beautiful as they had been on the day when they had arrived at Devereux House.

After his wife's untimely death, the late Earl had ordered all her personal belongings to be consigned to the attics—he could not bear to see them, he had said. They had been stacked in one corner. Cass looked doubtfully at them. She hardly liked to ask Jack if she could examine them—it seemed a sort of sacrilege, so she left them untouched. He never spoke of his mother at all—and his references to his father were brief and unflattering.

Hidden away from his mother's possessions, Cass unearthed a portable writing desk: an elegant thing with a green leather top. Opening it, she found a place for a small inkwell and some pens, their quill feathers moth-eaten and yellow. There was a locked drawer beneath the top. The key was missing so she could not open it, but it was such a dear little piece that Cass fell in love with it and ordered Bailey, her personal footman, to carry it downstairs for her, together with the superb portrait of Jack with the falcon.

That evening, Jack walked into the drawing-room to find that his portrait hung over the hearth, replacing a perfunctory and rather banal view of Rome. He was so surprised that he forgot to be tactful.

'Good God, Scrap! Where was that resurrected from?'

Cass, seated by Stroody, engaged in sorting and identifying the contents of a solander box of prints for Mr Hunt, went bright pink at the sound of her old nickname and stammered at him, 'It was in the attic. I like it, and it's a really beautiful painting, do admit. It ought to be downstairs now that you are Earl.'

'Beautiful!' snorted Jack. 'If I ever looked like that, which I doubt, I certainly don't resemble it any more. I think that it should have been left in the attic, not hung in here like a ghost at the feast to reproach me. . .' He fell silent.

Cass said gently, seeing that the portrait seemed to

distress him, and she had not anticipated it, 'If you really dislike it, Jack, then I shall ask Bailey to return it to the attic where I found it.'

She did not say that the handsome boy in the painting had been the imaginary companion who had lightened her loneliness when she had first arrived at Devereux House, for he might think her maudlin, but something in her tone struck him, for he replied, gently for him, 'If you really like it, then it may stay downstairs. But not here. I don't want to stare at it all day.'

'Then it may hang in my room,' Cass returned briskly. 'And now I have a favour to ask you. I found this dear little desk in the attic. I should like to use it myself, but if it was your mama's, and you find it painful to see me with it, then, of course, I shall respect your wishes and return it into store.'

Jack walked over to gaze at the pretty thing. He shook his head. 'I cannot remember my mama using that,' he said doubtfully, 'although it is possible that it may have been hers. But use it by all means. It were a pity to hide it away.'

'Like the portrait,' remarked Cass irrepressibly, looking at him from beneath her lashes, at which he shook his head at her impudence and registered again that the Scrap was growing up. He wished that he had not used his sister's demeaning nickname to her, and made a metal resolve to try not to do so again.

Two nights later they both attended Lady Leominster's great ball, one of the season's main events. She was busy throwing herself at the Prince Regent, being built very much in the style of the large and matronly ladies he favoured in these, his middle years.

'A massive four-decker,' Jack called her rudely after meeting her for the first time since he had left home.

He had remembered her as youngish and slim. She was a great power in the *ton*, and fortunately she soon made it plain that she approved of both Jack and Cass, so there was another social hurdle cleared.

It was inevitable that whispers followed Jack everywhere. 'Is it true,' it was hissed behind his back, 'that he was involved in the disappearance of the Star of Rizapore, and he barely twenty-one?' Everyone knew that his father had disowned him, but no one knew exactly why. Nor why his father had re-inherited him, as it were, after so many years.

Cass carried out her wish to have a Chinese turn-out, and decided that the world should see it at the Leominsters' ball. She and the dressmaker spent many happy hours designing it, and Jack was given the benefit of her new toilette shortly before they set out for the Leominster's palace in Westminster.

'My God,' he exclaimed simply, when Cass walked into the big entrance hall where he was waiting for her. He made her the most splendid leg, as though she were the Tsarina of All the Russias, the late great Catherine herself, or perhaps the Chinese Empress whom no foreigner was allowed to see.

Her dress was magnificent in its originality: the main body of it was of pale blue silk, and embroidered and appliquéd on the skirt were the Chinese men and women copied from the wallpaper in the big salon at Devereux House. It was low-necked, showing her pretty shoulders, and was clasped just above her small breasts with an ivory medallion that had the head of the Chinese Emperor painted on it. Her sash was of the palest pink silk.

On her head she wore a bandeau of twisted silks dyed in the delicate pinks, blues and greens of the clothing of the miniature Chinese, and thrust into it at one side was a cluster of tall feathers dyed in the same colours. Her train was decorated with irises, paeonies and bambo and, rampaging through them, a stylised tiger.

Her fan was originality itself, being composed of small silk flags, each with a different flower appliquéd on them, all of them mounted in an exquisitely carved ivory clasp, decorated with silver. On her small feet were the tiny brocade slippers with turned-up toes which she had dreamed of wearing ever since she had decided to be a Chinese lady.

Cass was quite overcome by the impression which she was obviously making on Jack. He was meant to notice her, but not to stare at her like that! 'You don't think that it's too much?' she asked him anxiously.

'Of course it's too much,' Jack told her. 'Much too much, Lady Devereux. You will knock everyone's eye out, that's for sure. Caroline Lamb and Emily Cowper won't be in it. Nor that new heiress—the plain one, Miss What's-her-name. You'll stun the lot. Did you think it up yourself?'

He wasn't cross, and he was taking note of her!' 'Yes,' she told him, suddenly shy. 'I have always wanted to be a Chinese lady, so when you said that I could do what I wanted within reason, I thought I would make myself one.'

'You have been a rifleman, a cavalryman, and now an Eastern princess, Cass. What next? Amelia will have a fit of the vapours every time she looks at you, whilst I think that Constantia may approve.'

'Fred certainly will,' Cass offered, watching him as she teased him with Fred's interest in her. 'He visited me the other day when the milliner delivered the ornament for my hair, and told me that he could hardly wait to see the whole creation.'

'Did he, indeed?' Jack was dry. 'So, you favoured the nephew with your plans whilst keeping the uncle in the dark.' He wondered why it was that he was so

annoyed every time Cass spoke affectionately of that
ass Fred Maxwell.

'Well, it wasn't meant to be a surprise for Fred, and
it *was* meant to be one for you. You always look so
splendid that I thought that it was time I kept up with
you.'

'Kept up with me! I think that Lady Devereux has
run several miles ahead of me. The only way in which
I imagine that I could create as great a sensation
tonight as you will would be if I were to dress up as
the Devereux Wild Man of the Woods and arrive at
Lady Leominster's waving a tree branch and clad only
in a loincloth made of leaves like our Grandfather
Adam.'

Cass gave a great peal of laughter at this outrageous
picture. She wiped her eyes with her Chinese-style
handkerchief, embroidered with a miniature manda-
rin, and looked altogether so enchanting that Jack
forgot himself.

A surge of desire ran over him so strongly that he
caught her in his arms to kiss the tears of laughter
away for her, but that, of course, was not all that he
wished to do—or did.

His mouth came down hard on that of his unconsidered wife's, one hand found itself in the curls at the
back of her head and the other was on her small
breast, where it fitted so sweetly and neatly that Jack,
continent these many months, found himself in a sweat
of desire and cursing his tight breeches against which
his treacherous body ached and strained.

As before, Cass kissed him enthusiastically back,
putting her own hands into the thickly clustered russet
waves of his hair and making them even more windswept than the style which his valet had created
for him. And all of this in the entrance hall, where
Miss Strood, coming in to accompany Cass to the

Leominsters' as her attendant lady, discovered her late charge being passionately embraced by her husband.

Her hands flew to her mouth. 'Oh!' she exclaimed, and Cass, opening her eyes, for she had descended into a dream of sensation under Jack's attentions, found herself looking at poor Stroody, who was standing there in an agony of embarrassment.

Cass stepped back. Both she and Jack—who was a little slow to recover, but then he was further overcome—were almost relieved by Stroody's arrival—for who knew where this unexpected passion might have inconveniently led them?

'Oh, Stroody, there you are!' Did her voice sound as strained and silly to Miss Strood as it did to herself? Husbands and wives of great station were not supposed to take their pleasure in public, nor be so woefully overcome as to forget themselves quite so enthusiastically as she and Jack had just done.

Cass now had no doubts at all about her true feelings for him. Not only did she lust after him so much that for him to touch her only slightly was to overset her to a degree where she had difficulty in not throwing herself at him, but she also loved him, and everything about him—even his brusqueries and sudden savageries when he forgot that he was Lord Devereux and reverted back to being plain-spoken Jack Devlin. She thought that she perhaps liked Jack Devlin best of all—the man he was when he was talking simply to Dickie and herself.

What she was not sure of was the nature of Jack's feelings for her. Something that Dickie had hinted at recently seemed to suggest that Jack had lived 'a monk's life' recently. And, if so, perhaps that explained why, whenever he gave her an idle kiss, he seemed to be so overcome. She was the available woman, that was all. And his wife, of course—whatever that meant to him. He seemed to like talking to her, so she ought to be satisfied with that.

And all this was running through her head whilst she sat by him on the way to the Leominsters' ball, Stroody opposite them. Miss Strood was busy thinking that if Cass would draw all eyes as a consequence of her inventive toilette, then Jack would also attract attention by the splendour of his physique, so perfectly set off by his fashionably tight clothing.

She was not wrong. Eyes followed the two Devereux everywhere. Lady Leominster gave a slight scream when she greeted them at the top of the grand staircase, one of the glories of Leominster House. 'Chinoiserie, my dear Lady Devereux, used to enhance dress and not our walls and furniture! How clever of you—you are setting a fashion that all will follow, I have no doubt.'

Her approval of Jack was internal rather than external. What a splendid specimen of manhood—and where had he been these last dozen years, to turn himself into such a nonpareil? Not handsome, of course, but better. However, even Lady Leominster, that plain-spoken and blunt *grande dame*, who rivalled Lady Holland in insolence to her guests, could not quite come out with anything as frank as what she was thinking when she greeted him.

Instead she said, 'Welcome, Devereux. You have been too long absent from our society. Mind that you don't go off a-wandering again—but not likely with a new wife, eh?' And she could hardly refrain from digging the grinning Jack in his ribs.

'So,' said his sister Amelia, coming up to them, 'you are the sensation of the season, Jack. What a turn-up. Surprising how short people's memories are!'

Jack agreed with her. A little of the friendship and goodwill being so lavishly displayed on his return, had it been offered to him twelve years ago, might have rendered his exile unnecessary. But Lady Thaxted gave him no time to answer. He attention was now turned on to Cass, who was quailing a little at the thought of what might be coming her way.

But the great guns which Lady Thaxted had been so eager to fire at her when she was plain and penniless Cassandra Merton were not to be so readily trained on Lady Devereux.

'Original,' she barked, raising her lorgnettes to inspect the mandarins, 'if nothing else.' A comment which was almost a friendly one compared with those with which she had been wont to favour Cass.

'Who did you find to make it for you? And was it her notion, or yours?'

'Madame Rosina, and it was my notion. The wall-paper in the salon in Devereux House inspired me.'

'Hmm. You are young enough to carry it off.' Which was a form of grudging accolade, rather different from the many other admiring ones which Cass received that evening.

But every rose had its thorns. Just as Cass was beginning to believe that Jack's return to the *ton*, his new wife by his side, was a triumphant success, something occurred to spoil it.

They were walking out of the great ballroom among many others who were looking for refreshment, when a man, a late arrival, came towards them, his eyes fixed on Jack, whom he had just seen from across the room.

He was wearing the flattering dress uniform of a colonel in that crack cavalry regiment the First Royal Dragoons. A magnificent order was pinned on his breast. He was as tall and broad as Jack but was running to seed. His blond locks were thinning, his face was purple rather than ruddy, and he had the beginnings of a paunch. Nevertheless, from a distance if not near to, he was a fine figure of a man.

Approaching Jack, the purple in his face increased. Cass felt Jack's grip on her arm tighten, heard him mutter softly, 'Oh, dear God, no.' It was immediately plain to Cass not only that they knew one another, but that they disliked each other exceedingly—something confirmed by the officer's first words.

'By God, I never thought that I'd come to the Leominsters' to be confronted by scum from the gutter! What in thunder are you doing here, *Sergeant* Devlin? And by what name are you passing in order to weasel your way into decent society?'

His sneering glance taking in Cass, he added, his voice high, so that everyone around them could hear what was said, 'You can either leave quickly of your own free will, Devlin, or I'll have the footmen called to remove you forthwith—and your latest whore with you.'

Jack had said and done nothing in response to the angry tirade loosed upon him until the sneer at Cass. Afterwards, Cass was to marvel at the speed of what happened next. Jack launched himself at the officer like an avenging angel and, before anyone could stop him, had pinned him against the wall, one hand on the man's throat, the other on his shoulder.

'Damn you, Spence. Sneer at my wife again and I'll kill you. This time you have no rank to pull over me to protect you from wrongdoing.'

Almost before Jack had finished speaking he was pulled away from his prey. His brother-in-law Thaxted, energetic for once, put a hand on Jack's shoulder as he tried to work himself free to attack Spence again. What Spence had said of him was nothing: it was the insult to Cass which had him frothing.

As enraged as Jack, Spence was being held back by his friends. He was roaring that 'that low cur, Devlin, who is fit only for the whipping post, should be thrown out of Leominster House forthwith'.

Into this maelstrom of baffled rage and fury, which had all the guests at the Leominsters' ball entranced, the Duke of Wellington sauntered, with the portly Lord Leominster, who had pleaded for his assistance in settling this untoward turn of events, at his shoulder.

He stared first at Jack, who had recovered his usual sang-froid, and remarked coolly, 'Devlin, eh? I thought that I knew you, but it wasn't as Devereux. I remember you now. You were at Salamanca in the charge. Your captain and lieutenant went down and you took over—saved your corporal by a piece of horsemanship I've never seen equalled.'

He turned his searching gaze on Spence, who had begun to gibber at him that 'this piece of filth must have passed himself off as a gentleman to be flaunting his doxy and himself here'.

'"Passed himself off as a gentleman", eh?' remarked the Duke, eyebrows raised. 'I agree, Spence, that he ain't that. A nobleman, now, that's different. I'd better introduce you to the Colonel, Devereux—missed Salamanca, didn't you, Spence? Something about an illness, as I recall. It seems that Sergeant Devlin here chose to serve in the ranks under that name when he was plain Jack Devereux, the late Earl's younger son. He's been Earl Devereux for the last six months, his elder brother dying before him. The lady whom you have just insulted is his wife. Apologies called for, I think.'

'Devereux? *That's* Earl Devereux? I beg leave to doubt it. He was the most insubordinate swine I ever...'

'Enough!' The Duke's voice was that of unthinking command. 'This unseemly squabble must cease. It is, after all, based on a misunderstanding. Leominster, I propose that you and I, together with Spence and

Devereux, adjourn to a private room to settle this matter one way or another, whilst we leave your wife to comfort Lady Devereux.' And he smiled kindly at Cass who needed no comforting at all.

'No!' Jack's voice was stern, also the voice of command. 'I will go nowhere until Colonel Spence apologises publicly to my wife for the insult which he put upon her.'

'Indeed, Devereux, most correct.' The Duke turned to Spence. 'As your Commander in Chief, Spence, I insist that you tender your regrets to Lady Devereux for your insult—which I am sure was unintended.'

So Jack *had* been in the Army, which did not surprise Cass even if it surprised everyone else. And Dickie was probably the corporal he had saved in the famous cavalry charge at Salamanca about which she had read to Jack's father. The room, which had been in a buzz at the revelation of what Jack Devereux had been doing for the last twelve years, fell silent as the Duke led his small party from the room after Colonel Spence had stuttered his apologies to her.

That embarrassing event over, she was compelled to endure the attentions of Lady Leominster who, obeying the Duke's command to her, flung a fat arm around Cass's shoulders and fluted, 'Oh, my poor dear child, what an evening you are having—and what a defender you have in Devereux. I am sure that Colonel Spence did not insult you intentionally. He quite mistook who you were.'

This was hardly comforting, since to take what Colonal Spence had said at face value would be to agree with him that Cass resembled a whore! What worried her more than the insult, intended or not, was that Jack might be pushed into fighting a duel. She hoped that the Duke would make both men see sense, but feared that he might feel it necessary to pay lip service to what men called honour and women thought was no such thing.

Lady Leominster insisted that Cass sit down with her on an elegant bergère in a small recess just off the ballroom from where they could still see the rest of her guests. A footman was sent to fetch Cass a glass of sherry wine. 'To restore you, my dear. Oh, and, Francis, be sure that you bring one for me as well. Such excitement is not good for the nerves. I declare that I am beginning to feel quite faint myself!'

She certainly didn't look it, was Cass's unkind reaction, but she said nothing and allowed herself to be mothered. Miss Strood, who had found an old friend in the supper room, another attendant lady whose mistress was occupied with her own affairs, also came rushing along to assist Cass on hearing the news. As was the way with gossip, the story of Jack's encounter with Colonel Spence had flown around the company, the tale growing with the telling—Spence had been lucky to escape with his life being one version.

Speculation was also rife about what would be the outcome of the meeting which the Duke and Leominster had arranged. One excited version had the Duke arranging a private on-the-spot duel—something which had not happened since Lord Byron's grandfather had fought a similar duel with a neighbour.

Not only Stroody came up to comfort Cass. Fred arrived, full of fizz and excitement.

'I say, Cass, is it true? The fellows are saying that Jack joined the Royal Dragoons as a ranker, rose to be sergeant, and that he was in the cavalry charge at Salamanca! Famous, ain't it? And why should Jack keep mum about it? Odd fellow, ain't he?'

Cass, knowing Jack, could understand why he had said nothing. To Fred she merely said, 'Oh, he's a very private man, Fred. He never talks about himself.'

'Explains that fellow he runs around with—Dickie—

don't it? The one who calls Jack "Dev". Depend upon it, they were in the Army together.'

This was shrewd for Fred—a sign that he was growing up at last, perhaps. Before he had time to say more, the Duke's party emerged from their 'confabulation', as Lady Leominster called it, and Jack came over to Cass, Colonel Spence going in the opposite direction to rejoin his friends.

Before Jack could say a word, Fred exclaimed eagerly, 'I was just sayin' to Cass what a fellow you are, Jack, to keep quiet about being in the Army. In the Peninsula with the Duke, were you? At Salamanca— and were you at Waterloo? I've always wished to speak to someone who'd been there. I thought once of joinin' the Army myself.'

Jack said shortly—Cass thought that he looked weary—'You wouldn't like it, Fred, and Waterloo was such a bloody business, saving your presence, ladies, that it's not the kind of thing I care to gossip about. I must apologise to you, Lady Leominster, for creating such a scene at your ball.'

Whatever other talent Jack possessed, thought the fascinated Cass, he had the talent to charm women— and of all ages too.

Lady Leominster rose and tapped him with her fan. 'Oh, no, my dear Devereux, no apologies, if you please. You have quite made the evening. My little party will always be remembered as the one where you defended your wife's good name so nobly—and your own, of course. And now I must leave you, for I am sure that dear Lady Devereux is longing to hear what the Duke has decided.'

She seized Fred by the arm and firmly led him away before he could continue his campaign to persuade Jack to give him a detailed account of all the forced marches, guerilla actions, cavalry charges and battles in which he had been engaged during his long exile in the British Army.

Cass patted the bergère cushions and persuaded her husband to sit beside her. She thought that while they were talking no one would interrupt them.

'Was your conference with the Duke as distressing as Waterloo, Jack?'

To Cass's great relief his grim face lightened at last. 'I might have trusted you, my dear, to behave with your usual common sense. A lesser woman would have treated me to an attack of the vapours! I suppose the correct answer is "Not quite". He read the Riot Act to both of us. To Spence for jumping on me without taking the trouble to find out who I was and what I was doing at Leominster House, and to me for jumping on Spence.

'Trouble was, I'd always wanted the chance to knock Spence down, or more preferably to kill him for his cruelty to the poor wretches whom he commanded. I was never able to because I'd have been shot for mutiny if I'd as much as laid a finger on him. When he badmouthed you, the temptation to try to do for the swine was too great.'

He was speaking to her in the plain language of the private soldier he had once been.

'The worst thing was that he was a coward who liked inflicting pain. Whenever a battle came along Spence invariably managed never to take part in it— there was always some reason for his absence. I'd never have made corporal or sergeant if he'd been about, but fortunately for me, and for the rest of us, he was on leave for some imaginary complaint for months on end, and the officer who took his place gave me my chance to shine.

'I even turned down a commission after Salamanca— I think that was why the Duke remembered me. I hoped never to meet Spence or any of the officers I served under again, but luck was not with me tonight.'

He paused, and Cass took the opportunity to ask what the Duke had decided about his quarrel with Spence. 'Oh—' Jack laughed '—it was Wellington at his best. He said that he wasn't having us fight over what was past and done. That I was out of the Army now, and not subject to Spence's discipline any more. That I should not have lost my temper, and we were to shake hands, not meet on Putney Heath.

'And that, he told Spence, was an order, and, although he could no longer order me, he hoped that my good sense would see that there was nothing to be gained by pursuing a vendetta against Spence. So, there is to be no duel with him, now or in the future, which I suppose is a great disappointment to everyone here—as well as to me.'

'Oh, no, Jack.' Some of the common sense, which Jack had praised her for evaporated. 'Never say so. Promise me that you'll never fight a duel. Please!'

The look Jack gave her was an odd one. 'Well, if I can keep my temper, I will. But I should have liked to kill Spence. He marked Dickie and me for life, and out of spite, too. Neither of us deserved what he did to us.'

Cass remembered Spence's shriek about the whipping post and thought that she knew what Jack was referring to. She shivered.

Jack was all attention to her when he saw the shiver. 'Would you like to go home, Cass? It's been a trying evening for you—and to find out that I was a private soldier in the Army must have been a bit of a shock as well.'

Cass did not tell him that she had already suspected that he had been a soldier. She wanted to ask him how he had met Dickie, and why he had joined the Army, but that could wait. Instead she rose, saying to him earnestly, 'Oh, no, Jack, we can't go home. We can't flee the world, can we? Most cowardly. If we stay people can talk to us, as well as behind our backs. For, of course, they are going to talk.'

'Well, as long as they don't drag up all that old business about my leaving home, then I don't mind.' Jack had stood up, and was offering his arm. 'You're a brave little thing, as I should have known when you accepted my offer of marriage, and you're right. Come, let us rejoin the ball. Having given everyone something to gossip about, the least that we can do is to show that we are above being hurt by it.'

'And were you truly at Waterloo?' Cass asked him as they walked towards the refreshment room, all eyes upon them.

'Indeed, I was—and wounded there. After that, they invalided me out with a small pension. The wound wasn't severe, but once the war was over Dickie and I weren't wanted—which is always the fate of the soldier in peacetime.'

A remark which, like many of Jack's, set Cass thinking, and which remained with her after the evening was over and she was in her lonely bed.

But before that she had to endure the two hours which Jack thought that they ought to spend at Leominster House before they could go home. They were never alone, for a horde of people, either through vulgar curiosity or through genuine sympathy, came up to speak to them, carefully avoiding as a topic Jack's earlier encounter with Colonel Spence.

'Dear Jack,' cooed Lady Luxcombe, who inevitably, Cass thought with unaccustomed sourness, came up to address her conversation entirely to him, offering Cass only a most perfunctory nod. 'Too many years have flown by since we last met. How much I regret the loss of those happy days we spent together before you disappeared from society.'

Jack was cool, at his most dour, his wife was relieved to note. 'Forgive me if I doubt your memory a little, Caro dear. I seem to remember that when last we met you expressed a desire never to see me again, and handed back to me the ring I gave you to convince me that all was over between us. But then, a penniless younger son, turned out of his home, was a somewhat different proposition from the Earl Devereux I now am, so perhaps I ought to forgive you.'

The beauty before him turned scarlet. Her husband, far from being annoyed, gave a sardonic laugh. 'You rather walked into that, my dear. Hardly gallant of you, Devereux, but truthful. May I compliment you on acceding to the title and on acquiring a wife whose youthful charm will, I trust, not be dimmed by over-much attention to what she thinks the world demands of her?'

He bowed to the startled Cass, then took his wife by the arm, saying, 'Come, my love, there are others to whom you wish to pay equally untruthful compliments, I am sure.'

'You were bosom bows, then, Jack?' asked Cass, watching Sir Charles manoeuvre his startled wife through the crowd. 'She told me so in the Park, but I was not sure that she wasn't saying so simply in order to put me down.'

'Now, that,' said Jack, his mouth twitching as it was wont to when talking to the 'biddable girl' whom he had made his wife, 'I don't believe. That she might be able to put you down, I mean. That would have been a notable first! But, yes. We were childhood sweethearts and betrothed into the bargain. She couldn't break with me quickly enough after I was disgraced.'

And that probably explained Jack's cavalier attitude to women. It was a trifle dispiriting, though, to discover that his first love had been such an outstanding beauty. And twelve years ago she had probably been more outstanding still. It made Cass even more unhappily aware that, however much she might improve her appearance, she was never going to be able to rival Caro Luxcombe in looks. Was *that* the sort of creature Jack had a *tendre* for?

'I suppose. . .' Cass was judicious in the extreme, trying to disguise how disturbing the discovery of Jack's one-time involvement with such a beauty was. 'I suppose that I ought to say how sorry I am that she treated you so vilely. Although in the long run it was all for the best. Imagine if you had married her!'

'From the perspective of twelve years later,' replied Jack, equally judicious, 'I quite agree with you, "oh, wise young judge", but it hurt damnably at the time, all the same!'

Of course it had. Jack had once used the phrase 'when the world fell in on me' to describe what had happened to him twelve years ago. It was hardly for Cass to be light-minded about his downfall. Undoubtedly, its reverberations were still echoing around society, as the expressions and conversation of their fellow guests bore witness. It was too bad. Cass was as sure as anything that he was innocent of wrongdoing.

Jack was not perfect, no man was, but she thought that he possessed a sense of honour and integrity best shown when he had insisted on keeping his word to Louis Fronsac when no one, not even Louis, would have expected him to do so. More, she could not imagine Dickie Dickson respecting anyone, as he undoubtedly respected Jack, if they were in any way false. Besides, his courage was undoubted, and this evening the Duke had borne witness to it.

If he were a pot, to be touched and tested, Cass thought that he would ring true. So, how had he come to be judged so harshly? What had happened? Had he been in some sense betrayed, and if so, how? And could she, his young wife, even at this late date, discover the truth of the matter and put right the wrong which had been undoubtedly done him?

And what a fanciful notion that was, fit only for the heroine of a Minerva Press novel! Cass shook her head, but he had called her his 'wise young judge' more than once, and if she were to resemble Portia in *The Merchant of Venice*, of whom the judgement had been made, then she must try to earn his description of her.

No one, least of all Jack, could have guessed what she was thinking as she smiled until her face ached, accepted the compliments her toilette had created and talked amusingly to the Duke, who after a short time had come over to her, to marvel privately at the composure of so young a woman—a child, almost—in the face of the night's events.

Between Jack's notoriety and her own determination to make her mark on the world, Cass was rapidly turning into the sensation of the season, as Harriet Ashburn had been the sensation of the year before— and both of them because of their character rather than their looks.

CHAPTER TEN

CASS was watching Jack shave himself. His so-called valet, who might have been expected to perform such a menial task for him, existed merely to look after his wardrobe. He was not even allowed to dress his master—except, perhaps, to assist him in the tying of his cravat. Jack still behaved in private as though he were humble Sergeant Devlin, however much he played the lord in public.

She had first wandered through the connecting door into Jack's bedroom one morning a week earlier, to ask that he allow her to take the perch-phaeton out for the first time on her own. Dickie had told her that he thought that she was ready to do so. She had taken the precaution of knocking on the door, and had entered on his muffled summons to find him shaving.

After he had given her his reluctant assent, she had continued talking to him, and had enjoyed this free and easy intercourse with him so much that it had become a habit for her to join him once she was dressed and to go down to breakfast with him.

Shaving fascinated Cass. She had never seen a man so relatively unbuttoned before, never seen one before he removed the previous day's growth from his cheek and jaw. Until this morning she had made no comment, but today could not restrain herself from saying, voice neutral, 'I'm glad I don't have to do that every day. It must quite take the gloss off being a man.'

Jack's razor halted in mid-stroke. 'And pray what gloss is that?' he enquired politely.

'Oh, being in charge of one's self. Doing as one

pleases. Never having to consider what a young lady of quality ought or ought not to do.'

'Really? Well, I must confess that I have never observed that such considerations have ever put you off your stroke, my dear wife. What was this Dickie was telling me last night? That that monster of yours, egged on by yourself, struck down some wretched pickpocket in Piccadilly last week, and sat on him until a constable was summoned, you reading him the Riot Act the while. Were you not in charge of yourself at the time?'

Cass turned pink. 'It was not quite as exciting as you make it sound. Besides, I had to do something. It was poor Stroody's purse that he snatched, and I could hardly let him get away when Caesar was there ready to pull him down when I gave the order.'

'Yes, I quite see your point.' Jack was grave, rubbing his right hand up and down his newly smooth cheek. 'And, by the by, who taught you how to handle Caesar in such a fashion?'

'Oh, that was Fred. He said that Caesar would make an excellent guard dog who would be able to protect me if I were attacked. I persuaded Fred to show me how to control him. You must agree that I couldn't stand by and allow poor Stroody to be pillaged.'

'No, indeed. Except that Dickie thought that there was rather more to the story than that. Your footman, who, I gather, ably assisted Caesar, told Dickie that when the constable came and the boy blubbered at him that neither he nor his mother had eaten properly for a fortnight—hence the botched robbery—you insisted to the constable that he, Stroody, the footman and yourself should go to the boy's home to verify the truth of what he said. Tell me, my wise young judge, did you do so?'

'I thought that it was only right. I wondered what I would have done if I had been starving, and committed a robbery so that my mother and I might eat and then had Caesar sit on me.'

Cass faltered. She was uncertain how Jack would respond to the news that the Countess Devereux and her cohorts had been driven in a couple of hackney cabs to Vetch Street in London's slums to visit a young thief's mother, even if they had all been chaperoned by a constable.

'I must say, Stroody made the most awful fuss, but even she was nonplussed when we arrived at Vetch Street to find that the poor boy had been telling us no less than the truth. There was a little baby there too, his brother, who was almost a skeleton. Their poor father had been killed when he was run over by a dray soon after the baby was born...and so I had to do something.'

Cass ran down. She was not sure how Jack would feel about the something, but since Dickie had told him so much he probably knew the end of the story anyway.

'Something?' Jack was shrugging himself into a beautiful black and white striped waistcoat—later in the day he was going to the House of Lords to take his seat there—something which he had never visualised himself doing. 'And what did the something consist of—if I may be told, that is?'

'Well, I thought that the boy could be a boot boy at Devereux House, and his mother a sempstress. She hasn't been able to get work, but the housekeeper told me the other day that she was short of staff, so the constable said that he would let the boy go if we stood surety for him and he and his mother were employed by us. Jasper, his name is, and the butler says that he is a hard worker, and his mother too. The baby is looking much better, you will be happy to hear.'

'I will?' Jack was busy trying to tie his cravat and failing to achieve anything wearable. 'D'you think that, as well as rearranging the lives of everyone with whom you come into contact, you could find the time to help me to tie my cravat? I don't want to fetch m'valet in just for that. I can only hope that. . . Jasper, is it?. . .is as honest as you believe him to be. I am grateful in the extreme that you relieve me of so much of the task of running this household.'

Cass had picked up his cravat, was holding it in her hands and gazing dubiously at it. 'Oh, now I know that you are funning me, Jack, but I did think that the whole episode came under the heading of those acts of mine about which I don't need to trouble you. There, how does that suit?' And she stood back to admire her handiwork, for, whilst Jack's cravat bore no resemblance to a Napoleon, or a Waterfall, or any of the other styles which men wore, it had a certain artless charm of its own, as she earnestly assured him.

'My dear—' Jack took her hand and kissed it '—everything that you do has a certain artless charm, including the sophistry with which you justify all your more *outré* actions. I shall regret the day when society is *not* gossiping about your latest exploit. I can also see that I must be exceedingly careful what I say to you in the future about what you may or may not do, or I shall arrive home to find that you have taken over from Lord Liverpool the task of running the country.' And he kissed her hand again, deciding that he liked the sensation.

Later, when they had eaten a late breakfast, almost a luncheon, and he had spoken to Greene, the butler, about Jasper and his family, and learned that they appeared to be willing workers as well as respectable people down on their luck, Jack returned to his room to make ready to go to the Lords. Whilst doing so he could not prevent himself from thinking about his young wife. She was coming to occupy more and more of this thoughts.

He had taken her in marriage as a convenience, believing that Cass would be so grateful to him for saving her from penury that she would make no demands on him. When he had first seen her he had deemed her to be a little creepmouse who would be overawed both by him and by becoming a Countess— a biddable girl, in short. What amused him was how wrong he had been to make any such judgement!

He had been reading Mary Shelley's newly published novel, *Frankenstein*, which incidentally, Cass had recommended to him, and he thought that, like Count Frankenstein, he had unwittingly created a monster—a nice one, perhaps, who would, he hoped, not land them both in a grand finale among the Polar wastes.

What intrigued him—no, puzzled him—was that more and more he was looking forward to coming home to her, to being with her. And she only just nineteen! And at the Leominsters' ball Caro Luxcombe, for all her beauty, had looked commonplace beside her. In planning a white marriage, he had seen himself acquiring a mistress, or mistresses, as soon as the problems of taking over as Earl Devereux had been overcome, but more and more to do so would have seemed to be a betrayal of Cass. . .

Which was odd, because he had promised her nothing and she had agreed, without any other coercion than the knowledge that she would not starve if she married him.

Jack frowned. He had promised Dickie that he would not hurt her, but now he no longer knew what would or would not hurt her. She was no longer a pawn on a chessboard to him, but someone who had claims on him. Was she slowly advancing up the board in order to promote herself to be Queen?

And would he mind if she did?

* * *

Cass wasn't exercised about being betrayed by anyone. She was too busy trying to discover the truth about a betrayal which might have taken place in the past to worry overmuch about the present.

That morning at breakfast she had casually asked Jack if she might continue her exploration of the attics.

'Now, why,' he had asked her, in the middle of buttering himself a roll, 'do you ask me for permission to do such a trivial thing, when ever since we were married you have been taking it upon yourself never to ask me permission to do anything important?'

'Such as asking you for permission to play the harp?' Cass had commented naughtily.

Jack had fixed her with a basilisk eye. 'You know perfectly well what I am talking about, and it is not harps. Of course you may rummage in the attic, so long as you promise to tell me if you discover an artistic masterpiece among the dust and cobwebs. A lost Leonardo, perhaps?'

So that had been that. She had solemnly promised to let him know of any treasure which she found there, and, not for the first time as he left her, he had dropped a light kiss on the top of her head.

At this rate, Cass had thought acidly, the servants will be thinking all the wrong things about our marriage. And why did he kiss me? Because I took his funning about the attics without making a fuss? One would think I spent my time thinking up things to provoke him.

And that had made Cass laugh to herself, for was not that exactly what she had been doing?—Although rummaging in the attics was not something she was doing to provoke Jack—no, indeed!

Not that Cass proposed to rummage in the attics straight away. First, she needed to find out exactly what had happened twelve years ago. She could make a prompt start by talking to Amelia Thaxted, who was due to visit her that afternoon and, by some means which did not look like mere vulgar curiosity, winkle out of her as tactfully as possible what Jack was supposed to have done, and whether it was connected with the Star of Rizapore.

Except that when Amelia arrived, graciously prepared to be as pleasant to Cass as though she had never described her as a millstone around the family's neck, tact was not needed, because not only did Constantia arrive with her, but Fred lounged in behind his mother and his aunt.

Cass knew quite well that tactful questions would simply have Fred making such innocent remarks as, Come on, Cass, what was all that about, hey?—as though she had been speaking in Greek or Aramaic, at least. Instead of using a rapier, a mace would doubtless do.

It was odd to have Jack's sisters trying to please her instead of the other way round! She ordered the tea-board to be brought in on hearing that, like herself, they would be dining late. Fred was off to Watier's, he informed her.

'Jack doin' the pretty at the Lords, is he?' This was not a question, but what Cass thought of as a typical Fred statement—that was a statement which was phrased like a question to avoid committing oneself and earning reprimand or correction!

'Wonder you didn't go to watch him,' he ended.

'He particularly didn't want spectators,' Cass said firmly. 'It's not as though he were going to make a speech, you know. He's simply taking his seat.'

'How odd to think of Jack in the Lords,' sniffed Amelia. 'One would not have thought it...' She paused. She had been about to say,...twelve years ago, when Papa had the footmen throw him out of Devereux House, but stopped. Perhaps it was not quite the thing to say to his wife.

This was the opening Cass had been waiting for. 'You know, my dear Lady Thaxted—' she began, only to be interrupted.

'I wish you may call me Amelia,' her sister-in-law said. 'Lady Thaxted sounds so formal.'

Cass bowed her head as graciously as she could. 'My dear Amelia, I have often wondered exactly what it was which provoked Jack's father to such an extreme course of action. I think it wrong that I, whom am his wife, should be the only person ignorant of what occurred. It may result in me saying something unfortunate, and that would be too bad.'

She saw Stroody turn a disbelieving eye on her, astounded by the unlikely notion that Cass would ever be troubled by what anyone might think of her.

'Oh, that had not occured to me, I do admit,' Amelia conceded graciously. 'But you must understand that none of us knew exactly what Jack had done, for Papa always refused to speak of it, but there seems to be little doubt that he stole the Star of Rizapore in order to pay his debts. In any event, the Star disappeared and has never been seen since. Was not that so, Constantia?'

Constantia, her sister's echo, thus appealed to, nodded her head eagerly. 'Indeed, sister dear, but recollect, the whole wretched business began when Papa wished Mama to wear the Star when they went to Court for some grand occasion. Mama rarely wore it—she disliked it, said it was too large and vulgar—but this time Papa insisted. I distinctly remember the excitement which followed Papa's discovery that it was missing from the chest where her jewels were kept.'

Amelia nodded. 'So there you have it, my dear.' She seemed to think that enough had been said on the matter.

Cass was not so sure. 'But why was it assumed that Jack stole it?'

An impatient sigh from Amelia was followed by, 'We were never told the details of the matter. I suppose that Papa had investigations made from which it appeared that Jack was the guilty party—hence his disgrace. Certainly he had paid off the debts he had acquired at Oxford—not that they were anything like as large as the value of the Star.'

'And did Jack admit that he had stolen the Star?'

Constantia took up the tale. 'Oh, no. He protested his innocence most vigorously. One supposes that it was that which annoyed Papa. He never liked liars, and, for some reason which I don't understand, he never liked Jack—did he, Amelia?'

'Indeed not. And he never mentioned Jack's name again. Which makes it all the more surprising that he left Jack everything—provided he married, that is.'

Fred, who had been following all this with his mouth open, exclaimed suddenly, 'Bit thin, all this—what was Jack supposed to have done with the rest of the money? Even if he handed the Star over to a money-lender or a fence, what did he do with what was left over after he had paid his debts? And if he didn't spend it, where is it now?'

Cass nodded thoughtfully. Even Fred, not the greatest of intellects, had worked out that Jack would hardly have joined the Army as a penniless ranker if he had had thousands to his name as a result of the theft. Or had he not dared to spend it? Particularly if he claimed to be innocent.

'But where did Jack get the money from to pay his debts?' continued Fred doggedly. 'Couldn't have counterfeited it, could he? Did my Grandmama have any idea exactly when the Star disappeared?'

'No, indeed.' Amelia's answer was quite definite. 'But one has to remember how broken Mama was by the whole wretched *brouhaha*. Jack was her favourite, you must understand, and to discover that he had stolen from her was altogether too much. Although Jack always claimed that he had paid off his debts with what he had won on the gaming tables, no one believed him! Poor Mama died almost immediately after Jack was turned out. She had a weak heart, and Papa always believed that it was the discovery of Jack's wickedness which killed her.'

His aunt's reply did not appear to satisfy Fred. More questions were in the offing. He opened his mouth again, only to have his mother remark irritably, 'Oh, really, Fred, no more, if you please. You are like a dog with a bone, and we must not distress dear Cass by hashing over the unhappy past.'

Dear Cass was not in the least distressed, and Fred was about to say so. It was plain that neither sister knew the whole of the story, nor any details of it. Jack had stolen the Star, their father had said so, and so far as they were concerned that was that. Like Fred, she thought that it was thin, but undoubtedly both sisters believed in Jack's guilt.

There was one more question which she had to ask, even if it upset Amelia.

'What about Philip, the heir?' she asked. 'Was he involved?'

'Philip?' both sisters exclaimed at once, and Amelia added, 'Oh, Philip had nothing to do with it. He was away at the time. In any case, you may depend upon it that stealing diamonds was not Philip's way at all — no, indeed.'

Remembering Philip, Cass was inclined to agree with them. On the other hand, despite what Amelia had said, it had to be admitted that the Star might have disappeared long before its loss had been discovered. She decided not to say so, and listened instead to Fred, who was still doggedly defending Jack, saying in a grumbling voice, 'Well, I can't see Jack stealing diamonds and lying about it. More likely to have boasted that he had done it, if you ask me, hey, Cass? Only it's not his sort of thing at all, I'd lay odds.'

Cass thought so too, but did not say so aloud. What did surprise her was Fred's newly discovered vein of shrewdness and his defence of his uncle.

'Sterling feller, Jack,' he finally offered, as though he were doing an inspired bit of mind-reading, and then, to everyone's satisfaction, including Cass's, he let the matter drop. There was no point in hashing over the Star's disappearance further when there was apparently nothing more to be learned.

Her manner did not show it, but the whole conversation had left Cass feeling dispirited. It seemed to her that it would be almost impossible at this late date to clear Jack, when two and possibly three of the principals were dead. To make matters worse, she was quite sure that Jack would refuse to discuss the theft of the Star with her. But, like Fred, she was now sure that he had not stolen it. It certainly didn't fit.

Later, when Fred left for Watier's, he said to her in a low voice as he bowed his farewells, 'Don't want to distress you, Cass, but you ought to know that Colonel Spence has got hold of the wretched business we were discussing this afternoon and is going round London blackguarding Jack over it.

'He can't challenge Jack to a duel, nor can Jack challenge him, because of the Duke's edict. Depend upon it, though, Spence is going to do as much damage to Jack as possible. But what will happen when Jack finds out, hey? Best you keep an eye on him, Cass,' he ended anxiously.

Two things struck Cass, one of them being that Fred must think that she had some influence over Jack, and the other that she had been right to suppose that Fred was growing up. Was it associating with Dev and Dickie which was doing the trick? Cass knew that they had been teaching Fred, not only to use the small

sword and the sabre, but the finer points of horsemanship and the correct driving of a carriage. His father
had never been interested in such athletic pastimes
and had always shown little interest in Fred, leaving
his upbringing to servants and his mother.

It was almost as though Fred, who thought and
spoke off him as Jack and not as uncle, was finding in
him the father he had never had, and that Dickie was
taking the place of all the men who should have
trained him in manly pursuits.

She took this thought back with her to the drawing-
room, and after Amelia and Constantia's departure
made her way to the library, where Mr Hunt was
engaged in examining a rare copy of a herbal, which
he had found hidden at the back of an armoire in a
rarely used bedroom.

'Lady Devereux, how may I assist you?' He was
pleased to see her, but did not show it. As he had
supposed, she had not found much time to visit him
now that she was Countess.

'I don't exactly know,' Cass confessed. She had once
thought that she ought not to discuss Jack's downfall
with him, but needs must when the devil drives had
become her motto. 'You said once, before I married
Lord Devereux, that you would help me if you could;
now I would like you to try to do so. I gained the
impression when I asked you about the Star of
Rizapore that you knew more than you were telling
me about its disappearance. I should be most obliged
to you if you were to tell me all that you know.'

This was daring of Cass, for she had nothing but a
vague intuition that Mr Hunt knew more than he told
about practically everything which had passed in
Devereux House since he had arrived there.

Mr Hunt was looking dubious. Cass was Countess,
but she had not bludgeoned him with her rank and
ordered him to obey her, but had spoken to him as

though she were the simple Miss Cassandra Merton she had once been. He decided that he would honour her with the truth.

'If I were to say that I never believed that the present Earl stole the Star of Rizapore, it would not be because I am trying to please you now that he is your husband, but because, at the time, I thought that it went against the grain of what I knew about his present lordship. You will allow me to speak plainly, m'lady?'

'As plainly as possible, Mr Hunt. It is always my wish, whoever speaks to me.'

'Yes, I know that that was true when you were Miss Merton, but. . .'

'But you did not know whether that still held good now that I am Countess?'

He nodded.

'Whatever you say to me, Mr Hunt, will remain between the two of us. You may speak freely and frankly to me.'

'Very well, m'lady.'

'And you may be seated whilst you do so.' And Cass sat down on the other side of the large map table where she had been used to work before she had married Jack.

'First, you must understand that when your husband was plain Jack Devereux he was quite a different man from the stern one he is now. He was somewhat of a wild boy, but not in any way vicious. He was always cheerful and considerate to the staff, which was more than I could say of his elder brother—you asked me to speak plainly, so I do.'

Cass nodded for him to go on. 'His father, for some reason, did not care for him, and made his partiality for his heir plain. Not that that worried Mr Jack, you understand. He was very fond of his mother, and she of him. As I remember, he came down from Oxford that year about a month before it was discovered that the Star was missing. I remember distinctly that he came into the library to borrow a book shortly after he arrived home—he was always an avid reader, even though his greatest love was everything to do with horses and field sports.

'He told me that he proposed to spend the vacation reading, that he had wasted his first year at Oxford and had run up a lot of debts, but had been able to pay them off because he had had a run of good luck at the gaming tables. He also said that he had made up his mind never to gamble again, that it was a foolish thing for a younger son to do. You see, he was basically steady behind the natural exuberance of youth, though I wondered whether he would keep to his resolution. It was an easy one for a man to make, but a difficult one to adhere to.'

Cass interrupted. 'Dickie Dickson said once when he was teaching me to drive that Jack never gambled—he was twitted about it, he said, when he was in the Royal Dragoons.'

Mr Hunt nodded in his turn. 'As I thought. He was always strong-minded—as he is now—only much more so now than when he was a boy. I think that hardship may have changed and strengthened him, if you will forgive me for passing judgement on him.'

Cass thought so too, but said nothing to Mr Hunt, who continued his tale. 'I remember when the jewel was found to be lost—it was supposed a thief had got in, or a servant was the culprit. And then m'lord discovered that Mr Jack had suddenly paid off his debts, and at the same time the Runner he had employed to find out who had stolen it must have told him that Mr Jack was involved somehow.

'M'lord sent for Mr Jack, accused him of the theft, which Mr Jack denied, and then sent for the footmen to throw him out, after telling him that he was never

to come home again, that his allowance was to be
stopped. He did not need it, m'lord said, for he had
what was left over from the theft of the Star, and must
live on that. He said that Mr Jack was fortunate not to
be handed over to be tried as a common criminal and
hanged.'

So far Cass had heard nothing which Amelia and
Constantia had not already hinted at to her. But she
wondered how it was that Mr Hunt knew so much
more of the details of the scandal than they did.

Her expression must have given her away, for Mr
Hunt said drily, 'Servants always know more than their
masters think they do, m'lady—as you should be well
aware. But that was not the end.

'After Mr Jack had gone—never to be seen here
again until the day of the will-reading when he
reappeared, a changed man—m'lady went in to m'lord
in his study, and it was impossible for us not to know
what was said; they cared little who heard them. She
was hysterical, cried out that she knew that Jack was
innocent, and that m'lord must change his mind. He
had always been very tender to his Countess, but over
this he was adamant. He said that Jack was no son of
his, deserved to be hanged, and that his name was not
to be mentioned again.

'But she would not give way. They argued and
shouted so violently that the staff were frightened, and
ran to find out what was happening. M'lord walked
out of the door with m'lady on her knees, clinging to
his legs. He swore at her—which was a thing he never
did—raised her up and threw her against the wall. He
said that it was her fault that Jack had disgraced him.

'By now the noise they made was so great and
m'lord's anger was so strong that a crowd of us had
gathered, fearful of what might happen, and at this
point m'lady screamed suddenly that she could prove
that Jack was innocent. When m'lord told her that she

was beside herself, and he would send for a mad doctor to have her confined in an asylum, m'lady began to answer him, but never finished what she began. She had a fit, fell to the ground, and never spoke or moved again. They said afterwards that her heart had always been weak, and that shock had stopped it.

'The shock nearly killed m'lord too. He was never the same man again. He had been of a high temper, but his temper had killed his wife, whom he had always loved and been careful of in his distant manner until that day—and he hated Mr Jack more than ever, for it was easier for him to blame his Countess's death on his son than on himself.

'And that is all I know.'

'And Lady Thaxted and Lady Constantia—did they know of this?'

'No, nothing. M'lord told them that Mr Jack's wickedness had killed their mother and that was that.'

'And do you think that my husband stole the Star?'

'To be honest, I do not know what I think. The simplest explanation, which philosophers frequently say is what we must believe, is that Mr Jack stole it, and that his mother refused to believe the truth—but, as I said earlier, that goes against all I know—and knew—of the present Earl.'

'And the Star has never been seen or heard of again?'

'Never. It disappeared. M'lord thought that it might have been recut after Mr Jack stole it and handed it to a fence or a receiver, and that it no longer existed in its original form. He had the Runners search for it, but they never even traced the fence, let alone the Star.'

He fell silent. 'I fear that I have told you little more than I imagine you already know.'

Cass rose, which had Mr Hunt rising too. 'Well, at

least I now know rather more than everyone else
thinks they know, when I previously knew nothing.
What surprises me is that I never heard anything about
the disappearance of the Star of Rizapore during all
the years I lived here—years in which I came to know
Jack's father quite well. He was a most unhappy man.'

'That you heard nothing is not surprising, for if
m'lord ever found out that anyone spoke of Mr Jack,
or the Star, they were dismissed on the spot without a
character.'

'Thank you, Mr Hunt. You may be sure that I will
not pass on anything of what you have told me. I am
also sure, although I have no grounds for saying so,
that the Earl does not know exactly how his mother
came to die, and I would prefer that he did not. I think
that the knowledge would trouble him greatly.'

'Indeed, m'lady. And may I say, although you may
think it impertinent of me, that you are making a most
gracious Countess—although it is no more than I
expected. M'lord is a lucky man—in you and in his
friend, Mr Dickson.'

All the way back to her room Cass thought of what
she had been told. Mr Hunt's account of the theft had
not been quite the same as Amelia's and Constantia's.
In his, Jack's mother had not died of shock at Jack's
wickedness, but because she believed him to be innocent and his father would not listen to her.

Slowly a shadowy possibility began to take shape in
her mind. But until she could find some evidence to
support that shadow, there was nothing she could do.
An early visit to the attics was imperative.

CHAPTER ELEVEN

'WHAT next?' Jack had come home after a session at Louis Fronsac's. He believed in keeping himself in trim by exercising every day. As he drove home he made up his mind to propose a ride in the Park to Cass. Dickie had told him that she had already mastered the perch-phaeton and he would ask her to let him be her passenger.

He entered the drawing-room to find that Cass was at the big table in front of the window with a man whom he had never seen before instructing her in the art of watercolour painting. Miss Strood, acting as chaperon, sat before the empty hearth engaged in her canvaswork.

'Oh, Jack!' Cass rose with a swirl of skirts. 'I am so pleased that you have arrived early, before Mr Swallow has finished teaching me. I am sure that you would wish to hear from him that I am making excellent progress at a skill which I have always wanted to perfect but have never been able to do so before.'

'Like playing the harp?' enquired Jack smoothly as he walked over to inspect the watercolour on which Cass had been working. It was pinned to a sloping board and was a view of the gardens at the back of Devereux House as seen through the drawing-room window.

'Exactly!' Cass was all artless charm. She watched his face twitch as he examined her painting. It was with no surprise that he found that it was excellent, and that Mr Swallow's eager praise of m'lady's undoubted talent and her willingness to be instructed was not simply due to his desire to flatter a Countess.

It came to him with the force of a revelation that Cass excelled in everything she did, and that had she not married him all these talents would have died a-borning.

This aroused in him a fierce protectiveness towards her which he had not suspected he possessed. He had become aware that she was testing and teasing him by engaging in a series of activities designed to challenge any preconceived notions he might have had that she was a 'biddable girl' resigned to carry out only his wishes. He thought that Dickie might have been better employed in worrying whether *he* was the one who was going to be hurt, and not his young bride.

'Excellent,' he offered at last. 'A tribute to both student and teacher, if I may say so, sir.'

He was, Cass noted, as polite to Mr Swallow as he was to all those who might be considered to be beneath him in station.

'You come pat, sir,' Cass said. 'My lesson has just ended.' And she walked over to where Jack was holding out his hand to Mr Swallow, who was shaking it with an expression of complete disbelief at such enormous and unaffected condescension. 'You look full of something, my dear, what is it?'

She was reading his mind again—was he really so transparent? 'If you have finished your lesson, then I propose that you drive me to the Park. Dickie tells me that you are ready to drive the phaeton in public, and who better to accompany you on your first excursion than your husband?'

Not only Mr Swallow's eyes widened at this public declaration of affection, but so also did Miss Strood's and Cass's.

She made him a deep bow. 'If you say so, sir. Your wish is my command.'

'Now that I do not believe! But I do say so, and I also ask that, if possible, you surprise me a little with your toilette. I should not like to think that you had lost an opportunity to demonstrate your powers of invention!'

Cass could not help giggling. It was almost impossible for her to wrong-foot him. Just as she thought that she had disconcerted him a little he turned her guns against herself, or, in terms of the cavalryman he had once been, he charged her defensive positions and overran them.

'I will try not to disappoint you,' she shot back, before thanking Mr Swallow. Jack compounded his earlier graciousness to his subordinates by saying to Miss Strood as Cass walked to the door, 'Stroody, my dear, you look a little peaky. Would you like Dickie to follow us in the landaulet, with you as a passenger?' And then he spoiled her treat a little by adding, 'You may take Caesar with you so that Cass may give him his daily walk in the Park.'

Even the prospect of chaperoning Caesar could not ruin Miss Strood's pleasure at being given the opportunity to play the lady in Hyde Park.

'Most kind of you, m'lord,' she twittered at him, her face flushing and softening so much that Jack thought, not for the first time, that she must have been quite a pretty girl when younger. Not that she was so very elderly. He judged her to be in her late thirties, and therefore not many years older than himself. But, as women's years were counted, she was well past her last prayers whilst he was still a most eligible *parti*—eligibility and age having little to do with one another where men were concerned: money and position counting for everything.

So it was quite a little procession which entered the Park, particularly as Fred Maxwell arrived at the mews on horseback just as Cass walked in. She was not wearing one of her military rigs, but a naval one. Her deep blue riding dress with its silver buttons and high

snowy cravat was surmounted by an admiral's hat à la
late Lord Nelson, correct even down to its white
cockade.

Even the Imp, who had rushed to be m'lord's tiger
and had been disappointed to learn that he would not
be needed, looked impressed when she appeared in
the yard. He and Cass were much of a size, and in
some odd way the Imp thought that this rebounded to
his credit, and, like Dickie, worshipped m'lady from
afar—and sometimes from anear.

She had admired his skill in playing the horn, and
had asked him if she could try to blow it. One of the
pleasures of being Countess was that she could enjoy
herself by doing all those things which had been
forbidden to lowly Miss Merton. The Imp had
responded enthusiastically and, amidst a great deal of
merriment from the watching grooms caused by Cass's
initial failures, had taught her the correct signals used
to warn tollgate keepers that they were coming
through, and those which demanded that the slow
coaches in front allow them easy passage.

All this was known to amused Dickie, but not to
Jack. Cass was not quite sure how he would respond
to the notion that his Countess was playing at being a
tiger!

As for Dev and Dickie, when they saw her new
outfit they reacted as one. Both of them began to clap
and cheer, Jack shouting, 'Three times three for
m'lady! Huzzah! Huzzah! Huzzah' Miss Strood, who
had not seen Cass's admiral's uniform before, looked
her surprise, and Fred leaned down from his splendid
chestnut to remark, 'Admiral Devereux to the main-
mast, hey,' straightening up with a naval salute.

Cass blushed her pleasure before Jack, waving the
groom to one side, helped her up into her phaeton,
which, picked out in blue and silver as it was, complemented her toilette—or was it the other way round?

Curious eyes followed them everywhere. Colonel Spence's blackguarding of Jack, plus the knowledge that he had spent twelve years in the ranks, intrigued society no less than his speedy marriage to Cass, a nobody whom no one knew.

Cass was relieved to see that they were not being cut—if anything, people seemed to be going out of their way to speak to them. Which, of course, proved nothing. Their main interest, doubtless, was in seeing how she and Jack reacted to the reviving of the scandal about the Star. What they were not aware of was that Jack had no notion that the scandal had been publicly revived, and by a man whom he thought of as an enemy. The later he learned the news, the better, so far as Cass was concerned.

She concentrated on her driving, earning a quiet bravo from Jack when, at his suggestion, she finally drew to a stop and handed over the phaeton to one of the grooms who had accompanied them. Her toilette, as well as the elegant figure she cut walking along with Caesar, Jack on one side of her and Fred on the other, leading his horse, was the sensation of the afternoon.

'It's not her looks, *voyez vous*, which makes her remarkable,' explained the French military attaché, 'because she is piquant rather than pretty, but the whole *tout ensemble*. One admires not only her air of charming self-control, but the manner in which she wears her original clothes as though she is not aware that they are original. Her husband is a lucky man, one would dare say, because, depend on it, she is an original in every way!' His knowing smile said everything which he could not utter aloud.

Both Jack and Cass would have enjoyed the joke on them if they had heard what he was saying, seeing that their relationship was quite otherwise from what he was undoubtedly thinking. Amelia Thaxted, angry at the commotion which her brother and his wife were provoking, beckoned them over to her carriage. Her eyes said what her tongue did not dare utter. That Cass's admiral's uniform was outrageous and that Caesar, by reason of his size and beauty was even more so, and that Jack really ought to inform his wife that she owed it to her new station to be as modestly correct in her attire as possible.

'So,' she exclaimed, a trifle shrilly, 'you have arrived to satisfy everyone's curiosity, I suppose.'

'On the contrary, my dear sister. I make a point of never satisfying anyone's curiosity. M'lady and myself are here merely to take the air and allow Caesar a longer walk than the grounds of Devereux House can afford him.'

Jack was as smooth as he sometimes could be. His likeness to a chameleon had never been stronger. What Cass would have liked to see, but would never now have the opportunity to do so, was how he had behaved when he was a simple trooper. Not, she was beginning to think, that Jack was a simple anything. On the contrary—as he had just said to his sister.

'Hmm!' was her only answer to that. 'I am to suppose that you do not care that the old scandal about the missing Star has been revived, and that Colonel Spence is tattling your guilt about London again?'

Jack went quite still. Cass felt his hand on her arm tighten. His voice, though, when he answered his sister, was as controlled as ever.

'Indeed, one would have *supposed*—' and he leaned on the word which his sister had used '—that society— and Colonel Spence—would have more interesting and up-to-date matters to discuss than something which was dead and buried long ago.'

Amelia threw caution and common sense to the winds. She had long dominated all those about her, and could scarcely believe that she could not dominate

Jack. 'Oh, fie on you, Jack!' she trumpeted. 'How can you say such a thing when you have so melodramatically returned from the dead and taken a wife who chooses to flaunt herself as though she were a light comedy actress on leave from Drury Lane! Of course everyone is tattling about you. You would have done better to have stayed at home and persuaded Cassandra to adopt a more modest garb.'

At that, Jack's hand left Cass's arm. She felt quite giddy with anxiety about what he might say and do in response to his sister's strictures. She heard Fred's indrawn breath, and then his indignant, 'I say, Aunt, steady on.' He had felt the edge of his aunt's tongue many times in the past, and had always bent before it. Like Cass, he was a trifle fearful of what Jack might say.

Jack put up a hand to silence Fred. He stood back. Bowed. And, his voice so cold and neutral that even on a day as warm as this one could well believe that it would freeze ice, said, 'So happy to be given the benefit of your advice, sister. You will, of course, permit me to ignore it—and the unkind remarks that you have made about my wife. I think that you have forgotten that she is no longer a penniless dependant whom you may insult at will. You will also forgive me if I inform you that I find the company of Miss Strood and Dickie, my friend, infinitely perferable to yours.'

He turned his back on the startled Amelia, to whom no one had ever before spoken in such a cold and controlled fashion, and walked Cass, Caesar and Fred to where Dickie and Miss Strood, who were talking together, were stationed under a tree.

'I think,' he announced to Dickie, 'it is time that we returned to Devereux House. I have some thinking to do.'

He was strangely quiet on the drive home, resembling more the grim man who had mocked the

Devereux family the first time Cass had seen him rather than the more easy one he had become since she had married him.

They were in the house before he asked her, his voice distant, 'Did you know, Cass, that Spence was spreading gossip about me? I think that you did.'

Cass was tempted to say Know what? but the set of his mouth discouraged her, as in the past it had discouraged more than one man who might have tried to temporise with him.

'Yes,' she told him, as quietly as she could, rather like, she thought afterwards, an animal trainer gentling a particularly angry lion. 'Fred told me the other afternoon.'

She did not say, I would have told you at a suitable moment, because that would not have been the truth.

Jack's expression lightened a little on hearing that she had heard the gossip so recently. 'I shall have to do something about Colonel Spence, you know,' he told her.

Cass was aghast. 'Oh, no, Jack, you promised the Duke—and me—that you would not fight a duel with Colonel Spence.'

'Nor shall I. But I shall find some means to humiliate him, make him pay for what he is doing now—and what he did six years ago.'

His tone was so quietly savage that Cass wondered at her own temerity in so frequently bearding and teasing him. She wondered what it was that Colonel Spence had done which was so dreadful. Curiosity got the better of her.

'Is it because—because he had you flogged?'

Jack's feral eyes were hard on her. 'Who told you that?'

'No one—or rather, something Colonel Spence said to you at the Leominsters' ball. . . I thought. . .'

His whole posture eased a little. 'Yes, I remember.

But you are quick to have understood that. I see that I must never underrate you. Yes, he had me flogged—and that was because I knew something to his discredit, and an officer can always find a reason to send a ranker to the whipping post if he is so minded. But it was the reason I ended there which was important, rather than the punishment itself.'

'And what exactly did Colonel Spence do which was so dreadful?'

Jack's face closed as though he had drawn a shutter over it. 'Oh, Cass, I can't tell you that. Not only would it not be right or proper, but it is not my secret to give away. It is someone else's, long dead. Somehow or other I intend to make Spence pay for what he did—as well as for his continual insults to you.'

'Yes, but Jack, when he says that there is something strange about our marriage—that is the truth, is it not?'

'It is not a truth which concerns him, and when I have it out with him I shall take good care that your name is not mentioned.'

'But,' persisted Cass, worry in her voice, 'if you are not going to fight him, Jack, what will you do?'

For the first time he was easy, the hint of laughter plain in his voice—a hint that always gave her pleasure. 'Oh, I am a most inventive man, Cass. Depend upon it, I shall think of something. And if I don't, then Dickie will.'

Cass asked him a question which she had long wanted to pose to him. 'How long have you known Dickie, Jack?'

'Since the first day I joined the cavalry. I was the arrogant raw recruit who thought that I was God's gift to horsemanship and who had never known what discipline meant from the day I was born. Without him I think that I would have gone under. He took pity on me, God knows why, and eased my way into the life which I had chosen without the remotest notion of what it would really be like. I had been used to giving orders. . .not taking them. . .and hardship was unknown to me. And now you know the debt I owe to Dickie. He saved my life.'

'Dickie says that you saved his.'

'At Salamanca, yes. But that was in return for saving mine by making a man out of me when I was only a silly spoiled boy. One thing that I learned was that it is as necessary to be able to take orders as it is to give them if one is going to be able to command one's self, let alone other men.'

And that is why Jack is different from any other man I have ever known, Cass thought when she was alone in her room. He has walked through what the poets call the fire, and has come out at the other end strengthened, not consumed. All of the other men whom I have ever met have only known a life of ease. She thought of Fred, and wondered what sort of man he might become if he were made to suffer and endure as Jack had done.

And by what means did Jack intend to make Colonel Spence pay?

Jack was apparently about to pursue Spence without delay. He came into the drawing-room where she was waiting for the tea-board to be brought in after a rather late dinner, which he had eaten in the most distracted fashion, almost as if she were not there. At the end of it he had informed her abruptly that he intended to spend the rest of the evening at Watier's.

He was dressed to kill, and Cass wondered for the hundredth time why a man who was in no way conventionally handsome should look so impressive that wherever he went every eye followed him. She had been introduced to Lord Granville, reputed to be the most handsome man of his generation, and that judgement was still true of him, even though he was in early middle-age. He was also very charming, after a gentle fashion, which was quite remote from Jack's brusque downrightness.

And yet. . .and yet. . . Jack charmed too—not only herself, but any woman who met him. Men, as well, were happy to meet him and to call him friend. Even Spence's repeated slandering of him had not yet possessed the power to damage him.

Miss Strood raised her head curiously when Cass said, 'You hope to find Colonel Spence at Watier's?'

'Rumour says that he spends most nights there—but I don't intend to break him at the gaming tables, Cass.'

'I know. You don't gamble. Dickie said so. So what will you do there?'

Jack's grin was a shark's. 'Pretend to.'

'Oh-h-h.' Cass's sigh was one of exasperation. 'I wish that I might come with you. I know fine ladies gamble. But not at Watier's.

Now this statement of Cass's was not an innocent one. She had a reason for wishing to know what Jack's reaction might be to women gambling. She watched his whole body stiffen. He said, curtly for him, 'Women gambling are worse than men doing it, and that is bad enough. But women, being ignorant of much of the world, have no notion of the kind of tricks to which professional gamesters are prone—particularly when such swindlers have made sure that their victims have drunk heavily before they play.

'The late Duchess of Devonshire is a prime example. The sharks destroyed her ruthlessly. She lost thousands upon thousands at play to professional swindlers like Henry Martindale, at both Almack's Ladies Club and elsewhere. Her debts were so great that it is said that she could not calculate how large they were, and Coutts the banker, who lent her money to help her to pay them, lost a great deal of his by doing so.

'I trust, Cass, that you have no intention of emulating her. It can only bring distress and ruin on you, if you do. Do not compel me to make you swear that you will never engage in it.'

There was such passion in his voice that Cass hastened to assure him, quite truthfully, that gambling had always seemed to her the oddest of addictions. It held no attraction for her. 'To play whist for counters is as far as I am inclined to go—is not that so, Stroody?'

Jack left for Watier's with Stroody's fervent assurances as to Cass's lack of interest in play ringing in his ears. He might have been surprised at the conclusions which his young wife drew from his fervent attack on play—and particularly on women gambling.

His intended prey was already at Watier's, as Jack had expected. Spence was half-cut although the evening, in gambling terms, was yet young. So much the better for Jack's purposes if he were in drink. Jack despised heavy drinking because it destroyed a man's judgement, something he had frequently witnessed during his time in the cavalry.

Jack was well aware that the man that the Army had made of him was very different from the man he would have become if he had remained a idle and indulged younger son. That man might well have been an effete young aristocrat, incapable of the kind of sustained effort and self-control which had become his hallmark when he was half of Dev and Dickie. That man would have passed over or despised Dickie, not recognised the sterling worth of him.

Spence stared at Jack from the table where he was sitting, surrounded by his toadies. He whispered something offensive about Jack to them, loud enough for

Jack to catch what he was saying. He heard his name, and what Spence said was venomous enough for his companions to break into loud and drunken laughter.

'You were saying, Spence?' Jack observed pleasantly. His voice was as urbane as he could make it.

'Lost your manners did you, Devlin, serving among the scum? Oh, I do beg your pardon, *Devereux*. Now, why do I always forget who are you are, I ask myself? The stench of the gutter clinging to you still, I suppose.'

This came out as unpleasantly in manner as it was in speech, and all his sycophants laughed again.

'I tell you this for your own good, Devlin, I mean Devereux, as I frequently tell those who may not know that you enjoyed yourself among the dregs for twelve years. Every dog to his vomit—and you certainly clung to yours—as well as to the whipping post!'

There was more laughter as Jack remained impassive. He despised Spence so thoroughly that nothing the man could say had the power to hurt or to annoy him.

'And do you also tell them why you had me strapped to the whipping post, Spence?' Jack's voice held only mild interest in it, so that the crowd which had gathered around them, hoping to see some fun, felt a little disappointment. Devereux was plainly not going to be provoked.

'For insubordination, Devlin. For insubordination to your superior officer, as you well know.'

'No, I don't know.' Jack's voice was still low and level. 'Would you care for me to tell them the real reason, Spence?'

'Hold your lying tongue, Devlin. I've no need to explain why I inflicted condign punishment on a piece of filth who was on the point of mutiny.'

'Not good enough, Spence, especially when it comes from a man who managed to avoid fighting in most of the battles of the campaign in which he was supposed to be taking part. Was it your other interests which incapacitated you—or was it simple cowardice which kept you permanently behind the lines? Of course, that made it easier for you to indulge your fancy for—'

Spence saw the accusation coming. He could not allow it to be said aloud that Jack Devereux knew what few did: that his taste was for handsome young men or boys rather than for pretty women. Such things might be hinted at, and the person hinted of might remain in society, but for it to be publicly stated meant social death.

He stood up, leaned forward, pushing the table before him, so that cards and counters, glasses and bottles were flung about, and struck Jack across the mouth. Jack had been expecting the blow, but made no attempt to avoid it—indeed, he had taunted Spence in order to provoke such a reaction.

'Damn you, Devereux, take that back.'

'Not I,' responded Jack, gingerly feeling his bruised lips, 'and I shall want immediate satisfaction for the blow, Spence, be sure of that. My choice of weapons, you must agree.'

Heads nodded in all directions. Yes, indeed! Here was a fine to-do, a splendid piece of gossip to travel around the drawing-rooms of the great and mighty, the cousinry who ruled England and its growing Empire.

Spence's face whitened for a moment, and then he gave a relieved little laugh. 'Damme, Devlin, you cannot demand satisfaction from me. The Duke expressly forbade it. He is my Commander-in-Chief— I cannot disobey him.'

'Oh, damme, Spence, you may forget that. I don't intend to come after you with swords or pistols, or even my fists. No, indeed. What I have in mind is something quite different. They tell me that you are a great whip, and I fancy myself a little in that line, so my proposal is that we race our curricles and four from London to Brighton, tigers up, on a day to be named.' He looked lazily around the room.

'I will send my seconds to you tomorrow morning to make formal arrangements for the race. My principal you already know, he being the lately Corporal Dickson of the Royal Dragoons, and Fred, my boy,' he added, turning to Fred Maxwell, who had been an interested spectator to the proceedings, 'you will do me the honour of backing Dickie, I trust?'

'Delighted,' exclaimed Fred. To be a second in a bloodless duel would be something to boast about when this evening was long past. 'But what penalty do you propose for the loser, Jack? If I may be so bold as to ask.'

'You may, indeed. I propose that the loser forfeits his horses, curricle and tiger, and writes a humble letter of apology to the winner, withdrawing all slanders and accusations previously made. The letter to be posted up on the front door of this Club, if the proprietors so agree. How about that, Spence?'

The hum which went round the room was one of admiration for Jack's ingenuity in circumventing the Duke's ban on a duel between himself and Spence. More than one man wondered what the Duke's reaction would be to Jack's impudence.

Greatly relieved that he was not being asked to commit himself to a duel to the death which he was sure that he could not win, Jack's prowess with small sword, pistols or fists being public knowledge, Spence snarled, 'Send your seconds to me and mine in formal fashion tomorrow, Devereux—though I would rather you spared me having to deal with that oaf Dickson again.'

Part of his relief came from his conviction that his

own ability as a driver must be better than Jack's—
Jack's recent involvement with horses having been
that of riding them, rather than driving them.

'My choice of weapons and my choice of the seconds
who represent me, Spence.'

Jack turned on his heel. One of the few men ever to
enter Watier's and not to gamble there.

Fred Maxwell caught him by the arm. 'Hey, Jack
you do intend to make up a table while you're here, I
hope.'

His uncle shook his head. 'Not I, Fred, and if you've
any sense you'll not linger long either. The sharks are
out for blood, and the wolves lurk in the undergrowth!
Beware.'

He left, having achieved what he had set out to do.
And now there remained only the race—which he
must win, not only for his own sake but for that of the
poor boy who had shot himself after Spence, his
superior officer, had used his rank to assault him. . .

The only pity was that the Duke's veto meant that
he could not use a pistol to dispose of the cur once
and for all.

CHAPTER TWELVE

OF COURSE, there was no way in which Jack could keep what he had done from Cass, seeing that the whole world knew of the challenge and the race. He worried less about what the Duke might think, although he hoped that his actions would not lose him the great man's goodwill.

Later in the week, he met Wellington in Hyde Park, walking a dog nearly as large and formidable as Cass's Caesar. 'Oh, Devereux, I trust I see you well,' was his amiable offering to Jack. 'Ingenious devil, ain't you? Might have known that you'd find some way of wriggling around my veto. Bound and determined to meet him in one way or another, are you? Wouldn't do for you to lose, but you do know that the fellow is a splendid whip, however worthless all his other accomplishments are?'

'Dickie's a better,' was Jack's reply, volunteered with his most impudent grin.

'Corporal Dickson—the man you saved at Salamanca,' returned the Duke, who was reputed never to forget any soldier, private or officer whom he had personally encountered. 'But Dickson ain't racing him, Devereux. More's the pity.'

'Dickie taught me.' Jack was brief.

'Well, it's to be hoped that you know the road to Brighton, and show Spence a clean pair of wheels...' With which riposte the Duke took off his hat, bowed and saying, 'Remember me to your lady wife, Devereux—whichever of our country's regiments she is representing today,' he was off down one of Hyde

Park's paths. Bowing heads and doffed hats followed him on his triumphal procession.

Well, it was a better reception to the news than Cass had given him, that was for sure! He had been shaving, or rather had just finished and had been wiping his razor on a towel, and she had been reclining on his bed, leafing through yesterday's *Morning Post* when he had said, as off-handedly as he could, 'There's something you ought to know, Cass.'

Cass had put down the paper. She had just been thinking what a cosily domestic scene she was part of, the only drawback being that she was still Jack's wife in name only. She had spent the previous evening wondering how she could delicately hint to him that she rather fancied the notion of being the Countess Devereux in every sense of the word, but tact in such a matter had seemed hard to come by. . .

'Oh, what ought I to know?'

'I challenged Colonel Spence at Watier's last night. . .'

He had purposely been ambiguous, in order to see her reaction. She had jumped to her feet, her face ashen, flung down the *Morning Post*, and exclaimed in a stricken voice, 'Oh, no, Jack, how could you? You know that you promised the Duke that you would not duel with him. I should never have thought that you, of all people, would go back on your word.'

Jack liked that, 'you, of all people'. It showed that his wife had a proper appreciation of his true value. It almost made him regret having teased her. Almost. It had been worth it if only to break the steadfast calm to which she usually treated him.

'I deceived you, Cass. Forgive me. What I challenged Spence to was not a duel *à l'outrance*, but instead to a race from London to Brighton, tigers up, with the loser to forfeit horses, curricle and tiger, and to write a letter of apology to the winner withdrawing all slanders, now and for ever. The letter to be posted up on Watier's front door.'

Cass had never thought that anything which Jack could propose would make her feel so frantic.

'Oh, Jack, how could you? You must know that if you lose it will mean social ruin. I don't care about that for my sake, but for you... You have been accepted again after all these years—and to lose that in such a fashion...'

She was so different from his usually calm, well-controlled, sardonically amused wife that Jack was entranced. Why, I do believe that she must care for me a little, he thought, and then, more soberly, Or does she care for losing her own position as Countess? Yes, that must be it.

'First of all,' he told her earnestly, 'I don't intend to lose the race. With Dickie's help I could win the chariot race at Byzantium if we could go back in time! And, secondly, I don't give a brass damn about whether I am a social pariah or not. Oh, I don't object to coming to London once a year and playing at being Earl Devereux for a few short months, but what I really want to do is to go back to Coverham and try to put things straight there. I hope you don't mind, Cass, if we live there most of the year. London's a fine place for a short time, but I want the open country again, and my dogs and horses. The only things that I shall miss are the mountains of Spain, but they are gone for ever, and the jolly days with them.'

'Jolly days!' Cass was sidetracked, as he had perhaps intended that she should be. 'What was jolly about being a ranker in a campaign and in a country notorious for its danger?'

He was near to her now, his feral eyes hard on her. He put down his razor, took both her small soft hands in his callused large ones. 'Oh, Cass, one never enjoys life more than when one might lose it at any moment!

Especially when one is with comrades whom one loves and trusts. I can't explain it.'

Cass's analytical mind was at work again. 'But weren't you afraid, Jack?'

'Of course I was. I would have been a fool else.'

They were eye to eye now, and he had pulled her so close to him that they were breast to breast. They were breathing as one, and Cass was conscious of his body as she had not been since the night of their marriage. She could see again the faint shadow of his beard, where he had shaved it close to his skin. She could feel the strong beat of his heart and was aware that her body was responding to his, wanted to push itself even closer to him, wanted his to take her over. . .

She muttered hoarsely, 'I think that I do understand you a little, Jack, but my knowledge of life is so limited. . .' She paused. For some reason she was having difficulty breathing as well as thinking and speaking. She pulled one hand away from his and stroked his warm cheek, astonished to find how soft it was compared with the rough lines of his strong jaw.

Jack bent his head and muttered as hoarsely as she had done, 'You must see that I have to bring matters to a head with Spence, Cass. Not only did he betray the men he led, but he has the impudence to carry on his vendetta against me, and I cannot rest until I have silenced him. For both things, and more besides, he deserves to be punished.'

'So long as *you* don't suffer, Jack.' The words trickled out of her like thick honey slowly poured from a jar. Cass's lips parted, and her small pink tongue came out to lick them feverishly.

'Yes!' Jack's voice was suddenly commanding, and after the one explosive word left his lips they came down on Cass's, and his tongue emerged to lick Cass's so that she gave a small shudder of ecstatic delight, closed her eyes and abandoned herself to sensation. . . but not for long.

The busy intrusive world was with them again. It was Dickie knocking on the door, come to discuss with Dev how best to win the race, and how best to organise everything connected with it.

For a moment they remained locked together, until Jack stood back with another explosive monosyllable jerked from him. This time it was 'Damn!' He shook his head as though to clear it as he spoke, adding apologetically—and unfortunately—'Sorry, Cass. I shouldn't have jumped on you like that.'

Sorry! So, he was sorry, was he? Well, so he should be! It was a penance to begin to make love to his wife, was it? And leave her aching all over for she knew not what! Well, he knew what was what, and she hoped that he was aching too.

Jack was. All the time that he was talking to Dickie. He decided that he would make it up to Cass for jumping on her by being tenderly considerate to her in future, and not forcing his rough self on her. He was quite unaware that what Cass desired most of all was to have his rough self forced on her!

But—as he might have guessed, he thought rue-fully—when he was finally alone with Cass again, she was even cooler than she usually was with him—quite in the boughs, in fact.

She immediately precipitated a bad-tempered argu-ment with him by remarking in a lofty voice, 'Of course, I shall expect to be installed at Brighton for a few days before the race, so that I may cheer you on Marine Parade when you arrive there before Colonel Spence. I shall take Stroody, and I expect that Dickie will add respectability to our household—he having to be there as your principal second to receive you and check that all is in order.'

This all came out so grandly that Jack stared at her

in amazement before saying regretfully, 'No, Cass, I don't want you to be involved in this in any way. It is between Spence and myself, and the matter is not one with which women ought to be concerned... Stroody may keep you company in London.'

Cass sprang to her feet again. It seemed to be an action which she was doomed to repeat that day. It was all Jack's fault, of course. He was being even more provoking than usual, when by rights she ought to be provoking him.

'Oh, no, Jack, please. Do allow me to go to Brighton. I am your wife, and I ought to be there to support you.'

But for once he was adamant, so that finally Cass announced, as cuttingly as possible, 'I suppose that I am being a fool to ask you to allow me to share the more important parts of your life. I understand now that I may do as I please so long as I confine myself to trivialities. After all, you made the terms of our marriage quite clear to me before our wedding, so I cannot complain.'

She knew that she was being unreasonable—childish, even, but she couldn't stop herself. The knowledge that she loved and desired him was strong in her, and equally strong was the bitter conviction that he did not really want her. He could scarcely have signalled his rejection of her more strongly than by refusing to allow her to support him when it would have been most natural for her to be allowed to do so. She was simply a toy which he occasionally allowed to amuse him, and she must never forget that.

'Now look here, Cass—' Jack began, exasperated, but she would not allow him to continue. Head high, she waved a dismissive hand at him and sailed from the room.

'Jumped on you like that.' What a thing to say! All the way to her room the words echoed in Cass's head, whilst Jack, frustrated, made for the tantalus and drank down a bumper. He would never understand women—never. Here was Cass, usually such a wise and sensible little thing—barring a few odd quirks about uniforms, dogs, painting, shorn hair and harps—behaving like a termagant. All my fault, he told himself savagely, forgetting myself because she felt so sweet and soft, and jumping on her, so that I frightened the poor little thing away.

He spent the next half an hour trying to think of something he might buy which would please or amuse her and restore her to her usual equable self. Failing to do so, he flung off to the stables again to tell Dickie what had happened between himself and Cass and ask for advice on how to handle her.

Only Dickie began laughing like a madman, finally clapping Dev on the back, exclaiming weakly, the tears running down his face, 'Go and put your head in a bucket of water, Dev, before I do it for you!'

All these excitements had not prevented Cass from pursuing her search for clues as to the true fate of the Star of Rizapore among the discarded objects in the attic.

To no avail. On the morning after her quarrel with Jack, she did not go to his room as she was wont, and instead, after breakfast, made one last and fruitless search among the dust wearing a stout brown holland apron over one of the prim dresses from her previous incarnation as Miss Cassandra Merton.

Later, she was to think that what followed showed how useless it was to expect life either to conform to one's expectations or to behave in the rational way which the great philosophers on the one hand, or novelists on the other, seemed to assume that it did. As so often happened, accident rather than reason was to show Cass the way forward.

Hot and tired—for the summer sun beat hard on the attic roof—and still wearing her apron, she made for the library to try to winkle some more information out of Mr Hunt. She found him shaking his head and pondering over a pile of books set out on a side-table—books which to Cass's certain knowledge had been there for at least six months, and for some reason had never been moved.

Something in her expression, however, moved Mr Hunt. He picked up the top volume, a splendid thing, quarto in size and bound in royal blue leather with an elaborate gilt trim, and announced distractedly, 'These were the books which the late Lord Devereux was reading when he was taken with his apoplexy. I have never liked to reshelve them: it seemed too much like burying him all over again. When I see them I half expect him to come through the library door, knowing that they will be there, on that table, waiting for him.'

He put the large volume down sadly. He had always respected m'lord, and in turn he had been one of the few people to whom Jack's father had spoken as a friend.

'Later this morning—' his tone was a trifle dramatic '—I shall return them to where they belong. There is a new Lord Devereux now, and it is him I must consider.'

Cass nodded. She thought that it was hardly the moment to begin badgering Mr Hunt about the past. Instead—and why, she never knew—when he moved off after she had assured him that she had no purpose in her visit but to pass some time among the treasures which he guarded so diligently, she picked up the beautiful book to discover that it was an early edition in the original Latin of Caesar's *De Bello Gallico*.

It reminded her also of Jack's father, and she riffled through it, admiring the elegance of the type and its lay-out, until she came to a page where two sheets of writing paper had been inserted—presumably by the late Earl, since it was his writing on them. Curious to discover what notes and comments he had been making on the text he had been studying so shortly before his death, Cass picked them up and began to read.

To discover that, instead of learned analysis, the first sheet was headed 'Memorandum—to be acted on immediately'—the last five words being heavily underlined. Curiosity held her rapt. Perhaps there might be something here which would throw light on the missing Star and Jack's disgrace. But to her astonishment the first item on the sheet was headed by her own name!

It might have been wrong of her, but she could not resist the temptation to read on. In his small precise handwriting the late Earl had written:

Item: Miss Merton is a good little thing and has lightened my recent lonely days. My will must be revised as soon as possible so that she may feature in it—I will send for Herriot this afternoon.

So he had not forgotten her, after all. Only his sudden death had prevented her from figuring among the beneficiaries of his will. Until this moment she had not admitted to herself how much her passing over by the man whom she had come to know and pity for his loneliness during the last months of his life had hurt her. He had not forgotten her; he had remembered her only moments before death had claimed him so suddenly.

Then there was a gap in which the Earl had written the same name over and over again, in a hand which betrayed much agitation. The name was that of his dead wife—Clarissa.

On the next line his writing had assumed its normal pattern, but what he had written served only to mystify Cass even further.

Item: It has been borne upon me during the past year, during which time has lain heavy on my hands, that I may have done my son John an injustice. I must give further orders that he is to be sought and found as soon as possible. For all I know he might already be dead. Pray God that it may not to be too late for me to right the wrong which I have done him. Herriot must be told to alter that part of the will dealing with his inheritance. . .

The last words were barely legible, as though the writer had been losing control of his pen. He must have begun writing them even as the apoplexy had struck him. Mr Hunt had reported that, on hearing a cry, he had gone at once to the Earl, to find him slumped forward over his books, dying. In the confusion which had doubtless followed he must have thought that the papers in the book merely recorded the notes which m'lord had been used to make when reading.

Cass thought that it was a great pity that Jack's father, usually so precise and sure in his reasons for any judgements which he made, had given no hint in his memorandum as to why he had changed his mind about his son's guilt. It made her even more determined to try to discover the truth.

And had the discovery of that truth served to kill the Earl? And was it not sadly possible that now that he was dead the proof of Jack's innocence might never be found? Meantime, as soon as possible, she must show Jack what his father had written of him. For surely he would be consoled by the fact that his father had died aware that he had misjudged him.

But Jack wasn't consoled. He had been having a lesson from Dickie designed to improve his driving skills, although Cass wondered what there remained for him to learn. He came in full of the race, and the plans which he and Dickie had for winning it, and the arrangements for fresh horses, with their attendant grooms, to be ready for him at the three staging posts on the Brighton Road.

When he had finished his large nuncheon he quizzed the obviously impatient Cass. He told her between mouthfuls that driving and physical exercise always made him hungry, and that after his driving lesson he had been sparring, not with Dickie, but with a large footman who had once been a boxer of sorts.

'I must be in splendid fettle for the race,' he explained. And then, teasingly, his eyes dancing, he asked her, 'Now what news are you big with, m'lady wife? I can tell you are full of something.' But his manner changed when he grasped that for some reason Cass was not responding to his mild provocation.

'Oh, Jack,' she said simply. 'By accident I found some papers of your father's in the library this morning. I think that you will want to read them straight away.' And she handed him his father's memorandum. 'They were in the copy of Caesar's *De Bello Gallico*, which he was studying when he died.'

Jack read them, his face stony as he did so. Cass had no means of knowing what he was thinking. She had thought that he would be pleased, but he handed them back to her remarking, curtly, 'So? Why the excitement, Cass?' For it had been plain to him that the discovery had moved her—even though it had not moved him.

'I thought that you might be pleased to know that your father had changed his mind about your involvement with the Star and that he was thinking of you shortly before he died.'

'He was thinking of his son John who no longer existed. You know, Cass, that time is past and gone, and I would prefer that it remained dead.'

'Your father was so lonely, Jack.' Cass was remembering him in that last year. It had been almost as though he were lost in the magnificent palaces in which he'd lived, all purpose in his life gone with the deaths of his wife and his elder son. As for his younger son, he had been lost to him as the result of his own actions.

If she had thought to move Jack she was much mistaken.

'If he was lonely, he knew whom to thank. In the end he drove everyone away from him, as well as myself. My mother was frightened of him and Philip was quenched by him and his demands. As for myself. . .' He shrugged. 'You cannot offer me a single reason why I should feel pity for him.'

Cass picked up the papers. The forlorn words written on them had touched her, but she was honest enough to see why they had not touched Jack. Perhaps he might feel better if his innocence could be demonstrated to the world, but she was not sure of that either. In any case, Jack's mind was fully occupied with the coming race, and he began to speak of it again; he was expecting Fred Maxwell that afternoon, to assist with the final preparations.

'Young Fred is beginning to grow up,' he remarked, his father dismissed. 'I have the impression that he has never been given any real responsibility before. It is quite wrong of my brother-in-law not to have had him schooled in the management of the vast estates which he will one day inherit. It never ceases to astonish me that great landowners leave their heirs to live a life of loose ease instead of training them for the future. Small wonder that so many inheritances are gambled away!'

This was typical Jack. Beneath the outwardly hard and careless manner of the ex-soldier was, Cass was beginning to discover, a deep-thinking man thoroughly aware of his own responsibilities.

She drew a bow at venture, wondering whether she

might hurt him by what she was about to say, but say it she must. 'It might be an odd thing to suggest, Jack, and I know you suffered greatly as a consequence of it, but might not your father have done you a favour by throwing you into a world where you had to learn that men have duties as well as privileges, or have only duties and no privileges? Indeed,' she added hastily, 'you said something like that to me some time ago.'

Jack nodded and bent down to kiss the top of her newly shorn head, to let her know that she had not angered him. 'Wise child that you are, I have sometimes thought that myself. But, Cass, you were right about one thing. I learned my lesson in the most damnable fashion, and I would not like to think that Fred or any other young man I know would have to go through such a hell to learn wisdom—if I have learned wisdom, that is, which I sometimes doubt.'

He rose and walked to the door, turning to say kindly to her, 'Leave it, Cass. I know that that old business of the Star grieves you, but it doesn't grieve me. I'm a pretty imperfect fellow, and the best way I know to continue to defy my father is not to allow his opinion of me to matter to me either way—whether he thought me guilty or innocent.'

But, whatever he said, he could not persuade Cass that the truth need not be known... Perversely she was more determined than ever to continue her search—although how, she could not think. The official papers of the late Earl and his Countess were closed to her, and she knew no way of gaining access to them. Mr Hunt had said, in response to an apparently idle question, that they were locked away in boxes in Jack's study, and only Jack possessed the key which would unlock them. To question Mr Hunt further might not be wise; to begin to interrogate old servants might cause the sort of gossip which she particularly wished to avoid. Perhaps what she ought to do was write out a list of further possibilities to explore—but what they might be was difficult to imagine, since all roads now seemed to be closed to her.

Instead, Cass retired to her own little drawing-room, away from Jack, Stroody and the world, to read a Minerva Press novel where the heroine appeared to be able to do everything during the late wars to win freedom for the country in which she lived except actually lead troops into battle! If only her own problems could be solved so easily.

There were times when she wished that she had never heard of the Star of Rizapore, and this was one of them. On the other hand, she would not wish to exchange Jack for the wilting hero of *The Maid of Freedom* for all the Crown jewels lodged in the Tower of London!

CHAPTER THIRTEEN

'STROODY! Are you listening to me?' It was bad enough that Jack was rejecting her by refusing to allow her to go to Brighton, but now Stroody was beginning to behave in the most peculiar manner.

She would stop speaking to Cass in mid-sentence, to look out of the window at nothing with a rapt expression on her face. Worse, she was given to not hearing Cass at all. Worse still—or was it better?—she had given up wearing her drab toilettes in favour of those which, if not exactly girlish, were much younger-looking than anything which Cass had ever seen her wear during the six years they had been together. She had redressed her hair too, which had softened her face by relieving the austere sternness of her expression.

She had also taken to reading from Cass's growing collection of novels, and, although she laughed at much of the Minerva Press's output, she also told Cass how much she had enjoyed Miss Jane Austen's novel *Persuasion*, that story of autumnal love.

Vagueness, love of dress and the reading of novels were not things which Cass had come to associate with Stroody. Why, if novels were to be believed, one might almost have thought that she was in love! She certainly mooned after Jack, but surely that was not why she had improved her appearance so dramatically.

'So sorry, my dear.' Stroody was apologising for her distraction. 'I'm afraid I didn't catch what you were saying.'

'That it is the outside of enough that Jack will not allow me to go to Brighton. He has said so with the force of a papal interdict! I cannot see why not—you could accompany me, so everything would be proper.'

'Mr Dickson quite agrees with Jack that you should not go. Colonel Spence is an exceedingly unpleasant man, and the less you have to do with him the better.'

'Oh,' exclaimed Cass, 'what a stupid reason that is, because I shall have nothing to do with *him* at all! I shall sit in the rooms Jack is hiring in Brighton. I believe that they overlook Marine Parade, so that I should be able to watch him drive to victory.'

Cass had not the slightest doubt that Jack would win, even though Dev and Dickie were not quite so certain of the outcome. Through bitter experience both of them agreed with the old adage that 'The best laid schemes o' mice and men Gang aft a-gley'.

'Nevertheless,' said Stroody commandingly, with the kind of shrug and intonation which she had employed when Cass had been her charge and was expected to obey her, and which she had not used since Cass's marriage.

It struck Cass as more than a trifle odd that Miss Strood should call Lord Devereux 'Jack', and Dickie Dickson 'Mr Dickson'. But everything connected with Dev and Dickie was odd, and perhaps Miss Strood was making a kind of third in the coalition, or perhaps a fourth, if Cass was to be counted as a member of it—which she sometimes doubted!

She was about to say so when Lady Thaxted and Lady Constantia were announced, and was compelled instead to endure the delights of the company of Jack's sisters, who had come to complain about Fred's involvement with the race to Brighton, which now appeared to be society's only topic of conversation.

After Amelia Thaxted had at length drawn breath, Cass remarked quietly that Jack had said that he thought that Fred's involvement, far from being a bad thing, was having a steadying influence on him.

This brought loud cries of disbelief from both ladies. 'As though Jack, of all people, knows anything about steadying influences,' scoffed Constantia.

'We had thought,' offered Amelia Thaxted magisterially, 'that you might be prepared to ask Jack to relieve Fred of his duties. But one sees that you are thoroughly under his thumb, and are consequently not to be relied on.'

'Is not that where all wives ought to be?' sighed Cass wickedly.

Neither of the sisters had any answer to this piece of wisdom, until Constantia said thoughtfully, 'Mama was never under Papa's thumb, I do know—although the whole world thought that she was. He was so involved in his political life that she behaved more or less as she pleased. Not that she ever did anything wrong, you understand,' she hastened to add.

Amelia Thaxted, usually silent about her parents, chose for once to speak of them. 'Mama was part of the set around the late Duchess of Devonshire. But, of course, Mama always behaved with the utmost discretion. Quite unlike the Duchess, who plunged heavily and whose morals left much to be desired.'

This Cass knew to be true. But what interested her more than Jack's mother's morality—or lack of it— was that, judging by what Constantia had just said, he might have been referring to his mother when he had railed against those gamesters who tricked and exploited gullible women. Was it possible that she had, like the Duchess, gambled and gambled heavily—and lost?

'Did you know,' she asked Stroody, after the sisters had left, 'that Jack's mother was part of the Devonshire set?'

'You must remember that I was not employed at Devereux House until years after the Countess's death,' Stroody replied, a trifle cautiously. 'But Mrs

James, our former housekeeper, once hinted some-thing to that effect. It was not widely known, she said, because Lady Devereux was most discreet—she never took lovers, and no one ever suggested that she gam-bled, let alone that she wagered more than she ought.'

But suppose everyone was wrong? Cass was sud-denly in a fever of speculation. Why had Jack spoken so fervently against women gambling and virtually made her promise that she would never do so? And what had Lord Devereux discovered that had made him change his mind about Jack? And why had he scrawled the oft-repeated name of his dead wife on his memorandum?

She left Stroody, who had gone into another of her odd trances, her canvaswork unattended on her knee and her eyes focused on something in the distance, and wandered off to her room to think. It was time that she compiled her list of possibilities. To do so, she sat down at the portable writing desk she had rescued from the attic, pulled up a sheet of paper, dipped her quill into its little inkstand, and began to write.

Item: I have already explored the attic, examined everything in it, and it contained nothing which would throw light on the mystery of the Star.

The moment she re-read the words, something struck her with the force of a blow.

Of course she had not examined everything which was or had been in the attic! For had not her desk come from the attic? Although she had meant to open and examine its little drawer, she had forgotten to do so. Jack had said that he did not think that the desk had been his mother's, but he might be wrong. It was stupid of her not to have searched it before—but somehow she had come to take it for granted as hers, and had forgotten its history.

But she possessed no key to the tiny lock of the

drawer beneath the desk's top. She would be compelled to force it open. Cass picked up her brass paperknife, inserted its point into the lock and began to turn it gently. She had no wish to mar the perfection of such an elegantly crafted piece of furniture, so her progress was slow. A locksmith would doubtless have had it open in a trice, but she could not ask anyone to help her. The secret, if the drawer did contain a secret, must be hers alone—and then Jack's.

One final twist and she felt the tumblers move: her delicate task was over. Trembling a little, Cass pulled open the drawer—to find that it contained a number of letters and receipts. Thrust to the back of the drawer were several small objects wrapped in paper, and one which was not: an elegant little miniature which portrayed Jack's mother as a young girl. Her name was scratched on the back. Yes, the writing desk had been his mother's.

She slowly read the letters and receipts, and what she found there had her heart pounding and her face turning white as their import slowly sank in. If she had ever had occasion to doubt Jack's innocence, she dounted it no longer.

Next she unwrapped and examined the small objects. These, too, she put on one side, after carefully restoring them to their protective paper, before dropping her head and covering her face with her hands whilst her thoughts turned and twisted inside her brain like a newly trapped animal, frantic in its cage.

What to do? Before Jack's repeatedly stated objections to her desire to clear his name she would have run downstairs and confronted him with what she had found, but the memory of what he had said, coupled with the surprising nature of what she had discovered, made her reluctant to do any such thing. Besides, he was fully occupied with planning for the race which was to take place in two days' time, and she wished to do nothing to disturb his fierce concentration on it.

The papers and little parcels had lain there, forgotten, for more than twelve years, and could surely wait a little longer—until the race was over. Then Jack must be informed of their existence and it would be for him to decide what to do with them. Cass thought that she knew what his decision would be, but she could not pre-empt it.

At last, she took her hands from her face and straightened up in her chair. For the time being she must carry the burden of her knowledge alone. The maturity which she was rapidly gaining and which Jack mocked—tenderly, she had come to recognise—told her that she was doing the right thing. Had he not repeatedly said that she was his 'wise young judge'?

Slowly, she gathered together the papers and the other small treasures which she had found, for she could not leave them in an unlocked drawer, and fetched out her new dressing-case, which was among the many presents which Jack had given her on their marriage.

It had a lock—not a strong one, it was true—but, being personal to her, no one in the household was likely to try to open it without her permission. She unlocked it, placed the papers and little parcels carefully inside, locked it, thought a moment and then left the case in plain sight. To hide it might occasion comment, which she did not want.

And then, big with her new knowledge, Cass went downstairs, being as charmingly bland as she could in order to give nothing away to Jack when she greeted him on his return from yet another lesson from Dickie.

It was true, as Amelia had said, that all society was agog over the race between Jack and Spence. It had been arranged to start at Westminster Bridge, and beside the two principals and their supporters there were bound to be a great many spectators. Enormous sums of money had been wagered, much of it by Spence himself, who could not believe that Jack Devereux, who had been in the ranks for so long, could truly challenge a gentleman who had been driving all his life.

Virtually the only persons not betting on the race were Dev and Dickie. Dickie had already left for Brighton, after seeing that Jack's change of horses, with attendant grooms from the Devereux stables, were in place at the three stops they were making on the London to Brighton Road. Devereux servants had also been despatched to Brighton to staff the house which Jack had rented on Marine Parade.

'I have arranged for you and Stroody to come down to Brighton a few days after the race, when all the excitement will have died down,' he told her at dinner on the afternoon before the race in an attempt to mollify her.

Unknown to Jack, Cass did not need mollifying. She had decided, after finding his mother's letters, that her anger at being left behind was childish. She had half a mind to tell him so, but did not. It might be offering him too much of an advantage over her if she admitted that he had been in the right.

Instead, she inclined her head with a gracious smile and offered him an olive branch. 'Thank you for your consideration, Jack. It is most kind of you.'

Jack looked sharply at her. He was not used to a Cass who agreed with him so easily, and was inclined to wonder what was in the wind. But her smile was so sweetly innocent—he had no idea of what a work of art it was—that he was quite deceived, and decided that she had had a change of heart.

'Young Fred has been a brick,' he went on, 'but I do wish that he had not wagered so much on my winning the race. Anything might happen. The Brighton Road is always crowded, what with over twenty stagecoaches leaving daily, as well as the world and his wife tooling alongside them in every kind of carriage you can imagine. Depend upon it, few of their drivers are reliable whips, and both Spence and I will be in danger of un unintended collision. I would not wager a farthing on the outcome, even though Dickie and I feel that we have the beating of Spence.'

He yawned, his large capable hand before his mouth, his wicked eyes laughing at Cass over it. 'To speak of more pleasant things, the Imp is delighted with his new clothes, especially made for him, and actually spoke to me today! He has been practising on the yard of tin—beg pardon, Cass, the horn—ever since he knew that the race was on, ready to sound it at every stage and every tollgate.'

'I know.' Cass's expression was demure, she was making her confession about her sessions with the Imp on the horn, at last. 'He let me have a go on it one afternoon, when you were at the lawyers. It takes a deal of blowing, I can tell you, but by the end I managed a proper tantivy!'

Jack laughed his pleasure at this unlikely news. One of the things about him which pleased Cass was that he did not expect her to be missish.

'Now, that I am sorry not to have heard. What a girl you are, Cass! Do you have to try everything which comes your way? Harps, horns—why, I am in a constant pother as to what you may be doing next.'

But his voice was kind, and when they retired to bed he gave her a friendly kiss as they parted, saying, 'I'm sorry to have had to disappoint you over going to Brighton to see the end of the race, but pleased that in the end you took it so well.'

The look Cass gave him for that was a glowing one. So glowing that only the knowledge that he was to race in the morning prevented Jack from making further overtures to her of a more passionate kind, which he hoped that Cass might welcome.

Devil take it that he had ever suggested the bargain to her! But she had seemed such a poor little thing when he had first met her, and he had been fearful that the mere notion of having him as her true husband would scare the wits out of her. Besides, if he were truthful, the idea of getting into bed with such a timid mouse had held no attraction for him at all. It would have seemed like an assault on a child.

But, whatever she had been then, Cass was no child now; she had grown and changed in every way from the day that he had married her. It would not be true to say that she was quite transformed—Cass would never be a beauty—but she had something better, and something which, Jack knew, would last longer: a charm in which character and spirit met, to attract not only him, but other men.

He had seen them looking at her and he admitted wryly that the knowledge that other men desired her had him desiring her the more. He told himself sternly that there was nothing of love in what he felt for her, for love was an illusion which, persisted in, might bring pain and sorrow. More, the kiss which he had just given her had burned his lips, but had, apaprently, left her unmoved.

He was not to know that it had burned Cass's cheek, for she had given him no indication that it had affected her. What she felt for him was unknown to him, what he was beginning to feel for her was. . . He refused to admit the truth.

So both of them went lonely to their separate beds, but the balance of power between them was changing, and as it changed so did they, and Jack's biddable girl was beginning to assume an importance in his life which he could never have imagined when he had first

seen her, wide-eyed and pale-faced in the library at
Devereux House.

Cass woke early the next morning. She put her head
through the connecting door to find Jack's bed empty.
He was already up, but not downstairs. She could hear
him singing, and then cursing as he bathed in the little
room which opened off his bedroom. She laughed to
herself a little, for she knew that he always cursed
when he poured cold water over himself. She
invariably had to restrain her own unruly imagination
when she imagined what Jack might look like naked,
and this morning, excited as she already was, was no
exception.

Her erratic musings were halted when she heard
footsteps outside in the corridor. For once Jack was
allowing himself to be shaved and dressed by his valet,
in order to reserve his strength for the race. Cass drew
back into her own room and hastily washed and
dressed herself. She knew that it would be some time
before Jack was ready for the day. She would be in
the dining-room to eat breakfast with him, trying not
to say anything which would disturb or annoy him.
She had promised Dickie that.

The day was so young that even Miss Strood was
not yet up, and Cass made for the stairs in a mixture
of excitement and trepidation. As she reached the top
step she could hear a loud noise and agitated voices
downstairs, and then the sound of running feet as
someone rushed urgently up the winding stairway.

It was Fred Maxwell, his usually carefree face
drawn, his easy composure gone.

'Cass! Is Jack up yet? They seemed to think not
downstairs.'

'He's having a bath and should be with his valet
soon. Why, Fred, what is it? Why all the tohu bohu?'

'I haven't time to gossip, Cass. I must speak to Jack. At once!'

'Only tell me what is wrong before you do. He won't thank you for disturbing him while he's dressing.'

Fred always gave in to Cass, and he did so now with a long-suffering sigh.

'It's the Imp. He slipped out of quarters last night, when he was expressly told not to, and he was nobbled. Sim, the head groom, thinks that whoever did it used a woman to lure him. It was probably done on Spence's orders, or by someone who had bet heavily on him. Whoever it was had him thrown down in the stable yard some time last night. He was found early this morning, unconscious and bleeding, one leg broken, quite unable to be Jack's tiger today.'

'Oh, dear.' Which was really an inadequate way to greeet such dreadful news, Cass thought. 'But surely, Fred, Wattie can take his place. They're much the same size, and he's nearly as skilful as the Imp.'

'The devil take it, he went down badly with the pox—saving your presence, Cass—two days ago, and is fit for nothing, and Sim says that there's no one else anywhere near the same size and weight to act as tiger instead. Jack's virtually lost the race before it even starts: Spence will have a great advantage over him!'

Cass's mind reeled. The Imp nobbled! And Jack's race lost before it was even begun. It could not be. It should not be if she could help it. Inspiration struck, either from on high in heaven or from low in the other place. Cass never knew which. She caught Fred by the sleeve as he tried to pass her on the way to tell Jack the dreadful news.

'Fred! Don't go. There is a way out, but Jack mustn't know.'

Fred stopped in mid-stride and turned an astonished face on her. 'There is? What the devil is it?—saving your presence, Cass.'

'Oh, damn my face and my presence,' shot back Cass through her teeth. 'Do you think that I don't know what language men use on their own? I am not a fine lady, Fred. I spent most of the first twelve years of my life living in the stables at my stepfather's home! Just listen and don't interrupt.

'I am the same size and nearly the same weight as the Imp, so the curricle's balance won't be spoiled. I can use the yard of tin, and have enough common sense to do for Jack on the journey what the Imp would have done. Only Jack mustn't know. He'd never let me do it. Smuggle me down to the stables and I'll persuade Sim that for Jack to have me as his tiger will be better than him having to renege or lose.'

'Good God, Cass. Of course not! What a thing to suggest!' And Fred turned and made for Jack's room again.

Cass tried to pull him back by the arm. 'Can you think of anything better?' she cried fiercely.

There was such passion in her voice that Fred stopped dead in his tracks.

'He'll never forgive me if he finds out that I helped you to do such a thing.'

Cass stamped her foot. 'Oh, damn that, Fred! Are you going to stand by and allow Jack to be a laughing stock who has to go on his knees to apologise to Spence without even having the chance to race him properly? Did Sim think that the balance had been tipped against Jack winning?'

Fred nodded miserably.

'Then let me do it. Please, Fred, please.'

'You might fall out and be injured.'

'I could catch my foot in my skirts and fall downstairs and be injured now, Fred.'

They stared at one another. Time was passing. Fred gave a great sigh, then said in a melancholy voice, 'I must be mad, and Sim will probably stop you anyway, but yes, you've made your point. You can be the Imp.'

'Sim won't stop me doing anything,' announced Cass grandly, 'because I am Countess.' She pulled at him again. 'Quickly, take me to the stables at once, in case Jack decides to forgo his breakfast and go straight to the stables.'

'Oh, he won't do that,' stated Fred confidently. 'He said that a good meal before battle is advisable, and that although most couldn't choke it down, he always could. He only felt sick afterwards.'

As I shall, thought Cass. But I haven't time to worry about what I propose to do now.

Sim moaned and groaned, said he would have to ask m'lord permission for m'lady to dress up as the Imp and take his place, and what would everyone think?

'Less than if Jack loses the race,' Cass fired at him. 'Now, bring me the Imp's livery and I'll change into it at once.'

Sim gave way at last, mournfully agreeing that m'lord was not to know what m'lady proposed to do, and if m'lady and Mr Fred had chosen to run mad it was no affair of his. 'I shall tell him that I was only following orders,' were his last words as he let Cass into the Imp's room, which he shared with two of the grooms at present working in the yard, and showed her where his splendid uniform was kept.

Cass was greatly relieved that Jack had decided to exchange the Imp's top hat for a jockey cap for the race. Crammed down on her brows, it hid her face as the top hat would not have done.

She practised walking with the Imp's slouch, and had mastered it by the time she trotted into the yard where the curricle was already standing, burnished and polished until it was fit for the Tsar of all the Russias to ride in. The horses were being rubbed

down, and every groom knew what m'lady was about
to do without m'lord's knowledge and permission, so
every interested eye was upon her.

Fred's expression was a wonder, as was Sim's. 'Good
God, Cass, you look exactly like the Imp in that.' Sim
nodded in unhappy agreement. 'If I didn't know it was
you, I would have sworn you were the Imp.'

Cass wasn't sure whether this was a compliment or
not. She pulled the jockey cap even further down on
her forehead, and turned her mouth sideways into the
Imp's characteristic lop-sided scowl. He didn't like
anybody. Except possibly ladybirds, who lured him to
his doom.

'I'm not concerned with whether you think that I
look like the Imp, but with whether Jack will recognise
me,' she retorted, and she looked anxiously at Fred
and Sim.

'Not he,' announced Fred, with more confidence
than he felt. 'He'll only see the Imp because that's
who he'll be expecting to see, and in any case he'll be
thinking too hard about the race to take much notice
of you.'

'But what will happen when I have to talk to him?'

'Now look here, Cass,' advised Fred, kindly but
tactlessly, 'you do talk a lot, you know, but the Imp,
he don't say much. Just grunts, nods his head, and
touches his hat. Wouldn't know he'd got a tongue.
You do that, Cass, and you'll be A1 at Lloyds.'

Cass nodded agreement, registering that Fred was
growing up before her very eyes. Jack was right. Fred
still had his helter-skelter mode of speech, but he was
beginning to examine and order his world much as
Jack did. He would never have noticed the Imp's little
ways in the past. Associating with Jack was resulting
in Jack's shrewdness rubbing off on him.

Had Jack changed her as well?

No time to think of such things, for Fred, one eye

on the gate into the yard through which Jack would shortly be coming, was continuing to advise her, in the voice of an elderly uncle.

'You will be a good girl, Cass, and button your mouth, won't you? And if Jack does find out that you're not the Imp, the later in the race the better. He'll be less inclined to stop.'

Yes, Fred was rapidly turning into a Machiavellian schemer! What next?

Cass grunted her assent in the Imp's best surly manner, and pulled at the peak of her cap in lieu of a forelock.

'Splendid, Cass. The Imp to the very life. That's the ticket, ain't it, Sim?' Fred was full of optimistic enthusiasm. But then he added anxiously, 'You won't fall out of your seat if Jack has to turn suddenly if some ass cuts across him, will you?'

Cass nodded again, her face still screwed up like the Imp's.

Fred couldn't help himself. Before Sim and all the grooms—some of whom would have liked to cheer m'lady, who was not only showing herself to be a good plucked 'un, but who was also busy putting one across m'lord—he kissed Cass on the cheek.

'What a girl you are, Cass. Jack don't know how lucky he is to have you,' Fred exclaimed, unwittingly echoing what Jack had said to her earlier. He gave a hearty laugh. 'I'd admire greatly for Stroody to see you. Depend upon it, she would never recognise you in that rig!'

And all that Cass could think of when Jack finally arrived, ready for the race, and his eyes flickered unconsideringly over her, seeing only the Imp in his new livery, was that she was going to be present at the end of the race at Brighton after all—and with Jack!

What larks!

* * *

Cass was soon to discover that she had let herself in for a great deal of hard work as well as a great deal of excitement. She was told to hold the wheelers with Sim considerately holding the lead horses for her whilst Jack climbed into the driving seat. He was feeling a little disgruntled because Cass had not turned up to have breakfast with him or to see him off; it was plain that she had not forgiven him for not allowing her to go to Brighton to see the end of the race.

He had no notion that it was Cass who handed him his whip; and then, while she clung onto the yard of tin, Sim hoisted her into her little seat behind Jack. She pulled her cap even further down over her eyes, and nodded and grunted in the Imp's most disobliging fashion when Jack called, 'Ready?' to her and to Sim, who was still holding the leaders. He immediately set off for Westminster Bridge, well in time to be there for the scheduled start.

Fred had already gone ahead in his curricle and two, having told the startled Miss Strood that he had ordered the Devereux chaise to take her and Cass's maid to Brighton and that she would make sure that her own clothes and Cass's were stowed away in the boot.

Miss Strood had cried out in agitation, 'But where *is* Cass? And does Jack know of this change of plan?'

Fred had roared at her, 'Never mind that. That's taken care of. Just make sure that you are on the way once Jack has left the yard. You're not to go troubling him about this—he needs all his energies for the race, not for worrying about you and Cass. And now I must be off if I am to be at Westminster Bridge before Jack.'

There had been something so masterful about the usually easygoing Fred that Miss Strood did as she was bid, grumbling to herself the while. Was Cass trying to circumvent Jack by travelling in Fred's curricle to

Brighton in defiance of all that she had promised her husband? She sincerely hoped not, but who knew what the dominant creature which Cass had become would do?

Cass herself, remembering to sway and turn with the curricle as Jack drove towards Westminster Bridge, could only be pleased that Dickie had let her take the Imp's place once when Jack had been absent one day. She had begged Dickie to allow her to see what life was like in the tiger's seat.

He had driven her carefully out of the yard, down the short avenue and almost to Piccadilly, where he had turned before driving her back. It had not been exactly like being behind a first-class whip racing to Brighton, but at least it was better than never having been there before. Dickie had made her promise not to tell Jack about her ride, but the sight of her eager, pleading face had undone him—like many of the staff at Devereux House, he could deny Cass nothing.

She wondered what Dickie's reaction would be when he found out that she had taken the Imp's place—and what society would say if it ever discoverd what a hoyden she was being. Wearing the Imp's livery and taking his place! Excommunication would almost certainly be her doom! Well, pooh to that, if, by taking the Imp's place, she was giving Jack a chance to win his race.

CHAPTER FOURTEEN

Dev and Dickie had planned the race with some care. The road to Brighton was a turnpike in good condition and there were a large number of posthouses along it. They were almost sure that Spence would only make three stops on the way, and commonsense dictated that they should do the same.

The principal causes of lost time which might lose them the race were if the change-over of horses at any or all of the three stages was slow, if any of the many unskilled drivers or coachmen were to cut across them without warning, thus causing an accident, or if they were held up by other traffic taking the centre of the none-too-wide road and refusing to allow them to pass, rather than allowing them to pass whenever the tiger blew his horn hard, signalling that they wished to do so.

The compensating factor here, they agreed, was that Spence would have the same problems to face. Dickie had made the grooms practise the change-over before they were despatched to the posthouses, but he couldn't duplicate the real problems they might face in an inn yard crowded with ingoing and outgoing stagecoaches, mailcoaches, chaises, barouches, cabriolets and curricles as well as slow gigs and lumbering farm carts, all wanting to change horses rapidly at the same time.

Fortunately, Cass knew the route which Jack was taking, and the names of the inns at which they would change horses, as well as the names and situation of the many tolls on the road. She had sat entranced on one of the mounting blocks in the yard at Devereux

House, watching Dev, Dickie, Sim and the grooms at work, despite all Stroody's moans to Jack.

'Whatever are you thinking of, Jack, to allow your wife to spend her time among grooms in a stable yard? Whatever would your sisters think if they found out?'

'Whatever. . .' was her constant cry.

'Who's to tell them?' he had retorted briskly. 'Better for Cass to pass her time with Dickie and me than to sit in someone's drawing-room exchanging gossip all afternoon.'

'But such rough fellows. . .' she had wailed at him.

Jack had been brisker than ever. 'Oh, come on, Stroody. I'm a rough fellow, as well you know. None rougher. And I don't seem to have done her much harm, do admit.'

'You've changed her, Jack.' Stroody's tone had become a trifle tragic.

'But for the better, Stroody, you *must* admit. No, if Cass wishes to watch Dickie and me get ready for the race, who am I to stop her? I have had to disappoint her by not allowing her go to Brighton for the finish; it would be cruelty itself to spoil her pleasure in the preparations.'

And, fortunately, that had been that. Stroody had not ceased to moan, but had continued to wail at Cass behind Jack's back, until Cass had forbidden her to mention the words 'race', 'grooms' or 'stableyard' to her again.

No time to think of that now—though, indeed, afterwards Cass found it difficult to remember much of the race at all.

She remembered Westminster Bridge and the cheering crowd, and the sight of Colonel Spence standing by his curricle, watch in hand, hoping perhaps that Jack might be late instead of early.

Fred had just arrived with Lord Worcester, who had been deputed to start the race. Cass had privately wondered whether he would be steady enough to do it correctly, but, like Fred, he seemed to have assumed some of the gravitas of his uncle, Lord Granville, who had once had to rescue him from the clutches of the notorious Cyprian, Harriet Wilson, to whom he had unwisely promised marriage.

Cass sometimes thought how unfair it was that conduct which would ruin a woman could actually add to a man's reputation rather than detract from it! But musing on Lord Worcester took second place to musing on what her responsibilities were during the race, and how she could manage to deceive Jack for as long as possible, as Fred had advised. Much of her concentration centred on knowing when to sound the yard of tin and worrying how she would manage to cope during the change-over at the first posthouse, the Crown in Croydon.

Jack, on Dickie's advice, had allowed Spence to draw away from him at the start. 'If he goes too hard too early, you should easily overtake him at the end of the stage, when his cattle are tired and yours aren't. He's a bit of a hothead on the box, so rumour says.'

Sure enough, Spence began by driving at a spanking pace, and soon disappeared from view. Cass, her heart in her mouth, and worried that Dickie's judgement might be wrong, had to sound the yard of tin twice in the first mile. First to pass a mailcoach, which was driving a hard pace of its own, and secondly to warn a postchaise that they wished to overtake.

The mailcoach allowed Jack an easy passage, but the postchaise was not so obliging, and Cass was amused to hear Jack give vent to a string of colourful invective, which only ended when he finally swept by, one wheel almost in the ditch at the side of the road. Cass gave an exhausted and valedictory toot as they drove clear, and then—unseen by Jack—a triumphant grin. One thing, her vocabulary was certainly being enlarged—but she was sure that most of Jack's curses were fit for nowhere but the taproom and would certainly not be acceptable in a lady's drawing-room!

One of the steeper parts of the course was Brixton Hill on the way to Croydon, and Dickie had assured Jack that if he did not press his own horses too hard he would be certain to catch Spence soon after that, for Spence's horses would be blown after climbing the hill as a result of his pushing them too hard too early.

'But don't overtake,' Dickie had warned. 'Follow him home to Croydon. Gammon him by persuading him that you are a slowcoach, fearful of a hard drive. Make him over-confident as early as you can, and then you can take him later in the race.

'The word is that he'll be stopping at the King's Head in Croydon—it's a stage the gentry always use, and consequently there's likely to be a crowd there, slowing the change down. Best that you change at the Crown—its only drawback is that there's a chance that you might be held up by farmers' gigs, but it's a risk worth taking.

'Don't push too hard when you do leave Croydon. If you're ahead, let him pass you at the halfway mark, and then follow him as though you are fearful of passing him. He'll push his horses all the harder, and you'll be tooling along nice and easy in his wake, not sweating yourself or the cattle.'

'How does Dickie know all that?' Cass had wondered to Jack one afternoon.

'Before he became a cavalryman he was a groom, and also had a spell as a coachman for a silly young gentleman who lost all his money. He's driven the Brighton road more than once,' had been Jack's answer.

What Cass did remember more than the drive itself was the odd incident or two, and the change-overs at the three stages. At Croydon neither she nor Jack needed to get down, their grooms rushed at them, led their first four away and harnessed their second at top speed and they were on the road again, narrowly avoiding massacring a flock of geese which a boy was desultorily herding out of a side road as they swept by.

'Goose for supper tonight, Imp,' Jack yelled, turning his head a little, so that he could be heard over the sound of the wheels and above the slight breeze of their passing. 'If we win today, I'll buy you enough bumpers to put you to sleep for a week. Sound your horn, boy, we're coming up to another stagecoach.'

So they were, and this one was not so obliging as the first, but Jack was not troubled by that, for it allowed Spence to catch him up again. After Jack had finally swept by the coach, with Cass hanging on for dear life as they took a stiff corner immediately afterwards, there was the Colonel, coming up behind them at speed.

He passed them once they had negotiated the corner, and waved a derisory whip at Jack as he did so. Jack, following his and Dickie's plans, obliged him by letting him go ahead without trying to race him at all, and then fell in behind him, nursing his horses, and himself, as they made for Horley and The Chequers—the only good posthouse, Dickie had said.

Horley Cass would always remember, because not only was it the halfway point of their fifty-odd-mile journey, but it was also the scene of her downfall.

Spence, arriving first, had been held up there, his men being unable to pass a postchaise waiting in the yard until it left. As a consequence, Jack was obliged to wait, once the chaise had gone, whilst Spence's cattle were changed. Both men remained on the box, and Jack, to pass the time, ordered ale for himself 'and my tiger'.

Cass gave a faint groan on hearing this. She had

never drunk ale in her life, and more than once had seen the Imp down his pint at one go, swiping the back of his hand across his mouth at the end to mop up the foam. She was sure that she would ruin everything by choking over it.

But what gave her away was not that, but Jack's climbing down from the box whilst waiting for his horses to be changed in order to give the supposed Imp his pint pot of ale. An act which had condescending eyebrows raised by various watching gentry at the sight of a dandified whipster waiting on his tiger.

Cass was compelled to lean forward to take the ale, so that for a moment she and Jack were face to face.

There was no help for it. For the first time Jack looked the Imp directly in the eye, and saw—Cass!

Desperate dark eyes met feral yellowy-green ones. Jack immediately gave off the reek of danger like a panther. He swore, colourfully, adding more unwanted words to Cass's vocabulary, and then, like the Imp, backhanding it at the end, he drank down the pot of ale in one go instead of handing it to Cass. His eyes never left hers. They were wicked, and she knew immediately what Dickie had meant when he had once hinted that Jack in a rage was a frightening sight.

'The devil!' he roared. 'What in hell's name are you doing here, Cass? What bloody stupid game are you playing with me? Were you so determined to defy me over coming to Brighton for the end of the race that you stooped to this piece of folly?'

His aspect was so fierce that Cass, usually courageous, almost gibbered with fright. She clutched the yard of tin to her for comfort.

'No game,' she finally managed, her voice shaking. 'No folly, and no time to tell you much, Jack. The horses are almost ready for you to start. The Imp was nobbled last night, his leg broken, and there was no one else to be your tiger—so I volunteered.'

Jack's language grew more colourful still. '"Volunteered"! What the devil was Fred about, and Sim too, to allow you to do such a mad thing? Get down at once. I'm damned if I'll have you risking life, limb and reputation just for me to win a stupid race! The race is over. I give up. Think of the scandal if I let you go on and it came out that you'd been my tiger, dressed as a boy. Lady Caroline Lamb never did anything half so hair-raising!'

'And I'll be damned if I'll let you throw it away when you can win it, even with me as your tiger! Oh, Jack, please, you can't let Spence beat you. Who knows? He probably arranged the nobbling. Fred and Sim are sure that he did. And think of the poor young boy for whom you want revenge. After all, you didn't even know it was me up at the back, did you? You thought I was the Imp. Didn't I blow the yard of tin beautifully for you? Except for losing my breath a bit when that nodcock in the postchaise wouldn't let us pass!'

She gave Jack her best smile, not as a piece of artful persuasion, but because the excitement of the race had gripped her too, and she did not want it to end in failure.

Jack's heartstrings were tugged by the smile. He gave her an unwilling grin, impressed, despite himself, by her gallantry. 'So you did, you monstrous child. What the devil shall I do with you, Cass? Beat you, or. . .?' He had to check himself from saying 'bed you' to the eager face beneath the jockey's cap, which was looking down at him so pleadingly.

'Dammit, Cass, if you promise not to get yourself killed, we'll go on. But if at any time you find it too much for you, tell me, and I'll withdraw.'

'Huzzah,' shouted Cass, and blew a merry blast on the horn to scatter the by-standers crowding the archway, aware that there was some drama going on, but also unaware of what it consisted of. Jack resumed his seat on the box, and the groom holding the leaders for him released them.

They were out of the inn yard and on the open road again, now well behind Spence, but safely en route for Cuckfield, the last stage. Fred had been right. Jack would have stopped her at the beginning, had he known who she was, but well into the race, with determination written all over him, he was ready to beat Spence to Brighton with his unbiddable girl in the tiger's seat behind him. . .

After that, for Cass, the race was a blur. Excitement gripped her even further as they followed the distant Spence, slowly drawing nearer and nearer to him. Jack was careful not to overtire his cattle in a reckless attempt to be up with his rival too soon. He was not driving his best matched four; they were waiting for him at the Talbot in Cuckfield, the next and final stage before Brighton itself, ready to give him the turn of speed which would—he hoped—take him past Spence just before they reached the winning post.

He contented himself with tooling along a powerful set of greys, dependable if not over-speedy, which pulled together in the most matchless fashion. Strictly speaking, in a curricle the horses did not actually pull, for it was so arranged that they pushed against their collars to draw the carriage along. This, like many other matters, Dickie had carefully explained to the entranced Cass.

But she was not thinking of Dickie, or of anything but holding on as they passed through more tollgates, Jack waving his ticket and Cass tooting the horn to warn the keeper to allow them through smartly. They were nearly up with Spence now, Jack's steady driving being a better strategy than Spence's of driving like the wind at the beginning of the stage only to lose speed increasingly as his horses tired.

As before, they arrived at the stage almost together. Jack fetched Cass a glass of lemonade, seeing that she had lost her refreshment at Horley, again creating amused and condescending comment on a man who waited on his servant. Jack ignored them, as he ignored Spence's jeering words to him before he drove out of the yard.

'Get ready to write that letter of apology, Sergeant, and find someone to teach you to drive before you race anyone else down the Brighton Road!'

To Jack's amusement Cass turned, and, raising the yard of tin to her lips, brayed loud and discordant defiance at him, and then they were off themselves, and the horn became a warning signal again as they charged after Spence. Jack drove his cattle a little harder than he had done before, dodging traffic to stay nearer to Spence on this stage, only allowing Spence to draw away when he began to push his horses too hard, too soon, in an effort to shake Jack off.

They sped through Crawley, little between them; the people in the main street were waving their hats at them and cheering, for it was plain by the speed and nearness of the two carriages that their drivers were racing, and shouts of 'Brighton be that way!' followed in their wake.

It was now early afternoon and the weather was glorious, so that Cass's hair and brow were damp with perspiration and she wondered how Jack was faring in his heavier coat, breeches and boots. She began to worry a little that he would not pass Spence after all as they crossed the beautiful Vale of Sussex, glowing in the sun, and Jack still remained obstinately in the rear, although Cass knew enough about horses and driving to be aware that he was far from pushing them to the utmost.

It was plain that Spence thought that he had the race won. Once he half turned and shook his whip at them, and his tiger blew derisory toots on the horn in their direction. Brighton drew nearer and nearer, and still they lagged behind until Jack, turning his head, shouted at Cass in his best Sergeant Devlin's voice, 'Now, Cass! Now! Hold onto your hat!'

His whip, sparingly used so far, was tickling his horses' flanks, and they were speeding at last, rapidly catching Spence, for Jack's horses were still fresh, having been driven well within their limits, whilst Spence had flogged his hard in an effort to put a winning margin between them.

Brighton was before them and they were almost up with Spence, who was vainly whipping at his labouring team, the horses puffing and blowing despite all his desperate urgings. For a moment Cass thought that a postchaise, which Spence had just passed, would delay them, but it remained to one side on hearing her horn, and they were by it and on Spence's tail. Cass was clinging on for dear life, and Jack was shouting to his team, 'On, on, my beauties, one more push and we're there.' And now they were racing level, and Cass could see Spence's tiger glaring at her.

And then—oh joy!—it was Spence himself she was level with, leaning forward and desperately flogging his cattle, as Jack later said, as though they were four Sergeant Devlins he was trying to kill—and then they had beat him and were by him, and leaving him behind.

Brighton was theirs, the race was theirs—they had won it in the nick of time when it was nearly over.

The Imp was avenged, and the boy Jack had told her of, and Jack's unmerited flogging was finally paid for. Jack's whip was above his head, off his splendid horses' backs as they drove down Marine Parade, the sea below them. They had left Spence furiously labouring in their rear, falling further and further behind them, he having led Jack all the way, almost until Brighton itself.

A large crowd lined Marine Parade, cheering as Jack's curricle came into view. Dickie was among them, and half the fellows Fred and Jack knew in London. Only Jack knew that the diminutive tiger on the groom's seat was Cass, who had blown him home after the nobbling of the Imp. She was defiantly sounding her horn as the race ended. Never mind that few of her toots had been strictly orthodox, and that the Imp would have winced at them; they had served Jack's purpose, and that was enough.

Jack drew to a stop where Dickie and Spence's discomfited second were standing. He swivelled round to face Cass, his own face one grin, its harshness relieved by his pleasure and his gratitude. 'Oh, Cass,' he almost choked. 'We did it, and I can never thank you enough.'

Only the presence of the watching crowd of people holding out their hands to shake his prevented him from jumping down and taking her into his arms. For a moment Cass thought that he was about to do so, and wondered what in the world the spectators would make of Jack Devereux passionately embracing his tiger!

She willed herself to sit still until the curricle finally stopped, and then she was down and standing between Jack and Dickie, the jockey cap pulled firmly over her eyes to disguise her as much as possible. She was trembling, as much from excitement as weariness after the four-and-a-half-hour journey. Dickie was exclaiming that Jack's time was very nearly a record.

Spence's arrival went almost unnoticed. He refused to dismount and sat, grim-faced, watching the furore round his victorious rival. He had lost not only a race which he had felt sure that he would win, but his position in society. Like Cass, he watched Dev and

Dickie embracing in what Cass thought of as a manly fashion, but brought a sneer to Spence's lips.

Neither of the two principals took any notice of the other, although the two seconds present at the finish shook hands, and agreed that Jack had won fair and square. Jack was too busy thanking Dickie to take much notice of anything else before the excited spectators separated them, shouting and cheering. Remembering Cass, whom he had temporarily forgotten in his exultant celebrations with Dickie, Jack detached himself from the crowd, which was slowly beginning to disperse, and started to cross the road to where she stood, Dickie following some little way behind him.

Whether it was the sight of the pair of them rejoicing over Jack's hard-won victory which pushed Spence over the edge of sanity, no one was ever to know. He was still seated in his curricle, the reins dangling loosely from his hands, his horses blowing hard and one of his grooms lightly holding the right leader, when he suddenly raised his whip. He caught his wheelers hard across their flanks and drove straight at Jack, who was now in the middle of the road with his back to him. He was howling something incomprehensible as he did so.

Cass let out a shriek of warning which would have been too late even if Jack heard her. She was shouting his name even as Dickie leaped forward, pushed Jack out of Spence's way with one lunging thrust—and took the sideways impact of Spence's leader, having thwarted Spence's last murderous throw at the man who had finally ruined him.

Both Jack and Dickie lay in the road. Jack rose slowly to his feet in time to see the crowd scattering before Spence, who had patently lost control of his horses which were rearing and plunging as they careered down the road. His mad gallop only ended when he was finally thrown over their heads, to lie on the ground as still and unconscious as poor Dickie.

Cass ran forward and fell on her knees beside Jack.

Dickie's eyes slowly opened. He was moving, trying to sit up, and Jack was saying feverishly, 'Lie still, man, lie still! What the devil possessed you to do that?' He looked up to meet Cass's anxious stare, exclaiming with rough authority, 'Cass, my love, you can't stay here. As soon as I know that Dickie is in safe hands, I'll smuggle you into our lodgings.'

'No, let me stay, Jack, please. I might be able to help.'

Jack shook his head. 'No, Cass. You've been an absolute trump already. You've done quite enough for one day. I don't think Dickie's seriously hurt, thank God, and you need to rest.'

No sooner had he spoken than they were surrounded by the curious and the caring. An apothecary had appeared from nowhere and began to minister to Dickie, who was now sitting up and saying weakly that there was nothing wrong with him. Spence's second had arrived, apologising for his principal's behaviour.

Cass thought afterwards that it was good thing that she'd appeared to be only an unconsidered tiger, for no one took any notice of her. Presently she pushed her way through the noisy throng to sit on one of the benches which overlooked the sea and waited patiently for Jack to come to collect her. The euphoria of winning the race had disappeared in the shock of what Spence had tried to do to Jack and had done to Dickie.

Jack came to her after a little while, his face no longer strained and haggard with worry.

'Dickie's not too badly hurt. The sawbones says he's shaken and his left arm is broken. He's taken him to his surgery nearby for treatment and rest, which allows me to see you home. You look all in, and no wonder.'

'I am a little tired,' she admitted at last—excitement and effort were taking their revenge on her. 'Oh, Jack, I'm so happy that Dickie isn't badly hurt. What a brave thing to do, to save you from Spence's wicked attempt to kill you.'

'I know. I don't deserve him. That's twice he's saved my life, Cass.'

They walked to the house which Jack had taken just off Marine Parade, where he managed to smuggle Cass in, without anyone remarking on them, and up to her room. She refused to allow him to help her to undress, telling him to go to Dickie and carry her love and best wishes with him.

'And you may tell him, and no one else—although I suspect the story may get around—that I was your tiger and blew you to victory.'

Jack's reply was to kiss her cheek gently and advise her to try to rest a little before doing her bidding.

And after that Cass shrugged herself out of the Imp's coat, pulled off his constricting stock—why did men wear such stupid things?—and lay down on top of the bed.

Perhaps it might not be a bad thing, after all, to try to rest. And, thinking so, she fell asleep.

CHAPTER FIFTEEN

SHE was in the curricle again, and they were approaching the tollgate on Kennington Common; she tooted the horn, Jack waved a ticket at the keeper and they were through, but instead of careering along the road they were rising into the heavens! Cass let out a little shriek which disturbed Jack. He turned to look at her and they instantly began to fall... Someone was shaking her gently.

Cass opened her eyes; she had been dreaming, and it was Jack who was bending over her and shaking her awake. She was lying on top of a bed in a strange room. Memory flooded back. Cass sat up and swung her legs over the side of the bed.

'Jack! How's poor Dickie?' The words flew out of her. Jack, still in the clothes he had worn for the race, was pulling off his coat and his stock, so that like her he was left in his shirt and breeches. He answered her even as he sat down in a big armchair by the empty fireplace and began to tug off his boots.

'Dickie's as well as can be expected with a broken arm—it's a mercy that that murdering swine didn't kill him. But he'll mend as good as new, if I know Dickie.'

While he was speaking, and quite as though she were actually the Imp, Cass moved over to assist him to pull off his boots. For a moment Jack began to demur, but then he accepted her help, looking down at her bent dark head with an expression which would have surprised Cass had she seen it, it was so tender and loving.

'And Colonel Spence?' she asked, both hands

around his left boot as she eased it off. 'What about him?'

'Dam' bad luck,' said Jack with a callous grin, 'that he didn't kill himself. But he came pretty near, I'm told. It'll be some time before he walks again, if ever.'

'Oh, Jack, it may be wicked of me, but I cannot feel sorry for him after what he tried to do to you.'

'No need to feel sorry, my wise young judge. He brought it on himself. Feel sorry for poor Dickie.'

His boots now off, Jack stood up and stretched himself, his arms high above his head, relief on his face, 'And you, my mad but gallant wife, to whom I owe the race, how are you feeling?'

The joy of winning, which had disappeared when Spence had made his murderous attack on Jack and had hurt poor Dickie, was with Cass again.

Her face alight, she put down his boots and looked fully at him for the first time that day. Mostly she had seen his back, and when she should have been rejoicing with him she had not even been with him.

And now he was in her bedroom, looking tired but triumphant, with Dickie not dangerously hurt and his enemy vanquished. Her Jack, and no one else's. Jack of the strong face and body and forthright nature. Something sweet and powerful, which Cass had never felt before and which she hardly recognised, shot through her.

'Oh, Jack,' she cried, her face alight, 'we did it, we did it! Oh, Jack.' The words flew from her, unbidden. She had not meant to say them, but somehow they said themselves. 'Oh, Jack, I love you so.' And she hurled herself at him, to throw her arms around him and hide her face against his broad chest. 'I nearly died when I thought that Spence was about to kill you. . .'

His arms were about her, his lips were in her hair, and then his big hand was under her chin and he was

tipping her face towards him, so that his filled her
world as hers filled his.

'You mean that, Cass, you truly mean it?'

She nodded her head, and then, suddenly shy, hid
it, to murmur into his chest, 'Yes, but if you don't feel
the same way about me, I shall quite understand.'

This brave declaration moved Jack nearly as much
as his wife's courage during the long day.

The arms around her tightened as his mouth bent
towards hers, but before he claimed it he said hoarsely,
'Oh, God, Cass, I don't deserve you. You saved me
today by taking the Imp's place, and, God forgive me,
I only married you in jest, to anger my relatives—
particularly my sisters.'

His kiss was fierce and passionate, and now his
hands had left her back and were undoing the Imp's
little shirt. Cass drank him in, letting her tongue tangle
with his, savouring the feel and taste of it, and when
he at last lifted his mouth from hers, for his very
breathing's sake, she told him, still shy, 'It doesn't
matter, Jack. I always knew why you married me.'
And then she moaned as Jack's hand at last slipped
inside her opened shirt to stroke her breast, creating
another new sensation which, oddly, was both sweet
and sharp at the same time.

'Ah, but I didn't know why I married you, Cass, I
only thought I did. But I do now. Let me prove it to
you.' And slipping the shirt from her shoulders he let
his mouth move on her breast, sucking and pulling at
it as though he were her child, and she, slight young
Cass, was his mother. His hands were cradling her
buttocks, which fitted as sweetly into them as her
breasts had done.

Again, the sensation Jack was provoking in her was
a mixture of pain and pleasure, but the curious thing
was that near to him though she was, nearer than she
had ever been, Cass wanted to be nearer still. So much

so that when, with a little groan, Jack lifted her onto the bed, to follow her there, she obligingly slipped off her shirt for him, so that even that should not lie between them.

He hung over her, his face softer than she had ever seen it, stroking her and kissing her all over. He admired most of all the delicate perfection of her small, pink-tipped breasts, and then, when he had slipped off her breeches, his hands stroked the black curls which covered her most secret parts. But even that was not enough for them, for if he was drinking his fill for her she needed to see him, to stroke the strong body which had driven them to Brighton, and which so far she had felt only through his clothing.

Her hands were pulling away his shirt, and when she undid his breeches flap he helped her to remove his breeches completely, so that at last Cass saw him, stark and plain.

And, oh, what a sight he was. For if he was worshipping the delicate perfection of her perfectly proportioned body, then Cass was entranced by the sheer brute masculinity of him, of his muscled shoulders and chest—the chest covered with curling hair of a darker hue than that on his head and rougher, the curls spiralling up to the base of his neck, and then arrowing down to his narrow waist to fan out again and cover, but not completely, the secrets of his sex.

Roused, fully erect, and looking down at Cass, his eyes almost blind now, Jack was consumed by the first true and selfless love of his life. 'Oh, my darling love,' he muttered huskily, his harsh cheek against her soft one, his hands stroking what the curls hid. 'I fear for you. I am so big and you are so small, but, oh, Cass, let me love you, and forgive. . .forgive. . .if I hurt you.'

Cass put her arms around him and pulled his head down to hers. She could feel the ridges on his back, the stigmata of the flogging which Spence had ordered, as well as his rippling muscles. All that registered with her was that he had called her his darling love. She could forgive him anything, even though their first mating might mean pain for her. He had taken her small hand and had placed himself in it, so that she could feel the throbbing energy of him.

'Make me complete, Cass, as I make you,' he whispered urgently, his body already thrusting against her hand, seeking the fulfilment which only she could give him.

In answer she whispered, 'Oh, please, Jack, please, and soon.' For, pain or no, all that her body was crying for was union with him, something which she had come to need in the long weeks of their unconsummated marriage.

'Slowly, my love, slowly,' was Jack's reply to that, for, although he burned to take her with all speed, he must try to make her pleasure equal to his, for without that his own would be spoiled.

And, thinking that, again he marvelled at himself, for although he had never been selfish in his loving, he had rarely before considered his partner as he was now considering Cass. But then he loved Cass, and he had not loved those who had preceded her in the same all-consuming fashion.

So, slowly, slowly, although his body fought against delay, he sought to ready her for the final act, so that when at last they were united she gave only one great gasp of pain, but after that the joy of being one with him subsumed and transcended everything else, pain included.

To reach the heights of loving, Cass was discovering, meant to lose the self. Paradoxically, through the most supreme enjoyment the flesh could experience that same flesh disappeared, the mind disappeared, and the sensations which took over were beyond the understanding of either mind or body. Afterwards, she was sensible enough to know that not everyone scaled such heights, but only those who were united with their other half, their second self, and, in seeking the pleasure of that other, achieved what selfishness alone could never ensure.

The supreme joys of love were sometimes called the little death for that reason, and even Jack, no stranger to the act of love, was surprised by the strength and force of what he and Cass had unleashed between them.

Afterwards, panting, they lay side by side, their breathing slowly returning to normal. Jack had his right arm around Cass, so that she lay against his heart, her head cradled on his shoulder. Her left leg was tucked between his two powerful ones, so that when, to tease him a little, she bent it and ran her foot upwards towards his groin, she could feel his muscles pull and flex at the sensation created by her passing.

He encircled her small ankle with his left hand and said thickly, 'Provoke me once more like that, madam, and you will be beneath me again.'

Cass said sweetly, 'Is that a threat or a promise, sir?'

One thing that had surprised her was the sheer physicality of lovemaking. There was nothing decorous or graceful about it, and she thought that Jack's powerful body had helped to make her pleasure as great as it had been.

There was no doubt that she complemented him in every way. Her slight grace met his Mars-like physique; the delicate flower of her face lay on the pillow beside Jack's harsh and craggy one: Cass could not decide whether he more resembled Vulcan or Mars in the many portrayals of the Greek gods which filled Devereux House. She put up her hand to brush back the reddy-brown locks of his hair which had fallen forward across his forehead.

'What happened to our bargain, Jack,' she whispered

in his ear, 'and your determination not to have an heir as a revenge on your father?'

'What bargain, Cass?' His voice was teasing her and, before she could answer, he kissed her on the lips, a butterfly kiss. 'Oh, that bargain. I must have been mad to suggest it.' Then he said, a trifle anxiously, 'You don't regret what we have just done, I hope? And if we have a child, as well we might, you won't regret it?'

'Regret it—' Cass was so shocked by this suggestion that she sat up '—oh, Jack, no never. The only thing I regret is that we didn't break the bargain before.'

Jack gave a great shout of laughter, and pulled her down beside him again.

'You minx, Cass! You deserve a kiss for that!' And he gave her one. 'And there I was, holding off from making love to you, because I was sure that you were frightened of me. Now I know why Dickie laughed at me and told me to put my head in a bucket when I told him I was fearful of distressing you by forcing myself on you!'

Cass let him pet her—she was beginning to feel drowsy. She wondered whether Stroody had arrived in Brighton yet, and what she would think when she discovered that she and Jack had gone to bed in the middle of the afternoon—for there was no keeping that a secret.

Let them think! They were husband and wife, were they not? And truly so now. A small contented sigh escaped her, and, sighing, she slept. Jack felt her breathing change, and knew the reason for it. Satisfactory lovemaking was so often followed by sleep, or so he had found in the past.

He remembered the Spanish woman, Luisa, who had followed the Army and him during the campaign in the Peninsula, only to die so cruelly before it was over in a massacre by the French of the camp-followers who had been trapped behind the French lines. Their child had died with her. He had married her, or rather had been handfasted with her over a campfire, and doubtless if she had lived he would have brought her back to England with him when the war was over.

But he had married her out of loneliness, for companionship, not for love. That had been given to Caroline Luxcombe, and she had repaid him by throwing him off when he had most needed her support.

But Cass. . .she was a different thing altogether. The girl, who was now a woman, who had twined herself round his heart from the moment he had seen her scared white face in the library on the day of the will-reading. Who would have thought it, that he would have found his true wife in the very last place where he might have looked for one?

And such a wife, who loved him fiercely and would defend him fiercely, whose sheer courage was such that it almost awed him—and whom he had married without intending to bed her, and look where that had got him! He dropped a kiss on her rosy cheek. She mewed a little as he did so, and burrowed against him, and, thinking of her, and the future, which suddenly seemed bright and clear before him, he, too, fell asleep.

It was dark when they awoke—to make love again. A servant had come to the door while they slept, had knocked, heard no answer and had gone away again to report to his comrades in the kitchen that, 'M'lord and m'lady apparently need no one else but each other today,' and to hand a censored version of this to Miss Strood, who had now arrived and dined alone. Fred had gone off into the night to find some boon companions to celebrate Jack's victory in Jack's absence.

After lovemaking came more talk. Cass had picked up the Imp's shirt to wear as a nightgown, she having none of her own. 'You won't dismiss the Imp, will you, Jack?' she asked anxiously, 'He's only a lad, and he can't have known that he was being most cruelly bammed in order to handicap you, if what Fred and Sim thought was true.'

'He deserves dismissal,' returned Jack lazily, but, having achieved happiness himself in such an unlikely fashion, he was in no mood to be harsh with anyone—other than Colonel Spence, that was. 'I shall ring a fine peal over him when we return to London, you may be sure of that!'

'And when do we go back, Jack?' Cass sat up, the shirt round her shoulders, looking, Jack thought, like the most gallant boy he had ever seen—although it had been no boy who had joined so lustily in their lovemaking a moment ago.

'Soon,' was Jack's sleepy answer. 'I have a mind to be off to Coverham as soon as possible, when all the business in London is done with.' He gave a great yawn. 'It's been a long day, Cass. You will let me stay in your bed, won't you, my darling?' It was not the habit of the aristocracy to sleep all night with their wives, but before Luisa had been killed Jack had come to enjoy sharing a bed with her nightly.

'You called me "my darling" again, Jack.' Cass found that, despite having been as close and intimate with Jack as a human being could be, so that she felt that the strength and masculine scent of him would be with her for ever, she was oddly shy in speaking to him about such important matters as whether he loved her or not. 'Did you mean it?'

Jack sat up vigorously, pulling Cass with him. Then he slipped off the bed, his face alight with joy, and fell on one knee before her. 'Of course I meant it. Oh, Cass, all these weeks that we've lived together I've been trying to tell myself that you were nothing but the outward sign of my revenge on all the Devereux, and that my final revenge on my father was the bargain I made with you that we should have a white marriage. How stupid can a man be?

'Of course I love you. I think that I began to love you on our wedding day, and all your little naughtinesses committed to attract my attention only served to make me love you the more. Will that do, my darling? Or must I make a pilgrimage to Jerusalem and carry out some knightly task to convince you?'

'Coming back to bed would be best of all,' volunteered Cass. 'It feels empty without you.'

So he did—to their mutual pleasure.

On their return to London Cass was met in the hall at Devereux House by an enthusiastic Caesar, who carried on, Jack said, as though she had been all the way to St Petersburg and back again at the very least, instead of to Brighton a mere fifty miles away!

They had been fêted at Brighton, and it was just as well, Jack thought, that no one was privy to the fact that Cass had been his tiger, for she would surely have had her head turned. She was undoubtedly one of the season's greatest successes without that piece of scandal adding a lurid lustre to her name.

Dickie, as Jack had foretold, was healing rapidly, and so was Spence's tiger who, although he had been thrown onto his head, had not been seriously hurt. But his master was still confined to his bed, and the rumour that he might never walk properly again turned out to be the truth.

Not that this news worried Cass. She was too happy to trouble much about anything now that she was truly Jack's wife, and only her doubts about the best course for her to follow after her discovery of Jack's mother's papers and trinkets cast a small shadow on her happiness.

She had not believed that Brighton was the proper

place to tell Jack of what she had discovered about the mystery of the disappearance of the Star of Rizapore. It would wait their return to Devereux House. This was particularly so since Jack's winning of the race against Spence seemed to have silenced most of those who had reservations about him because of what he was supposed to have done twelve years ago.

It was odd to be back in London with everything changed between Jack and herself. Other things seemed to have changed too.

Stroody was no longer *distraite*, but there was an odd glow about her which even Fred had noticed. And Fred had changed as well. He was growing steadier than ever, and one sign of it was that he had ceased to moon over Cass and was chasing one of the pretty daughters of the Londonderry family. He was still friendly with Cass, but in a brotherly fashion, jokingly calling her 'aunt', and it was plain that he had at last accepted that Jack could be trusted to make her happy.

Cass was in the small drawing-room, a week after her return, and Jack had left her to go to the stables to enquire after the condition of both the Imp and Dickie. The Imp, at first repentant and remorseful after his accident, had returned to being his usual surly self once he had realised that Jack was prepared to forgive him for disobeying orders, thus allowing himself to be nobbled.

She was engaged in writing an acceptance to an invitation to a ball at Lady Jersey's when Stroody came in. She was not carrying her embroidery, which was rather like saying that the King had left off his crown when engaged in a State occasion.

'Dear Cass,' Stroody began, without any kind of elaborate preamble,'forgive me for interrupting you when I can see that you are busy, but it is essential

that I speak to you immediately about a most important matter which concerns us both.'

Whatever could be causing Stroody to sound so
urgent? Cass registered that Stroody's face was paler
than usual, and that she was twisting her hands nervously together.

'Of course, Stroody dear. I am, at present, engaged
in little of consequence.'

'It cannot have escaped your notice, I am sure, that
recently I have spent a great deal of time in the
company of Mr Dickson, by virtue of your own
increasing involvement with Jack.'

This sentence did not serve to enlighten Cass as to
what was distressing Stroody. Rather, it served only to
bewilder her.

'Yes, I had noticed that, and that since he has
broken his arm you have been keeping company with
him whilst Jack and I are otherwise engaged. I thought
that it was most kind of you, seeing that he must be
lonely now that Jack and he are no longer fellow
soldiers and companions in arms, and must, of necessity, spend much time apart.'

'Exactly, my dear. Most perceptive of you.' Stroody
stopped for a moment and changed colour. She was
flushing now. 'It may not, then, come as a complete
surprise to you that George—Mr Dickson, that is—
has asked me to marry him and that I have accepted
him.'

Not come as a complete surprise! Cass felt as though
all the breath in her body had been knocked out of it!
First the use of the name George, not Dickie—with all
that that implied of familiarity—and then the thought
of Stroody marrying, and being lost to her. She was
struck dumb. So much so that Stroody hurried on, to
save them both embarrassment.

'You see, Cass dear, we are both lonely people, and
both much of an age. George is forty-five and I am

thirty-seven, still young enough to have a child. He does not want to marry a flighty young thing, and you must see, now that you are growing older and Lord Devereux has become your friend as well as your husband, that you do not need me any more.'

'Oh, Stroody!' Cass had recovered herself, and had taken her companion by both hands and pulled her down to sit by her on the sofa. 'If this is what you want. But will you not find it difficult to be here and to be Dickie's wife?' She could not call him George; that was for Stroody.

Stroody shook her head. 'Oh, no, my dear. We shall not stay with the Devereux household. George's father is a saddler in Islington in comfortable circumstances. George's older brother has died, leaving no family, and his father, a widower, wishes him to return to learn the business before he grows too old to teach him. I shall have a cook and a little maidservant, George says, and I may run his money matters for him as well.'

So here was a turn-up, indeed! Cass felt that tears were not far away. But she must not cry; she must not. It would be selfish of her to wish Stroody to stay with her for ever, a useful and willing companion. For here was a chance for Stroody to be no longer a dependant, but to be Mrs Dickson, someone in her own right.

As though she could read Cass's mind, Stroody said hurriedly, 'Oh, Cass, I know that I am a gentlewoman, and that George is not a gentleman, but consider—I face a lonely old age, no gentleman will ever propose marriage to me, and I like him and he likes me, and we can make one another happy. You do understand—say you do!'

Cass kissed her on the cheek. 'Of course I understand, and I hope that you and George will be very happy. But I can no longer call you Stroody, and in all the years that we have been together I have never used your Christian name. Dear Emma, now that we are to be married women together, pray allow me to do so.'

Emma Strood kissed Cass back. 'You are a good girl, Cass, and a credit to my teaching. I am so happy to see that you and Jack have come to an accommodation at last. He may be rough and ready in many ways, like George, but, like George, he is a good man. And if I am to leave you, it is in the knowledge that you do not really need me any more.'

'Oh, but I shan't lose you,' announced Cass gaily, 'for I shall insist on visiting Mrs George Dickson frequently, and taking tea with her and her husband, and with any luck we may discuss babies together, instead of embroidery and French verbs! Think of that!'

And then she said, in a changed voice, 'Does Jack know? For I believe that it may be more of a shock for him than for me.'

Emma consulted her little fob watch, pinned to her lace-bordered fichu. 'I calculate that George is telling Jack about our wish to marry at almost exactly this very moment. We were agreed that you should be told at the same time.'

Cass kissed her again. 'What a scheming pair you are!' And included in that comment was Cass's sudden understanding that Dickie and Stroody—as she now thought of them for the last time—were both well aware that she and Jack had not lived together as husband and wife until after the race to Brighton, and that their coming together had been a joyous one.

And had they decided on marriage because they had both lost their roles in life—as only friends and protectors of much loved charges—and now needed to assume new ones? Emma Strood already looked younger and happier than Cass had ever seen her in all the years which they had spent together. Cass hoped that Dickie would be as kind to her as he had been to Jack and to herself.

CHAPTER SIXTEEN

'So you see, Dev, Emma and I are to be married as soon as it can be arranged. I thought. . .a special licence. . .'

'Of course. Let me help you with that, Dickie. And Dickie, are you sure that you will not stay with me? I can find you a place here—or one at Coverham, should you so wish. . .' And then he added, a little ruefully as he saw the expression on his friend's face, 'No, I can see that you think it will not answer. You wish to be independent, most right and proper. But, oh, I hate to lose you. . . I thought that we should remain Dev and Dickie to the end.'

Dickie shook his head. 'No, Dev, you know better than that. Not only are you Earl now, but you also have Cass. You don't need me and Emma does, as Cass doesn't need Emma—she has you.'

Jack thought of all the long days and nights, and the pains and the pleasures which he had shared with Dickie—and of how much he owed him for turning him from a boy to a man, and a man who knew how to suffer and to endure.

No, he must let Dev go. They must become George Dickson and John Augustus Devereux, to meet occasionally as old friends, to smoke a pipe together and to reminisce about the past before a roaring fire in a comfortable house, remembering times spent over a flickering campfire in the open. . .

'You have your duty as Lord Devereux—to your lands, to your household and to your tenants,' said Dickie quietly, 'and I have my duty to the father I left behind when I first became a groom and then joined the Army, not wanting to work for him, but to be my own man. My own man! In the Army! Now I must do for him what I would not do all those years ago, as you must take up your burden—only we have two good women to help us, for Emma trained Cass well, as you must admit.'

And so Jack said later to Cass, after they had dined and were alone together. Emma and George had been excused all duties, and Lord and Lady Devereux were both trying to come to terms with the loss of their friends.

'We have to grow up, I suppose, Cass,' Jack said, drinking his burgundy. 'Although I am rather elderly to learn new tricks. I shall miss Dickie.'

'Stroody—I mean Emma—calls him George,' remarked Cass. 'I find it as hard to think of him as George as it is to think of Stroody as Emma.'

'I find it almost impossible,' sighed Jack. 'He called me John Augustus—I preferred being Dev. He had so few responsibilities—and all of them clear-cut, whereas none of John Augustus's are.'

They wandered out of the dining-room and into the drawing-room which overlooked the garden, Jack leaving the half-empty bottle of burgundy and his glass on the table. Once he might have drunk heavily after such a blow as losing Dickie, but now he had Cass, and drinking himself stupid would not help her. Dickie had hinted that he trusted Jack to look after her, and he must not fail him.

He could tell that something was troubling Cass. She had carried her little reticule into dinner with her, swinging from a clasp at her high waist. She was looking particularly charming in apricot organza and was wearing a small pearl necklace and a circlet of seed pearls threaded through her dark curls. It came to him that these days what she wore was in some sense immaterial; what mattered to him was essential

Cass, and the Cass whom he loved most of all wore no clothes at all.

'What is it, Cass?' he finally asked her after they had discussed Lady Jersey's coming ball and the latest gossip about who was in and who was out in the small world of the cousinry in which they lived. 'What is troubling you?'

'Oh, you read me so well,' sighed Cass. 'Did you read me that first day, in the library?'

'Not correctly at first, I do admit. I thought you meek and mild—a biddable girl whom I could marry and forget in a marriage of pure expedience. . .'

Jack was being honest with her, so she would be honest with him. She said swiftly, 'Do not reproach yourself for that, Jack,' for she had seen the shadow on his face, and wished to remove it. She put out a hand to touch his. 'For I married you for the same reason. Expediency governed my decision as well. I only married you because you offered me and Stroody a home and a future. I could not then guess how much you would come to mean to me. . .'

His answer was a loving kiss. 'And, that being so, Cass, you will tell me what troubles you, will you not?'

Cass nodded. She took from her reticule the small pile of letters and papers which she had found in her desk. She held them out to him.

'The little writing desk I found in the attic did belong to your mother. I broke open its locked drawer and found these papers inside. I think that anyone reading them would soon work out the truth about the disappearance of the Star of Rizapore. They clear you, Jack, of any complicity in the theft. More, they seem to show that in the strictest sense the Star was not stolen at all. They also explain what your mother was trying to tell your father when she died.'

She had Jack's full attention now. He was holding the papers, making no attempt to look at them—and why should he? He undoubtedly knew the gist of what they contained.

'Why have you given them to me, Cass? And what you are trying to tell me about my mother's death?'

Cass was compelled to reply, even though his whole aspect had changed. He was stern, unsmiling, looking at her as though she were indeed the 'wise young judge' he had so often called her.

'Oh, Jack, you must see that you could use the papers to clear yourself. And, as for your mother, Mr Hunt told me something that is not generally known— indeed, your sisters are not aware of it. Immediately before your mother suffered her fit she was trying to tell your father that you were innocent, and she could prove it. He refused to listen to her. The papers show that she was telling the truth at last.'

Jack bent his head and crumpled the papers in his hand. When he straightened up there were tears in his eyes.

'I'm glad you told me that, Cass. But, if you have read the letters, then you must understand that I cannot use them to clear my name. To do so would mean that I must implicate someone whom I loved dearly, and who, I think, after what you have just told me, loved me.'

'But, Jack—' she began. She must argue this case even though she knew that he would surely reject it. 'Only think, to be able to clear your name. To prove that you were not a thief and a liar...'

He leaned forward and placed his hand over her lips. 'Not at the expense of someone long dead—and you must know to whom I refer. My mother asked for my help, and I freely gave it. I acknowledge that when I did so I could not have guessed the price I was about to pay: the loss of all I loved, what remained to me of my father's love, and the world's esteem as well as my translation to another, harsher world.

'But it doesn't matter any more, Cass. And you must forgive me if I refuse to tell you the details of what these letters only hint at... Let the past stay dead, Cass. It happened; it's over. Let my sister Amelia and others twit me about it as they will. What happened to me in consequence may have been for the best.

'I never knew what friendship truly meant until I joined the Army as a private and met Dickie. I never knew what duty meant until then. I never knew what love meant until I met you, and if I had remained Jack Devereux I would have married Caroline Luxcombe, and think what that would have done to me! And if I am still a selfish brute, I am less of one than I might have been if the Star had never disappeared and I had never been ruined. My one and only wish, and it is a foolish one, I know, is that the Star had never existed.'

Her took his hand from her lips, and she murmured hesitantly, although she knew that it was useless, 'But your honour, Jack?'

'If you had never read the letters, Cass, and I had told you that I did nothing wrong, and that I have nothing to reproach myself with, and had asked you to trust me, would you have honoured me by doing so?'

They were face to face, eye to eye, but it was neither love nor lust which was moving them.

'I have always honoured you, Jack, from the moment I met you. And once I truly knew you I had but one wish—and that was to prove to all the world that you could never have stolen the Star. Of course I would have believed you—as I believe you now.'

He stood up, the papers in his hand. There was a small fire burning in the grate, although the evening was warm.

'And that is enough for me, Cass. In return I honour you, because you refuse to drag from me every last detail of what happened twelve years ago. Your love and trust is all I need. I want no public recognition.' He waved the papers at the fire, his purpose plain. 'You will allow, Cass?'

Cass nodded. She had started on her odyssey to prove Jack's innocence to all the world. Against all the odds, she had discovered the evidence which would exculpate him—but neither he nor she wished to use it.

'Burn them,' she told him, 'so that none of those who come after us may use them after a fashion with which we would not agree.'

Jack nodded, and pitched the papers into the heart of the fire, where they blazed up brilliantly for a moment before falling into ash. The past was dying before them. He put his arm around Cass's shoulders and hugged her to him. 'I little knew the treasure I was acquiring when I asked you to marry me, Lady Devereux. You are a far greater star than that of Rizapore, and no blood and shame of conquest taints you.'

He kissed her cheek tenderly. There was no hint of sexual passion in his caress. They had, for the moment, gone beyond it. Later they would find their love again, and celebrate it, but for the moment they were honouring Jack's sacrifice. Perhaps it was as well that as they stood there, saying farewell at last to the sad past, they were interrupted by the arrival of the Devereux lawyer, Mr Herriot, demanding that Jack attend instantly to the present and the future.

Cass wondered what the solemn man of law would have made of what had just happened, but her demure bow to him, and her renunciation of Jack's company so that he might attend to the business of the Devereux inheritance, betrayed nothing of what had so recently occupied the new Earl and his wife.

* * *

Later, much later, when it had begun to grow dark, and Jack was still closeted with Mr Herriot, whom he had invited to stay the night at Devereux House, Cass walked out of the glass doors of the Chinese drawing-room and into the night.

Emma was on the sofa, seated by her George. They were busy planning their future, and Emma only looked up briefly to say to Cass, 'The evening is chilly, my dear. Should you not take a shawl with you if you wish to stroll in the grounds?'

She made no demur when Cass refused, returning to the delightful task of arranging her move to Islington and her new life there. Devereux House and her one-time duties were taking second place to her future. The world was turning rapidly, and what had been urgent in the past was tending to become meaningless in Emma Strood's new present.

Cass wandered down a gravelled path to the small ornamental stretch of water known as the lake, even though it was little more than a pond. Before it was a wooden summerhouse on whose veranda Dev and Dickie had been wont to smoke and chat in the warm summer evenings.

Never again. That, too, had passed, but new vistas were opening before them, as they were opening before Cass. There remained but one thing for her to do, and if it were to be done, it must, as Shakespeare had once said in a vastly different context, be done quickly.

On her way to the lake she had passed the windows of the room where Jack and Mr Herriot had now reached the end of their business for the day; Jack had just handed his visitor a glass of port, and Mr Herriot was raising it to him. He and Jack had begun to get on famously, after some early mistrust on both sides had been overcome. Another milestone passed.

The water lay before her, calm and still. The rails and

ducks which sailed on it during the day were asleep. Cass stared across it, sat down on the wooden bench before the summerhouse and opened her reticule. She took something from it, and held the something in the palm of her hand. The rising moon caught it and struck sparks from it.

The Star of Rizapore! Lost and found again.

It had been in the last packet which Cass had taken from the desk. She had opened it with little thought of what she was about to find. She had stared at it in disbelief, as she stared at it now. Nothing in the letters and papers in the desk had explained why she had found it there.

And now she held it in her hand, having intended to give it to Jack. But to do so after what he had said to her—that he wanted the past to be dead—would have meant that he would have had to revive it after all. To restore it to its original position as the greatest of the Devereux heirlooms would simply have meant that its reappearance and its disappearance would have had to be accounted for, and the scandal would inevitably have been revived again.

Cass shivered. Its reappearance meant that she could still not be quite sure of what exactly had happened twelve years ago. She had no doubt that Jack's mother, desperate because she could not pay her debts of honour incurred whilst gambling, had taken it and pawned or sold it. The letters and the receipts plainly showed that to be true. And then, when she had become fearful that its loss might be discovered, she had involved Jack after such a fashion that he had been suspected of stealing it, and in consequence had been exiled by his father.

But how had it returned to Devereux House? Had Jack recovered it too late to save its disappearance from becoming known?

Jack knew.

But Jack was not telling, would never tell. He had asked for her trust, so she could not question him. For, of all the people in the world, Cass trusted Jack the most. And was not that right and proper, seeing that she was his wife?

And if Jack wished to protect the memory of his mother, who had died in the act of defending him to his father, about to confess her guilt, who was Cass to try to tell him that he was wrong? She must respect his wishes.

The past was the past, and though its acts might reverberate through time they could not be recalled or changed. And life, real life, was not like a novel, where all loose ends were neatly tidied away at the grand finale. In real life, some puzzles remained puzzles, and there were some problems which would admit of no solution, and true maturity consisted in recognising this.

Cass held the lovely thing in her hand, thinking of all the misery it had seen, both before and after it had been captured in blood in India, to become the stone which had led a lonely woman to her doom. How many other deaths had its bright beauty unwittingly caused, besides that of Clarissa Devereux? The stone itself might not be evil, but it created evil in others, and, as well as Clarissa, Jack, his father and perhaps even Philip had all been damaged by it. And she, Cass, wished that she had not found it.

Jack had asked that she trust him even if he did not tell her everything he knew. Only in the act of love could one soul—and that only briefly—meld and merge with another. Away from it, each individual had to make his or her own decisions and hold to them. As she trusted Jack, who had kept part of the truth from her, so he must trust her to use her judgement and do the right thing. He had called her his 'wise young judge', and for his peace of mind she must be one. He had said, most passionately, that he wished that the Star had never existed.

And so thinking, Cass stood up and tossed the Star of Rizapore high into the air, where it seemed to hang for a moment, a small sun, shooting out its rays before it fell into the waters of the miniature lake. For a moment the ripples created by its fall disturbed the lake's surface until, once again, it was as calm and still as though the Star had never existed. The Star of Rizapore had disappeared for ever.

Its passing lifted a burden from Cass's back which had lain heavily on her from the moment she had found it. She made her way lightly and easily along the path to the house, and there, walking towards her, was Jack, come to find her.

'My dear,' he said, 'Herriot has retired to his room, and I missed your company.'

His simple words were enough to set Cass's feet on the level plains of acceptance, understanding and renunciation, from whence sprang a love more lasting and more true than that expressed only in inflated terms, dealing with flames and hearts afire. The words told of need, and of the desire for companionship, which was the other face of love. She would have passion enough with Jack, she knew, but his words told her that she would have more than that. He was her friend as well as her lover; she was truly blessed.

'I needed air for a moment,' Cass said—which was true, no lie, but it was not all the truth.

'And so did I.' Jack took her arm and began to lead her back towards the house. 'You are cold, my love. You will let me warm you, I trust?'

Cass nodded her agreement.

'Good. I thought that you might like to come to bed with me, Lady Devereux. It grows late.'

Cass turned her face into his broad chest.

'I am always ready to go to bed with you, Lord Devereux.'

Laughter was in his harsh voice again. They were easy with one another.

'I know, Cass, I know. Long may it be so.'

They walked out of the dark of the garden into the light of the house, twin souls who had known both rejection and suffering, and had found a love which was to endure and sustain them through the long years to come.

THE WOLF'S PROMISE

by

Alice Thornton

Dear Reader

When I heard *The Wolf's Promise* was to be included in the Regency Collection I was thrilled, because the location of the story is particularly special to me. The book is set in West Sussex, the country where I was born and grew up, and where my family roots go deep. My father has lived all his life in the same country road—moving only half a mile from his birthplace when he married—and it's a family legend that my mother's forebears were involved in the Sussex smuggling trade. I was a shy little girl, and I was entranced by the idea that I might be distantly related to the daring, romantic adventurers of the past. But when I grew older and did some real research on the 'Gentlemen', I found they weren't always as noble and heroic as I'd pictured them. That left me with a dilemma. I'd always wanted to write a book featuring smugglers—but should I make them the good guys or the bad guys . . .?

I hope you enjoy this chance to discover my solution to that dilemma as much as I enjoyed writing it.

Best wishes.

Alice Thornton

Alice Thornton grew up in Sussex. It is a family legend that her ancestors in the county were involved in smuggling. She was a shy little girl, and she was fascinated by the idea that she might be distantly related to bold and daring adventurers of the past—who were probably not shy! When she grew up she studied history at York University, and discovered that smugglers were often brutal men whose main ambition was to make money. This was disappointing, but she still feels justified in believing in—and writing about—the romantic and noble heroes of earlier ages.

Other titles by the same author:

Ten Guineas on Love
An Unsuitable Match

PROLOGUE

West Sussex 1793

IT WAS cold and dark on the beach. A black night sky arched over the endless expanse of sand and gusts of icy wind buffeted the Earl. He shivered and turned up the collar of his greatcoat. He could hear the crash of the incoming tide away to his right, but he couldn't see much further than the circle of light thrown by the lantern Sir William had snatched from the riding officer.

'Damn it! The scurvy villain *lied* to me!' Sir William exploded.

He was staring at the marks in the ridged, damp sand where the kegs had been hauled up onto the beach in a long daisy-chain of contraband.

'Or perhaps your informant was himself misled?' the Earl of Ellewood suggested, stamping his feet to keep warm.

It was quite clear what had happened. The smugglers' landing had been here, while Sir William's small party had been lying in wait on an empty beach two miles to the west.

'They're a cunning lot,' the riding officer began nervously. It made him anxious to have the local magistrate, two of the magistrate's men, and a visiting earl assisting him in his duty. 'It would be just like them to feed you false. . .'

'Be quiet, damn you!' Sir William growled. 'If you were any good at your job, neither the Earl nor I would be wasting our time on this God-forsaken

beach! Well, their tracks are clear enough. We'll follow them. Lead the way.'

He handed the lantern back to the riding officer and
swung himself into his saddle.

'Yes, sir.' The riding officer shuttered his lantern
until only a thin beam of light was visible. Then he
climbed up onto to his horse and bent low in the
saddle so that he could still see the smugglers' tracks.
His lack of enthusiasm was very evident.

Sir William and his men followed the luckless riding
officer, but Lord Ellewood did not immediately join
them. He was frowning in the darkness.

'I think Bess has picked up a stone,' he called. 'I'll
catch up with you in a minute.'

'As you wish.' Sir William's voice drifted back in
the darkness. 'Damn sorry about this, Henry. I was
hoping to show you some action tonight.'

'The night's still young,' the Earl replied.

He watched for a few seconds as the others rode
away. Then he looked down at the dark, stirred-up
sand and pinched his lower lip thoughtfully. The tide
was coming in quickly; many of the smugglers' marks
had already been washed away, but he was sure he'd
seen the deep footprints of heavily laden men and
horses going down *towards* the water—not away from
it.

There was probably a reasonable explanation for
that, and he knew so little about the smuggler's craft
that he wasn't inclined to make a fool of himself by
voicing his observations.

But it was certainly a fact that Sir William had been
tricked into waiting on a beach two miles to the west,
yet the very obvious tracks leading away from the
landing point also headed in a westerly direction.

Lord Ellewood began to lead his mare east along
the beach, keeping close to the tideline. There was no
moon in the dark sky. It was hard to see what lay

ahead, but the stars provided some light, and now that he was away from the riding officer's lantern the Earl's eyes adjusted to the darkness.

Two hundred yards along the beach he found what he was looking for. A track of damp, churned up sand leading inland from the sea. Horses and men had passed this way not long ago.

He felt a surge of gratified pleasure that he had guessed right, and his heart began to beat faster with excitement. There was no time to go back for Sir William. Without hesitation he followed the tracks up the beach towards the black shadows of the dunes.

The sea rumbled behind him; dried seaweed crackled beneath his salt-caked boots, and ahead of him he could hear the wind whistling through the thin, exposed grasses of the dunes—but he could barely see where he was going and he trod almost blindly towards his goal.

He was nearly among the dunes when the light of a lantern blazed suddenly in his eyes.

His heart thudded in startled alarm. He flung up a protective arm to his face, squinting into the glaring light and black darkness ahead, unable to see how many people confronted him. He had heard nothing to warn him of their presence.

He struggled to see beyond the lantern light, remembering all the stories Sir William had told him of smugglers beating or even killing anyone they believed to be a danger to them. Was he going to be battered to death without even seeing his attackers?

'I'm sorry, my lord,' said an apologetic voice, 'but I'm afraid I can't let you go any further.'

'What the hell do you think you're doing?' the Earl rasped, more angry than frightened. 'Who are you?'

He heard someone chuckle in the darkness behind the lantern.

'No one important.' The voice sounded like that of

a young man—pleasant, educated and confident. 'In case you can't see it, my lord, I should warn you that there is a pistol levelled at your heart. It will be better for both of us if you don't make any sudden moves.'

'You damn murderer! You'll swing for this!' Lord Ellewood grated furiously.

'I haven't murdered anyone yet,' his opponent pointed out mildly. 'I would infinitely prefer it to remain that way—but the matter lies in your hands.'

The Earl's first moment of surprise and fear had passed and he began to relax. As far as he could tell, the other man was alone, and he didn't seem to have any immediate plans for violence.

'What do you intend to do with me?' he asked more temperately.

'Nothing,' said the young man. 'We could discuss the weather—it's remarkably dry for the time of year, don't you think? Or you could tell me the latest scandals from London—and when the conversation begins to pall, you will be free to go back to the Manor.'

'What if Sir William catches up with us first?' the Earl enquired politely.

His eyes were beginning to adjust to the lantern light which was not, in fact, all that bright, and he could discern the dim outline of his waylayer. The young man was bare-headed in the wind. He was also tall, but he seemed to be lightly built and Lord Ellewood felt confident that, if an opportunity arose, he would be able to turn the tables on his opponent.

'He won't,' said the young man confidently.

'What have you done to him?' the Earl demanded angrily, taking a hasty, unconsidered step forward as he spoke, suddenly afraid for his friend.

'Stand still!' Unexpected menace in the assured voice brought the Earl to an abrupt halt. 'Thank you. I believe I've already mentioned I'm not partial to murder.' After his initial sharpness, the young man sounded friendly again, and almost reassuring. 'But I've no doubt Sir William will find tonight's chase more exhilarating than the average foxhunt.'

The Earl drew in a deep breath, allowing the sudden tension to ease from his body.

'You've sent him on a wild-goose chase?' he said at last.

'As you say,' the youth agreed. 'Until your arrival I thought I'd lost the toss, but now I see I was mistaken,' he added politely.

The Earl grunted, unimpressed by the implied compliment.

'I'm sorry to detain you in such an inhospitable place, my lord,' said the young man apologetically. 'If you had gone with Sir William you would have been a great deal warmer! But I won't keep you much longer. If you wish, you can retrace your steps now.'

'That's hardly more enticing than my current situation!' Lord Ellewood retorted.

The young man laughed.

'I don't suppose it is,' he admitted. 'Allow me to make some amends.'

He put the lantern down, balancing it carefully between two tufts of grass half-way up a dune. The Earl's eyes narrowed speculatively, wondering if this would be a good moment to spring at his companion—but the pistol continued to point steadily at his heart. The young man was both watchful and cautious. It seemed increasingly unlikely that he would make a mistake.

He delved in his pocket with his free hand.

'Catch!' he said, and tossed something to the Earl.

Lord Ellewood barely had time to react. He fumbled the catch and nearly dropped the flask.

'Brandy?' he asked dryly, unscrewing it.

'What else? I'm not particularly fond of it myself,

but it might compensate for the bitter wind around your ears,' the young man replied. 'You've had an unrewarding night, my lord.'

'I'm not so sure.' The Earl swallowed a mouthful of fiery spirit. 'At least I can claim to have bandied words with a smuggler. . .'

'Free trader,' the young man corrected him pleasantly. 'Sir William bandies words with us all the time—but not usually in circumstances of much benefit to him.'

A sudden gust of wind blew up a swirl of dry, gritty sand from the dunes. The mare snorted and reared backwards, lunging away into the darkness.

Startled, the young man turned his head—and the Earl seized the brief opportunity. He leapt towards the smuggler, knocking him to the ground without difficulty.

The pistol fired, but the Earl had already thrust it to one side. He was heavier than his opponent, and he'd had the element of surprise in his attack. He had no doubt that the youth had pulled the trigger involuntarily as he fell backwards.

They struggled among the dunes in an untidy confusion of flailing limbs. It was far too dark to see his opponent and Lord Ellewood fought by instinct, trying to subdue the youth without inflicting real damage. But the young man was strong, and agile as an eel. He twisted and broke free with a powerful lunge, disappearing among the shadows of the dunes.

The Earl sprang to his feet, drawing his sword instinctively as he glanced around, alert to any indication he was about to be attacked from the darkness.

The lantern was still resting undisturbed between the tufts of grass, sending its pale beam of light towards the sea. The wind hissed through the dunes, but the Earl could hear no other movement from the shadows surrounding him.

The mare had bolted, frightened by the pistol shot and the noise of the fight.

The Earl backed away, his boots crunching on the shingle as he returned to the firm sand of the seashore. He wasn't a coward, but he had no desire to run on to an unseen blade among the dunes.

Then a dark shape rose silently from the shadows, sword in hand, and sprang towards him.

It was an untidy fight, illuminated only by the distant stars and the inadequate lantern. Twelve years earlier the Earl had served in the America Wars. He had both training and experience on his side, but his opponent was familiar with the ground and very, very fast.

Even so, the young man was soon outmatched. There was a sickening slither of steel, his sword was wrenched from his hand, and he found himself flat on his back in the sand.

'Now I'll see you!' the Earl growled, his blade at his defeated opponent's throat. 'Get up! But be warned— if you make one false move I'll run you through!'

The young man got to his feet displaying neither fear nor panic. He was breathing quickly from his exertions, but otherwise he was as much in control of himself now as he had ever been. The Earl smiled grimly in the darkness, aware of a certain measure of respect for his opponent. Smuggler or not, the youth had fought bravely and bore himself well in defeat.

'I must take a few more lessons before I cross swords with you again, my lord,' he said boldly.

'You'll not have the opportunity.'

The Earl picked up the lantern and shone it straight into the young man's face.

The youth had been expecting it, and he neither flinched away nor threw up a hand to protect himself from the light. The tip of Lord Ellewood's sword was still grazing his throat; but his dark brown eyes stared fearlessly at the Earl from a lean, intelligent, and extremely youthful face.

'How old are you?' the Earl demanded sharply.

'Fourteen,' said the boy.

'My God!'

From his opponent's composure and self-confidence Lord Ellewood had assumed the youth to be a good deal older.

They stared at each other in silence for several tense moments, then the boy grinned impudently.

'Take care, my lord,' he said, glancing at the lantern the Earl was holding. 'It's an offence to show a light so close to the sea. If Sir William catches you, he may be obliged to clap you in irons.'

'You should be flogged at the cart's tail for your insolence!' the Earl growled, half angry, half amused by the boy's disrespectful boldness.

'Or hung in a gibbet until my dry bones fall through the iron cage as a warning to others?' the boy suggested softly.

'No!' Lord Ellewood exclaimed, startled.

He paused, considering the implications of the boy's comment. The lad's connection with the smugglers might be difficult to prove, but there was no doubt that he had waylaid—and attacked—the Earl; for that charge alone he could expect a heavy penalty if he ever stood in the dock. His youth would offer little protection.

'Do you intend to be a smuggler all your life?' Lord Ellewood demanded abruptly. 'Or was this escapade just a moment of brief, high-spirited folly?'

'No.' The boy held the Earl's gaze for a few more seconds without attempting to clarify his ambiguous answer, then he turned away to look towards the sea, unheeding of the sword still held at his throat.

The first grey light of dawn was rising in the east and Lord Ellewood no longer needed the lantern to distinguish the boy's features. The youth was almost as tall as the Earl, and his black hair was wildly tousled by the cold, salty air—but his eyes looked steadily towards the distant, silvery horizon, almost as if he saw his future there.

Lord Ellewood smiled sardonically. Despite the threatening sword, his prisoner had obviously decided that the risk of being precipitously dispatched was minimal—but the Earl wasn't quite ready to confirm that assumption.

'Stand still!' he said harshly, thrusting the sword tip a little closer to the boy's neck. 'Don't give me an excuse to save the hangman work.'

'I am unarmed and at your mercy,' the boy pointed out calmly. 'I'm sure no man whom Sir William calls friend would take advantage of such a situation. What do you intend to do with me?' he added matter-of-factly.

'Damned if I know,' the Earl admitted frankly, although his sword didn't waver. 'You're too good for gallow's meat. Perhaps I ought to have you pressed. A few years of naval discipline might make a man of you!'

'A very courteous offer, but I have other plans,' the boy replied instantly.

'I daresay you have,' said the Earl dryly, 'but you should have thought of that before you held a pistol on me. You have the voice and manners of a gentleman, boy. News of this night's escapade might seriously damage your family's reputation and standing—don't you think?'

There was silence for several long moments. The boy's eyes were still fixed on the horizon and he did not look at the Earl. Lord Ellewood almost began to wonder if the youth had heard what he'd said. Then the boy replied,

'Yes, my lord.'

The Earl grunted and sheathed his sword. The boy turned his head sharply at the sound. For an instant he seemed poised for flight—but he didn't run; and there was a question in his eyes as he met Lord Ellewood's gaze.

'Which is the quickest way back to the Manor?' the Earl asked, without attempting to explain his actions.

The boy stared at him for a few moments, a frown in his dark eyes as he tried to decipher the Earl's intentions. Then he bent to pick up his own sword.

'I'll show you,' he said. 'We'll go along the beach. It's quicker and more comfortable for walking.'

'An important consideration, since I am now on foot,' Lord Ellewood agreed caustically. 'I suppose you don't have a horse hidden among the dunes?'

'I regret not, my lord,' the boy apologised.

'I imagine you must be well known to Sir William,' said the Earl, as they began to walk along the beach.

'We have met,' said the boy cautiously.

'Hm.' Lord Ellewood turned over several possible ways of dealing with his erstwhile prisoner as they strode, almost companionably, along the damp sands.

'Why didn't you run when you had the chance?' he asked abruptly. 'You must know I couldn't catch you in the dunes.'

'You've seen my face,' said the boy simply. 'I'd like to know what you intend to do next. As you just implied, Sir William would certainly recognise my description.'

'I see,' said the Earl dryly. 'I dare say you could be long gone before he came in search of you.'

'But my family couldn't—as you also pointed out— and my father's practice would suffer. Inflict your punishment on me, my lord, whatever it is—but not on them.'

The boy turned as he spoke and looked squarely into the Earl's face. The force of his personality was reflected in his keen, dark eyes. Lord Ellewood was powerfully struck by the coiled spring of potential within the youth.

For a moment it seemed as if they were well matched: the shrewd-eyed, experienced man and the fearless, black-haired boy. They had more in common than the Earl would willingly choose to admit.

'I'll not betray your secret,' he said curtly. 'But I suggest you find more legitimate outlets for your ambition in future. The gibbet is a sorry place for anyone to end their days.'

'Thank you.' The boy spoke without over-emphasis, but the Earl caught the undercurrent of sincerity in the light voice.

'That way, my lord,' he said, turning to point inland. 'Follow the track for half a mile. Then turn right onto the lane. Turn left at the crossroads and Sir William's house is a mile further up on the right.'

'Thank you,' said the Earl.

He hesitated, suddenly reluctant to part from his companion. He was extremely curious about the boy but, in the circumstances, it probably wasn't advisable to try to pursue their acquaintance.

'My name is Benoît Faulkener, my lord,' said the boy, clearly and unhurriedly, surprising the Earl once again.

'Very French,' Lord Ellewood replied casually, not quite sure why the boy was sharing this information with him. 'I'd heard that most of the smugglers have contacts across the Channel.'

'My mother's French,' said Benoît. 'My father is the doctor in Arundel. My friends call me Ben. It seems unlikely that you will ever be my friend, my lord, or that you will ever need my services. But, if you do, I'll not forget what I owe you.'

The Earl stared at him in undisguised astonishment as he realised the implications of the boy's words.

'You're offering to repay me for my silence?' he exclaimed.

'At any time, and in any way you choose, my lord.' Benoît stepped back and bowed with something of a flourish.

The Earl laughed disbelievingly.

'Your effrontery is extraordinary!' he declared, unable to imagine any circumstances in which he might need the boy's help. 'Take care that one day you don't overreach yourself.'

Benoît grinned, the fresh dawn sunlight emphasising the distinctive contours of his dark face and the gleam of his strong white teeth as he returned the Earl's gaze.

'That may happen; but I'd rather try, and fail—than live knowing I'd never had the courage to try at all!' he declared boldly. 'Good day, my lord.'

He turned and strode away across the open fields which fronted the beach, leaving the Earl alone on the cold, windswept sands.

CHAPTER ONE

Early March 1809

THE pale winter's day was nearly over when Lady Angelica Lennard arrived at Holly House. She had been anxiously anticipating this moment for hours, but now she was here she was almost reluctant to climb down from the carriage.

'I'll knock on the door, my lady,' said her coachman.

'Thank you.'

As she waited for the door to open, Angelica glanced quickly around. It was too dark for her to see much, but she was acutely aware of how isolated the house was. It was situated a few miles south-west of Arundel, on the flat, windswept coastal plain of West Sussex. There wasn't another house within half a mile. It was an ideal place for a master smuggler to set up his headquarters.

Angelica suppressed a shiver. She was used to the teeming bustle of London and, even without the possibility that she was walking into a smuggler's lair, she would have found the absence of visible human life disturbing. There was not even a light showing from one of the windows to suggest the house was occupied.

It wasn't raining but there were heavy clouds in the sky, and an icy wind wrapped her skirts around her legs and tugged at her bonnet. She did her best to ignore the discomforts of the weather. She was conscious of her maid's dour presence beside her. Martha had made no secret of her disapproval of this errand. Angelica was equally determined not to reveal her own misgivings.

The front door opened and a maidservant looked cautiously out into the gloom, lit from behind by a pale light in the hallway. Angelica summoned up her courage and stepped briskly forward.

'Good evening,' she said pleasantly. 'Am I correct in believing that this is the residence of Mr Benoît Faulkener?'

'Yes, m'm.' The girl looked at her suspiciously.

'Good! My name is Lady Angelica Lennard. I would like to speak to your master, if you please,' said Angelica firmly.

'The master's not at home. . .'

'Then perhaps you would be so kind as to allow me to wait for him?' Angelica took another step towards the girl. She'd come this far; she was determined not to be turned away when she was so close to her goal.

'Oh, I don't know. . .'

'What is it, Tilly?' An older woman appeared behind the maid, and the girl gladly gave way to her.

'Good evening, ma'am.' Angelica introduced herself again. 'I would be grateful if you would allow me to wait for Mr Faulkener.'

'Is my son expecting you?' The woman spoke with a hint of a French accent. She was in her early fifties, and her dark hair was greying, but she studied Angelica with shrewd brown eyes.

'No, ma'am.' Angelica replied steadily, although her heart was pounding a nervous tattoo within her chest. 'He does not know me. I have come to deliver a letter to him from my father. It is very important.'

Mrs Faulkener looked thoughtfully at her visitor for a few more seconds.

The shadowy bulk of the carriage rose up behind Angelica, but the light from the hall illuminated her face and picked out gold highlights in her blonde hair. She was very pale, and her expression seemed strained, but her candid blue eyes met Mrs Faulkener's gaze with an almost innocent steadfastness. The Frenchwoman nodded slightly.

'It must be important to have brought you all this way,' she said. 'Come in, my lady. Tilly, direct the coachman to the stables.'

'Thank you.' Overwhelmed with relief that she had so far been successful in her mission, Angelica followed her hostess into a sitting room at the back of the house.

'You must be cold, sit by the fire.' Mrs Faulkener spoke in a brisk but not unwelcoming voice. 'Would you like some tea?' She tugged on the bell pull .

'You are very kind,' Angelica said awkwardly. Now that the first moment of confrontation and relief was over, she was feeling increasingly ill at ease.

The sitting room was comfortable but unpretentious. It contained two armchairs on either side of the fireplace, a small, well-polished sideboard, and an occasional table beside one of the armchairs. The chairs were upholstered in rich, russet brown, but they were slightly shabby and old-fashioned. It was a room for living in, not for show, and it offered a welcome contrast to the bleak, dark, lonely fields outside.

All the same, Angelica could not feel entirely comfortable. It was clear from the neat pile of linen, the scissors and pin-cushion that she had interrupted Mrs Faulkener in the middle of doing her mending. It was an unexpectedly mundane scene to discover in a smuggler's house, and Angelica was thrown off balance. It had never occurred to her when she set out to find Benoît Faulkener that anyone else would be involved in their meeting; or that she would be forced to engage in social niceties with a member of his family while awaiting his arrival.

'I'm so sorry to intrude upon you like this,' she said impulsively. 'I really didn't mean to. It's just. . .'

'I met your father once, several years ago when he

was visiting Sir William,' said Mrs Faulkener calmly. 'My late husband was a doctor in Arundel. The Earl is a very fine gentleman. Ah, Tilly—' she turned her head as the maid came into the room '—Lady Angelica will be spending the night with us. Please prepare a room for her. We would like some tea, and no doubt her maid is also hungry.'

'Yes, m'm.' Tilly glanced at Angelica curiously, and then retreated with appropriate discretion.

'Oh, no!' Angelica leapt to her feet in agitation. 'I'm sure I needn't put you to so much trouble. I only wish to speak to Mr Faulkener and then. . .'

'You came down from London, did you not?' Mrs Faulkener raised an enquiring eyebrow. 'And Benoît will not return home for several hours. You can hardly travel back in the middle of the night.'

'But there must be an inn. . .' said Angelica helplessly.

'There are several,' said Mrs Faulkener equably. 'But you will be much more comfortable here.'

For a moment Angelica felt uncharacteristically daunted. She had been mistress of her father's household for several years since the death of her mother, she was used to being in command; but there was something rather disconcerting about the Frenchwonan's self-assurance.

Then Mrs Faulkener smiled, the expression softening the rather severe lines of her face.

'I will be glad to have your company at dinner,' she said. 'I doubt if Benoît will be back in time, and I get so bored when I have to eat alone.'

It was after nine o'clock when Benoît Faulkener finally returned to Holly House.

Contrary to her expectations, Angelica had enjoyed a surprisingly relaxed meal with Mrs Faulkener. The Frenchwoman had been a pleasant, undemanding hostess and, much to Angelica's relief, she had asked no awkward questions. But after dinner, when there was nothing to do but return to the sitting-room and wait for Benoît Faulkener, Angelica had become increasingly nervous.

She had to control a start when at last she heard a door bang and muffled voices in the hall. Mrs Faulkener nodded to her reassuringly and went quickly out of the room.

Angelica stood up instinctively and turned towards the door. Her mouth felt dry and she moistened her lower lip with her tongue before catching it nervously between her teeth.

Despite the cascading blonde curls, which had inspired her name as a baby, and which had never darkened as she grew older, there was nothing ethereal about her appearance. At the moment she was pale with anxiety, but under normal circumstances her cheeks were rosy and her blue eyes merry.

She was very well liked, but she had never been considered a classic beauty. Her personality was too forceful, her mouth was too wide and she laughed too readily. In addition, and most regretfully, her figure was considered a trifle too robust. It was true that she had a trim waist and long, slim legs, but she moved with an energy and determination which offered no concessions to the die-away airs fashionable among some of her contemporaries.

It was impossible to imagine that a zephyr of wind could carry her away like thistledown—or that she would find such an experience to her taste. Angelica preferred to keep her feet firmly on the ground.

She was dressed now in an elegant but suitably understated gown of soft blue silk which seemed unexpectedly vivid against the predominantly brown furnishings of the sitting-room. Martha had insisted on packing an adequate supply of clothes for her mistress's foolhardy mission, and now Angelica was grateful.

The dress had a modest neckline, but it was gathered in beneath her full breasts by a narrow ribbon which hinted at the voluptuous figure hidden by the demure folds of her skirts. She had thrown a long, fringed stole over her shoulders, and her glowing blonde hair was pinned up in a classical chignon of curls. Although she didn't know it, she shone like a candle in the shadows of the little room. All in all, she was as ready as she ever could be to confront a smuggler in his own home, but she felt uncharacteristically unsure of herself—and completely unprepared for the coming encounter.

She gasped as she remembered something, and snatched up her reticule. She dragged out two letters and cast the reticule aside, swinging hastily back to face the door as she heard footsteps approaching the room.

The door opened and the candles flickered in the sudden draught. Long dark shadows swooped up and down the walls as Benoît Faulkener entered the room. Angelica caught her breath, her hands gripping the letters painfully hard as she fixed all her attention on her host, trying desperately to divine what kind of man he was.

He closed the door quietly and returned her gaze with equal curiosity but considerably less intensity. He was tall, slightly over six foot, lean and sinewy, with a deceptive, whipcord strength. His hair was raven black and his skin tanned. He had high cheekbones and a slightly aquiline nose. There were small creases at the corners of his eyes, as if from squinting through bright sunlight and seaspray. His mouth was firm yet sensitive, but it gave away few secrets.

Apart from his white cravat and the frill of his shirt sleeves beneath his cuffs, he was dressed entirely

in black, which emphasised his lean height and
corresponded well with Angelica's somewhat exotic
preconceptions of him. After her father's description
of their dramatic encounter on the seashore, she had
never expected Benoît Faulkener to look like an
average gentleman—though what she had been anticipating she would have been hard pressed to say.

In fact, he looked more like a pirate than a smuggler. Her first, confused thought was that she wouldn't
have been surprised if he'd been wearing a golden
earring and a red kerchief, and carrying a cutlass. It
was as if he had brought the briny expanse of the
ocean into the small room with him. In his invigorating presence, the hitherto cosy chamber seemed to
become claustrophobic and cramped.

Angelica's full lips parted slightly in amazement.
She stared at him as if transfixed, still clutching the
letters against her breast.

A hint of amusement appeared in Benoît's alert,
watchful dark brown eyes. He had a mobile, intelligent
face; his resemblance to his mother was elusive but
unmistakable.

'Good evening, Lady Angelica,' he said politely,
bowing slightly in her direction. 'I'm sorry you've had
such a long wait for me. Had I known you were here,
I would have returned sooner.'

Angelica blinked. After an evening spent with the
still very French Mrs Faulkener, she had somehow
expected Benoît to sound equally exotic. In fact his
voice was pleasantly deep, but unambiguously English.

'I've brought you a letter from my father,' she said
baldly. It wasn't what she'd intended to say, but her
customary self-assurance had deserted her.

'So my mother said. Please, sit down again.' He
gestured courteously towards a chair and then went
over to the sideboard.

Angelica's gaze followed him. She knew she ought

not to stare at him quite so intently but she couldn't help herself. Even if she hadn't already been so curious about him she would have felt compelled to watch him. He moved with a controlled, crisp grace which she found unaccountably rewarding to see. He was certainly the most assured man she had ever met; yet she sensed that his self-confidence wasn't founded on empty arrogance, but upon hard-won experience. Perhaps he really would be able to help her.

'Would you care for some brandy?' he asked courteously. 'You've come a long way today, and I don't imagine you are finding your errand an easy one.'

Angelica had been so preoccupied with her reflections on his potential character that, for a few moments, she barely understood what he'd just said to her. She glanced blankly at the decanter he was holding, and then a natural association of ideas popped unbidden into her mind.

'Is it smuggled?' she exclaimed, before she could stop herself.

He had been pouring the brandy, but at her comment he glanced sideways at her. There was a gleam in his dark eyes, and she saw a slow smile form on his lips. He was clearly amused by her gauche outburst. She blushed hotly, wondering furiously how she could have been so unsophisticated as to speak her thoughts aloud.

'I doubt if much of the spirit drunk in this county has had duty paid on it,' Benoît replied urbanely, completely unruffled by her question. 'Except for that in Sir William Hopwood's house, of course.'

'Thank you.' Angelica took the brandy he offered her, returning his gaze as calmly as she could.

She had already put herself at a disadvantage with him; she had no intention of allowing him to see the extent of her inner confusion.

'Of course, you must know Sir William,' said Benoît

conversationally, as he sat down opposite Angelica
and stretched out his long, black-clad legs across the
hearth. 'He's one of your father's friends. But I don't
believe you yourself have ever visited this part of the
country before, have you?'

'No,' Angelica replied, more harshly than she
realised. His words had conjured up an old, painful
memory. 'We were going to visit Sir William one
spring—but then my mother died,' she added.

She would not normally have said as much to a
stranger, but she was thoroughly unsettled by the
situation. Asking a favour from a man she didn't
know, even one who owed such an enormous debt to
her father, was turning out to be even harder than
she'd anticipated.

'I'm sorry,' said Benoît quietly.

Angelica glanced at him quickly and then looked
away, gazing into the fire as she tried to get a grip on
herself. She knew she was being completely ridiculous.
She had come to perform a simple errand and she was
turning the whole thing into a foolish melodrama.
After a moment she put the brandy glass down on a
hearth stone with a firm click and lifted her head to
look squarely into her host's eyes.

'Thank you, sir,' she said briskly, sounding much
more like her normal self. 'But it happened several
years ago, and I'm sure you are more interested in
what I am doing here now.'

'I imagine you've come to reclaim my debt to your
father,' said Benoît matter-of-factly, crossing one
black-booted ankle over the other and taking a sip of
his brandy. Unlike Angelica, he was completely
relaxed. 'I confess I'm curious as to the exact nature
of your request.'

'You do intend to keep your promise, then?'
Angelica exclaimed, staring at him, her surprise audible
in her voice. She had assumed he'd done no more than

make a brash, boy's declaration all those years ago. She'd been quite certain that she would have to struggle to persuade him to keep his promise—perhaps even obliquely to threaten him.

Benoît looked up and met her eyes. He hadn't moved a muscle, but she was suddenly conscious of the immense force of his personality. Like a sleek black wolf slumbering by the winter fireside—he looked peaceful, but you roused him at your peril.

'I always keep my word, my lady,' he replied coldly. His voice was dangerously soft, and it contained an undercurrent of pure steel. 'But I do not yet know what service the Earl requires of me. Perhaps you would be good enough to give me his letter.'

He moved suddenly, leaning forward and stretching out an imperative hand towards her. Her heart leapt in momentary fright at his unexpected gesture and she instinctively hugged the letters against her breast.

'My lady,' he said impatiently, a hard gleam in his eyes. 'It would be foolish for you to come all this way and then refuse to give me the letter.'

Angelica hesitated, her gaze locked with his. She could see no apology in his eyes for having alarmed her—but neither did she have any intention of apologising for doubting his honour. She felt the same sense of apprehension, yet strange exhilaration, that sometimes gripped her at the sound of an approaching thunderstorm. The storm was unpredictable and uncontrollable, but after the endless silence that preceded it the noise and the lightning flashes could be so exciting.

'I know what's in it,' she said suddenly, still making no move to give it to him. 'Papa dictated it to me yesterday evening. It might be better if I try to explain.' She stood up restlessly, and took a few hasty steps, but there wasn't enough space in the small room to pace as she would have liked.

'Dictated it?' Benoît glanced at her, a slight frown in his eyes.

'Papa has been blind for more than a year,' she said curtly, the abruptness in her voice a measure of how painful she found it to make that admission.

'I'm sorry. He was a fine man.'

'*He still is!*'

Angelica spun around to confront Benoît in a swirl of flashing blue silk and dazzling, golden curls. Spots of colour glowed on her cheeks and her eyes burned like angry sapphires. Benoît's quiet words of sympathy had touched a raw nerve, jolting a far more vehement response from her than she might have wished.

'My father is a brave, noble man—not a common smuggler, a *thief*!' she blazed furiously. 'My God, he spared *your* life. How dare you speak of him as if he's *dead*!'

She broke off abruptly and turned her head away, blinking back treacherous tears as she tried to regain control of her emotions. She could not possibly explain to a stranger the bitter, black despondency which had consumed the Earl from the instant he'd realised he would never see again.

Lord Ellewood had lost far more than his sight when his carriage had overturned—and so had all those who loved him. Sometimes Angelica wondered despairingly if he would ever again be the same man she had loved and admired for so much of her life.

For a few moments after her outburst there was silence in the sitting-room. The clock ticked steadily on, and a log collapsed with a shower of sparks in the fireplace, but neither Angelica nor Benoît paid any attention to their surroundings.

Benoît was watching her with slightly narrowed eyes. He didn't seem to be particularly offended by her explosion of anger, but she had certainly succeeded in commanding his full attention.

He stood up almost lazily and went over to her, looking down at her thoughtfully. She glanced at him briefly, but she couldn't bring herself to meet his eyes. She was too afraid he would see the pain behind her anger, and she was ashamed on her father's behalf, as well as her own.

'I beg your pardon,' he said quietly. 'I had no intention of insulting your father. I have no doubt that he is still a fine and noble man. But he was also a very active man—and the loss of his eyesight must have hurt him grievously.'

'It has,' she whispered.

Benoît's unexpected understanding of her father's plight disturbed her almost as much as his earlier words had upset and angered her. She found she was trembling with a mixture of confused emotions. She didn't object when Benoît took her hand and led her back to her chair. He picked up her brandy glass and gave it to her, then sat down again himself.

'I hate to disappoint you,' he said lightly, once more sounding completely relaxed and at ease, 'but I haven't been actively involved in the smuggling trade for nearly fifteen years. I am now an entirely respectable and, I regret to admit it, unromantic businessman.'

Angelica choked on the brandy and began to cough, her eyes watering. She started to rummage in her reticule, and then found that Benoît was presenting her with a spotless linen handkerchief.

'So I'm afraid you won't hear any ponies trotting beneath your window tonight,' he continued, as she dried her eyes, 'or see any mysterious lights shining from the landing casement. In fact, you will probably find your stay here as uneventful as a night under Sir William's roof.

'Actually,' he added reflectively, 'you may find your stay here rather more restful than it would be with

"Blunderbuss Billy". I believe he has a habit of setting the whole household in an uproar whenever he goes out to chase my erstwhile companions in crime.'

Angelica smiled, in spite of herself.

'I can imagine,' she said, trying to summon up her usual good-humoured composure. 'I'm sorry, sir. I had no right to speak to you so bitterly just now. Papa only told me about his meeting with you yesterday. I really wasn't sure what to expect of you—but I assure you I will keep your secret as faithfully as Papa has always done.'

'Thank you, my lady,' said Benoît gravely. 'Is your father well in every other respect?'

'Yes,' said Angelica, biting her lip. 'It was a carriage accident. The coach overturned and splinters of wood and glass went into his eyes,' she added, almost as if she felt impelled to do so, though Benoît hadn't asked for further details. 'He broke his arm and suffered a raging fever for several days, but now everything is mended except his eyes.'

She tried to sound matter-of-fact, but she couldn't disguise the bleakness in her voice. The Earl's body might have healed, but his spirit was still sorely wounded. Benoît watched her shrewdly, but he didn't comment.

Angelica glanced down, dragging her attention back to the business in hand, and was dimly surprised to realise that she was still holding the two letters. One of them had already been creased and stained; now they both looked the worse for wear. She tried to smooth them out in an instinctive, almost automatic gesture.

'So what is it your father wants me to do for him that he is no longer able to do for himself?' Benoît enquired, a trifle impatiently, as the silence lengthened.

Angelica looked up.

'To rescue my brother from Bitche,' she said simply.

Outside, the wind was growing stronger, and she could hear the patter of raindrops against the window. A storm was blowing up, isolating Holly House even further from the outside world. She had heard no movement from anyone else in the house for some time. It would be easy to imagine that she and Benoît were the only two people awake and breathing on the face of the earth. She certainly had the very real sense that he was the only person who could help her, and that this was the moment of truth.

'I see,' he said at last, his deep voice expressionless. 'You want me to travel through more than two hundred miles of French-occupied territory and then rescue your brother from one of Bonaparte's most notorious prisoner-of-war fortresses.'

'Papa spared you—and your family. Now we're asking for a life in return,' said Angelica with breathless urgency.

She leant towards him, her golden curls dancing, unconsciously holding out her hand to him in a pleading gesture, trying with every fibre of her being to compel him to agree.

She was desperately anxious for her brother to come home. She was sure the Earl's black moods were made worse by his unspoken fears for his son's safety. And Harry had always been so cheerful and lively. Perhaps *he* would be able to find a way of helping Lord Ellewood to come to terms with what he had lost—all Angelica's efforts had failed.

'A dramatic rescue is hardly necessary,' said Benoît dryly. He was still leaning back in his chair, dark and imperturbable, infuriatingly unresponsive to Angelica's beseeching blue eyes. 'All your brother— what's his name. . .?'

'Harry. He's a midshipman.'

'All Harry has to do is sit tight and behave himself,

and he'll be exchanged in due course,' said Benoît. He took a sip of brandy, and watched Angelica over the rim of his glass. 'There's no need for all this melo-drama over a perfectly straightforward situation.'

'But it's not straightforward!' said Angelica passion-ately. 'Maybe you haven't realised, but the French have stopped making automatic exchanges of their prisoners. When the war broke out again in 1803 they even detained civilians—women and children. Many of them are still being kept prisoner at Verdun. Papa says such infamy is in breach of every civilised code of war!'

'I'm sure many people think so,' said Benoît softly, still intently studying Angelica, an enigmatic ex-pression in his eyes. 'But I also understand there is a school at Verdun, with several young midshipmen among its pupils. Why is Harry not one of them?'

'He wouldn't give his parole,' said Angelica flatly. 'He has already tried—and failed—to escape once. That's why they've sent him to Bitche. It a punishment depot, isn't it? You seem to know all about it.'

'Only what I hear,' said Benoît mildly.

His expression revealed nothing of his thoughts, but he was frowning slightly and Angelica at least had the satisfaction of knowing that he was giving the problem his full attention.

'The fortress was built by Vauban, I believe,' he said after a moment's reflection. 'It's situated on the sum-mit of a great outcrop of rock. Not an easy place to escape from.'

'Harry's done it once already,' said Angelica proudly. 'Look!' She passed him the older of the two letters. 'We receivad this only yesterday from one of the *détenus* at Verdun.'

'Thank you.' Benoît put down his brandy glass, unfolded the crumpled paper and began to read.

'This paragraph here!' said Angelica impatiently,

dropping onto her knees beside his chair, so that she could see the letter too.

Harry and his friends were at liberty for nearly three months. After many difficulties they reached the coast in safety, but they could not find a vessel to take them across the Channel. The French are strict in their surveillance of all boats at night; Harry was recaptured near Étaples and marched back to Verdun in shackles. . .

'You see, the main problem was finding a boat to get to England—that is why Papa thought of you!' Angelica exclaimed eagerly, her golden curls bouncing in her excitement. 'According to Sir William, the war hasn't made any difference to the smugglers.'

'But I'm not a smuggler any more,' Benoît reminded her, a gleam of appreciation in his eyes as he looked into her ardent face. 'Hush! Let me finish the letter,' he admonished her, as she opened her mouth to make a hasty retort.

She bit her lip in vexation and sat back on her heels in a rustle of impatient silk. She wasn't used to being spoken to like that, but she didn't want to alienate him if he might be able to help.

He smiled faintly, as if aware of her impatience, and carried on reading.

She watched him anxiously. If it was true he was no longer a smuggler, perhaps he couldn't help her. But he must still have relatives in France, and she retained the deep conviction that if he wanted to do something he could find a way.

The Earl's correspondent continued:

I saw Harry when he arrived here at Verdun, but I was only able to snatch a few words with him. Following his failed escape attempt he is regarded by the French as a *mauvais sujet*, criminal and the worst possible escape risk. He has been sent back to the fortress in Bitche, a punishment depot, but I am sure he will try to escape again as soon as the opportunity arises.

It is ironic, is it not, that if the French had offered him parole his own sense of honour would have held him more surely than any shackles? But the French don't really understand where midshipmen fit into the naval hierarchy. They often don't offer them the same privileges they allow commissioned officers. Of course, it might be different if they realised he was your son, but so far they don't seem to have discovered the connection. I remain your humble servant, James Corbett.

'You see!' Angelica declared, unable to remain silent any longer. 'It is a matter of life and death. Harry will surely try again, and next time he may be killed. I know that some of the prisoners have been killed trying to escape. All he needs is a little help. One small boat in the right place.'

She knelt up, gripping the arm of Benoît's chair in both hands.

'You don't even need to go to France,' she said earnestly, her lucid blue eyes fixed on Benoît's face as she concentrated all her powers of persuasion onto him. 'James Corbett sent his mistress over to England to carry out some business for him and she smuggled the letter out in her clothes—the French seem to be very lax in some respects—and she will be returning soon to Verdun.

'All we need is the name of someone Harry can safely approach to give him passage over the Channel. Fanny can take the information back to James Corbett.'

'And how will Corbett get a message through to Harry?' Benoît asked sceptically, raising one black eyebrow. 'And what happens if the name of the "safe person" falls into the wrong hands? What kind of tragedy would I be responsible for then, if I did as you suggest?'

Angelica bit back an angry retort. She knew Benoît's objections were valid; in her frustration and anxiety she wasn't thinking clearly. But his lack of a positive response to the problem aggravated her almost beyond bearing.

'There *must* be a way!' She struck the arm of his chair in her exasperation. If you won't go to France yourself—'

'Did I say I wouldn't?' Benoît covered her hand with his, and Angelica gasped as she suddenly realised how informally she had been behaving with him.

He was still sitting in the armchair, and she was kneeling on the floor beside him in a position which was neither dignified nor ladylike. In her wildest imagining she had never expected their interview would end up like this.

His hand was tanned, with strong but elegant fingers. She was instantly conscious of the warmth and potential power in his grip, and felt an answering spark at his touch which no other man had aroused within her.

She had been drilled in habits of strict decorum, but she also lived in a fashionable, glittering world in which flattery and flirtation were commonplace. She had received thousands of compliments during her few Seasons, and many eligible and not so eligible gentlemen had kissed her hand—but none of them had produced such an immediate response in her.

She hesitated, unable to look away from his face. His gaze was strangely compelling, though she still couldn't decipher the expression in his guarded brown eyes. She was torn between a desire to snatch her hand away and a fugitive wish to prolong the moment.

Then she remembered it was her duty to Harry—and her father—to do everything she could to persuade Benoît to help.

She smiled a trifle uncertainly at him, her anxiety and hope apparent in her candid blue eyes.

'You mean you will go to France?' she said, almost pleadingly.

'Perhaps.'

'*Perhaps*!' she exclaimed, drawing her hand away, consternation in her expression. 'But. . .'

'Let me have your father's letter,' said Benoît briskly.

'Why? I've told you everything it contains,' she said rebelliously.

'Nevertheless, I'd like to see it,' he replied equably. 'This one belongs to you.' He handed back James Corbett's letter and stood up.

Angelica was taken by surprise by his sudden action. She tried to stand up too, but she'd been sitting on her legs, and she was already stiff from the long hours in the coach. A flurry of pins and needles made her gasp and sink back to the floor.

Benoît reached down and took both of her hands in his, drawing her easily to her feet. She winced slightly as the tingling in her left leg made it extremely uncomfortable to put her full weight on her foot, and he steadied her with a light hand on her waist as she took an involuntary step sideways.

She looked up at him, very conscious of how close together they were standing, and the almost casual intimacy of their actions, which nevertheless did not seem entirely unnatural.

His brown eyes were as watchful as ever, but they didn't lack warmth.

'You're right,' he said, and he was so close his deep voice seemed to reverberate through her. 'I do owe your father a life—and that life would appear to be your brother's. But it will be best if you leave it up to me as to how I rescue him. I will write a reply to your father's letter and you may take it to him tomorrow.'

'But what are you going to *do*?' Angelica demanded. 'And when are you going to start?'

'That's my business,' Benoît retorted firmly. 'Does your father know you're here, by the way? He must have changed a great deal since my brief meeting with him if he allowed you to beard me in my den without a murmur.'

'Of course he knows!' Angelica exclaimed indignantly, stifling the uneasy awareness that she had informed the Earl of her intentions by the cowardly expedient of leaving him a note.

The Earl had wanted his secretary to bring his letter to Benoît, but Angelica had been deeply suspicious of asking a smuggler to rescue Harry. She hated doubting the Earl's judgement, but since his accident his decisions had often been erratic and even unreasonable. Harry's life was too important to entrust to a stranger on the strength of one brief meeting, sixteen years in the past. Angelica had been determined to discover what Benoît Faulkener was like for herself.

Benoît smiled. His dark face hung dizzyingly above Angelica's and she closed her eyes. The candle flames had begun to merge together in a glowing, misty haze. Now that she had finally put her case to Benoît—and he had apparently agreed to help—she was suddenly overwhelmed with weariness.

She was dimly aware of an almost imperceptible touch on her hair, so light that she couldn't be sure it hadn't been a draught from the window disturbing her curls, then Benoît put his hand on her shoulder.

'You're swaying like an aspen tree in a summer gale,' he said, sounding amused. 'You've had a tiring day. I suggest you go to bed. You've done your part. Tomorrow you can safely return to your father.'

Angelica opened her eyes, insulted by the idea that she could be worn out by the carriage ride from London and irritated by Benoît's calmly amused dismissal of her.

'Don't patronise me, sir,' she said coldly. 'I am a little weary, but I am quite equal to my responsibilities. If your inordinately secretive disposition means that you prefer not to discuss you plans with me, so be it—but don't pretend it's because I'm not capable of understanding their complexities!'

Benoît stepped back and inclined his head in acknowledgement of her comment, but he didn't trouble to retaliate.

'After you, my lady,' he said, opening the door for her. 'I am sure we will all see things more clearly after a good night's sleep.'

Angelica gritted her teeth and walked out of the room with as much dignity as she could muster.

CHAPTER TWO

'WE'LL be going back to London today, my lady?'
said Martha grimly as she brushed Angelica's hair.

She wasn't much more than thirty, but she'd culti-
vated an air of old-maidish disapproval from an early
age.

'I expect so,' Angelica replied distractedly.

She had fallen asleep almost the moment she had
climbed into bed the previous night. She'd had no time
to reflect on her meeting with Benoît. She knew so
little about him, and she wanted to be sure she was
doing the right thing in entrusting Harry's safety to
him.

Martha sniffed disparagingly.

'Nasty, damp, miserable, unfriendly place,' she said
sourly. 'I don't know why we came here at all.'

That was, quite literally, true. Angelica hadn't
thought it prudent to explain the whole story to her
maid. She had simply said that Benoît Faulkener was
an old acquaintance of the Earl, and that he might be
able to help Harry.

'I came to deliver Papa's letter,' said Angelica
calmly.

'No good will come of it,' said Martha grimly. 'It's
an ungodly household. Comings and goings at all
hours. Secretive servants... You mark my words, Sir
William was right when he told the Earl Sussex was
nothing but a nest of villainous—'

'What are you talking about?' Angelica interrupted
quickly. 'What do you mean, comings and goings at all
hours?'

'Far be it from me to talk ill of strangers,' said

Martha, looking down her nose disdainfully, although her shrewd eyes watched Angelica closely in the mirror. Her mistress might not have told her everything, but Martha was quite capable of making her own deductions about the situation.

Angelica returned her maid's gaze suspiciously.

'What have you found out?' she demanded imperatively.

'They gave me a little attic room, overlooking the back of the house,' said Martha, her lips pursed with, for once, genuine distaste. 'The wind rattles through the casement something shocking—and the draught under the door... I got up to see if I could fix it and then I heard voices. Someone came to the house late last night, but they didn't come openly. There were no lights, just low voices.

'Then the Master himself went out. I saw him, and I heard the horses. You can be sure I didn't go to sleep after that. I waited for him to return, which he did. Two or three hours later, and on his own. But I'm asking you—what kind of a carry-on is that for a respectable household?'

'There might be a perfectly innocent explanation,' said Angelica slowly, not sure whether what she was hearing was good or bad news from her point of view.

'Oh, yes, and I'm a Chinaman,' said the maid scornfully. 'If it was all so innocent, why did they look at me as if I was mad this morning when I mentioned I'd heard visitors last night? "Oh, no," said the cook. "It must have been the sound of the wind you mistook, Miss Farley. You being more used to city life than the sounds of the countryside. No one came to the house last night."'

'I see,' said Angelica. 'I admit, it does sound suspicious.'

'That's what I've been telling you!' Martha

exclaimed triumphantly, momentarily forgetting to be disapproving.

'But it may not be altogether a bad thing if what you suspect is true. . .'

'*What*?'

'Think! Martha!' Angelica twisted round in her chair to face the maid, seizing both the woman's hands in her eagerness. 'The reason Harry's escape failed was because he couldn't find a boat to bring him across the Channel. Who better than a smuggler. . .?'

Martha stared at her mistress for a moment, then she nodded grimly as if she wasn't entirely surprised.

'I guessed it might be something like that,' she said heavily. 'But how do you know they won't take your gold and then betray Lord Lennard to the French to make an extra profit on the deal?'

'I don't—yet,' Angelica replied. 'But it may be the best chance Harry has. I have to do everything I can . . .for Papa's sake. . .'

Martha pressed her lips together, accepting Angelica's argument, although she didn't like it very much. But she knew better than anyone how hard the past eighteen months had been for her mistress. No one had been able to break through Lord Ellewood's morose mood. He had shut himself up in his Town house and refused to receive old friends.

For months Angelica had done little but read to her father and try to persuade him to take up his life again—but nothing had helped. If Lord Lennard's return could change all that, then Martha as well as her mistress would do anything to hasten it.

'Very well, my lady,' she said. 'Tell me what you want me to do.'

'Just keep listening for the moment, I think,' said Angelica, smiling ruefully. 'You've been more alert than I, so far.'

Martha sniffed disparagingly.

'Only because they put me in a room with half rotten window-frames,' she said caustically.

It was quite late when Angelica finally went downstairs. She was wearing a deep rose-pink travelling dress, with a soft shawl thrown around her shoulders in deference to the winter draughts.

Despite her uncertainty about the situation, she looked much brighter and less anxious than she had done the previous evening. There was a warm glow in her cheeks and a sparkle in her blue eyes. She moved with the vibrant sense of purpose which normally characterised her. Martha's gossip had intrigued rather than alarmed her, and for the first time in months she had something other than her father's problems to think about.

There were two doors at the front of the hall. She knew one led into the dining-room, and she was about to go over to it when she heard voices coming from the other room. The door had been left slightly ajar and she recognised Benoît's voice immediately. The other voice sounded familiar, but it was only when Benoît referred to him by name that she realised he was talking to Sir William Hopwood.

She caught her breath in horrified consternation. Her first thought was that her father had sent him to fetch her back, but then reason reasserted itself.

There would hardly have been time for the Earl to get a message to Sir William. Besides, her father had cut himself off from the rest of the world so thoroughly that he was unlikely to think of calling upon his old friend for such assistance.

Her second thought was that it would be extremely embarrassing if she did meet Sir William. It would be very difficult to provide an unexceptional explanation for her presence to him, and he was bound to be surprised and suspicious. She was about to hurry back upstairs when she suddenly realised that the subject of their conversation was of profound interest to her.

'My men are sure one of the ruffians escaped in this direction,' said Sir William gruffly. 'They're equally sure one of the others was hurt when he was thrown from his horse, but the fools lost track of them in the storm. Did you hear anything last night, Faulkener?'

'I regret not,' said Benoît coolly. 'Apart from the wind, of course.'

'Dammit! I wish I could believe you,' Sir William growled.

'Are you suggesting I'm *lying*, sir?' Benoît demanded, but he sounded more amused than outraged.

'You know damn well I am,' Sir William retorted. 'Not that it'll do me any good. There were times when I thought I'd caught Toby, fair and square—but somehow he always managed to outwit those porridge-brained men of mine. And you're as slippery as a greased pig.'

'What a flattering comparison,' said Benoît appreciatively. 'I'm sorry you don't find your men entirely to your satisfaction. I'm sure I could pick out some sharp-witted fellows to take their places.'

'I dare say you could,' said Sir William grimly. 'But I'll thank you not to interfere in my business.'

'I wouldn't dream of being so impertinent,' Benoît responded smoothly. 'Are you positive you won't take some refreshment?'

'Dammit! Faulkener! Why do you persist in siding with these villains?' Sir William burst out. 'If only a few of us made a stand, we could stamp out this infernal business in no time!'

'Who am I to go against tradition?' said Benoît lightly.

'*Tradition*!' Sir William exploded. 'A tradition of murder, terror, blackmail. . .*treason*!'

'Treason?'

'What do you call trading with the enemy? My God! I've even heard that smugglers row over to France from Dover with belts of guineas round their waists to pay for Bonaparte's armies. Don't you call that treason? When good English gold is being used to equip our enemies?'

'I won't argue with you on that point,' said Benoît coldly. 'But you might ask yourself, who supplies the guineas? Not the poor men who risk their lives in the Strait of Dover. It's merchants in the City—men who may never come within a mile of the coast—who send the gold to Napoleon. Why don't you discuss the subject of treason with them?'

'My God! Faulkener! How can you excuse the villainy of these base scoundrels by laying the blame on others?' Sir William demanded fiercely. 'If I had my way, every merchant or banker who sent gold to Bonaparte would be stripped of his possessions—but that doesn't justify what the local men do. They're lazy, workshy, and they'd rather spend the night dishonestly landing raw spirit than doing a decent day's work.'

'Perhaps if they were paid a decent day's wage for a decent day's work, they might not be so keen to risk their lives and their health on the beaches,' Benoît retorted sharply.

'By heaven, sir! I might have known you'd have a revolutionary spirit in you,' Sir William breathed, horrified. 'It's your French blood. Next you will be telling me that all men are equal and the government should be overturned. You're in league with the Frogs!'

Benoît laughed.

'My good sir,' he said, chuckling, 'when I take it into my head to overthrow His Majesty's government, you will be the first to know. In the meantime, I regret I cannot help you with your current problem.'

Angelica had been standing, transfixed, at the foot of the stairs, hardly able to believe what she was hearing. But now she suddenly realised Sir William was about to leave and she was in grave danger of being discovered. She hurried back upstairs, nearly tripping over her skirt, as Benoît and Sir William emerged into the hall.

She paused, just around the bend in the stairs, and listened to Sir William's departure. Her heart was beating rapidly with excitement and alarm, and she tried to still her breathing to a normal rate. It would never do if Benoît suspected she'd been eavesdropping.

His argument with Sir William had given her pause for thought. Asking the help of a smuggler was one thing—but what if he really was a traitor to England? He had made no greater attempt to deny that charge than he had to deny he was involved in smuggling.

She pressed her hand to her mouth in horror. What if Benoît really was a revolutionary? Some of the things he'd said certainly implied he had radical ideas. Until this moment the fact that he was half-French had seemed important only because it meant he might be in a better position to help Harry. She had met a number of *émigrés* in London, and most of them heartily loathed Napoleon. It had never occurred to her that Benoît might actually support the Corsican monster.

She heard the front door close behind Sir William and took a deep breath. She had a strong desire to run back up to her bedchamber, but she could hardly spend the rest of the day hiding there. The sooner she faced Benoît the better.

She draped her shawl more becomingly around her shoulders, and walked sedately downstairs. He had been about to return to the room he had occupied with Sir William, but he looked up at her approach.

'Good morning, my lady,' he said politely. 'I trust you slept well.' She thought she detected a glint of amusement in his brown eyes, but in the dimly lit hall it was hard to tell.

'Very well, thank you,' she replied calmly, although her heart was beating faster than she would have wished. 'My maid tells me there was quite a storm last night, but I'm afraid I was dead to the world.'

'I'm glad you were comfortable,' said Benoît. 'Come and have some breakfast.' He held open the dining-room door for her.

'Thank you.' Angelica went into the room, feeling a strange frisson of something that wasn't quite nervousness as she passed beside him.

For a man who could only have had a few hours sleep, he looked surprisingly vigorous. She was profoundly disturbed by what she'd just overheard—yet she couldn't suppress an unruly surge of excitement at being once more in his presence. There was a virile energy in his lean body which provoked an immediate response in her own ardent nature.

But she wasn't entirely comfortable with that piece of self-awareness, so she tried to distract herself with more mundane considerations. She noticed that he was once again dressed entirely in black—apart from the white cravat. She wondered vaguely if he took it off when he went out smuggling, or whether he just took good care to cover it up. She supposed it must be very convenient for him to be always dressed for business, whatever the hour of day or night.

There was no one in the dining-room, and Benoît pulled on the bell rope. Angelica hesitated. She was feeling extremely unsettled, and she knew if she sat down at the table she would feel trapped. The curtains were open so, partly out of curiosity, partly from a desire to appear at ease, she went over to the window.

The dining-room looked out to the front of the

house. After the previous night's storm, the sky was a surprisingly bright and clear blue. She saw a holly tree close to the window, and in the distance some short-stemmed daffodils were dancing in a light breeze. They were the first she had seen that year.

'Spring is on its way,' said Benoît behind her, making her jump. She hadn't realised he was so close. 'You should have a relatively pleasant journey back to London.'

Angelica gasped, all coherent thought driven from her mind by his unexpected proximity. She was grateful she had her back to him and he couldn't see her confusion. It would never do to let him think he had her at a disadvantage.

She bit her lip, her eyes fixed on the daffodils, at a loss for an immediate reply. She had discharged her errand and she had no real grounds for refusing to go; but she didn't want to leave. She couldn't abandon Harry's fate in the hands of a man about whom she harboured such terrible suspicions.

'It certainly is a beautiful day,' she compromised, turning to face Benoît just as the maid came in.

It was a mistake. He was too close and she had no avenue of retreat. He looked straight into her eyes for a few seconds, almost overwhelming her with the electric force of his personality. Angelica felt as if she had been stripped naked by the unexpected intimacy of that brief contact. She struggled to appear cool and unflustered, but her cheeks burned with embarrassment as she lifted her chin almost defiantly to meet his gaze.

He smiled, and turned his head to speak to the maid.

Angelica relaxed slightly, and discovered she'd been holding her breath. She controlled a desire to drag in a shaky lungful of air, and began to breathe normally again, berating herself for acting so foolishly. Surely she was far too sophisticated to be overawed by a provincial smuggler? But she couldn't resist the urge to watch Benoît as he spoke to the maid.

His black hair glinted blue in the bright sunlight. She could see the tiny lines around his eyes from all those times when he must have squinted to see in poorly lit conditions; but he was far more tanned than she would have expected of a man who spent most of his time working at night. For the first time it occurred to her to wonder how active a part in the smuggling trade he took. He surely wouldn't land the kegs and carry them up the beach himself?

He glanced at her, and she felt her cooling cheeks begin to flush again. A glint of amusement flickered in the intelligent brown eyes, almost as if he had guessed what she was thinking, then he said,

'Would you prefer tea or coffee with your breakfast, my lady?'

'Oh. . .coffee, please,' she stammered, suddenly remembering Sir William's strictures on the subject of smuggled tea, although she had a dim recollection that now the duty on tea had been so greatly reduced it was no longer an important item on the smugglers' inventory.

'I have written a letter to your father,' said Benoît, holding a chair for her to sit down. 'I will give it to you presently.'

'Thank you,' Angelica said vaguely.

Her errand was becoming far more complicated than she had ever anticipated. Not only did she have to face the possibility that Benoît might be a traitor; she also had to find a way of dealing with her own irrational attraction to him. She couldn't believe he had aroused such a strong response within her—no one else ever had. It was probably just a symptom of her anxiety over her father and Harry.

'You'll be sorry to learn that you've just missed

seeing an old friend,' said Benoît pleasantly, sitting down opposite her.

'I have...I mean, have I?' Angelica stammered, flushing guiltily.

'Sir William Hopwood,' said Benoît helpfully.

'Oh, *Sir William*!' Angelica exclaimed, trying to sound suitably surprised. 'What a pity...I mean—'

'It would certainly have been entertaining watching you trying to explain your presence here to him,' Benoît observed, grinning. 'Your eloquence and his bewilderment—or perhaps I have that the wrong way round. As you no doubt know, the worthy baronet is seldom at a loss for words.'

Angelica bit her lip, wondering if Benoît suspected she had overheard his conversation with Sir William.

'I would have done my best not to embarrass you, sir,' she said stiffly. 'Obviously I would have been unable to give Sir William a true explanation for my visit. I am a person of honour—even if you are not.'

'But I'm not a nobleman's son,' Benoît pointed out, completely unruffled by her comment. 'No tradition of chivalry flows through my veins. I'm just the son of a poor, hardworking country doctor.'

'Which is how you come to live in such a large house and wear such fine clothes,' Angelica flashed, before she could stop herself.

'I earned those,' he replied, an enigmatic gleam in his eyes as he met her hot gaze.

'Yes! By illegal—' She broke off as Tilly came back into the room with a heavily laden tray.

'Thank you, Tilly,' said Benoît.

Angelica waited until the maid had left the room, almost grateful for the interruption. She found Benoît both disturbing and infuriating, but it was hard to imagine he was in league with his country's enemies. On the other hand, what did she really know of him?

'Do you deny that this house was purchased with

the profits of smuggling?' she demanded, when they were alone again.

'I would do so with alacrity, if I didn't think the answer would disappoint you,' he answered immediately, a faint smile playing on his lips. 'I believe I told you before that I'm an unromantic businessman.'

'Are you suggesting I find anything. . .*attractive* about the idea that you are a smuggler?' Angelica exclaimed, colouring angrily at the implication that she might find him attractive in any way at all.

'Well, obviously you do,' he pointed out reasonably. 'From your point of view, if I don't have any connections with the smugglers I'm unlikely to be able to help you. Your principles as a good, law-abiding citizen— the kind Sir William would welcome as a friend—are at war with your sisterly devotion. It's quite understandable if sisterly devotion wins the day.'

Angelica glared at him.

'I don't find this funny, even if you do,' she informed him through gritted teeth.

'Of course I find it amusing,' he retorted, grinning. 'I haven't been so entertained in months. On the one hand I have you, a monumentally respectable citizen under normal circumstances, I am sure, hoping and praying I am a dastardly smuggler—and on the other hand I have Sir William berating me for not taking a more active role in the suppression of the malevolent trade. How could I ever hope to satisfy both your expectations?'

'I don't wish you to be a smuggler,' Angelica denied grimly. 'I simply hoped you might have means of communicating with France. . .What do you mean— "monumentally". . .?'

'A slip of the tongue,' Benoît assured her instantly, but she distrusted the gleam in his eye. 'I meant no disparagement of your character or figure. How old are you, by the way?'

'Really, sir!' she exclaimed, affronted. 'I don't see what business—'

'Not much more than five-and-twenty,' he mused, idly playing with a silver teaspoon. 'Not on the shelf yet.'

'I'm twenty-three,' she snapped.

He grinned and she flushed crossly, suddenly realising how easily she had allowed him to bait her, and with the most obvious ruse in the world. She had intended to learn more about him, but instead it was he who had prodded her into an unwary disclosure.

Before she could think of anything to say to retrieve her position, he stood up.

'I'll leave you to finish your breakfast in peace,' he said magnanimously. 'I wouldn't want any guest at Holly House to suffer from a disturbed digestion. Come into the library later. I'll give you the letter for your father.'

'The library?' said Angelica, raising her eyebrows in delicately disbelieving enquiry, as if wondering what a mere smuggler might know of books or learning.

'The room where you overheard me talking to Sir William,' Benoît explained helpfully. 'Enjoy your breakfast, Lady Angelica.'

Angelica was too hungry to allow her confused emotions to interfere with her breakfast. She had a healthy appetite which even Benoît's provocative manner couldn't disturb; but she was too distracted to pay much attention to what she was eating.

She kept remembering his conversation with Sir William, and the suggestion that perhaps his sympathies lay with the French.

He was in many ways an infuriating man, and one with whom she would never normally have exchanged a single word.

He had the appearance of a gentleman but, as he

had reminded her himself, he was only the son of a provincial doctor. His handsome figure and quick wit might be enough to open the doors of her fashionable world but, unless he also had the wealth to support him, he was unlikely to make a permanent niche for himself there. Perhaps an ambitious, but nameless, man might well feel post-Revolutionary France did have more to offer him.

On the other hand, although she felt as if she'd been at an almost permanent disadvantage ever since she'd met him, he had treated her with a tolerable measure of courtesy—if you could discount that half-amused, half-mocking gleam in his brown eyes whenever he looked at her. It seemed incredible that he might actually be her enemy.

'Good morning, my lady.' Mrs Faulkener came quietly into the dining room, interrupting Angelica's speculations.

'Good morning.'

Angelica hadn't seen the Frenchwoman since her first meeting with Benoît. She wondered how much he'd told his mother about her reason for coming to Sussex—and what she ought to say to the woman. No mother could be happy at the possibility of her son undertaking such a difficult and potentially dangerous task; Angelica couldn't help feeling uncomfortable in Mrs Faulkener's presence.

'I hope you feel more rested this morning,' said Mrs Faulkener pleasantly, nothing in her manner revealing any underlying hostility towards her guest. 'Benoît tells me you will be going home today. Cook is preparing a basket of food for you. It's a long, weary drive back to London.'

'Thank you. You've been very kind!' Angelica exclaimed, touched by the Frenchwoman's thoughtfulness. 'I'm so sorry to have imposed myself upon you like this. I truly never intended. . .'

'All your thoughts were fixed on your goal,' said Mrs Faulkener calmly. 'That's only natural. I hope you have found the outcome of your visit satisfactory.'

Angelica stared at the Frenchwoman, wondering if there was some hidden meaning behind the words, but Mrs Faulkener seemed quite sincere.

'Has Mr Faulkener not explained why I came?' she asked curiously.

Mrs Faulkener smiled, a hint of quiet pride and amusement in her eyes.

'My son has never been one to betray someone else's secrets,' she said sedately. 'Even to me. If you came here seeking help, my lady, I am sure he will be able to provide it. Excuse me, I must see how Cook is getting on.'

Angelica gazed after her, deriving a degree of reassurance from her words. Mrs Faulkener clearly considered her son to be a man of honour, but she had also admitted that Benoît didn't tell her all his secrets—was he likely to tell her if he really was a French spy?

Angelica patted her lips with her napkin and stood up decisively. She wouldn't obtain any answers dawdling over her breakfast.

The door to the library was properly closed this time, but she turned the handle without hesitation. It was a larger room than she had anticipated, and she paused on the threshold, taken aback by its size and bright airiness. There were windows on two sides, and broad, clear beams of morning sunlight streamed in to illuminate the books and furnishings. A cheerful fire burned in the grate—but what caught her eye and completely arrested her attention was a picture over the chimney breast.

'That's not real!' she exclaimed, forgetful of everything else in her surprise.

Benoît had been sitting at a large desk, but he stood up at her entrance.

'I hate to contradict you,' he said, smiling, 'but I'm afraid it is.'

'But those colours. . .' Angelica stared at the picture. She guessed it portrayed a scene from somewhere in the Caribbean; she had seen many engravings of similar scenes. What had transfixed her were the colours. She couldn't imagine that the sky or the sea could ever be such vivid, vibrant hues.

'I was there when the artist painted it,' said Benoît, watching her fascinated, disbelieving expression. 'I can assure you that it's a faithful record of what he saw.'

Angelica went to stand beneath the picture, half raising her hand towards it. She still found it hard to credit that such lucid, brilliant colours could be real.

'Have you never left England, my lady?' Benoît asked quietly, coming to stand beside her.

She shook her head mutely, unable to take her eyes off the painting. After the dark gloom of an English winter, and the bleak, anxious journey she had made the previous day, the vibrant colours seemed to sing within her, satisfying a hunger she hadn't even known she had had.

'The quality of the light is quite different,' said Benoît, 'even in the Mediterranean. And the Caribbean is a whole new world. How long was Harry at sea before he was captured?'

'A year,' said Angelica distantly. 'He was so eager to go. He was in a frigate on the way back from the West Indies when. . .'

'Then when you see him again, you must ask him to verify the truth of my picture,' said Benoît lightly.

Angelica turned slowly, still dazzled by what she had just seen and lifted her eyes to his face. With the splendour of the Caribbean sun behind her, she suddenly realised his tanned skin could owe nothing to a dark English winter. She had been so sure he was a smuggler that she had missed some obvious clues. When she had first laid eyes on him she'd even thought he looked more like a pirate than a smuggler, but then she'd dismissed the idea.

'If you're not a smuggler, what are you?' she blurted out, sounding completely disorientated.

He grinned, and she saw a flash of strong, white teeth against his dark skin. There was a glinting light in his eyes which was almost a challenge.

'I told you, my lady. I'm a respectable businessman.'

'I don't believe you,' she said flatly.

He laughed aloud, an unexpectedly full-bodied sound which only served to strengthen the image of piracy in her mind. She had a confused image of him standing on a quarterdeck, a cutlass in his hand, as his crew boarded a helpless merchantman.

'You're the second person to call me a liar this morning!' he remarked. 'Now Sir William knows I'm so lacking in the honourable qualities of a gentleman that I'm unlikely to call him to book for his words—but what about you, my lady? I can't *call* you out, but I could *turn* you out. Oh, no, you're leaving anyway so that threat lacks force. How would *you* suggest I obtain satisfaction?'

A familiar, slow smile played on his lips, and the challenging gleam in his dark eyes was very evident now. He was standing relaxed, yet poised, and there was no mistaking the provocative way in which his gaze lingered on her eyes, her hair and her rosy lips.

She gazed back at him, her blue eyes wide and questioning, her lips parted slightly in surprise. She had tried to convince herself that she had misinterpreted what had happened earlier; but the fiery spark of intimacy she had sensed between them in the dining room was even stronger now—and this time there was no maid to interrupt them.

Despite her attempt to remain cool and detached, Angelica's heart beat out an uncontrollable rhythm of excitement. Men had flirted with her before, but never like this—if Benoît was flirting. He had not uttered a single elegant compliment. But she could feel the virile power of his personality, even across the few feet of empty space which separated them. It half-frightened her, but it also made her blood sing.

She had spent the whole of her life comparing other men to her father—and none of them had ever measured up to him. She didn't know whether Benoît was a smuggler, though he was certainly involved in some shady business; he might even be a French spy—but dealing with him could never be boring.

She turned slightly away from him, resting her fingers gently on a large globe. She'd finally recovered her self-possession, and it was time he learnt that she couldn't be overawed by a quick tongue and a bold look. She was the Earl of Ellewood's daughter—not a giggling chambermaid.

'I don't know, sir,' she said lightly. 'I believe, in an affair of honour, it is the gentleman who receives the challenge who has the choice of weapons, is it not?'

'Are you suggesting you have already challenged me, my lady?' Benoît raised one quizzical black eyebrow. 'I thought it was the other way around.'

'Is it?' She paused, her hand poised delicately just above the globe, a faint smile on her lips. 'In that case, I will chose no weapons and thus you will have no opportunity to show me your mettle.'

'A very feminine solution to the problem,' he retorted. 'It ensures that you can accuse me of any dark deed you wish, secure in the knowledge that if I dispute your interpretation, you will refuse to pick up my gage.'

'If you were a gentleman. . .'

'But we have already established that I am not.'

'. . . you would not contradict a lady's opinion,' Angelica concluded serenely.

'But think how insulted you would feel if I were foolish enough to imply that you are incapable of understanding complex ideas,' he retaliated. 'I've made that mistake once already, my lady.'

'So you have.'

With a quick flick of her wrist, Angelica set the globe spinning. Oceans and continents flashed beneath her hand, merging into each other as the world revolved.

She had a giddy feeling that she had set much more in motion this morning than she fully realised. She didn't know how to stop it and she didn't know if she wanted to do so. She hadn't realised just how frustrated she had become with the enclosed life she'd led for the past eighteen months.

Benoît reached past her and stilled the globe with a deft touch.

'I've always had an ambition to circumnavigate the world, but perhaps not at quite such a breakneck speed,' he observed dryly.

'You mean you haven't already done so!' Angelica exclaimed in mock amazement, seizing gratefully on the change of topic.

'Not yet. As I believe I've mentioned several times, I've been earning a living. But one day I fully intend to sail in the wake of Vasco de Gama.' Benoît turned the globe slowly beneath his hands, lightly tracing his planned course over the surface of the polished wood.

Angelica glanced at his face. For a few moments his features were in repose, neither challenging nor concealing anything. His eyes rested on the world as if he thought it was a wondrous place—and life an endless adventure.

She looked at the picture on the chimney breast and wondered, a little wistfully, if she would ever have the

opportunity to see the colours of that glowing world
with her own eyes. Harry had, and she knew her father
had, but it had never occurred to the Earl to tell her
about them—and now he was blind.

Benoît reached over and picked up a letter from the
desk. He offered it to her.

'This is for your father,' he prompted her, when she
didn't immediately take it.

'What does it say?' she asked, receiving it rather
reluctantly and noticing that it was already sealed.

'My lady!' Benoît exclaimed. 'Do you make a habit
of enquiring into other people's private correspond-
ence?'

'Papa will ask me to read it to him, I might as well
know what it says now,' Angelica replied, a dull note
in her voice.

Some of the brightness seemed to have gone out of
the day. Ahead of her lay only a weary journey back
to London, an unpleasant interview with her father
explaining what she'd done—and then a long wait to
find out if Harry really would be be rescued.

'That's his privilege,' Benoît agreed, unperturbed.
'He sent me a letter and I have replied directly to him.
That's my privilege. It might also make him feel less
humiliated by the situation if he has the opportunity
to break my seal himself.'

'Yes, perhaps,' Angelica replied almost inaudibly.
She doubted if her father would appreciate Benoît's
tact. He loathed his dependence too much to be
consoled by such courteous gestures.

She weighed the letter in her hand, remembering
her earlier doubts about Benoît She found it almost
inconceivable that he might be intending to betray
Harry to the French—what good would it do him?
The information that Harry wanted to escape was
hardly going to be news to his captors. But she did

wish he had given her firmer assurance about what he meant to do.

She looked up and found that he was watching her, a half-smile, and perhaps a question, in his eyes.

'You were right, sir,' she said slowly, 'it was a very tiring journey yesterday. It's lucky the storm didn't break earlier in the day. We had enough trouble jolting over the ruts and boggy places in the road as it was.'

She went over to the front window, looking out at the driveway and the bobbing, yellow daffodils. There were one or two shallow puddles on the ground, reflecting the blue sky above.

'I confess, I am a little daunted at the prospect of setting out again so soon,' she said hesitantly, as if reluctant to admit a weakness.

'Come now, Lady Angelica,' Benoît said bracingly. 'This doesn't sound like you. What happened to being "equal to your responsibilities"? I'm sure you won't let a little discomfort stand in the way of your duty. Besides, the Earl's carriage is very well upholstered.'

Angelica bit her lip. She disliked intensely the role she had created for herself, but she couldn't think of any better excuse to stay at Holly House another day.

'I'm sure the journey to London must seem infinitesimal to a man who has sailed halfway round the world,' she said grittily, 'but to me it is not so. I do not enjoy having to admit such foolish sensibility to a stranger, but the prospect of climbing into the coach again this morning fills me with horror.'

'Now that I can believe,' Benoît said appreciatively. 'It's always best, when telling lies, to stick as close to the truth as possible.'

Angelica swung round indignantly, sparks in her blue eyes.

'Were you planning to challenge me?' he asked

softly, before she could speak. 'I warn you, my lady, I will pick up the gage.'

He was standing beside the desk with the still vigour which characterised him, simultaneously relaxed yet alert. There was an intelligent, amused understanding in his brown eyes which was very disconcerting.

Angelica hesitated, thinking better of what she'd been going to say. She knew she was on shaky ground. Her own nature would not allow her to play the part of a nervous, vapourish female, even if she wanted to do so; sooner or later she would betray herself.

'Nevertheless, I would be grateful if you would allow me to intrude upon you another night,' she said, as serenely as she could. 'If the weather remains dry the roads will be in much better condition tomorrow. It will be easier for the horses.'

'Of course, we must consider the horses,' Benoît agreed smoothly, a gleam in his eye. 'But how long will the Earl tolerate the absence of his daughter? I should hate to have Sir William come storming in here accusing me of kidnapping you. He might suspect me of trying to hold the Earl to ransom for your safe return.'

Angelica gasped. Not once, in all the time she since had decided to deliver her father's letter herself, had that possibility occurred to her.

'You wouldn't!' she exclaimed, caught between indignation and disbelief.

'I might, under certain circumstances,' Benoît said reflectively, startling her even further. He smiled at her expression. 'No, my lady, you're quite safe with me,' he assured her. 'But I think we might send a message to your father that you're still here. He must be more aware than most of the possibility of accidents on the road.'

Angelica nodded, unable to argue with Benoît's suggestion. For all his black moods, she knew the Earl was probably desperate with worry for her. It upset her that she was causing him so much distress. But it was an unbelievable relief to have escaped briefly from the dark, gloom-enshrouded house in Berkeley Square. One more day could not hurt.

'I'll tell my mother you are staying while you write a note to the Earl,' said Benoît briskly. 'Feel free to use the desk. We'll send him my letter at the same time.'

'Oh. . .' Angelica wanted to protest, but she couldn't think of an unexceptional way to resist his eminently reasonable suggestion.

'You will have to curb your curiosity in that respect a while longer,' said Benoît, with dry amusement, removing it neatly from between her fingers. 'Excuse me, my lady.'

He went out, leaving Angelica alone. She looked around, her eyes drawn once more to the brilliant painting over the fireplace. She was staying for Harry's sake, she told herself. There was a great deal about Benoît Faulkener that still needed investigation before she could finally trust her brother's life to him.

But was there also something here for her? She spun the globe idly, and then noticed for the first time the model of a ship standing alone on its own table. It was beautifully made, with a well-polished hull, deli-cate spars and intricate rigging. She went over to it, hardly daring to touch it. It was resting on a wooden plinth, but the sails billowed as if it were scudding through the waves, free and unrestrained.

For eighteen months the Earl had rarely left the familiarity of his own home. For the first time she wondered if he would be happier if they travelled; if he could feel the wind on his face even though he could no longer see it bending the trees? It had to be so.

When Harry came home they would *make* Lord

Ellewood emerge from his self-made prison. They would take him out so that he could sense the teeming world all around him, and they would *make* him start living again. Because if they didn't, she could not bear to contemplate what the future would be like.

She remembered suddenly that she was supposed to be writing him a note, and hurried back to the desk, half afraid that Benoît would be back before she had finished.

CHAPTER THREE

'WELL, my lady,' said Benoît, when a messenger had been dispatched with two letters for the Earl, 'how would you like to spend the day of repose you have won for yourself? In a comfortable chair by the fire—or perhaps you'd rather lie down for a few hours?'

'You are very considerate, sir,' Angelica replied coolly, trying not to let him provoke her, 'but I think I could endure a little more activity than that. Perhaps you might permit me to look at some of the books in this well-stocked library.'

Benoît inclined his head politely, an ironic gleam in his eyes.

'Be my guest,' he said graciously. 'Are you very fond of reading, my lady? If you tell me your taste, I may be able to select just the thing for you.'

'I have read a great deal to Papa,' said Angelica.

She wandered over to the nearest shelves, idly running her fingers along the leather spines of the books. Then she paused, her hand resting lightly on the edge of the shelf as she looked up at the rows and rows of books.

'You haven't read all these?' she said suspiciously.

'By no means,' Benoît replied urbanely. 'Most of them belonged to old Mr Fanshaw, the previous owner. He had very eclectic tastes, not all of which I share. But there are also my father's medical books, and I have added others on subjects which interest me.'

'The Great Discoverers—the New World?' Angelica guessed, glancing at him for confirmation of her suggestion.

'Among other things.' Benoît watched, smiling slightly, as Angelica looked back at the shelves.

Her dusky pink gown was more subdued than the blue she had worn the previous evening, but nothing could dim the vivid glory of her hair. Her full-breasted figure radiated energy and a barely contained zest for life. She didn't belong in front of rows of dusty books.

Then she sighed, clearly unaware that she had done so, and Benoît frowned, his eyes narrowing a trifle as he studied her.

Angelica had just realised that she was sick of books and everything they stood for. There had been too many days and nights when she had read endlessly to her father from texts that she didn't understand or that didn't interest her.

Books had become the only substitute for life the Earl was prepared to accept. He was more willing to listen to the words of long-dead philosphers than the voices of old, and once-valued, friends. Angelica turned abruptly away from the shelves.

'On the other hand,' said Benoît smoothly, before she could speak, 'if you don't feel too bruised from your journey yesterday, perhaps you might like to explore some of the surrounding countryside.'

Angelica glanced at him, startled and not quite sure of his meaning.

'I take it you do ride?' he said, lifting an enquiring eyebrow.

'Of course, but—'

'Then since this is your first visit to this part of the country, I would be honoured to show you around,' he offered politely.

He spoke in the unexceptional tone of a good host doing his best to entertain a difficult guest, but there was an amused glint in his eyes as if he had read Angelica's mind and knew exactly how she felt about a day spent in the library.

'The scenery isn't spectacular, but we're quite close to the sea,' he added encouragingly.

'I know,' Angelica replied dryly, wondering why he always managed to make her feel at a disadvantage.

He grinned, unabashed at her implicit allusion to smuggling.

'What do you say?' he asked, the challenging light in his eyes almost daring her to decline his offer.

She hesitated, meeting his gaze with fearless, lucid blue eyes. She already knew she was going to go riding with him—it would be far too craven-hearted to refuse his implicit challenge—but she couldn't help wondering, briefly, about the propriety of his suggestion. She stifled her conscience with the thought that she was extremely unlikely to meet anyone she knew.

Above all, the prospect of riding freely in the crisp open air was irresistible, and she was suddenly filled with exuberant anticipation. She smiled, her expression lighting up with unexpected radiance, her blue eyes almost dazzling with luminous excitement. She met his gaze without reservation, unaware of the impact her happiness might have on him.

'I would be delighted, sir,' she said eagerly. 'Oh!' Her face fell. 'Unfortunately I didn't foresee the need to bring a riding habit. I'm afraid. . .'

Benoît had been watching her internal struggle to justify riding with him with an appreciative half-smile. But now he was gazing at her with an arrested expression in his eyes, almost as if he had been taken by surprise by something. He seemed to absorb her last, disappointed words with an effort, but then he responded with his customary competence.

'I dare say my mother will be able to make good that deficiency,' he said briskly, ringing the bell. 'I will have a couple of horses saddled and we will set out as soon as you are ready, my lady.'

* * *

Angelica had no time to reflect on the wisdom of her decision. Besides, she was too excited at the unexpected treat in store for her to worry overmuch about propriety. She dressed as quickly as she could in the old-fashioned riding habit Mrs Faulkener lent her, eager to get out of the house and anxious not to keep Benoît waiting.

'Well, it's not what I like to see you wearing, and it's to be thanked that no one we know will see you in it, but it will do,' said Martha grudgingly, although she was secretly pleased to see the renewed glow of life in Angelica's eyes.

Angelica's preoccupation with her father's problems—and her increasing anxiety about him—had worried Martha. But she had been unable to think of any advice which might help.

'Oh, Martha, it's fine!' Angelica protested buoyantly, hastily checking her appearance in the mirror.

The riding dress was charcoal grey, severely cut and very plain. It was a trifle too loose around her waist, and it fitted very snugly across her bust, but it was undoubtedly smart. The doctor's wife had had style—still did have, Angelica reflected. There was nothing of the vulgar, provincial housewife about Mrs Faulkener.

Angelica cast one more glance at the mirror and turned to leave the room, but at the last minute she paused. She picked up her reticule and took out the letter from James Corbett, slipping it safely into a concealed pocket in the capacious riding skirts. It was the most valuable thing she possessed, and somehow it seemed to bring her closer to Harry. Besides, if it came to an argument with Benoît about how he was going to rescue her brother, she wanted to have all the facts at her fingertips.

It was wonderful to be outside in the fresh air. There wasn't much warmth in the March sunshine, but the sky was still a clear blue. The damp cobblestones

in the stableyard glistened in the bright morning light
and the horses were glossy and sleek. Angelica hadn't
been riding for a long time, and she could hardly
contain a thrill of anticipation at the prospect ahead
of her.

'It's a beautiful day!' she exclaimed, almost dancing
in her sudden light-heartedness.

'I can't argue with that,' said Benoît more sedately,
but smiling at the vivid picture she made in the
sunlight. 'This is Billy,' he added, rubbing the silky
nose of a neat bay gelding. 'My mother named him.
She said she perceived a resemblance to Sir William
in his countenance.'

'Oh, no!' Angelica protested instinctively. 'I
mean. . .'

The bay turned its head at the sound of her voice,
flicking his ears disapprovingly. Then he struck the
cobblestones a couple of times with an impatient
forefoot and pulled against the groom's restraining
hand.

Angelica laughed. 'I think I can see what she
means,' she confessed.

The groom grinned and spoke chidingly to the
horse.

'And this is Dorcas,' said Benoît, patting the
shoulder of a quiet chestnut. 'She's my mother's mare.
Allow me to put you up, my lady.'

He was standing right beside her, and she was
suddenly deeply conscious of his nearness. Her heart
began to beat faster and she knew she was blushing.

'Thank you,' she said in a muffled voice.

She was grateful that her face was turned away from
him, and that she could blame any colour in her cheeks
on the exertion of mounting.

He tossed her up with an easy, confident strength
which landed her securely in the saddle. He stepped
back and watched as she gathered up the reins. She

was very aware that she was under observation and
tried to compose herself, as well as her mount.

She told herself fiercely that she mustn't allow her
natural excitement at this welcome moment of freedom to blind her to the more serious issues at stake.
And she certainly mustn't let Benoît Faulkener use his
undoubted charm and quick wits to put her at a
disadvantage.

Despite that, she had to resist the urge to fidget
under his gaze, and she knew she was blushing even
more rosily than before. She was unbelievably relieved
when at last he nodded, as if satisfied, and swung
himself up onto the bay.

'Thank you, Thomas,' he said.

The groom stepped back and watched them ride out
of the stableyard.

Angelica was suddenly aware that she was going to
be quite alone with Benoît. In the past a groom had
always acoompanied her whenever she went riding,
but Benoît had apparently given no thought to the
matter.

She wondered for a brief, almost panic-stricken
moment whether she should insist that her coachman
accompany them. In the circumstances it would be a
perfectly reasonable request, but she decided against
it almost immediately. Benoît might do his best to
disconcert her, but she had no real fear that he might
molest her—and it would be easier to find out more
about him if no one else was within earshot.

She glanced at him surreptitiously. He was sitting
erect yet relaxed in the saddle, holding the reins in
one hand, his other hand resting lightly on his lean,
well-muscled thigh. He hadn't troubled to wear a hat,
and his raven hair glinted in the winter sunlight. He
was gazing south over the water meadows, his deep
set eyes resting on the horizon, momentarily forgetful
of her presence.

She could easily imagine him on the deck of his ship, looking out across the sea-swell. Her heart stirred within her at the picture she had conjured up, and she realised in stunned disbelief that she felt sad that it was a sight she would never see in real life.

'What is your respectable business?' she asked abruptly, trying to banish the disturbing vision.

Her question recalled his attention to her, and he flicked a quick look in her direction. There was a humorous gleam in his brown eyes, and a tantalising smile played on his lips.

'I would tell you anything you want to know, my lady,' he declared, 'but are you not afraid that once I have done so we will have nothing left to talk about?'

'Don't be ridiculous!' she snapped, flushing, determined not to let him make fun of her. 'This situation may be amusing to you, sir—but it isn't to me! My brother's life is very important to me. I'm not prepared to entrust it to someone I know so little about.'

He turned his head towards her, one black eyebrow raised interrogatively. There was a direct, challenging glint in his eyes which she found very disturbing.

'Are you suggesting you no longer want my help in rescuing Harry?' he enquired silkily, and she could sense the sleeping wolf within him beginning to stir.

Her thoughts were thrown into chaos, for she had not expected such an uncompromising response to her hasty remark. She glanced away, trying to regain her composure, and then looked up to meet his eyes.

'I don't wish to offend you,' she said steadily, 'but you have given me little reason to trust you. You're right, I did, quite unintentionally, overhear some of your conversation with Sir William this morning. He must have known you for many years, and if he has doubts...' her voice faltered slightly '...doubts about...'

'Ah, yes, if Sir William harbours doubts about me I

must be a treacherous, blackhearted scoundrel,'
Benoît interrupted smoothly, a disquieting smile on
his lips. 'What exactly do you fear, my lady? That I
am not equal to the task of rescuing Harry? Or that,
having done so, I might sell him back to the French? I
presume from a comment Corbett makes in his letter
that they don't know he is the Earl's son. I might be
able to get a very good price for him—although I dare
say I could force a higher one from your father.'

Angelica bit her lip, unable to face the expression
of aloof contempt in his eyes. There was an undercurrent of fierce inflexibility in his voice which she had
heard once before, and which was very difficult to
confront. She had inadvertently angered him far more
with her cautiously worded doubts than Sir William
had with his intemperate accusations. She lifted her
head, flags of bright colour flying in her cheeks, confusion in her wide blue eyes.

'Why are you so offended by my natural apprehension?' she demanded hotly. 'Sir William called you a
liar and you laughed out loud! All I know about you
is that you were once a smuggler and that you will tell
me nothing of how you intend to help Harry—and you
act as if I have bitterly insulted you by asking a few
questions! If you were in my place wouldn't you want
some indication of your good faith?'

Silence followed her impassioned words. The blue
dome of the sky arched above them, and a strong
breeze whispered through the damp grass beneath the
horses hooves. It was a very flat, open landscape. Even
in the bright sunlight it could not be called cosy, and
it was easy to imagine how a grey sky and biting wind
could transform it into a bleak, desolate wilderness.

There was a frown in Benoît's eyes, and his lean,
aquiline face seemed particularly hawk-like as he
turned his head to meet Angelica's heated gaze.

'It hadn't occurred to me that you might try to sell Harry to Papa,' she added bitterly.

'I know,' said Benoît coldly. 'You are not very consistent in your anxieties, my lady.'

'That's because I'm not used to thinking ill of other people!' Angelica flared back at him. 'You force me to be suspicious because you're so secretive.'

'On the contrary,' Benoît retaliated, an edge of steel in his voice. 'You came to Sussex with such deeply embedded preconceptions about me that you have shown no willingness to accept the truth. I told you last night that I haven't been actively involved in smuggling for fifteen years—but you still refuse to believe me!'

'What do you expect when you receive secret visitations in the night, and then tell Sir William you didn't hear anything but the wind!' Angelica demanded wildly, abandoning all caution.

To her surprise, Benoît didn't seem particularly disturbed by her accusation. She had expected an angry denial, but instead he stared frowningly between his horse's ears for a few moments.

'That must have been your maid,' he said curtly. 'Your room faces the front, but she slept in the attic. I heard she'd been asking a lot of questions this morning.'

'How do you explain that, sir?' Angelica challenged him, her chin lifted defiantly.

Her heart was beating uncomfortably fast, and her agitation communicated itself to the mare who tossed her head nervously, but Angelica was determined not to be overawed by her companion.

'I don't intend to explain it at all,' Benoît replied evenly. His expression was distant and uncommunicative. 'What happens in my house is my business, my lady.'

Angelica shook her head in frustration, her golden

curls trembling beneath the brim of the hat Mrs Faulkener had lent her.

'Then we are back where we started,' she said in angry exasperation. 'You will not explain, and my doubts will not be satisfied until I receive some earnest of your good intentions.'

'My word should be good enough for that,' said Benoît chillingly. 'You would not make such a demand of your father—or of Sir William.'

'But you have already proved yourself to be a liar!' Angelica exclaimed, firing up instantly. 'If you can lie to Sir William, why not to me? You don't need to remind me that you don't have honourable blood in your veins—you've proved that already!'

Benoît pressed his lips together in a thin, furious line. Beneath his tan he was very pale, and his hand gripped the reins almost convulsively. Angelica was light-headed with the effects of her own anger, but she was dimly satisfied that she had finally provoked a strong emotional response from him. He wasn't laughing at her any more.

'I wonder if you really understand the meaning of the word honour, my lady,' he said harshly. 'Do you? Tell me—is it to risk the lives of men, whose names you don't even know, in a search for vain-glory? Or to call out and kill a passing acquaintance for some supposed slight? Or does it mean betraying men who have known and trusted you all your life to satisfy one man's momentary frustration? Is that what it means, my lady? *Tell me*!'

His eyes, as they met hers, were granite-hard and uncompromising. He was icily furious and he was allowing her no quarter in their argument.

No one had ever confronted Angelica like this. Her social status and sex meant that on inconsequential matters she was used to having her opinion politely deferred to; and she had rarely had an opportunity to discuss more profound matters with anyone—even her father. The Earl had always indulged his daughter, but he would never have considered it appropriate to enter into a serious debate with her. Benoît's obvious willingness to do so was a new experience for her.

'No,' she said faintly, feeling very shaken, but unable, in all honesty, to disagree with him. 'Of course not.'

Benoît stared at her for a long, unyielding moment. She looked away, unable to meet his flinty gaze.

'Do you suppose that Sir William really wanted me to tell him the truth, this morning?' Benoît said at last, some of the uncharacteristic roughness smoothed from of his deep voice.

'What else. . .?' Angelica looked at him in bewilderment, grateful that he was no longer so freezingly angry. 'He was furious with you.'

'He very often is,' Benoît said equably. 'But he'd never have spoken to me again if I'd told him what he wanted to know—he respects loyalty, if nothing else. And I don't imagine you would have had much time for me either if I'd turned informer.'

Angelica's eyes fell beneath his sardonic gaze. She knew there was an element of truth in what he'd just said.

'We live in a complicated world, my lady,' he said more gently. 'It is not always easy for even the wisest man to decide on the best course of action.'

'I know that!' Angelica's temper flared up again at the almost indulgent tone in his voice. She hadn't enjoyed being challenged by him, but she preferred it to being treated as a child. 'Don't patronise me, sir! I am not a fool! And my original point still remains. I do not know anything about you except that you were once rash enough to put yourself at my father's mercy. I would like to know exactly how you intend to rescue my brother.'

'Since I do not yet know myself, you are likely to have to wait some time for that information, Lady Angelica,' Benoît replied blandly. He seemed to have his own temper well in hand now.

'My God! You're insufferable!' Angelica exclaimed. 'I have never known a more conceited, arrogant, cocksure. . .' Words failed her as she tried to describe his infamy.

'Have you run out of insults already?' He grinned wolfishly. 'I'm sure there's a dictionary in the library at home. You will have to look up some more.'

For the last few minutes the horses had been ambling along a narrow, tree-lined lane, but Angelica had been too engrossed in their argument to pay much attention to her surroundings. Suddenly the lane petered out and the beach opened up before them, stretching out to east and west in a long, smooth expanse of shimmering sand.

Angelica was taken completely by surprise, and Benoît smiled faintly at her obvious amazement. She sat and gazed about her, utterly forgetful of his last provocative comment. Her riding skirts rippled in the sea breeze, and she could taste the salt in the air. It wasn't the first time she had seen the sea. She had visited Brighton several times with the Earl, but their family estates were in the midlands, and her first glimpse of the sea after such a long absence was an exciting experience for her.

She slipped her foot free of the stirrup and slid down to the ground, almost without realising what she was doing, and let Benoît take the reins from her without a murmur of protest. She picked up her skirts and crunched down over the large round pebbles onto the firm sand, her eyes fixed wonderingly on the horizon.

In some small, logical part of her brain she knew there were places on the south coast where France was

closer than London—but staring out to the horizon it
didn't seem so. It seemed as if the glittering expanse
of water might go on for ever.

She could see the white wings of seagulls as they
soared above the waves and then dipped down with
raucous calls to the surface of the water. She could
smell the dried seaweed on the stones, crisp with salt
and sand, and hear the rolling murmur of the waves.
The sea was going out, and wading birds crowded the
tideline, hurrying back and forth in a never-ending
quest for food. The glistening wet sand was ridged and
furrowed with the regular pattern of the waves, and
here and there a pool of seawater reflected the light of
the sky above.

She walked down the beach, heedless of the wind
tugging at her skirts and whipping her hair into her
face. She'd almost forgotten Benoît, and he made no
effort to remind her of his presence as he followed
her, leading the two horses.

Then the wind snatched her borrowed hat, bowling
it along the shining sands at a brisk pace.

'Oh!'

She clutched ineffectually after it, and then picked
up her skirts, intending to run after it.

'Leave it!' Benoît caught her by her upper arm,
swinging her around to face him, laughing at her
consternation.

'But I can't lose your mother's hat!' she protested.
'She's been so kind to me.'

'I doubt if it will be wearable, covered in salt,'
Benoît pointed out, grinning. 'It won't be difficult to
replace.'

'I suppose not,' said Angelica doubtfully.

She was acutely conscious of his grip on her arm. It
was cold on the beach, but the warmth of his hand
seemed to burn through the sleeve of her habit. He
was standing very close to her, and the wind whipped

her skirts against his legs, almost as if to bind them together. She knew she ought to withdraw herself gracefully from his grasp, but she looked up and met his eyes and couldn't quite bring herself to do so.

A few minutes ago she had been arguing with him more fiercely than she had ever quarrelled with anyone except her brother, but there was no anger in his expression now. There was an unfamiliar but exquisitely disturbing warmth in his brown eyes as they rested on her face. He dropped the reins and lifted his other hand to her waist.

'The horses will run away,' she said, hardly recognising her own voice. A pulse was beating rapidly in her throat. She could scarcely breathe with the pressure of unfamiliar anticipation.

'They'd go back to the stable if I told them to,' said Benoît, with soft confidence. 'But they won't run away.'

'Just the kind of trick a smuggler would teach his horse,' Angelica said breathlessly, still trying to maintain some resemblance of normality, as he drew her a little closer towards him.

'Blame Thomas, not me,' Benoît replied, smiling. 'He gets bored when I'm at sea. He even taught Billy to count.'

'*What—*?'

Angelica's surprised exclamation was cut short as Benoît drew her neatly into his arms. He held her breast to breast, his dark face dizzyingly close to hers for an electrifying moment.

'This time there's no doubt your eyes are open,' he said, half-humorously. 'Remember that, when you next accuse me of not being a gentleman.'

'I don't. . .'

Benoît's mouth covered her parted lips and stifled whatever it was she had been going to say. Shock held her rigid for several seconds. She had never been kissed like this before, and nothing in her previous experience had prepared her for dealing with such a situation.

The wind wrapped her skirts around them, locking them together. She could feel the heat of his body burning through her clothes. He was holding her firmly in his arms. She was acutely aware of the power in his lean, hard-muscled body, but his lips were gentle and persuasive on hers. Her heart was racing; strange, exotic warmth slowly filled her veins. Her empty hands opened once or twice in vague uncertainty then, almost of their own volition, they slid up over the ridged black cloth of his sleeves to rest on his shoulders.

She felt his tongue stroke her lower lip in sensuous exploration, and a fresh wave of burning sensation flooded her. She closed her eyes, feeling disorientated and exhilarated. She had nothing to compare this experience with, and no way of moderating her response to him.

His hold on her tightened. He slid one hand sensuously up her back to bury it in her windswept golden curls, dislodging a few hairpins as he did so. She trembled at his touch, clutching erratically his shoulders. Her legs felt weak and she leant against him, needing his support.

The muted roar of the sea and the harsh cry of the gulls receded to the edge of her awareness. Benoît filled the whole of her consciousness. Her lips were swollen and throbbing with the desire he had aroused in her—and then he slipped his tongue gently between them and she felt as if her heart stood still.

Nothing had prepared her for the intimacy of this moment. His tongue confidently explored her mouth, gently probing, overwhelming all her senses. Part of her wanted to pull away and protest at the liberty he was taking, but another part of her wanted to surrender completely to his love-making.

Her arms slipped around his neck and she clung to him, her lips parted to allow him the soul-shattering intimacy he sought, not actively returning his kiss, but not denying him either.

It was Benoît who at last drew back, and she could hear his ragged breathing as he continued to hold her against him, her face resting against his shoulder. Her heart was hammering in her ears, she was deaf and blind to the world around her. She was content to remain in his arms for a several long moments before reality finally reasserted itself.

Then she lifted her head in horror as she realised what had happened and tried to wrench herself out of his grasp. He held onto her firmly.

'We'll both fall over if you do that,' he murmured provocatively. 'Which might be quite pleasant, but I'm sure it's not what you have in mind.'

Angelica gasped in embarrassed, furious indignation and helped him unwind her traitorous skirts. Then she stepped back quickly and lifted her burning eyes to his face.

He grinned at her, a rakish light in his eyes. He was slightly flushed beneath his tan, but he was once more his customary controlled self.

'Don't blame me, my lady,' he said before she could speak, an unexpectedly humorous lilt in his deep voice. 'I only meant to snatch a quick kiss. It was your own passionate nature that betrayed you.'

'How *dare* you?'

Sudden fury blazed through Angelica. Her over-excited emotions were in a complete turmoil, and she was too keyed up to think clearly. The only thing she knew for sure was that it was all Benoît's fault. Without stopping to think, she struck out wildly at him.

He caught her wrist before her hand connected with his cheek.

'Let me go!' she spat at him, pulling away from him and nearly stumbling over her skirts.

'No.'

She tried to wrench her arm out of his grasp with a vicious twist and his hold on her tightened until she winced.

'Stand still, Angelica,' he said sharply, almost as if he was talking to a naughty child.

She obeyed him, partly through surprise at his tone, and partly because she was startled by the use of her name.

'I haven't hurt you, and I'm not going to hurt you,' he said calmly, releasing her wrist. 'Believe it or not, both your morals and your person are quite safe in my hands—so don't attack me because your ideas about yourself have been thrown into confusion.'

She stepped back, rubbing her wrist absent-mindedly as she glared at him.

'Look!' He reached out and spun her round by her shoulders, moving so fast that she didn't have time to protest 'There's a whole world out there.' He faced her towards the horizon. 'Different people with different cultures and even different ideas of honour. Don't accept everything you've been told about life without question. Make up your own mind.'

He was standing behind her, his hands firm and insistent upon her shoulders, his words ringing in her ears.

She didn't pull away from him. She stared out to sea, feeling her hair whip about her face. The waves kept rolling up the beach, slightly further away now than they had been before. The sky seemed huge, it filled her vision; small white clouds had appeared in the distance.

'Papa always said—*says* you need good information to make a good decision,' she said at last.

'The Earl is a wise man.'

'So how am I supposed to make up my mind about you when I don't have any information?' she demanded, turning to face him.

He smiled almost gently, and reached out to tuck an errant curl behind her ear.

'You have a lot of information, my lady,' he corrected her gently. 'More than most, I might add. You just don't know how to fit it all together.'

'It *is* my brother's life we're talking about,' she said, almost pleadingly.

'Is it?' he asked, an enigmatic gleam in his brown eyes. 'Come along, my lady,' he added, before she could speak. 'The horses have been standing in the wind long enough, and there's something you might be interested to see further along the beach.'

She let him put her into the saddle without a word. She was deeply bewildered by what had happened, and more unsure of herself than she could ever remember being. He had challenged her preconceptions on several levels and she needed time to think.

She gathered up the reins and followed Benoît down towards the tideline. They turned east and Benoît urged Billy into a brisk walk across the wet sands. Disturbed sea birds flew up in raucous flurries, scattering and then returning to their foraging in the glittering water as soon as the horses had passed by.

'Where are you taking me?' Angelica asked, struggling to sound as if nothing exceptional had happened.

'Can't you guess?' Benoît shot her a glinting, almost mocking glance.

'No. How should I know?' she replied crossly. 'I hate guessing games.'

'Then you shouldn't have embarked upon one, my lady,' he replied, his voice carried to her on the wind blowing in across the sea. 'Shall we see how well you can put Dorcas through her paces?'

Angelica didn't hesitate. She leant forward, all her concentration instantly centred on showing Benoît just what she was capable of. The mare sprang forward eagerly and the bay matched her instantly. The two horses raced along the bright sands while the seagulls wheeled in the sky above them, shrieking their disapproval of such unmannerly disturbance.

There was a wild joy for Angelica in the sudden burst of speed. After the complications of the past two days this moment of untrammelled freedom was pure pleasure. She knew that when they stopped she would once again have to face all the growing complexities of her situation—but not just yet.

The horses matched paces, and Angelica made no attempt to outdistance Benoît. There had been too many challenges between them already; she did not want even a hint of competition to tarnish this perfect interlude. It was comforting to allow herself the brief illusion that he was merely an undemanding companion, and not...what was he? A friend or an enemy—or a chance met stranger she would never see again after today?

At last the horses slowed, falling back into a canter, a trot and then a walk. Angelica had time to look around and, for the first time, to become aware that she must have left most of her hairpins scattered behind her along the beach. She lifted a hand to her tangled, salt-sticky hair in mild consternation.

Benoît observed her gesture and grinned.

'That's a sorry sight to present to your long-suffering maid,' he teased her. 'She'll probably take one look at you and hand in her notice.'

Angelica opened her mouth indignantly, but then her sense of humour overcame her and she smiled wryly.

'She'll certainly have something to say about it,' she admitted ruefully. 'And she'll be horrified I lost your mother's hat. I just hope we don't meet anyone.'

'Sir William,' Benoît suggested wickedly. 'I believe he often rides on the beach.'

'Oh, my God!' Angelica let go of the reins with both hands and reached up to run her fingers through her unruly hair.

Blonde tresses which fell almost to her waist were blowing in unrestrained glory around her shoulders, shining like spun gold in the bright sunlight.

'What am I going to do?' she exclaimed in distress as the full enormity of her situation dawned on her. 'I'll never be able to find all my hairpins. I can't ride round the countryside looking like a hoyden!'

Dorcas had come to a natural stop, and Billy followed suit. Benoît dismounted and looked up at her, resting his left hand lightly on Dorcas's withers.

'Come down, my lady,' he commanded her softly, the light in his dark eyes daring her to refuse.

Her breath caught in her throat as she found herself snared in the compelling intensity of his gaze.

'I can't do much about your plight when you're perched several feet above me,' he pointed out reasonably, although there was a smile playing on his lips which made the blood tingle in Angelica's veins.

'I don't see what you can do anyway,' she objected, trying not to let him see how powerfully he was affecting her. 'Not unless you've any experience as a lady's maid.'

'None at all,' he said cheerfully, 'but I've plaited a few horsetails in my time.'

For some reason Angelica found his unflattering comparison reassuring, and she unhooked her leg from around the pommel and slipped down into his waiting arms. He set her neatly on her feet, but continued to rest his hands on her waist for a few seconds. She

looked up at him with uncertain blue eyes, not quite
sure what he intended, and he smiled crookedly.

'If you don't want a repeat of what happened the
last time you looked up at me like that, I suggest you
turn around,' he said softly.

Angelica gasped and turned so quickly she nearly
tripped over her flowing skirts.

Benoît chuckled and drew her hair gently over her
shoulders. She was standing on the lee side of Dorcas,
and it was relatively easy to smooth the wild tresses
into a manageable handful.

'You turned your back with unflattering haste, my
lady,' he chided her, his hands light and unbelievably
stimulating in her hair. 'My manly sensitivities are
deeply wounded. I had no idea you found my attentions quite so objectionable.'

Angelica gripped the stirrup leather for support and
closed her eyes. She felt trapped between the mare
and Benoît. She wanted to step briskly away from
Benoît's hands and declare that she could fix her hair
for herself. But she remained standing where she was,
caught under the spell of his seductive touch which
sent delightful shivers running up and down her spine.

Despite the tangles in her sea-blown hair he managed to divide it into three relatively equal portions
without causing her too much discomfort. Then he
plaited it neatly and Angelica was almost disappointed
when she realised he had finished.

'Hold that.' He put the heavy braid over her
shoulder and she obeyed without question. She heard
a faint ripping sound and glanced round in surprise to
see him tearing a strip from his handkerchief.

He grinned and she caught a glimpse of his strong
white teeth.

'You may not appreciate my love-making, but you
can't deny I'm resourceful,' he said outrageously.

She blushed and turned her head away as he took

back the braid and tied it firmly at the end. Then he folded it under and tied it again at the top of the braid, creating a relatively neat club of hair at the nape of her neck.

'Not bad,' he said judiciously. 'Although I don't think you maid is going to be afraid of the competition.'

'I don't know how I'm going to explain it,' said Angelica as she turned to face him, desperately trying to strike a normal note. 'First your mother's hat, now this.'

'You can blame it on me, if you like,' Benoît offered generously. 'You can tell them I pulled out most of the pins when I kissed you.'

'*What*?' Angelica pressed her hands against her burning cheeks, a victim of so many conflicting emotions she didn't know which one to give voice to first.

'I could pretend that nothing untoward happened between us earlier,' Benoît said deliberately. 'No doubt that would be the gentlemanly thing to do.' He met her disturbed gaze with a half-mocking, half-challenging light in his brown eyes. 'But the sooner you get used to the idea that I did kiss you—and that there's a very strong likelihood that I'm going to do so again before long—the better we shall proceed.'

'Oh!' Angelica whirled away from him. 'How can you be so *unfeeling*? I came to see you in good faith— to ask for your help. And you...you...'

'Took advantage of your innocence?' Benoît supplied helpfully when words failed her. 'Abused your trust? But you didn't come to Sussex entirely in good faith, did you? You're a strange mixture of trust and suspicion, my lady. On the one hand you question my motives and my integrity at every turn—and on the other you are content to wheedle an extra night under my roof and ride out with me alone as if you have no fears for your safety in my company. Should I be flattered or insulted?'

Angelica shot him a quick glance, feeling quite unable to answer his guestion. She drew in a deep breath, trying to regain her self-control.

'I believe you were going to show me something, sir,' she said, with as much dignity as she could muster. 'Or was I mistaken?'

'No, you weren't mistaken.' From the dark gleam in his eye she knew she wouldn't be permitted to continue with her evasion indefinitely, but at least she had won herself some respite.

'Take a look around and see if you can guess where we are,' he said.

She glanced at him frowningly and then stepped away from the horses, not really sure what she was supposed to recognise. The beach hardly seemed any different than it had done further west. The tide was still going out behind her, the wet sand gleamed, and whispering, thin-grassed sand dunes rose up before her.

'I don't. . .it was *here*!' she exclaimed as light suddenly dawned. '*This* is where Papa had you at his mercy!'

'As you say,' said Benoît dryly, although there was a hint of appreciative amusement in his eyes at her phraseology. He wasn't naïve enough to suppose her unflattering description of the incident had been entirely accidental.

'Tell me what happened!' she demanded.

'Your father came along the tideline, just as we have done,' said Benoît, apparently quite willing to tell the tale. 'He knew the tide was coming in, and he guessed we'd used it to cover our tracks and send Sir William off on a wild-goose chase.'

'He was a match for your devious schemes,' Angelica declared proudly, her blue eyes shining.

'Obviously,' said Benoît, grinning at her evident satisfaction. 'When he got to about there—' he indicated a point a few more yards down the beach '—he found the tracks going inland, so he followed them. I was waiting to intercept anyone who did so.'

'And he vanquished you!' said Angelica, with relish.

'Although I don't remember him taking such an unholy pleasure in his victory as you are doing,' Benoît remarked dryly. 'But it's true he didn't have a kiss to avenge.'

'You never give up, do you?' said Angelica wrathfully. 'Since I have not the slightest intention of allowing the incident to be repeated, it would be more courteous—and more tactful—if you would let the matter drop.'

'That sounds remarkably like a challenge, my lady,' he said good-humouredly.

There was a bright, unreadable light in his eyes, and she caught her breath as he took a step towards her. She was convinced he was going to kiss her. But he went past her and picked up the mare's reins.

'We should be moving on, my lady,' he said politely. 'The day is passing, and I wouldn't want you to exhaust yourself before your gruelling journey home tomorrow.'

'You are very thoughtful,' said Angelica through gritted teeth, wondering why she suddenly felt so deflated.

'Just trying to be a good host,' he replied self-deprecatingly. 'I've never had a member of the aristocracy grace my home with their presence before. I want to take good care of you.'

Angelica bit her lip, not sure whether to be amused or indignant. He met her gaze, a hint of warm understanding as well as the familiar, glinting humour in his brown eyes, and she felt reassured. He held out his hand and she went over to him immediately, letting him lift her once more into the saddle.

It was impossible to feel entirely relaxed in his company, he was too unpredictable. But he wasn't boring and she did, instinctively, trust him. He was unconventional and frequently disconcerting in his manner, but if he'd wanted to take advantage of her she'd given him the perfect opportunity—and he hadn't made use of it.

By imperceptible degrees, her opinion of him was rising. It might well be reasonable to entrust Harry's safety to him. She still refused to entertain the notion that she had any other reason for being interested in Benoît Faulkener.

CHAPTER FOUR

'Look.' Benoît interrupted her thoughts. 'It's the mouth of the Arun,' he explained, as Angelica glanced at him questioningly.

He had led her a few more yards along the beach while she'd been reflecting on his personality.

'Over there—' he pointed diagonally inland, across the river '—is Littlehampton. Arundel is three or four miles north—as the crow flies, not as the river bends. And there—' he gestured across to a construction on the east river bank '—is the battery which s supposed to defend us from Napoleon's invading hordes.'

'Won't it?' Angelica asked, catching the note of dismissal in his voice.

'It might,' said Benoît sceptically. 'It used to be armed with ten eighteen-pound guns, but they replaced them with several thirty-six pounders a few years ago. It's not in the best state of repair, but it does command both the entrance to the river and the eastern shoreline. Anyone stupid enough to sail within range is liable to get a good hammering—always supposing that it is sufficiently well manned and that the gunners are awake.'

'But if there was any danger of such an attack it would be adequately manned, wouldn't it?' Angelica persisted.

The invasion scares of earlier years had pretty much passed her by. It was only standing here, on the exposed foreshore, that she suddenly realised how vulnerable England might be to a seaborne offensive.

'Possibly,' Benoît conceded, throwing a quick glance

in her direction. 'But it's almost irrelevant. The best way of gaining control of the river would be to land a party of marines on *this* bank. They'd be protected from the guns by the dunes. They could work their way inland and eventually attack the battery from behind. Once it was taken, the French would have free passage up the Arun.'

'My God!' Angelica exclaimed in horror. 'You make it sound so easy!'

'Make no mistake, my lady,' said Benoît calmly, 'it would be easy. I would engage to do it with a handful of men.'

'Then why isn't something done?' Angelica demanded forcefully.

'Because they'd have to fortify this bank,' said Benoît reasonably. 'Which would take money and a determined effort by the Board of Ordnance. It's not that they don't know the dangers—they just don't have the resources to tackle them.'

Angelica looked around almost wildly, as if she half-expected to see hordes of armed Frenchmen emerging from the dunes.

'They won't come tonight,' said Benoît confidently, seeing the alarm in her expression.

'How can you be so sure?' she exclaimed nervously.

In London, safe within the security of the Earl's town house, the dangers of the war had seemed very remote. She had been afraid for Harry serving in one of the King's ships, but she had never experienced any personal sense of threat. Even Sir John Moore's devastating, three-hundred-mile retreat, which had ended in the Battle of Corunna less than two months ago, had had little impact upon her enclosed world.

Benoît grinned at her obvious alarm.

'Instinct,' he said unhelpfully. 'Don't worry, my lady,' he added more gently. 'I think there's very little danger of Napoleon landing an army on English soil.'

Angelica frowned, reassured by his words, but irritated that he hadn't bothered to explain further. It was annoying that he should assume a brief comment from him would be enough to calm her anxieties. She coiled a few strands of Dorcas's mane idly around her finger.

'It's hard to make up my own mind when I have so little information to work with,' she said slowly. 'Why not?'

'Because even Frenchmen can't walk on water.'

'What?' She looked at him suspiciously, afraid he was laughing at her, but there was no indication in his expression that he was mocking her.

'It's not easy to transport and disembark an army,' he enlarged upon his answer. 'It took a week or more for Wellesley to disembark of our troops in Mondego Bay last year—and they didn't have to contend with an attacking local militia while they were recovering from seasickness and reassembling their guns.'

'*Would* the local people fight?' Angelica said doubtfully. 'Wouldn't they run away? Sir William says the county is riddled with lazy, disaffected. . .'

'Possibly,' said Benoît dryly. 'But the same men who take up cudgels to protect their livelihood from Sir William, might show equally little respect to anyone trying to invade their homes—don't you think?'

They had begun to ride slowly back along the beach, retracing their path, although the sea had further retreated and they no longer disturbed the wading birds at the water's edge.

'Think of the logistics of organising a full-scale invasion,' Benoît continued as Angelica frowned, trying to get to grips with what he was saying. 'Even supposing Napoleon has enough seaworthy vessels suitable for transporting a reasonably sized army—and I doubt very much if he does—he doesn't have enough skilled seamen to sail them. The French navy has never recovered from its losses at Trafalgar.

'It may be relatively easy for individual boats to slip back and forth across the Channel, but can you imagine the chaos of two or three hundred transports all sailing on the same tide—scattering, colliding and foundering in the unfamiliar waters along our coast? No, Napoleon may dream of marching on London, but I'm sure he's putting more faith in the destructive power of the Decrees he issued at Berlin and Milan.'

He paused then, shooting a quick glance at Angelica out of the corner of his eye before allowing his attention to rest on the shoreline ahead, as if there was nothing more to say.

Angelica waited for him to explain what the Decrees were, realised he wasn't going to do so without prompting, and drew in a deep, rather exasperated breath. It was not so much that she wasn't interested in what he was saying, but she was slightly humiliated to discover how little she knew, and at how much of a disadvantage her ignorance placed her.

'Ah, yes,' she said brightly. 'I remember hearing something about Napoleon's Decrees, although I can't quite remember...'

'At Berlin he outlawed all trade between England and French-controlled lands, whether in English or neutral ships,' said Benoît, only a slight twitch of his lips indicating that he was aware of her feelings. 'That was in November of 1807, and it effectively cut us off from the European carrying trade. Then at Milan, about fourteen months ago, he issued a new set of Decrees which outlawed any neutral vessel which submitted to a British search or touched at a British port.'

'But surely, if our navy is so superior...!' Angelica protested, shocked. 'How can he hope to enforce—?'

'Ultimately, I don't believe he can,' Benoît replied grimly. 'But the Decrees have certainly had serious consequences for British shipping and manufactures. The cotton weavers of Manchester rioted last year because the disruption of their industry had reduced them to starvation.'

Angelica stared blindly ahead, heedless of the increasing chill in the wind. Manchester was as remote from her experience as the Caribbean, but it was dawning on her that the war involved far more than the well-publicised battles fought on land or sea.

'We have retaliated, of course,' said Benoît, relenting from the black picture he had been painting as he saw her disturbed response to it. 'After the Berlin Decrees, England blockaded all European ports from which she was excluded, and only allowed neutral ships to use them if they also touched at a British port and paid a reshipment duty on their cargo.

'And don't forget that the French are suffering from the effects of Napoleon's blockade as well. All those goods they've come to rely on—sugar, coffee, cotton, spices, dyes, tobacco—are now in short supply. Unless they resort to accepting smuggled goods,' he added blandly.

Angelica looked at him sharply.

'Is that how you justify smuggling?' she demanded, momentarily wondering if that was what all this information had been leading up to.

'I'm not a smuggler,' said Benoît flatly, his face expressionless.

Angelica bit her lip. There had been no hostility in his tone, but she felt as if a door had clanged shut in her face. It was quite clear that, however much general information he was prepared to volunteer, he wasn't going to be provoked into revealing more personal details by such a clumsy sally.

'You certainly seem to know a great deal about the subject,' she said, forcing herself to smile unconcernedly.

'Any man who reads the newspapers and keeps himself reasonably well informed would know as much,' he replied, and she saw the gleam of his white teeth as he grinned.

She was reminded, once again, of his elusive resemblance to a great black wolf. He revealed only what he wanted to reveal, and his response was always unpredictable.

'We will win, won't we?' she asked suddenly. It was the first time it had ever occurred to her to wonder.

'Oh, yes,' he said confidently.

'How can you be so sure?' she demanded.

'Because however many markets Napoleon closes to us in the Old World, we will always be able to open up more in the New World,' he replied, with absolute certainty. 'It has already begun with the islands we've taken from our enemies in the West Indies. We will survive for as long as we maintain control of the sea — and we will win as soon as we can put an army on continental soil that's capable of consistently defeating the French.'

'And when will that be?' Angelica asked curiously.

Benoît shrugged. 'I'm not a soldier,' he replied. 'I cannot give an informed opinion on that. All I can say is that, although we took a beating last year in Spain and Portugal, we also won a couple of victories that prove once and for all that Napoleon's army is not invincible. Further than that, we shall just have to wait and see.'

Angelica sighed. It wasn't an entirely satisfactory answer, but there didn't seem to be much she could say to it. She glanced around, noting, with mild surprise, that Benoît had turned inland before they'd reached the same track they had originally followed to the beach.

'It's quicker,' he said, answering her unspoken question. 'The day is losing its bloom and you must be getting cold, my lady. I wouldn't want to be accused of giving you a chill. Besides, we mustn't overtax your strength—you've got a long journey ahead of you tomorrow!'

Angelica swallowed a hasty retort, aware that she was being deliberately provoked and determined not to rise to it.

'What do you mean, Thomas has taught Billy to count?' she asked, remembering something he'd said earlier, although carefully blocking from her mind the context in which he'd said it. 'Surely the most accomplished horse would have difficulty. . .?'

Benoît laughed. 'When we get back, I will arrange a demonstration,' he promised her. 'I'm sure you'll be impressed, my lady.'

It took a long time for Martha to restore Angelica's hair to some kind of order, and she grumbled at her mistress throughout the ordeal.

'How could you be so heedless. . .so lacking in common decency. . .to go stravaging around the countryside without a hat on your head and your hair looking like a bird's nest?' she exclaimed, as she tried to untangle the knots. 'You're not a gypsy, my lady! What would the Earl say if he knew about this?'

'I don't know,' said Angelica, a hint of rebellion in her voice, 'but since he's never going to find out it doesn't matter, does it?'

'And how could it have happened?' Martha persisted, ignoring Angelica's words, although she had no intention of ever betraying her mistress's lack of conduct to anyone, least of all the Earl. 'Your hat blowing away I can understand—this wicked wind—but your hair! I always take care to fix it firmly. I know how you bounce about when you're excited. You've never managed to achieve the elegant carriage suitable for a lady in your position. Who did it up again?'

'Mr Faulkener,' said Angelica, boldly meeting her

maid's eyes and desperately trying not to let a blush
betray her.

'Did he, indeed?' said Martha dryly, her eyes resting
thoughtfully on Angelica's glowing cheeks. 'I suppose
letting your hair down was part of your ploy to discover more about him, was it? You ought to be
ashamed of yourself, my lady!'

Angelica coloured uncomfortably; very little
escaped Martha's sharp gaze and Angelica wondered
just how much her maid had guessed about her ride
with Benoît.

'So how have *your* investigations been going?' she
asked brightly, trying to change the subject. 'Is this
house a haven for smugglers, or is there an innocent
explanation for what happened last night?'

Martha sniffed disapprovingly.

'To think that a respectable woman like me should
have to stoop to such devious behaviour,' she said
sourly. 'I'll have you know that I'm not accustomed to
playing the part of a spy, my lady. It's not what I'm
used to.'

'Oh, Martha!' Angelica exclaimed, caught between
laughter and exasperation. 'You're used to doing
whatever it takes to keep Harry and me out of trouble.
You know you are!'

Martha smiled austerely as she finally succeeded in
dragging a comb through Angelica's tangled hair.

'There can't be much regular smuggling organised
from this house,' she said, as disapprovingly as if she'd
just announced it was a den of iniquity, 'not by the
master, at all accounts. He doesn't spend enough time
here.'

'What do you mean?' Angelica said quickly. 'I know
he's recently returned from the West Indies, but—'

'This is the first time he's spent more than a few
weeks at home since his father died, two years ago,'
Martha continued, as if she hadn't heard Angelica's

interruption. 'According to what I hear, he's worked his way up from ship's boy to junior partner in a shipowning business. Very proud of him below stairs, they are.'

Angelica stared at her maid, quite speechless for several moments. Martha smiled with grim satisfaction at her mistress's astonishment.

'It seems he went to sea when he was fourteen years old,' she said. 'By the time he was twenty-one he was master of a merchantman trading to the West Indies. He was employed by a man called Josiah Crabtree, who had a fleet of four ships. Very fond of Mr Faulkener the old man is, seemingly. Mind you, he has good reason to be—Mr Faulkener brought his ship safely through a hurricane after he'd only been in command a few months.'

'He did?' said Angelica breathlessly.

Her eyes were shining with excitement at Martha's tale. It was easy to imagine Benoît on the bridge of his ship, waves crashing all around, the wind shrieking and timbers creaking as he fought the elements themselves in his determination to bring his vessel safely home.

'So I'm told,' said Martha dryly, her eyes on Angelica's glowing face. 'When he thought he'd learnt as much as he could, he left Mr Crabtree and bought a ship of his own—started up an independent business. He's got three ships now—and last year Mr Crabtree suggested they go into partnership. From what I hear, Mr Crabtree's still got a soft spot for Mr Faulkener— like as not he'll make him his heir.'

'Good heavens!' said Angelica faintly.

In a matter of minutes, Benoît had been transformed in her eyes from little more than a pirate adventurer to a man of substance. It was true she had realised some time ago that he didn't earn his living

from smuggling, but her notions of what he had
become instead had been extremely hazy.

She had taken it for granted that he had captained
his own ship, but she hadn't given much thought to
the capacity in which he had done so. She had still
tended towards the idea that he must be involved in
some illegal or semi-legitimate business—perhaps as a
privateer, licensed by letters of marque to prey upon
enemy shipping. It was hard to believe he might really
be as respectable as he had claimed to be yesterday
evening.

'How did you find out all this?' she asked wonderingly, thinking about her own lack of success in
discovering more about her host.

'His people are very proud of him,' said Martha
repressively, as if she were revealing a discreditable
secret. 'It wasn't hard to get them to boast about his
achievements.'

'What about last night?' Angelica said. 'Did you find
out any more about that?'

'No.' Martha frowned with dissatisfaction. 'Close as
clams on that subject, they were,' she said irritably.

'Never mind,' said Angelica, suddenly feeling very
cheerful. 'At least we're making progress.'

'And how do you work that out, my lady?' said
Martha dourly. 'You came here in the hope he was a
smuggler, and therefore in a good position to rescue
Lord Lennard. We've just found out that he's spent
the best part of the last fifteen years at sea. Hardly the
best news from your point of view, is it?'

'I suppose not. On the other hand. . .' Angelica's
words trailed off.

She was remembering that, although Benoît had
refused to explain what had happened the previous
night, he had as good as admitted that his visitor had
been one of the men Sir William was searching for—
men who had known and trusted Benoît all his life.

He might not still be actively involved in smuggling, but he knew men who were.

'Thank you, Martha,' she said. 'I knew you wouldn't let me down.'

Not long later, Angelica ran lightly downstairs and burst into the library. Benoît had been sitting at his desk, writing, but he looked up at her arrival and grinned.

'So much energy, my lady,' he teased her. 'I was sure you would need to rest upon your bed for several hours before you would feel strong enough to rise for dinner.'

'Oh!' Angelica stopped short in confusion, suddenly remembering that she ought to make at least a pretence of being fatigued.

Benoît stood up and went behind her to close the door. She revolved on the spot so that she could keep him under observation. He made her nervous when she couldn't see him.

'Or perhaps you came to find a soothing text to lull you to sleep,' he suggested, a familiar half-mocking, half-humorous gleam in his eyes.

She met his gaze and her heart skipped a beat. Until a few minutes ago she had been so sure that he was completely ineligible that she had done everything she could to suppress the attraction she felt for him. But now it turned out that he was, after all, relatively respectable—although obviously not a suitable match for her father's daughter.

She tried to tell herself that it didn't matter to her what he was; she would be gone tomorrow. But it did matter—and she was beginning to realise and accept that fact.

'Why didn't you tell me you were a shipowner?' she demanded impetuously.

Benoît grinned and she remembered the wolf in him.

'Your maid obviously took the lesson about the persuasive powers of the sun and the wind more deeply to heart that you have done,' he observed dryly, although the mockery in his eyes was quite gentle.

'What do you mean?' Angelica exclaimed breath-lessly, confused by his words and disconcerted by the expression in his eyes.

'Despite her forbidding appearance, I understand she can display a warm and charming nature when the occasion warrants it,' Benoît explained helpfully. 'She certainly seems to have made a favourable impression on Thomas. Apparently she even got him to show her some of the tricks he's taught the horses. He's very taken with her.'

'Good heavens!' Angelica's attention was briefly seized by the incredible and fascinating picture of Martha sweet-talking the groom.

'Alas, my lady,' said Benoît, with laughing, teasing regret in his eyes. 'If you'd only pursued the same technique with me, think how much you might know about me by now.'

'What?' Angelica stared up at him with enormous, startled eyes, her lips parted in genuine surprise.

She saw the expression in his dark eyes change, and threw up her hand instinctively to ward him off, taking a hasty step backwards as she did so.

'No!' she exclaimed.

He grinned.

'You disappoint me, my lady,' he taunted her gently. 'With so much at stake, are you really not prepared to make a small sacrifice for your brother?'

Angelica swallowed. It was dangerous to keep look-ing into his eyes. What she saw there made her feel light-headed with excitement, and barely able to control her emotions. This wasn't how Martha had done it, surely?

'You mean if I. . .if I let you. . .' Her voice failed her and she tried again. 'If I. . .you'll tell me how you're going to rescue Harry.'

He smiled and her heart turned over.

'You could always try the experiment,' he suggested softly.

'That's. . .that's *blackmail*!' she protested breathlessly.

Benoît's smile broadened.

'But at least you'll have the consolation of knowing you did it for Harry's sake,' he consoled her, the enticingly wicked gleam in his eyes almost irresistible.

'Oh, dear!' said Angelica faintly, as he took her in his arms. 'Perhaps you ought to tell me first, sir.' She made one last attempt to remain in control. 'Then I could decide whether. . .'

Benoît laughed softly.

'You should have thought of that before, my lady,' he advised her.

It was too late to protest, and perhaps she didn't really want to. She lifted her face quite willingly to his, closing her eyes instinctively as his lips found hers. She'd believed that she was at least partially prepared for the experience, but she discovered almost instantly that she'd overestimated her new-found sophistication.

Last time he had kissed her they had been standing on a windswept beach and she had been dressed for the weather in a heavy cloth riding habit. This time she was wearing only a light muslin gown. She could feel every button on his waistcoat, every ridge of his clothes—and all the muscular strength in his body—in devastating intimacy.

She gasped, startled and a little disturbed, and pushed ineffectually against his shoulders. His hold on her relaxed slightly. He scattered gentle, feather-light kisses on her lips, her cheeks, and even her eyelids, until the tension ebbed from her body. Slowly, she began to feel more secure. Warm, billowing clouds of golden sunlight seemed to cocoon her in pleasure.

She slipped her arms around his neck, running her fingers through his crisp black hair in an unconsciously sensuous gesture. His lips became more insistent upon hers, tempting her with the promise of even greater delight to come if she allowed him the intimacy he demanded. She resisted briefly, half-afraid of what might happen if she capitulated. Then her lips parted beneath his and she surrendered completely to his kiss.

Instantly the spark of desire between them erupted into flames of scorching passion. The potent, surging energy within Benoît's whipcord body was matched by an ardent, unfettered response from Angelica which was quite beyond her power to control. Her zest for life found a natural outlet in the arms of a man who commanded both her respect and admiration.

She responded to him with an innocent, unselfconscious eagerness which startled, then enthralled him.

His hand slipped down her back, following the graceful curve of her spine, electrifying her senses with his seductive touch. She clung to him as he explored the voluptuous swell of her hip, before pressing her body closely against him.

She was standing thigh to thigh with him. She could feel his taut, powerful muscles against her softer flesh; and the hard, urgent desire in his body burned through her thin muslin dress. She was dimly aware that she was playing with very dangerous fire indeed, but she didn't have the strength to resist him.

He had burst into her confined, claustrophobic life like a whirlwind. Now she was riding on the back of the storm, exhilarated by the life-affirming passion they had unleashed between them.

He slid his hands up behind her shoulders and bent to kiss her throat, teasing her soft skin to even greater heights of sensitivity. She let her head fall back, leaning against his supportive hands as his lips left a fiery trail across her collar bone.

She was breathing in short, quick gasps, but her heart was drumming so loudly in her ears she couldn't hear the sound of her own excitement. She was consumed by conflicting sensations. Her legs felt too weak to support her, yet pulsating life scintillated through her body. She was full of glowing, warm languor—yet she was on fire with impatient anticipation.

Then Benoît straightened up, still holding her against, him, but in an enforcedly neutral embrace.

'My God!' he said hoarsely, his eyes dark with barely controlled passion. '*Ma douce séductrice!* You've come very close to completely unmanning me!'

Angelica felt the sudden rigid tension in his muscles and her eyes flew open in confused alarm. She fluttered in his arms, seeking reassurance more than escape. He was still fighting to contain his own fierce emotions, but he lifted his hand instantly to stroke her hair in a soothing gesture.

'Hush.' He held her against him. He was breathing very quickly. She was aware of his uncharacteristic lack of composure, but he still managed to sound wryly amused when he spoke. 'I promised I wouldn't hurt you, and I meant it. I just hadn't allowed for the effect of that passionate nature of yours.'

'Oh!' Angelica pushed herself away from him, taking refuge in indignation because she was too bewildered to know how else to react.

Her lips were bruised and swollen. Her skin still tingled from his kisses, and her body throbbed with the sensations his embrace had aroused within her.

She took a couple of irresolute steps, stumbling slightly because her legs no longer seemed to obey her wishes. She thought she would feel more in control if she put some distance between them, but away from the support of his arms she felt bereft and cold. She looked up at him, painful confusion in her lucid blue eyes.

He smiled crookedly, and reached out to stroke her cheek. She closed her eyes briefly at the sensations his gentle touch aroused within her.

'I think, perhaps, we have played this dangerous game long enough,' he said quietly. 'You will return to London tomorrow, my lady, and I've no wish for you to go back to your father hurt or distressed by what has happened to you here. It would be a poor reward for all I owe him, wouldn't it?'

Angelica stared at him, her blue eyes troubled and uncertain.

'I don't know what you mean,' she whispered.

'No?' He looked at her thoughtfully, an enigmatic gleam in his eyes. Apart from the unusual depth of colour in his tanned cheeks he seemed to be almost his normal, coolly controlled self—but Angelica could sense the ruthlessly suppressed energy in his lean body. 'Why aren't you married?' he asked suddenly.

'*What?*'

'You're twenty-three years old. Beautiful, desirable, a lady from the top of your golden curls to the soles of your elegant feet and—I suspect—something of an heiress to boot. So. . .why aren't you married, or at least betrothed?'

Angelica pressed her hands against her burning cheeks, suspecting at first he was mocking her, and then seeing from the steady expression in his eyes that he wasn't.

'I. . .Papa needs me,' she said with difficulty.

'He needs you now—he didn't need you two years ago,' Benoît reminded her. 'How long have you been out?'

'Since I was seventeen,' she replied, in a constricted voice.

'Five whole years for someone to catch your heart— or at least your interest,' he mused lightly, but there was an intent expression in his brown eyes. 'Didn't anyone light a spark within you?'

Angelica stared at him for a moment. Finally, after a desperate struggle, she succeeded in regaining some of her composure.

'I don't think that's any of your business,' she said steadily, managing to inject a cool note into her voice.

'Well, I'm not sure,' said Benoît slowly. He smiled suddenly. 'Even with my coaching, you're not very efficient at extracting information, are you?' he said provocatively. 'You should have demanded your fee long ago. I think I may invoke a time forfeit.'

Angelica blinked, momentarily confused.

'You were going to tell me how you're going to rescue Harry!' she exclaimed, remembering.

'Well, no,' he corrected her, a glint in his eye. 'I suggested you might find the experiment of kissing me worthwhile—but I didn't guarantee that I'd tell you about Harry.'

Angelica opened her mouth, drawing in a deep, indignant breath as she realised she'd been tricked.

'You devious, unscrupulous, ungentlemanly. . .' She glared at him with hot burning eyes, because she suddenly realised that what she felt was not indignant but hurt and betrayed. How could he have made such heartless use of her innocence?

Tears filled her eyes before she could stop them, glittering on her long eyelashes, and she turned away, humiliated that he should see her cry.

He was beside her in two long strides, gently turning her into the comforting circle of his arms.

'Don't!' She tried to push him away.

'Shush.' He stroked her hair gently, making no

demands upon her with his embrace. 'I didn't trick you that badly, *ma chérie*. And if you'd remembered to ask me, I wouldn't have teased you about it.'

Angelica knew she ought not to allow him to comfort her, but it was beyond her strength to push him away. His hands were soothing and his arms very protective. She had a brief, enticing vision of what it would be like if there was always someone there to turn to when she was hurt or afraid. It was a long time since she'd been able to turn to the Earl for support.

'That wasn't very gentlemanly of you,' she said at last, a catch in her voice, as she lifted her head to look at him.

'But I'm not a gentleman, *mignonne*,' he reminded her softly. 'We established that very early in our acquaintance.'

He paused; he was looking at Angelica, but there was a distant expression in his frowning eyes, and she could sense that he wasn't seeing her.

'My grandfather was a brickmaker who could neither read nor write,' he said abruptly, 'but he was determined his sons would do better in life than he had done, and he made enormous sacrifices to ensure that they did.'

He let Angelica go and went over to the globe, spinning it idly with his tanned, supple fingers.

'I don't think the old man ever travelled more than ten miles from his home in his life,' he said over his shoulder. 'He died soon after I went to sea.'

'He must have been very proud of you,' said Angelica almost hesitantly, recognising that she was being offered a rare insight into the making of Benoît Faulkener.

'He was proud of my father,' said Benoît. 'Yes, he was proud of me,' he added, as he saw her expression. 'But he didn't like it when we visited him, and he never consented to visit my parents in Arundel—less than twenty miles from his home. He said it wouldn't do to remind my father's patients that he was the son of a common brickmaker.'

Angelica bit her lip. She'd lived all her life in a privileged and sheltered world, taking for granted the advantages that had been bestowed on her. Now she was being confronted with an entirely different world, one which she'd only been dimly aware of until this moment. She realised that it must be hard for Benoît to speak so openly.

Benoît glanced at her, a sudden tension in his long limbs at her prolonged silence. What he saw in her face seemed to reassure him, and he added more lightly, 'Actually, I think the member of my family you'd find most interesting is Toby.'

'Toby?' The name sounded vaguely familiar but Angelica couldn't place it.

'My father's older brother,' Benoît explained. 'If it was Grandfather who had a dream of what his sons and grandson could achieve, it was Toby who ultimately made it possible. He learnt to read and write, and then got himself apprenticed to a blacksmith in Chichester. But he knew what was really needed to make the old man's dream come true was money. So he set about making some. It was Toby who paid for my father's training, his books and his instruments—and his first suit of clothes to impress his future patients. And it was Toby's inheritance which allowed me to buy my first ship. But he was still only a blacksmith in Chichester when he died.'

Angelica stared at him, her lips silently forming the word 'how', but she already knew and, even if she hadn't guessed, Benoît's wolfish smile would have informed her.

'He smuggled tea,' said Benoît, 'among other things. It was very profitable until they reduced the duty in the 1780s. We were running brandy the night I met your father. So you were right, my lady,' he concluded, a challenging glint in his eyes, 'this house is ultimately built on the profits of smuggling—or free trading, as Toby preferred to call it.'

Angelica gazed at him. She knew he wasn't ashamed of his antecedents; that, on the contrary, he was extremely proud af his determined and enterprising relatives. All the same, it couldn't have been easy to tell the tale and risk her possible ridicule. She was deeply impressed by both his moral courage in doing so, and his faith in her ability to understand.

'Why did you tell me this?' she said slowly.

He glanced at her, an intent, almost questioning look in his eyes, then shrugged dismissively.

'I cannot tell you how I will get Harry out of France, much less how I shall extricate him from Bitche,' he replied. 'Even if I knew, which at this point I don't, it wouldn't be wise. But I'd rather you didn't spend the next few weeks imagining me everything from a French spy to an extortionist. You may take this information as a—what did you call it this morning?— ah, yes, an earnest of my good faith.'

Angelica lowered her eyes, considerably shaken that he had remembered and finally responded to her angry demands. Then something occurred to her and she looked up, a spark kindling in her blue eyes.

'I don't believe I accused you of being a spy?' she protested indignantly.

'Bearing in mind what Sir William said to me this morning, and the vivid powers of your imagination— I'd be very surprised if that hadn't been among your suspicions,' Benoît retorted.

She saw the white gleam of his teeth as he grinned at her startled reaction, and surprisingly she felt reassured by his gentle mockery. It was hard to know exactly how she felt about Benoît Faulkener, but it was inexplicably comforting to know that, however quickly some aspects of their relationship changed, others remained the same.

'It was a perfectly reasonable concern on my part,' she said with dignity. 'And if you hadn't provoked Sir William into losing his temper, it would never have occurred to me!'

'Poor Sir William,' said Benoît appreciatively. 'It doesn't take much to enrage him. Do you know, he spent more than twenty years trying to get the better of Toby, but he never let his horses be shod by anyone else? He was very upset when Toby died.'

'You mean he liked him?' said Angelica wonderingly.

'They were, in a strange way, friends,' Benoît replied. 'Toby was a hard man, but he imposed a ruthless discipline on those who worked for him. For the twenty-five years or more he controlled the smuggling on this part of the coast there were none of the atrocities which have occurred in other parts of the county. The situation is far more unstable and unpredictable now that he's gone. There are several gangs vying with each other—' Benoît broke off, shrugging. 'Not that any of this is of interest to you,' he said briskly.

'It might be,' Angelica replied tentatively.

Benoît glanced at her sharply, then smiled faintly.

'No, it isn't,' he said firmly. 'Because none of this makes the slightest difference to Harry's rescue.'

'But if you no longer. . .' Angelica began.

Benoît laughed.

'My lady, you are so used to looking at the problem from Harry's point of view that you don't have a clear view of the picture,' he declared. 'It's true that Harry's main stumbling block was the Channel, but that's the least of *my* worries. I'm much more concerned about how I'm going to establish communications with him in the first place, and get him out of Bitche in the second.'

Angelica bit her lip. 'He's already done it once,' she said.

'Which will make it that much harder next time,' Benoît pointed out. 'Don't worry, my lady,' he added reassuringly, seeing her anxious expression. 'We will find a way.'

CHAPTER FIVE

ANGELICA was very quiet as she let Martha dress her for dinner. She'd had little time for reflection since her arrival at Holly House, yet so much had happened to her in the last twenty-four hours. Some of her most deeply held assumptions had been challenged. Even the familiar Martha had been revealed in a new and startling light. Did she feel frustrated by the limitations of her life as a lady's maid? Benoît had given Angelica so much to think about.

She touched her slender fingers briefly to her lips as she thought of how he'd kissed her. Her body stirred with the memory of his embrace, and the excitement he had aroused in her. He'd asked her if anyone had ever previously kindled a spark in her and she'd refused to answer—but she knew that, until today, they hadn't.

Five years ago she had gone out into society hoping to find someone to stir her heart, but every man she had ever met had been a pale, sickly shadow compared to the Earl. At first she had been disappointed, then resigned to the situation; and when the Earl had been hurt it had ceased to matter. He needed her, and depended on her, and she had done her best to be what he wanted her to be—if only she knew what that was.

But Benoît had changed everything. She wondered how easy it would be to go back to reading dusty books to her father, sharing the bitter limitations of the Earl's life since his accident, yet knowing there was so much more on the other side of the wall.

After tonight she might never see Benoît again!

This evening she would dine with him, tomorrow morning she would say a polite farewell to him, and that would be the end of her brief adventure.

She stared blindly at herself in the mirror, startled and rather dismayed by the powerful sense of loss which swept over her. She barely saw the huge, distressed blue eyes which gazed back at her out of a pale, troubled face. It was Benoît's eyes she saw, and Benoît's voice she could hear—teasing her, exasperating her, soothing her—and talking to her about things that mattered to him, confident that she was capable of understanding and responding to what he said.

Did he feel as sorry as she did that this brief interlude was nearly over? It hardly seemed likely. He had seen so much more of the world than she had—he must have known many women who interested or excited him. She felt an unexpected stab of an emotion which could almost have been jealousy and her hands clenched in her lap.

'Stand up, my lady, it's time you were dressed,' Martha interrupted her thoughts.

Angelica obeyed automatically, hardly aware of what she was doing, and allowed Martha to button her into a shimmering gown of pale ivory satin.

The long, softly gleaming skirt fell in a smooth, elegant line from just beneath her bosom to her feet, skimming discreetly past the curves of her waist and hips without entirely concealing them. The dress had a deep, square neckline which revealed the soft, creamy skin of her shoulders and throat, and a long train which whispered richly across the carpet whenever she moved.

Angelica frowned as she slowly became aware of what Martha was doing. For the first time she noticed that her maid had caught up her shining curls in a glittering diamond and sapphire comb, and that there were matching jewels in her ears.

'No!' she protested quickly, throwing up a hand and stepping back as she saw the pendant Martha was holding out. 'I can't go downstairs like this! It's a quiet dinner in the country—not a ball at Carlton House!'

'That's as may be,' said Martha quietly. 'But I think it's time he was reminded exactly who he's dealing with—and perhaps you need reminding too, my lady.'

Angelica stared at her maid for several long seconds, her skirts still caught up in one hand from when she'd stepped backwards so quickly, her other hand held almost protectively at her throat. She seemed vibrant with suppressed energy. The only colour about her came from the golden glow of her hair, the soft pink of her lips and cheeks, and the vivid blue of her eyes which was matched, but not overshadowed, by the sapphires in her hair and ears.

She didn't bother to ask who Martha meant by 'he' because she already knew. She stared at her maid, wondering how much Martha had guessed, and trying to read her thoughts in her expressionless face—but it was impossible.

'It that all you're going to say?' she asked at last.

'Yes, my lady.'

'I see.'

Angelica had been startled out of her preoccupation with Benoît more effectively by Martha's brief, elliptical comment than she would ever have been by the maid's more familiar grumbling. She glanced at the sapphire in Martha's hand and remembered her momentary jealousy at the thought of Benoît's other women.

Perhaps Martha was right. Perhaps it was time to remind Benoît he wasn't dealing with an unsophisticated country wench, but with the daughter of a noble and long-established family. She made no further objection as Martha fastened the pendant around her neck.

'I never told you to bring any of my jewels,' she observed, as the cool silver of the necklace caressed her warm skin, 'much less this dress. Why did you do it?'

'You never know when you might need to show your quality,' said Martha grimly, stepping back to look at her handiwork. 'Clothes are a useful reminder. And you can be sure I took care to hide your jewels from prying eyes.'

'You don't think there's much danger of me being robbed in this house then,' said Angelica, a half-smile on her lips.

But Martha might not have heard for all the notice she took of Angelica's remark. She studied her mistress intently, then nodded slightly, with evident reluctance.

'You'll do,' she said sourly.

Angelica hesitated as she approached the drawing-room door. Despite her earlier resolution she felt nervous and overdressed. She wondered if she'd made a crass and insulting mistake. There was nothing pretentious about the Faulkeners. In deference to their guest, Mrs Faulkener had had the fire lit in a larger room than the one she had occupied the previous evening, but it was still furnished very simply, with more regard for comfort than elegance.

Angelica was suddenly afraid that Mrs Faulkener would think she was showing off; and that Benoît would believe she was deliberately parading her consequence before him in direct response to what he had told her about his humble origins. That hadn't been her intention at all. She almost turned and fled back to her room, but it was too late. She turned the door handle and went into the room with as much nonchalance as she could muster.

She noticed, almost with relief, that Mrs Faulkener

was not yet present—then she gave all her attention to Benoît. He had risen politely at her entrance, but she saw a flicker of startled, warm appreciation in his eyes as they rested on her face. Her heart skipped a beat because surely that first, unguarded reaction to her appearance had been very revealing.

He recovered his composure quickly, looking her up and down with a coolly amused expression on his face. At last his gaze came to rest on the jewel around her neck, and his eyes narrowed almost imperceptibly.

'You are looking very magnificent tonight, my lady,' he said politely.

'It was Martha!' Angelica said breathlessly, hearing the cool note in his voice, and afraid that her fears had been well-founded. She lifted her hand instinctively to touch, and perhaps hide, the sapphire and diamonds at her throat.

'She insisted. . .' Her voice trailed off as she realised how impossible it was to explain what Martha had said. She looked at Benoît with luminous blue eyes which contained an unconscious appeal for understanding.

Benoît smiled, the warmth springing back into his brown eyes as he strolled towards her, moving with the controlled grace and latent power of the wolf he so frequently reminded her of.

'Martha is a formidable woman,' he said dryly. 'I must make sure I make her acquaintance before you leave, my lady. In the meantime, you may tell her that I have understood her message.'

'I don't understand,' Angelica said, in some confusion, although she was almost certain that she did.

How could she ever have been foolish enough to suppose Benoît would be too unsophisticated to comprehend the significance of her finery? She wondered briefly whether she truly understood it herself. Was

she trying to disconcert him with her magnificence—
or captivate him with her glamour?

Either way, she seemed to have met her match.

For the first time since she had known Benoît, he
was not dressed entirely in black. He wore a dark
blue, double-breasted tail coat which fitted his broad
shoulders admirably. A snowy white cravat fell in soft
folds beneath his chin, emphasising his dark tan, His
breeches were buckled just below his knees, and close-
fitting white stockings revealed his well-muscled
calves.

It was Angelica's turn to be surprised. She had
protested to Martha that she wasn't attending a ball in
Carlton House, but Benoît would certainly not have
been out of place in such a setting. He bent low to kiss
her hand with elegant assurance, and she could feel
the warm pressure of his fingers through her long
gloves. She looked down at his crisp black hair, feeling
strangely close to him, yet at the same time very
unsure of herself.

'Come and sit down,' he said. 'My mother will be
with us shortly, but she was delayed by a minor
domestic crisis. The cook's late brother—he was killed
last year in Portugal—turns out to have been a
bigamist.'

'What?' The force of Angelica's disbelieving exclamation owed much more to her chaotic feelings than
to what Benoît had just said, but at least he had
provided her with an excuse for her obvious confusion.

'Oh, it's quite true,' he assured her, grinning, as
he took the chair opposite hers. 'According to my
mother, the first bereaved widow arrived on the door-
step a couple of months ago, and the second one
came this afternoon. Apparently she gave quite a
dramatic performance—I'm almost sorry I missed it.'

'You're not serious?' Angelica didn't know whether
to be appalled or entertained at what he'd said.

'That she came—or that I'm sorry I missed the show?' Benoît enquired, a wicked gleam in his brown eyes. 'You're right, I doubt very much whether I would have found it as rewarding as a day spent in your company.'

Angelica blushed and turned her face away, uncertain how to respond to him. His directness always disconcerted her, and it was almost a relief when Mrs Faulkener came quietly into the room.

Dinner was an exquisite torment for Angelica. It was the first time she had ever spoken to Benoît in company, and she was acutely conscious of Mrs Faulkener's observant eyes as she tried to maintain a flow of light-hearted conversation.

But the Faulkeners were very easy and entertaining companions. Mother and son shared a similar sense of humour, and they had a relaxed respect for each other which impressed Angelica. She wondered if Benoît would show equal respect to his wife. Then she blushed and suppressed the fugitive thought as quickly and guiltily as if Benoît could read her mind. It was hardly any concern of hers how he treated his wife.

At last the two women left Benoît to enjoy his port alone and retired to the drawing room.

'You have been so kind to me,' said Angelica warmly. 'I cannot tell you how much I appreciate your hospitality. I feel so guilty for imposing on you a second night.'

Mrs Faulkener smiled as she sat down opposite Angelica.

'On the contrary,' she replied cordially, 'I am grateful for your company, my lady. We don't often have visitors. I'm only sorry that you must leave so soon.'

'Thank you,' said Angelica, uncomfortably aware that she had been so preoccupied with Benoît that she had spared very little thought for her hostess.

It would hardly be surprising if Mrs Faulkener did feel lonely, living in such an isolated spot and with Benoît away so often. Angelica resolved to be a more entertaining guest for the limited time she had left. She felt vaguely that it was important Mrs Faulkener should like her, although she didn't analyse why.

'Perhaps, in the summer, you could persuade your father to visit Sir William,' Mrs Faulkener suggested. 'It's a long time since the Earl came to Sussex, and I'm sure Sir William would appreciate it.'

'I will certainly try,' Angelica agreed, snatching at the idea eagerly. 'It would be such a relief! He hasn't left the house for months. . .' Her voice trailed away as she realised how close she was to openly criticising her father.

'It must be very painful for him,' said Mrs Faulkener quietly. 'And for you. It is hard to live in the shadow of someone else's unhappiness—particularly when you love them.'

Angelica looked down at her hands gripped together in her lap, seeing them through suddenly misty eyes. She was afraid if she spoke her voice would reveal how close she was to tears, so she didn't say anything, and in a moment Mrs Faulkener began to tell the story of the cook's bigamous brother.

When Benoît joined them, a few minutes later, Angelica had her feelings well under control. Even so, the sight of him after his brief absence caused her heart to leap into her throat and left her temporarily bereft of words. She couldn't believe she was acting so foolishly; anyone would think she was still in the schoolroom! Yet she had been mistress of her father's household for several years.

Her thoughts were interrupted by the maid who came into the room, looking a little flustered, and delivered a letter to Benoît.

'Thank you, Tilly.' He took it and broke open the

seal, reading it quickly. A frown creased his forehead as he nodded his dismissal to the maid.

'There'll be no reply,' he said curtly, standing up.

'What is it, Benoît?' Mrs Faulkener asked calmly.

He glanced at his mother and smiled, his expression clearing as he did so.

'Nothing serious,' he said lightly. 'It's from Sir William. He thinks he's caught a smuggler, but the man is claiming his innocence and says I can provide him with an alibi. It could wait till morning, but you know how excitable Sir William gets. It's probably best if I don't keep him waiting.'

Mrs Faulkener nodded, although there was a flash of annoyance in her eyes.

'Sir William is a good man,' she said with some asperity, 'but I wish he wasn't so prone to turn other people's lives upside down in his quest for the truth!'

Benoît laughed and turned to Angelica with a hint of apology in his eyes.

'I'm sorry, my lady,' he said sincerely. 'I hate to abandon you like this, but I will see you before you leave in the morning; and I will certainly keep my promise to the Earl.'

Angelica stood up instinctively, her hands gripped together anxiously.

'Do you know the man? Can you provide him with an alibi?' she asked, more bluntly than she'd intended.

She was remembering Benoît's absence the previous night, and wondering whether Sir William's letter had made more dangerous accusations than Benoît had chosen to reveal. She was suddenly frightened for him, although that was ridiculous. It was impossible to imagine that Benoît wasn't equal to any threat Sir William might pose to his security.

Benoît smiled as he took her hand, squeezing it reassuringly as he bowed with his customary grace.

'I certainly know the man,' he said easily. 'And it

doesn't sound as if Sir William has much in the way of evidence. I think he's just so exasperated that he's trying to frighten the poor fellow. It shouldn't be difficult to sort out. Good evening, my lady.'

Angelica watched him leave the room with an anxious expression in her eyes. For a moment she had completely forgotten Mrs Faulkener's presence.

'Don't worry, my lady,' said the Frenchwoman cheerfully. 'Whatever may have happened, Sir William is no match for my son. I'm sure everything will be all right—but I'm sorry he has broken up our evening!'

'It is a pity.' Angelica sat down again, reassured by Mrs Faulkener's unquestioning confidence in Benoît.

But now that he had gone she felt deflated and at a loss. The evening which had offered so much promise seemed to stretch emptily before her, and the weariness which she had falsely claimed that morning finally caught up with her.

It was months since she had been riding and her muscles were stiff and sore from the unaccustomed exercise. Until that moment she hadn't even been aware of her tiredness, but now all she wanted to do was lie down on her bed and sleep.

'My lady?' said Mrs Faulkener enquiringly.

'I'm sorry.' Angelica roused herself to smile at her hostess. 'I haven't been riding for so long—I suddenly feel very tired. Perhaps I ought to have another cup of tea.'

'Perhaps you ought to go to bed,' Mrs Faulkener suggested gently. 'I hate to remind you, but tomorrow you'll have to spend several hours in the coach.'

A flicker of reluctance crossed Angelica's face, partly because the idea of being jolted around in the carriage was unpleasant, but mainly because she didn't like the idea of leaving.

Although it hadn't occurred to her, her response to Mrs Faulkener's remark was giving credence to the hasty excuse she had made to Benoît that morning for staying another day at Holly House.

Her father's accident had never made her fearful of travelling, but Mrs Faulkener didn't know that. The Frenchwoman had a very clear memory of how strained and anxious Angelica had been when she first arrived. She found it easy to believe that Angelica was reluctant to travel more than fifty miles over bad, winter roads on her own.

'My lady, when Benoît returns, I will ask him if he'll take you back to London himself,' said Mrs Faulkener suddenly.

'What?' Angelica exclaimed, looking up in astonishment.

'He will be able to speak to the Earl in person, and you need have no fear that an accident might occur while he is with you,' Mrs Faulkener continued, warming to her theme.

'Oh, but. . .' Angelica began to demure, then hesitated.

There was no reason why Benoît shouldn't come to London to speak to her father. She wondered why the idea hadn't occurred to her before—and why Benoît hadn't suggested it himself. Surely it would be the natural thing for him to do?

'Good!' said Mrs Faulkener briskly, taking Angelica's consent for granted. 'I'm sure you will sleep much better tonight, my lady, now that's decided— and so shall I. I didn't like the idea of you travelling so far alone—even though I know you've got your maid and your coachman with you. But Benoît will take good care of you.'

She stood up, and Angelica followed suit.

'Good night, my lady,' said Mrs Faulkener. 'Now I really must go and talk to the cook. She was terribly upset this afternoon. She burnt the soup twice!'

* * *

Angelica began to walk slowly upstairs. Some of her tiredness had vanished, although she was trying not to admit to herself how much she owed her improved spirits to Mrs Faulkener's suggestion. If Benoît came to London. . .

She heard a quick, light tread on the stairs above her and looked up to see him coming down towards her, two steps at a time. Her heart gave a great bound in her breast and she caught her breath.

'I thought you'd gone,' she said foolishly, hoping against hope that he didn't know how powerfully his unexpected appearance had affected her.

He grinned.

'I'm on my way,' he said. 'But I think even Sir William at his most impatient would understand my reluctance to ride around the countryside in full evening dress!'

'Yes, of course!' Angelica exclaimed, wondering why she hadn't thought of that for herself.

Benoît was once again dressed in the familiar black riding coat and breeches which he had worn at their first meeting.

She hesitated, looking up at him as she wondered whether to mention his mother's idea to him.

'What is it, my lady?' he asked.

'Nothing.' The suggestion would sound better coming from Mrs Faulkener. 'I hope you're able to placate Sir William,' she said.

'Have no fear of that.' He touched her cheek lightly, and then, almost as if it was against his better judgement, he bent his head and kissed her quickly on the lips.

She half lifted her hand towards him, but he was already stepping back.

'Good night, Angelica,' he said softly. 'Sleep well.'

She turned and watched him run lightly down the

rest of the stairs, her hand pressed against her tingling lips, wishing she knew what was in his mind.

Then a look of puzzlement stole into her eyes. There had been something different about him. He'd been dressed in black as before, but something. . .if only she could think what. . .something had been—

He'd been wearing a black cravat!

In fact, he'd been dressed entirely in black, without even the white shirt frills at his cuffs to relieve the sombre impression.

Angelica's eyes narrowed as she remembered her earlier suspicions about why he chose to wear black—and her idle curiosity as to how he might conceal his white cravat when he was trying to avoid detection.

Now she knew. And surely he wouldn't dress in such a funereal fashion just to visit Sir William?

She stood stock-still for several seconds, then picked up her skirts and ran pell-mell upstairs. She burst into her room and tugged energetically on the bell pull, before struggling to extricate herself as quickly as she could from the formal satin gown. The tiny buttons resisted her attempts at speed and she pulled impatiently at the fastenings, hearing the fabric tear beneath her hands.

'My lady, what is it?' Martha arrived breathlessly. 'Are you ill?'

'Get me out of this dress,' Angelica said urgently. 'Hurry.'

'Why?'

'Don't argue, just do it!'

Martha did as she was bid, her lips pressed together in a thin, anxious line.

'Where's the riding habit?' Angelica spun around. 'Good.'

She almost snatched it from Martha in her impatience.

'Where are you going?' Martha demanded.

'I don't know,' Angelica replied briefly.

She seized up a dark shawl and wrapped it around her head, covering the bright golden curls.

'Come with me,' she said imperatively to Martha. 'I might need you to distract the groom.' A brief, reckless smile lit up her face. 'I understand you're good at it,' she added.

They ran downstairs, Angelica in the lead, cautious in her haste, but there was no one in sight. Mrs Faulkener was presumably consoling the cook in the kitchen, and Benoît had already left. They let themselves quietly out of the front door and hurried round to the stables, careful to keep in the shadows.

'What—?' Martha began.

'Shush!' Angelica silenced her quickly.

She flattened herself against the wall of the house, hardly daring to breath as she heard hooves striking on the cobblestones. Benoît exchanged a couple of words with his groom, and then she saw him ride past, less than twenty feet away, his dark shape silhouetted against the paler night sky. He was riding one horse and leading another, and Angelica was sure her instinctive suspicions had been correct. There might be a perfectly innocent explanation for why he should need to take a spare horse to Sir William, but she couldn't think of one.

'Come on!' she whispered to Martha.

'What's going on?' Martha whispered back.

'I don't know, but I'm going to find out!' Angelica declared in a low voice. 'You keep Thomas occupied while I saddle the mare!'

'*My lady!*' Martha's protest was no less vehement for being uttered in a tone that wouldn't have been audible from two feet away.

'Are you telling me you can't do it?' Angelica challenged her.

'Of course I can, but...' Martha realised she was

voicing her protests to empty air and abandoned her attempt to make Angelica see reason.

'Wait here,' she said as she caught up with her mistress.

'You'll have to get the saddle out of the tackroom while I distract Thomas. Be careful how you lead the mare over the cobbles or he'll hear her.'

Angelica huddled in the shadows and watched as her maid sauntered out into the stableyard. There was something subtly different about Martha, she even moved differently from the grim, sour-faced woman Angelica was so familiar with.

Even in the grip of the urgent excitement which filled her, Angelica was reminded of how much she had taken for granted before she came to Sussex. The world around her was changing shape before her eyes. Was that Benoît's influence?

'Good evening, Thomas,' said Martha.

'Miss Farley!' The groom turned as she spoke to him, unmistakable pleasure in his voice. 'Doesn't her ladyship need you?'

'She's asleep in bed,' Martha replied, a hint of laughter in her voice. 'She hasn't been riding for nearly a year—the exercise fairly tired her out.'

'I'd never have known. She looks good in the saddle,' said Thomas appreciatively.

'She should—the Earl spent hours teaching her,' said Martha indulgently.

She was standing very close to Thomas, and Angelica was sure she heard the groom's quick intake of breath as he looked down at her.

'I'd like to see *you* in the saddle,' said Thomas hoarsely. 'Are you really leaving tomorrow?'

'I'm afraid so,' said Martha regretfully. 'Unless I can think of a way to persuade her ladyship to stay. Do you have any suggestions?' She smiled up at Thomas,

moving slightly so that to look at her he had to turn
his back on Angelica.

Angelica stared at Martha in disbelief for a moment.
Then she collected her wits and darted silently behind
Thomas.

The tackroom was lit by a single lantern and
Angelica spotted the lady's saddle immediately. She
found a bridle, lifted the saddle down, careful not to
let the tack jingle together, and slipped out of the
tackroom and into the stables.

By the time she found the mare her arms were tense
with the strain of carrying the saddle in complete
silence. She'd had no choice but to allow her skirts to
drag on the ground. Fortunately, Thomas had hung a
lantern on a hook when he'd saddled the horses for
Benoît, and there was enough light for Angelica to see
what she was doing.

She heard voices outside, and knew that Martha had
led her eager suitor into the tackroom. She hoped he
wouldn't notice the missing saddle, then decided he
was too entranced by Martha to notice anything else.

She spoke softly to Dorcas and slipped the bridle
neatly over her head. It occurred to her briefly, and
incongruously, that she had less trouble dressing the
mare than she did herself.

As a child, she had spent far more time in the
stables than her mother had thought suitable, and she
had been fascinated by all aspects of horsemanship.
Now she was grateful for that early training. She
saddled the mare as quickly as she could and led her
out of the stables. Dorcas's hooves seemed to ring
loudly on the cobblestones and Angelica's heart leapt
in her mouth at the possibility that someone might
surprise her—but the tackroom door remained firmly
closed.

She paused by the mounting block and clambered
into the saddle, hoping she had tightened the girths

sufficiently to hold it firmly in place. The mare tossed her head, but made no other protest to the eccentric behaviour of her rider, and Angelica followed in the direction she had seen Benoît take.

He'd had several minutes' head start over her, but he hadn't been hurrying, and she was almost certain he was going towards the sea. Where else *could* he be going? She had a good sense of direction, and it wasn't too difficult for her to retrace their steps of that morning, but she was anxious in case she missed him — or overtook him unexpectedly.

She tied the shawl firmly under her chin and looked around at the dark, shadowy landscape. In this flat country surely she ought to be able to see him in the distance — but she might have been alone beneath the lofty stars.

It was very cold. The wind which had seemed almost invigorating that morning was now icy and hostile, cutting through her riding habit and chilling her bones. It sliced through the dank, winter grass beneath the mare's hooves and snatched Angelica's breath from her mouth.

She began to wonder if she was crazy. How could she hope to find Benoît in strange country in the middle of the night when, in truth, she had no idea where he was going? She only assumed he was heading towards the sea. And if she did find him, what was she going to do? Spy on him? Why?

She had acted without thinking, her pent-up and confused emotions finding release in a flurry of furious activity. At best she had made herself look foolish; at worst she might seriously jeopardise her friendship with Benoît — but she was desperately curious to know more about him.

Was he smuggling? Or was he involved in something else? She looked around at the dark, shadowy landscape.

Her eyes were unable to pierce the gloom for more than a few yards, and she suddenly felt afraid.

She remembered their talk of a French invasion earlier that day—and all the stories Sir William had told of smugglers terrorising or murdering people who had inadvertently surprised them at their work. Her heart began to beat faster as she realised she might have done a great deal more than simply make herself look foolish with this impulsive escapade.

She almost turned the mare for home then and there, but a tiny core of stubbornness within her refused to give up.

She rode on cautiously, glancing nervously around at the shadows. The sound of the mare's hooves suddenly seemed very loud, and she was uncomfortably conscious of how conspicuous she was perched on top of a tall horse in such flat countryside.

She had been a fool. It was time to turn back and hope no one would ever be the wiser—

Suddenly a dark shape loomed out of a nearby thicket, and a man lunged towards her.

Shocked, icy fear clutched at Angelica's stomach. Images of smugglers and wild-eyed French invaders filled her mind. She dragged on the reins, putting her heel to the mare's side in an unthinking, desperate attempt to get away—but the man seized the bridle and Dorcas submitted to his low-voiced command.

Angelica clung to the saddle like a panic-stricken limpet. Terrified thoughts of rape and murder drove every other consideration from her mind. She was determined not to let him haul her down. As long as she remained on Dorcas's back she should be able to get away—*if only he'd let go of the bridle!*

She slashed fiercely at her assailant with her riding crop, her actions made vicious by desperation. The mare snorted and tried to shy away—Angelica was jolted and bruised against the saddle pommel. The man moved fast in the darkness. She could hardly see him, and she'd had no warning of his intentions when he grabbed the crop and wrenched it out of her hand. Pain speared up her arm, startling her into an unwary cry of distress. Panic threatened to overwhelm her as she realised she was now almost defenceless.

'Angelica! Get down!' Benoît commanded in a furious undertone, barely controlled anger throbbing in his words.

She gasped in sobbing relief as his voice penetrated her terror and slid down into his arms, her legs all but giving way as her feet touched the ground. He half lifted, half dragged her into the shadows of the thicket, leading Dorcas with them. The other two horses were already there, standing like statues, though Angelica was in no condition to notice that fact.

'Quiet!' he whispered urgently in her ear.

He was holding her tightly from behind, one arm locked around her waist. As she drew breath to speak he clamped his other hand over her mouth. She was already thoroughly alarmed and now she experienced an irrational fear that he was going to suffocate her. Her heart hammered with fright. She'd known he was strong, but his strength had never been used against her before, and she was terrifyingly aware of how helpless she was in his arms. She struggled desperately, trying to kick back at his shin, but her long skirts impeded her.

'Quiet!' he commanded again, in the same imperative undertone, but his hold on her relaxed slightly, and Angelica's panic began to subside.

She became aware of the silence of the horses, and the tense expectancy in Benoît's body. Then she heard the muffled sound of hooves and realised that a sunken lane passed by on the other side of the thicket.

Benoît lifted her slightly in his arms and turned so that he could look in the direction from which the sounds were coming. Hidden in the shadows, staring out at an oblique angle towards the lane, Angelica could just see the dim silhouettes of ponies and men pass by.

There were more than fifty men in the gang, some of them carrying staves across their shoulders. They marched through the dark night in confident silence, as if they had an inalienable right to do so. Angelica knew that if they were surprised by Sir William they would fight; at least one of the magistrate's men had been seriously injured in a battle against smugglers—and another had been killed.

She closed her eyes, chill with horror as she realised that, if Benoît hadn't intercepted her, she would have ridden straight across the smugglers' path. What would they have done to her?

'What the hell are you doing here?' Benoît demanded furiously, when there was no longer any danger of them being overheard.

'I... You were wearing a black cravat,' said Angelica lamely, in a small voice.

She was still badly shaken by the realisation of how stupid she had been and in no condition to deal with his fury.

'For God's sake!' he exploded, his anger no less potent because it was so quiet and so controlled. 'What the devil did you think you were going to achieve? Do you know what might have happened to you if I hadn't been here? That gang has at least two murders to its credit already!'

Angelica bit her lip, tears filling her eyes. It was hard to defend herself because she knew she was in the wrong, but it was equally hard to apologise when he was so angry with her. The situation was made even worse because she couldn't see his face—all she could feel was his rigid, furious grip on his arm.

'I can take care of myself,' she declared, trying to put a spark of spirit into her voice and dismally failing.

'Not out here,' said Benoît categorically. 'What the hell am I going to do with you?'

'I was right, you aren't visiting Sir William, are you?' Angelica accused him, instinctively deciding attack was the best form of defence. 'You have no business scolding others when you make such a habit of lying yourself!'

'You little vixen!' said Benoît tautly. 'That's the last pert answer I'm prepared to take from you—lady or not! If you're going to trail around the countryside after me like a bitch in heat, then it's time you learnt to take the consequences!'

'How *dare* you?' Angelica struck out blindly at him, infuriated and bitterly insulted by his words.

She landed a glancing blow on the side of his face, then he dragged her into his arms. She struggled, pummelling at his chest and shoulders, and his hold on her tightened until she could barely move. She couldn't see his face, and she felt trapped by the black shadows of the thicket and the unyielding force of his arms.

'Let me go!' she commanded in a low, throbbing voice.

'No.'

She tried to wrench herself out of his arms, but it was impossible. She tried to kick him, but her long skirts and his well-made leather boots protected him from any harm.

'*Let me go!* You have no right—'

'Haven't I?' he interrupted harshly. 'It's too late to play the part of an aloof noblewoman, Angelica. I've made allowances for your innocence and your loneliness. But if you want to be treated like a lady, then you shouldn't act like a trollop following an army!'

'I didn't. . .!' she gasped, more shocked and hurt by his words than offended.

'For God's sake!' he ground out. 'Is this what you came looking for? Because if it is—by God you can have it!'

She caught her breath in protest as his lips found hers with ruthless efficiency in the darkness. Her arms were still trapped against his chest. He was holding her so tightly that she couldn't move and she could barely breathe. Shadows encircled them and the wind tugged at their clothes. His kiss was rough and almost punishing and offered her no escape. She struggled to resist him, appalled at the overwhelming surge of passion and anger she had unwittingly aroused in him.

She could feel the rigid tension in his body. She was dimly aware that his fury had very little to do with the fact that she had been trying to spy on him—or even that she'd accused him of lying to her.

Then, somehow, the nature of his kiss seemed to change. From being fierce and unforgiving on hers, his lips become warm and passionate. He was still holding her in a hard embrace, but one hand slipped up to cup the back of her head, and she felt her heightened, aroused senses begin to respond to him.

His lips were demanding as he claimed her open mouth, but he was no longer trying to punish her, and she felt a familiar, insistent tempo begin to pulse through her body. She clutched at the lapels of his coat, no longer struggling in his embrace.

Then he let her go—so suddenly that she stumbled back and fell, landing in a heap on the wet grass.

She drew in a gasping breath and dragged a shaking hand over her mouth, more confused than ever by his unexpected action. He was standing over her, and she looked up at him, sensing rather than seeing his presence in the darkness. She could hear his rapid breathing, but she was almost beyond coherent thought or feeling.

At last he crouched down beside her. She felt his hand near her face and flinched away, unsure of what he intended.

'Ne vous inquiétez pas,' he murmured reassuringly, and his touch was gentle on her cheek. 'I'm sorry, *mon ange*. I was angry, but I didn't mean to hurt you.'

'I. . .' Angelica began, but she couldn't continue; she simply didn't know what to say.

'Get up.' Benoît gripped her arms and lifted her to his feet. 'You mustn't sit on the grass,' he said, wry amusement in his voice. 'You're going to be cold enough before this night is over without being wet through as well.'

'Why?' Angelica asked vaguely.

She was less interested in the implication of his words, than she was in what had just happened between them. How could he be so furious one minute and so gentle the next? Then she remembered what he'd said about her acting like a bitch in heat—or an army trollop—and her whole body burned with embarrassment and distress. Was that how he thought of her?

'I can't send you back on your own,' said Benoît reasonably, apparently unaware of her inner turmoil.

'Not with both the Gentlemen out and Sir William and his men no doubt playing their dangerous game of hide and seek. And I don't have time to take you home myself—you'll just have to stay with me.'

'No. I meant why did you. . .?' she began uncertainly.

'There isn't time,' he replied, briskly but not unkindly. 'Not now. I'm already running late. And with so many others apparently heading for the same beaches things may turn out to be more complicated that I'd anticipated. Dammit! Perhaps I ought to send you back. Dorcas knows her way home—'

'No!' Angelica protested instinctively. 'Please. . .'

'All right. Come on.' He made up his mind quickly and threw her up into the saddle almost before she was ready.

She fumbled for the reins as he mounted his own horse.

'Pull your shawl back over your head,' he said quietly. 'At least you had the sense to hide your hair,' he added with mild amusement. 'You might turn into a useful companion-at-arms yet!'

CHAPTER SIX

THEY arrived at the beach not far from the place Benoît had brought Angelica to that morning—although he avoided the lane they had used before.

He travelled quickly but cautiously, and Angelica was aware that he was alert for the slightest unusual or potentially threatening disturbance. She didn't try to talk to him. She kept Dorcas close by his side, determined not to do anything more to anger him. She desperately wanted time to think about what had happened in the shadows of the thicket, but at the moment it was better not to let her attention be distracted.

The open fields ran almost down to the beach. Only a line of trees at right angles to the sea offered any shelter. Benoît paused in the lee of the trees, where the dense confusion of brambles provided some shelter from both the wind and prying eyes, and swung down from his saddle. Angelica hesitated, then dropped down to join him. He'd soon put her back on the mare if that's where he wanted her.

The wind had momentarily dropped, but Angelica could hear the sea, crashing on the sands not far away. The tide was in, just as it had been nearly twelve hours ago when she had first come to the beach. She could feel the damp air on her cheeks and taste the salt on her lips, but her vision was limited by the lack of moonlight. Only the cold, pale stars twinkled in the distant heavens. She wondered if this was how it had been for her father, when he'd tracked and found Benoît so many years ago. She was suddenly glad she had come.

'Stand here,' said Benoît briefly, moving her into position with firm but not unkind hands. 'And don't let your skirts blow in my face.'

She did as she was told, although it was only when she heard steel striking against flint that she realised he was using her body as a shield. The light flickered so briefly she doubted if even someone watching for it would have noticed it, and then he covered it and stood up.

'What is that thing?' she asked softly, indicating the strange object he was holding.

She'd barely had time to see it, but she already had her suspicions about its use—Sir William had told her of such things.

It was made of two tubes of metal. A short, rather stubby vertical tube with a conical lid, and a longer, tapering pipe, which extended at right angles from the side of the first tube and which could be covered and uncovered at will.

'Spout lantern,' said Benoît shortly. 'Stay here.'

She heard his boots on the pebbles, then she saw his dim outline against the paler sea as he stood on the beach. She guessed he was signalling, but the spout lantern meant that the only light visible was directed out towards any waiting boats. No wonder smugglers used them. The penalties for being caught signalling out to sea were severe—and even innocently lighting a pipe on the beach could get a man into trouble if the wrong people saw him.

She waited, shivering and hugging her shawl tightly around her head and shoulders. The wind had picked up again and it tugged viciously at her skirts.

She could hear the roar of the sea, much rougher tonight than it had been during the day. Nothing happened for a long time, and she huddled against the mare's shoulder for warmth and comfort.

She couldn't believe where she was or what was

happening to her. Nothing in her previous experience or wildest imaginings had ever prepared her for the events of this evening. She didn't know which was more unbelievable—the fact that less than an hour ago she'd seen a band of armed smugglers march within a few feet of her—or the strange and unprecedentedly intimate relationship she was developing with Benoît.

No one else had ever had such a profound effect on her behaviour, or so completely disturbed her peace of mind. She should be sleeping quietly in her bed now, not avoiding smugglers and riding officers on a black, windswept beach. What had he done to her that she could so unthinkingly abandon all modesty and decorum to follow him to an unknown destination?

She looked towards Benoît, and then beyond him, straining to pierce through the murky night and see what lay ahead for them. The stars above began to dance and blur before her overtaxed eyes; the shadows grew even darker and took on strange and alien shapes. She was no longer sure what was real and what was imagined. She gripped the comforting leather of the saddle, grateful for Dorcas's placid and solid presence. She had no intention of letting Benoit discover how nervous this long wait was making her.

Then she blinked, and lifted her head, hardly able to credit that she'd just seen the signal. The light flickered again, and then the sea was dark once more.

Angelica left the horses and the shelter of the trees and stumbled down over the shingle to join Benoît. He turned sharply at the sound of her approach.

'It's me,' she said softly, and sensed rather than saw his relaxation of tension. 'Are they coming?'

'Assuming we haven't confused our signals,' said Benoît dryly. 'I'd hate to find we were the unintended recipients of several hundred tubs of brandy meant for the Gentlemen we saw earlier!'

'I know we're not smuggling,' said Angelica, shivering at the possibility he'd just raised, and wondering where the men they'd seen earlier had gone. 'But what are we doing here?'

'You astonish me, my lady,' said Benoît, and she heard the gentle mockery in his voice. 'When I've done nothing more questionable than offer you a glass of brandy you accuse me of smuggling, and when I'm standing on a moonless beach sending signals to an unidentified vessel you acquit me of the crime! Here!'

In the darkness, she realised he had shrugged himself out of his greatcoat, and was holding it around her shoulders. She slipped her arms gratefully into the sleeves and hugged it tightly about herself.

'I'd say I'm sorry you're cold,' he said softly in her ear, his arms enfolding her from behind. 'But you shouldn't be here in the first place. How am I going to explain this to your father?'

'You won't have to explain anything,' Angelica protested, not sure what he meant.

The warmth of his body against her back was unbelievably comforting, and the soft caress of his breath against her ear sent a delicious tingle rippling down her spine. It was incredible that only a short while ago he had been rigid with fury at her.

'Papa won't know I followed you,' she murmured breathlessly as Benoît's lips brushed her cheek, devoutly hoping that she spoke the truth. 'All he wants you to do is rescue Harry,' she added rather incoherently.

'But what about you, my lady?' Benoît said softly, pushing her shawl back from her face.

'I want you to rescue Harry too!' she whispered, trying to maintain at least the pretence that they were having a normal conversation.

'I know.' Benoît began to explore the warm, delicate skin of her neck with soft, intimate kisses.

She gasped, and quivered responsively as glowing rivulets of pleasure radiated out from beneath his lips. Her eyes were open, but in the dark, lofty night there was nothing to see; she could only feel his arms around her, and hear his low voice reverberating through her body as he spoke to her, his mouth almost touching her skin.

'Is that all you want from me, *ma douce amie*?' he teased her, reaching across the front of her body to cover one of her hands with his as she clutched at his greatcoat.

'Of. . .course.'

She was still locked in his arms, the heat of his body burning through her back, his lips wrecking devastating delight beneath her ear. She was even beginning to forget why they were standing on the beach.

'Liar!' he murmured provocatively, biting gently at her earlobe. 'Besides, I might feel compelled to tell the Earl about this escapade myself.'

'What?'

She gasped with horror and tried to turn in his arms, but he prevented her quite easily. Fortunately she'd been too breathless to exclaim loudly, but it didn't stop him from admonishing her for her indiscretion.

'Shush!' he murmured infuriatingly, the familiar note of laughter audible in his low voice as he settled her comfortably in his embrace once again. 'Remember where we are! Besides, why not tell your father?' He returned to his thrilling explorations of her earlobe, his tongue running gently over the sapphire earring she had been in too much of a hurry to take off. 'Lord Ellewood might have some practical suggestions to offer about not wearing jewellery when tracking potential smugglers!'

Angelica drew in an indignant breath, but before she could speak Benoît lifted his head alertly.

'The boat's coming,' he said quietly, releasing her from his arms.

She looked out to sea. She couldn't hear anything beyond the familiar crashing of the waves, but she had no doubt Benoît was right.

'Go back to the horses,' he ordered, and went down to the tideline.

She started to walk up the beach, looking back over her shoulder, still not sure what to expect from the approaching boat. It was clear that Benoît was meeting someone, presumably one man who would ride the spare horse he had brought. But she still didn't know who the man was, although she was beginning to guess *what* he was.

She was still glowing from Benoît's embrace. The cold wind didn't seem so bitter any more. She smiled wryly. Twenty-four hours ago she would never have believed that she could care so little about whether Benoît was involved with a spy. But now she was far more concerned with how he felt about her, and how she felt about him. The man in the boat was just an unwelcome interruption to their conversation.

She hugged the greatcoat. She was much warmer than she had been. She reached the edge of the shingle and turned to look back at the sea. She could just hear the slap of oars on the water, and see the dark shadow of Benoît as he spoke to the men in the boat.

Then, somewhere to her right, she heard a man shout out. His harsh voice ripped through the peaceful, empty night—alien and frightening. His cry was followed by a pistol shot, raised voices and more shots.

Angelica jerked round in stunned amazement, staring blindly into the dark night. The noise was coming from further west. She blinked as she saw the brief flash as a pistol was fired. Her heart was racing in disbelief and alarm. She had almost forgotten the men they'd seen earlier, but now the danger from the smugglers had been made sickeningly real. A full-scale battle was taking place between Sir William and the smugglers only a few hundred yards down the beach!

'Angelica!'

She'd been momentarily frozen with horror, but at the sound of Benoît's voice she snatched up her skirts and ran towards him.

As she did so, she was vaguely aware of someone whistling—then Benoît seized her around the waist and dumped her without ceremony in the boat.

Another man, no more than a faceless shadow to Angelica, helped Benoît push the boat into deeper water, then they were rowing out into the black void of the Channel.

The boat rocked and pitched on the windswept waves. Angelica was quickly soaked with seaspray, and half-deafened by the thudding of her heart and the crashing of the water around her. Her skirt was already sodden from where it had trailed in the sea as Benoît lifted her into the boat. Four men manned the oars, with another at the tiller, and she huddled as small as she could, trying not to get in their way.

She had been terrified when she'd first encountered Benoît, but now that real danger threatened she felt more excited than afraid. She had no idea what would happen next, or where they were going—but she was with Benoît. She knew he would take care of her.

She could hear low voices as Benoît talked to the other passenger in the boat, but she couldn't distinguish what they were saying. This was the man they'd come to meet. She wondered who he was, but instinct rather than the evidence of her senses told her that he was hurt and in pain.

The black bulk of the cutter loomed suddenly above them. Benoît gripped her arm.

'We're going on board,' he said quietly. 'Take off

my coat, it'll get in the way. And take care as you
climb up, there's no hurry now.'

'I'll be all right.' She stood up, swaying as the boat
pitched, grateful for his steadying hands on her waist.

She slipped out of the greatcoat, then picked up the
front of her heavy woollen skirts and held them
clenched between her teeth. The creak of the wet wool
in her mouth made her want to gag, but she knew it
was safer than trying to spare one hand to hold them
up and she daren't trip over them.

'Good girl,' said Benoît. 'Here.' He guided her to
the ladder and she seized the rung.

It was a terrifying moment as she stepped out of the
rocking boat, but she hung on grimly and then made
the short climb. As she reached the top unseen hands
seized her and helped her over the side of the cutter.

'Good evening, miss,' said a dry voice. 'This is an
unexpected pleasure.'

'For me also,' Angelica replied, staggering slightly
as the deck tilted. 'Thank you.'

She was grateful for her companion's roughly
steadying hand, but she wished she could see him
more clearly, and she felt very isolated now that she
was no longer near Benoît.

She could only discern the dim outline of the man,
just enough to know that he was of average height and
stocky build. He spoke with an unmistakable Sussex
burr and she guessed from his voice and his stance
that he was no longer young. She wondered immediately if he had been one of Toby's cronies.

'What happened?' he asked sharply.

'I don't know exactly,' she said, not sure how much
she ought to say. 'There was a. . .disturbance. . .further
down the beach, then we came back with the boat.'

'We heard shots,' he said grimly. 'Blunderbuss
Billy's busy tonight.'

He turned as a dark shape appeared over the side.

Angelica just had time to realise that Benoît was carrying a man over his shoulder before her companion went to help lift him into the cutter.

'*Hell!*' The wounded man almost cried out as his leg touched the deck and she heard his quick, hissing intake of breath as he tried to suppress his agony.

'He can't walk,' said the stocky man, almost dispassionately. 'I said he was foolish to try to land, but he insisted. What are you going to do?'

'Can you land us this side of the Arun, on West Beach?' Benoît asked crisply.

'Of course. But he still cannot walk, and no doubt you sent the horses home. Besides—what of the lady?'

'The lady is more than equal to the situation,' said Benoît dryly. 'It's Adam I'm worried about. Get under way, George, I don't want to waste time.'

George grunted, then Angelica heard him giving orders to his crew.

Adam dragged in a groaning breath and Benoît dropped on one knee beside him. Angelica joined them, feeling the rough decking beneath her hands.

'Is he badly hurt?' she asked anxiously.

'He took a sword thrust just before they left France,' Benoît replied curtly. 'I don't know the details yet. George, I need some light!'

'In the cabin. I'll not have a light showing on this boat tonight.'

They lifted Adam from the deck, and Angelica winced in sympathy as she heard his barely suppressed groan of anguish.

In the cabin light his face was grey and strained, but there was no fresh blood on the rough bandages around his thigh. His breeches had been slit open and a clean pad pressed over the wound, then strips of cloth had been wrapped around his leg over his breeches. Benoît looked at the dressing carefully, but he didn't touch it.

'As long as it hasn't started bleeding again, we won't interfere with it,' he said briskly.

Adam gave a choking laugh. Angelica guessed he was about the same age as Benoît, although the lines of pain on his face made him look older. He was a thin, narrow-chested man, although she suspected he was a great deal tougher than he at first appeared. His eyes were shrewd enough, and he was bearing his discomfort with fortitude.

'Your father was right, you should have been a sawbones,' he said hoarsely. 'Sorry, Ben. I didn't mean to cause so many complications. Although I hadn't expected such a turnout for my arrival either.'

His eyes rested with open curiosity on Angelica as he spoke. The shawl had fallen back from her hair and the sapphire and diamond comb glinted richly in the lantern light. Her cheeks glowed with fresh colour and her eyes were bright with interest and concern. She didn't seem in the slightest bit disturbed by the ugly stains on Adam's leg or the uncertainty of her current situation.

'Neither did I.' Benoît smiled faintly as his eyes rested briefly on the glittering comb. 'Adam, I am sure you will be charmed to meet Lady Angelica Lennard.'

Adam's eyes widened in surprise and appreciation.

'Ellewood's daughter!' he crowed in delight. 'Ha! Your sins are finally catching up with you!'

'As you say.' Benoît's smile broadened. 'My lady, may I present Mr Adam Kennett? If he hadn't lost the toss sixteen years ago, it would have been him, not me, who waylaid your father that night.'

'I'm pleased to meet you.' Angelica held out her hand to Adam without hesitation. 'I'm so sorry you're hurt.'

'I'm sorry to meet you in such uncomfortable circumstances,' Adam replied ruefully. 'But this is no place for you. I don't know what Ben was thinking of to bring you.'

'He didn't,' she said awkwardly, not daring to look at Benoît.

'She wants me to rescue her brother from Bitche,' Benoît explained, 'but she knows too much about my unsavoury past to trust me—so tonight she followed me to see what dark deed I was about to perpetrate. Next time I will know better than to wear a black cravat in her presence!'

Adam stared at Angelica in amazement, then gave a crack of laughter which was cut short by a wincing stab of pain.

'Serves you right for being such a dandy!' he said gaspingly. 'Black cravat indeed! Well done, my lady! He needs taking down a peg or two sometimes—and so far the Lennards seem to be the only people who can do it. I'm *very* glad to meet you.'

Angelica blushed, avoiding Benoît's eye. Remembering everything that had happened that evening, she wasn't at all sure that Adam's enthusiasm was justified.

Adam stirred restlessly, his smile fading as he looked at Benoît.

'We'll be at West Beach soon,' he said breathlessly. 'Ben, you've got to take the news to London. I can't.' He hesitated, glancing doubtfully at Angelica.

'If I didn't think you could trust her, I wouldn't have told her your name,' Benoît replied instantly, taking Angelica completely by surprise.

'I guessed as much.' Adam closed his eyes for a moment. His face was pinched and, despite the fillip the unexpected discovery of Angelica's identity had given him, he was obviously weak and in considerable pain.

'Bonaparte's building a battlefleet in the Scheldt,' he said after a moment. 'There are ten ships of the line already in service, and more than that number

being built at Antwerp and Flushing. I've seen them.
If they aren't dealt with, they could pose a threat to
England's security. You must tell the Admiralty, Ben!'

'I will.'

Angelica had been looking from Adam to Benoît
and back again. Excitement, alarm and amazement
had all flickered across her face as Adam spoke, but
now she fixed her bright, glowing blue eyes on Benoît.
He did not seem perturbed by Adam's news, but she
was aware of the coiled, watchful tension which filled
him. He was alert and intent on the business on hand,
sure of his ability to overcome any obstacles. The
black wolf was poised and ready for action.

'Wait,' he said briefly. 'Shield the light.'

He ducked his dark head through the low cabin
door and went out on deck. Angelica unshuttered the
lantern and looked at Adam. He smiled wryly.

'I nearly get myself killed bringing that information
back, and all he does is snap orders at me,' he complained. 'I might have known I wouldn't get any
sympathy.'

He winced, and reached down towards his injured
leg.

'Don't touch it!' Angelica said quickly, catching his
hand. 'We don't want it to start bleeding again.' She
smiled encouragingly at Adam as he let his head fall
back wearily on the rough pillow. 'It will only hurt
more if you prod it!' she pointed out practically.

'I'm surprised you're not faint with disgust at the
sight of me,' Adam sighed.

'I've seen worse,' Angelica replied quietly.

She tried not to think of the frightening picture her
father had presented when they'd carried him home
from the accident. She'd swallowed her fear and her
nausea then because she'd had no choice. The memory
had given her a few nightmares, and she never wanted
to repeat the experience, but in general she wasn't

squeamish. Adam's injury caused her anxiety only in so far as it was a danger to him.

She heard Benoît's footsteps outside and, at his command, she shielded the lantern as he came in. He glanced quickly at Adam, then looked at Angelica.

'Let me have the jewels,' he said abruptly. 'I don't think Martha intended you to wander round the countryside in them. They're hardly inconspicuous!'

'I forgot I was wearing them.' Angelica took off the earrings and passed them to him, then tried unsuccessfully to disentangle the comb from her hair.

After a moment he gave an impatient exclamation and pushed her hands aside.

'You have less control over your hair than any woman I have ever met' he said in exasperation.

'Martha put it up!' Angelica protested, submitting to his hands, but feeling particularly foolish because she knew Adam was watching them, a curious expression on his face.

'I know she did! Hasn't it ever *occurred* to you to experiment with a hairbrush for yourself?' Benoît retorted. 'There. Now, make sure you don't let the shawl slip. Ready, Adam?'

'As I'll ever be.' Adam allowed himself to be hoisted up in Benoît's arms.

Angelica followed them out of the cabin, blinking in the sudden darkness. Now that her eyes had become used to the light, the night seemed even blacker than before. Only the stars twinkled above them. The coastline was nothing but a dark blur beneath the paler sky. She remembered the battery on the east bank of the Arun, its cannon waiting to fire on intruders and she shivered. Were they sailing into an ambush?

'What if we meet Sir William?' she asked suddenly. Would the magistrate assume they were smugglers and shoot them on sight if he encountered them?

'He's the least of our problems,' Benoît replied.

'Stragglers from that disturbed band of Gentlemen would be far more dangerous—but I doubt if they'll have come this far east.'

Angelica bit her lip at the possibility, but she refused to admit she was nervous.

'Then we'll just have to make sure we don't bump into any,' she said stoutly.

Adam gave a grunt of painful amusement as Benoît lifted him over the side of the cutter and carried him down into the waiting boat.

'No one can accuse the lady of being faint-hearted,' he gasped.

'By no means,' Benoît agreed.

'Good-bye, miss,' said George, from beside Angelica. 'I'm sorry I could not offer you more hospitality. Perhaps we'll meet again under more comfortable circumstances.'

'I hope so.'

Angelica picked up her skirts and climbed down into the boat, not at all surprised when Benoît caught her firmly around the waist and lifted her the last part of the way. She settled herself beside Adam as the boat surged through the waves. The oarsmen were strong and impatient for their work to be over. It had been an unlucky and unprofitable trip for them, though so far there had been no direct threat to the ship or her crew.

When they reached the beach, Benoît lifted Angelica out of the boat and carried her up onto the sand, wading through the shallow water. Angelica stood on the shore, tying her shawl more firmly under her chin as she looked around nervously. Dawn was still some hours away and the night was as black as ever. She had good evidence now that sometimes the shadows contained lurking danger, and it was much harder than it had been earlier to control her anxiety.

She strained to hear any unusual sounds, but all she

could hear were the waves rolling up the beach and the wind blowing through the sand dunes behind her.

She longed for the comfort of daylight, but she knew that the darkness protected them as well as potential enemies. She turned as Benoît came up the beach towards her.

'This way,' he said in a low voice as he reached her side, Adam slung over his shoulder.

Angelica followed him, careful to hold up her skirts as they headed into the dunes. It was hard to walk on the dry, shifting sands but, even burdened with Adam over his shoulder, Benoît was still moving quickly.

The wind blew up gritty, stinging sand in her face and whipped her hair painfully in her eyes. She slipped and fell to her knees, gasping for breath. Then she tied her shawl tighter, scrambled to her feet, and hurried after Benoît. Her skirts were a nightmare of wet, dirty, clinging wool. The wind cut through her riding habit and she no longer had the added warmth of Benoît's greatcoat.

She stumbled on, praying for the wind to drop, determined not to be left behind, or to force Benoît to wait for her. He had said that she would be equal to this, and she was going to prove him right. He had not asked for her presence on this trip, and she certainly wasn't going to give him cause to regret it.

The river wasn't contained between neat, high banks, and Benoît chose a route which swung quite wide of its main channel, avoiding as far as possible the worst of the marshy ground. Even so, Angelica found herself negotiating several streams of water which ran down into the river. Her skirts, legs and half-boots were soon plastered with mud. She staggered on, tripped over the uneven ground and pitched full-length in the quagmire.

She lay still for a moment, winded and almost grateful for the temporary respite, then pushed herself up onto her knees. She realised that Benoît had paused, and she sensed rather than saw that he was looking back at her. She gritted her teeth and shoved herself back onto her feet. If he could manage the walk burdened as he was by carrying Adam, then she could certainly do it hampered only by her riding skirts.

She caught up with him and they went on, neither speaking a word. She was aware of Adam's occasional hiss of pain, and knew his situation was far worse than hers.

At last they reached Littlehampton Harbour, and Benoît laid Adam down on the ground.

'Wait here,' he said in a low voice. 'I've got to find a boat to take us across the river.'

Angelica dropped on her knees beside Adam as Benoît went down cat-cautious to the water's edge.

The tide was going out; one or two boats were already beached above the waterline, and she could see the masts of ships and fishing boats against the sky as they lay at anchor in the harbour.

Adam drew in a deep, pain-racked breath and Angelica reached out to touch his shoulder comfortingly.

'It won't be long now,' she murmured, 'and then you can rest.'

Adam gave a sobbing gasp, quickly repressed, that could almost have been a laugh, but he didn't try to reply. Angelica supported herself on one hand as she pushed his wet hair back from his face, and waited for Benoît to return. She wondered exactly what he had in mind.

He came back very quickly and carried Adam down to a small rowing boat. He lifted Angelica into it and then rowed across the harbour. The fishing boats around them creaked and rattled continuously in the wind, but the oars of the rowing boat dipped almost silently in and out of the choppy water.

Occasionally Angelica saw a faint glint of reflected starlight in the wind-roughened black surface of the river, as Benoît negotiated the anchored vessels. She gripped the side of the rowing boat tensely, wondering whether there were watchmen on board the ships— and whether they would see and challenge the lone boat. But the harbour was dark and apparently devoid of any other human life.

At last the bottom of the boat grated on the shingle and Benoît lifted Adam out. Angelica climbed out before he could help her, uncaring that her skirts were trailing in the water. She was already so wet that it didn't make much difference; and she was growing sensitive to the fact that Benoît must be getting tired too, and that she didn't actually need to be lifted from place to place like a baby.

Benoît put Adam down in the shadows. Angelica knew without being told that once more they must wait for him. She crouched beside Adam, instinctively trying to make herself as small as possible, and wondered how he had been hurt. The French must have discovered he was a spy. Were they following him now?

She glanced nervously around the dark enshrouded harbour. Presumably Napoleon's agents would work very hard to prevent the information Adam had acquired from reaching London. If they found him he might be in considerable danger—along with anyone else who shared his knowledge. Angelica shivered at the thought. She must remember to ask Benoît a few questions as soon as she had the opportunity.

She heard quiet footsteps approaching, and lifted her head in alarm, instinctively leaning forward across Adam to protect him. Someone was coming. For an instant she was seized by panic—then she recognised

Benoît, though how she could be so sure it was him in the dim light she didn't know.

She struggled quickly to her feet as he picked up Adam, and followed him to an isolated building that stood between the harbour and the huddle of buildings which was Littlehampton.

She just had time to realise it was an inn—she heard the sign creaking above her head in the wind although she couldn't see the picture—and then she was standing inside a darkened room. A lantern was unshuttered and she blinked around in the dim light.

They were in the taproom. No fire burned in the grate, and the room was uncomfortably furnished with a rough wooden settle, a table and a few stools; but it was dry and out of the wind. She sighed with relief, and looked at her companions.

The lantern was held by an elderly man dressed hastily in his nightshirt and breeches. She guessed he was the innkeeper. He nodded with curious politeness to Angelica, but most of his attention was on Adam.

'Bring him straight upstairs, lad,' he said to Benoît. 'Best get him to bed as soon as possible.'

Angelica followed them unquestioningly up the narrow, uneven wooden stairs. Her freezing, sodden skirts dragged around her legs and she was almost too weary to move. Benoît carried Adam into a small, back chamber and Angelica dropped into the only chair the room possessed.

She knew instinctively that they were safe—at least for the time being. They were out of the screaming wind and Benoît would take care of Adam. She thought she ought to get up to see if she could help him, but from what she could see and hear it didn't sound as if he needed any assistance.

The lantern light glittered and misted before her eyes. She had strained her mental and physical capacities to their utmost during the past few hours, and

now that the immediate danger was over she was
desperately tired. She leant back her head and closed
her eyes. Disconnected thoughts and images of Benoît,
smugglers, spies and the windswept sea swam through
her mind—but none of them had any power to stir her
emotions. She was too tired to think clearly or even to
care what happened next.

She had no idea how long she had been sitting there
before Benoît lifted her up in his arms. She murmured
a wordless protest, but she didn't resist. Her arms and
legs were far too heavy to move of their own volition.
She didn't even open her eyes when he carried her out
of the room and into another chamber.

He sat her down again, untied her shawl and began
to unbutton the bodice of her riding habit.

'Come on, wake up!' he said, sounding amused. 'I
want to talk to you.'

She blinked at him, trying to clear her tired,
exhaustion-clouded mind.

'Yes,' she mumbled, lifting a heavy hand to scrub at
her bleary eyes. 'Of course. We must. . .decide what to
do next.'

Benoît grinned.

'I'll decide what we do next,' he declared firmly.
'And the first thing is to get you out of these wet
clothes. Get up!' He pulled her briskly to her feet.

Angelica winced as her aching muscles protested.
Then she tried to finish unbuttoning her riding habit
with stiff, unresponsive fingers.

After a moment Benoît pushed her hands away with
an impatient but tolerant gesture.

'I'll do it!' he said. 'How did you manage to get
covered in so much mud?'

'I kept falling down,' said Angelica vaguely. 'I kept
up with you though!' she added, on a note of triumph.

'I know.' Benoît pulled off her jacket and began to
unbutton her skirt.

Angelica didn't protest. In the bizarre and unreal circumstances in which she found herself, the fact that he was undressing her had hardly registered in her weary brain.

There was a fire burning in the hearth of the spartan bedchamber, and a candle stood on the mantelpiece. But it was still dark and shadowy in the small room, and the draught from the warped shutters made the candlelight flicker unevenly.

'Will Adam be all right?' Angelica asked anxiously.

She was too tired even to think of asking where they were, or how Benoît came to know the innkeeper. She just took it for granted that he was one of Toby's friends.

'Yes, I think so,' Benoît replied. 'But he'll be weak and in pain for quite a while. He's sleeping now.'

He pushed the wreck of her riding skirt down her legs to her feet as he spoke. It seemed quite natural to Angelica to rest her hands on his shoulders to keep her balance as she stepped out of the sodden mass of wool. She was barely aware that she was standing before him dressed in little more than her muddy petticoats.

'What about the men who hurt Adam?' she asked, voicing the fear she'd felt earlier in the harbour. 'Will they come after him?'

She looked up at Benoît as she spoke and saw that he was watching her thoughtfully.

'It's possible,' he said quietly. 'But there's a very good chance they won't be able to find him. George managed to elude pursuit in the Channel, and Adam's come from the Scheldt. No one would expect him to land this far west. That's partly why we arranged it so.'

Angelica was silent for a few moments as she absorbed this information.

'But if they know who he is, then they might expect

him to come back to his home,' she pointed out at last.

Benoît smiled faintly, affectionate admiration for her reasoning in his dark eyes.

'That's the biggest danger,' he agreed. 'Adam isn't sure how much the French know about him. It's probably not a major threat, but the less attention we draw to his presence the better.'

'But he is safe here,' said Angelica, not in any spirit of doubt, but simply stating what she already believed.

'The landlord is an old friend of Toby's,' Benoît confirmed her earlier suspicion. 'He'll take good care of both of you.' He sighed. 'I've got to go to London,' he said, almost reluctantly.

'Is Adam's news bad?' Angelica asked anxiously, jolted by the realisation that Benoît would have to leave soon.

He slipped an arm reassuringly around her waist, drawing her towards him. She rested her hands against his chest as if it was the most natural thing in the world that she should be standing within the circle of his embrace.

He gazed at her for a few moments, a curious expression in his eyes, then he smiled.

'Twenty ships hardly constitute a full scale invasion threat,' he said lightly, 'but they should be dealt with, nevertheless. The sooner I've informed the Admiralty, the happier I shall be.'

'You'll go to London immediately?' Angelica asked, feeling bereft.

'At once.' He reached up to stroke her tangled golden curls, a regretful light in his brown eyes. 'You'll be safe here until I return,' he continued, after a moment. 'I can't take you back to Holly House now— even if you weren't too tired to ride it will be dawn soon. You won't have any reputation left if you're seen jaunting around the countryside at this hour looking like a gypsy!'

'I don't care about that!' Angelica protested vigorously.

'I do,' Benoît retorted. 'I'm going to have enough explaining to do on your behalf as it is! I must call on your father when I'm in London.'

'Oh, my God!' The colour drained from Angelica's face as she thought about the Earl for the first time in hours.

She slipped out of Benoît's arms and turned away from him. She'd hoped she would never have to explain to her father why she'd followed Benoît to the beach, but the events of the night had made it difficult to conceal her impetuous actions. In his current state of mind the Earl was unlikely to be sympathetic to her motives.

'Angelica? What is it?' Benoît put his hands on her shoulders.

'Papa—' Angelica said, and broke off, hugging her arms across her body.

Not once since his accident had she openly voiced her feelings about the changes in her father to anyone— even Martha. It seemed the ultimate act of disloyalty. But she needed to tell someone.

'Papa's not the same,' she whispered. 'If. . .if. . .' She bit her lip, staring up into the dark corners of the ceiling as she blinked back tears. 'If Papa had been like he is now sixteen years ago you really would have ended in a gibbet,' she said in a rush, without turning round.

Benoît's hands tightened on her shoulders.

'His blindness has made him bitter?' he said quietly.

Angelica nodded mutely.

'I wondered.' Benoît sounded sad, but not surprised. 'Some of the things you've said. You're desperate to get Harry back, aren't you?'

'He's always so cheerful...optimistic,' Angelica whispered brokenly. 'Nothing *I've* done has made any difference.'

Then she finally responded to the steady pressure of Benoît's hands and allowed him to turn her into his embrace. She rested her head against his shoulder, trying not to give way to tears. There was no time for this conversation. Benoît had to go to London, and she had to stay and take care of Adam.

She felt Benoît stroking her hair and wished she could prolong the moment. She longed to tell him everything that had happened since the Earl's accident. All the bitter recriminations, the angry words—the despair. But even now she could not bring herself to do so. She lifted her head and met Benoît's steady gaze.

'He's not...easy...to speak to,' she said with some difficulty. 'You must be prepared for many changes in him. I hope—' She broke off. 'It would be better if I could come back with you,' she said, 'but I know you must reach London as quickly as possible. Tell Papa I'm sorry.'

'Don't worry.' Benoît's arms tightened around her reassuringly. 'I'll explain everything to him. Lord Ellewood need never know you followed me tonight. I'll tell him that Admiralty business prevented me from escorting you home straight away—which is true. I *will* take you home as soon as I get back to Sussex.'

Angelica smiled: then she glanced down, biting her lip. She was grateful for Benoît's quiet assurance. She believed he probably could make things right with the Earl. But his words had forced her to think of the future, and she knew how hard she was going to find it to go back to a life in which he had no part. She would wait with the Earl for Benoît to bring Harry back to them—and then what? Would she see Benoît again? Or would he consider his promise to Lord

Ellewood had been kept and sail away on the next tide?

'Angelica?' he said, softly questioning.

She summoned a smile and looked up at him.

'I'm sure you'll know just what to say to Papa,' she said confidently. 'Benoît. . .' She hesitated, focussing her attention on one of his shirt buttons. 'I'm sorry for the problems I've caused you tonight,' she continued breathlessly, after a moment. 'But I'm not sorry I came. It has been an. . .adventure.'

'You haven't caused me any problems,' he said, and his voice sounded very deep. He sighed. 'I really must go,' he said regretfully.

He bent his head to kiss her, and Angelica lifted her hand to touch his face, feeling the rough stubble beneath her fingers because naturally he hadn't shaved.

Benoît had meant it only as a light, farewell kiss, but as his lips met hers a tide of strong emotion swept over both of them. His arms locked around her and Angelica forgot her exhaustion and all her anxieties as she responded to him.

The events of the night had been so fantastic that they bore no relation to anything she had previously experienced. The shabby inn room contained no reminders of her status or the conduct normally expected of her. There was nothing to inhibit her instinctive response to the man she loved.

And she did love him. He was her embodiment of life and adventure. There could be no other man like him. She could taste the sea salt on his lips, and her spirit soared with elation. The unquenchable vigour in his hard, masculine body was intoxicating: she pressed eagerly against him, unashamedly matching the intensity of his desire.

Benoît moulded her vibrant body with sensitive hands, rousing her to new heights of excitement. She murmured wordlessly, her slim fingers pressing into his shoulders in a strong, convulsive grip as he kissed her just below her ear. She lifted her chin, gasping with pleasure as his lips and tongue explored the soft flesh of her neck and shoulder.

Her petticoat was far more revealing than any dress she normally wore, but she felt no shyness as his lips continued their downward investigation. She quivered in his arms, new currents of delight pulsing through her as his kisses alternately scorched and soothed the tender, exposed curves of her breasts.

The small fire in the grate provided little warmth, but Angelica was burning with the sensations Benoît awakened within her. The cool air against her damp skin only heightened her arousal.

She did not protest when Benoît picked her up in a swift, urgent movement and carried her to the bed. He laid her down gently, and sat beside her, his hand resting on her waist. Her heart beat a tattoo of excited anticipation and she looked up at him with open trust and love in her eyes.

His black hair glinted in the candlelight, and she could see his lean face was tense with desire as he leant towards her. She lifted her hand to touch his cheek, glorying in her freedom to reach out to him so spontaneously.

He turned his head, catching her fingers between his lips and biting them gently. Then he slid his hand up from her waist to cup her breast. Angelica caught her breath, her eyes locked with his. More than anything she longed to feel his touch against her naked skin, with no barriers between them.

The electric moment lengthened almost unbearably; and then Benoît bent to kiss the hollow between her breasts.

Angelica arched her back instinctively, lifting herself towards him, He slipped an arm beneath her shoulders—but then he paused, his rough cheek resting gently against her soft flesh. She could feel his warm breath against her skin.

She put her hands behind his head, feeling the sticky salt in his hair, holding him against her. Her body was crying out with longing for him to continue his lovemaking. She had been swept along by the riptide of their passion, and she felt frustrated by his delay.

But then he drew in a deep, shuddering breath, and sat up.

'You're a dangerous woman, my lady,' he said unsteadily, a glimmer of wry amusement in his dark eyes, and she realised that he had been fighting to regain control of his raging emotions.

'I am?' she murmured, her eyes locked with his, a provocative smile teasing her lips as she stretched her neck and shoulders luxuriously.

She felt both disappointed, yet incredibly moved by his efforts to control his desire for her.

'Like playing with fire,' Benoît almost groaned.

He reached out to stroke her cheek as if he couldn't help himself, but he didn't kiss her again. She could sense the fierce struggle he was having to contain his ardour, and she was amazed at how desperately she wanted to tell him that his restraint wasn't necessary. Only a deep-rooted shyness and some remaining shred of decorum prevented her.

He sighed, turning his head to brush the soft skin of her inner arm with his lips, sending rivulets of delight chasing through her veins.

'I always thought I was a man governed by self-discipline and reason,' he said wonderingly, 'but at this moment it would take very little to make me abandon both sense and duty. What have you done to me, my lady?'

'I don't know.' Angelica smiled mistily, unbelievably happy at his admission. Surely it meant he would *not* leave her when he had rescued Harry. 'What have *you* done to me, sir?'

'Nothing,' Benoît said quietly. 'I have never known such a passionate, high-couraged woman.'

He gripped her wrist gently for a moment, then he stood up, startling Angelica with the abruptness of his action.

'I will speak to your father as soon as I have been to the Admiralty,' he said more briskly. 'Don't worry, Angelica. I'm sure that when Lord Ellewood knows Harry is coming home, he'll feel more like his old self.'

'I hope so.' A shadow crossed Angelica's face as she thought of her father. She sat up. 'Benoît. . .?'

She felt confused. Not certain what was happening. One moment she was being carried along on the greatest surge of passion she had ever known—the next Benoît was calmly telling her he was going to visit her father. Was there a connection between those two things? Or. . .?

'I must go,' he said softly. 'Sleep well, *mon amour*. But make sure you put on the nightdress I obtained for you, and get *under* the covers before you do so. Otherwise you will be extremely cold when you wake up!'

'Now you sound like my old nurse!' Angelica protested, her heart singing as she just realised he had called her his love.

Benoît laughed, sounding unbelievably light-hearted.

'If I didn't have to go urgently to London, I might throw caution to the winds and demonstrate some of the essential ways in which I differ from your old nurse!' he retorted. 'Good night, Angelica.'

He turned and went swiftly out of the room, leaving her alone in the glow of the firelight. She could hear the wind rattling at the shutters, and there was a cold draught blowing around her shoulders, but until that moment she hadn't noticed it. She turned her head to look around at the barely furnished room. It contained none of the luxuries she was used to, but it provided her with everything she needed—except Benoît.

CHAPTER SEVEN

THE day was well advanced when Angelica woke up. For a few moments she felt bewildered by her strange surroundings, unsure of what had happened the night before. She was only aware of an unspecified glow of happiness. Then she remembered.

It was hard to believe that it wasn't just a dream. Had she really done all the things she remembered doing? Most importantly of all, was she right when she hoped and believed that she meant as much to Benoît as he meant to her? She replayed their final conversation in her mind, reassuring herself as she remembered the expression in his eyes, the loving touch of his hands and those last few words he'd uttered before he'd left:

'Sleep well, *mon amour*.'

Benoît didn't say things he didn't mean. She smiled happily and pushed back the bedcovers, ready for the next part of the adventure.

The fire had long since gone out and the room was bitterly cold. She gasped, shivering convulsively, then winced as she sat up, because her muscles ached from her unaccustomed exertions of the previous night.

She climbed resolutely out of bed and washed as well as she could with the icy water in the jug on the wash-stand. Then she grimaced at her reflection in the tarnished mirror. She hadn't realised just how muddy and bedraggled she was until she saw herself.

Her hair was a tangled disaster, her stockings ruined, her petticoats damp and grubby, and the half-boots unwearable. The riding habit was in little better condition.

Benoît had spread it over the chair to dry, but it was still damp and unpleasant to touch. She beat out as much of the mud and sand as she could, but wearing it was an unenticing prospect. Unfortunately, she didn't have much choice. She flinched as the clammy wool touched her skin, then buttoned it up decisively.

At last she sat down and contemplated the wreckage of her hair. There was a comb beside the water jug. She picked it up and tried to drag it through her knotty curls. After nearly half an hour she finally managed to reduce her hair to some kind of order, but her eyes were watering from the discomfort and her arms ached from holding them above her head so long.

She let her hands drop into her lap and wondered what she was going to do now. She'd retrieved a few hair pins, but it was a mystery to her how she was going to put her hair up and make it stay up. She almost wished Martha was with her, but that was defeatist thinking. After all she'd accomplished the previous night, she wasn't about to let a little thing like doing her own hair stand in the way of her newfound independence.

She persevered until she'd achieved a result she wasn't entirely unsatisfied with, and then wondered what to do next. No one had come near her, and although she knew she wasn't supposed to draw attention to herself, she was very hungry. She was also concerned about Adam.

She got up and went to the door, listening to see if she could hear anything, then she opened it a crack. Voices floated up from the taproom downstairs, but the landing was empty. She slipped out of her room, down the corridor and into Adam's room like a wraith in her bare feet.

There were two men in the chamber and they both looked up sharply as the door opened. Adam was lying in the bed, his face pale and strained; Thomas the groom was sitting beside him on an upright wooden chair.

Thomas leapt to his feet as Angelica came in, then visibly relaxed as he saw who it was.

'Good afternoon, my lady,' he said gruffly, not sounding particularly pleased to see her.

'Hello, Thomas,' Angelica replied.

She had been momentarily startled to see the groom, but now she realised Benoît must have sent him to take care of Adam.

She walked over to the bed, her long skirts dragging across the floor.

'How are you?' she asked Adam, studying him carefully and a little anxiously.

'I'll do.' He smiled and held out his hand to her. 'I'm sorry you had such an uncomfortable time of it last night, my lady.'

In the background, Thomas snorted disparagingly, and Angelica saw a small smile flicker in Adam's eyes as he returned her gaze. She turned to look at the groom.

'That was a fine trick you played on me, your ladyship!' he said truculently, a scowl in his eyes. 'And Martha! A tricksy, meddling, deceitful—!'

'Oh, no!' Angelica protested instinctively.

'I'm not normally one to speak out of place,' the groom continued, as if she hadn't spoken. 'But I tell you to your face, my lady, I'll not be made a game of like this! Jaunting about the countryside as if you were in Hyde Park. And who do you think would have been blamed if anything had happened to you—that's what I'd like to know!'

Angelica flushed guiltily.

'I acted on the spur of the moment,' she said placatingly. 'I'm sure no one would have blamed you, Thomas.'

'Made a right fool of me, she did,' he grumbled, unappeased.

'Oh, no! I'm sure she didn't mean you to feel like that!' Angelica protested, realising that Martha's diversionary tactics had seriously hurt Thomas's pride. 'It was just. . .'

'Blind loyalty to you!' Thomas said grimly.

Angelica bit her lip. She had no idea how Martha really felt about the groom, and she didn't think it would be sensible to make false claims on her maid's behalf, but she did feel guilty about Thomas.

'In a right stew, she was, when the horses came home without you,' he said, with grim pleasure. 'Only way I managed to stop her following me today was to threaten to tie her up. And she still made me bring some things you might be needing!'

He gestured to a nondescript bag on the floor.

'Poor Martha,' said Angelica guiltily. 'I'm sorry, I didn't mean to give everyone such a fright.'

She lifted her eyes and looked at the groom as she spoke. Her luminous blue eyes were clear and sincere as they met his.

He grunted wordlessly.

'You'd best sit down,' he said grudgingly, offering her the chair. 'Though this is no place for the likes of you, my lady.'

Angelica laughed.

'I know you don't mean that!' she exclaimed. 'You're probably thinking that it serves me right!'

The groom looked at her for a few seconds, then he smiled, very grudgingly.

'When it's dark I can take you back to Holly House if you like,' he said. 'We can go out the back way.'

'What about Adam?' Angelica asked immediately, glancing at him in concern. 'Surely Ben—Mr Faulkener—sent you to look after him?'

Adam pulled a face.

'I can look after myself,' he said.

Angelica turned back to the groom, a question in her eyes.

'There's a nasty wind blowing,' he said immediately. 'I wouldn't want you to take sick on top of everything else, my lady. And Joe—that's the innkeeper—his wife died a while back. He hasn't time to keep coming up here.'

'In that case, I'll certainly stay,' said Angelica firmly. She didn't really have any desire to leave. Benoît had told her to wait for him here and that's what she intended to do. 'Only. . .' She glanced around, seeing the remains of some bread and cheese on a plate. 'I *am* very hungry,' she added. 'Do you suppose. . .?'

'Be my guest,' said Adam grandly. 'I haven't much of an appetite at the moment, I'm afraid.'

'I'll see what I can do,' said Thomas, and went quietly out of the room.

'You don't need to stay,' said Adam, when he'd gone. 'Thomas is just being overcautious. No one's going to bother me here. And even if they do,' he added carelessly, 'there's nothing you can do to help.'

Angelica had been eating the bread and cheese as quickly as she respectably could, but at Adam's dismissive words she lifted her eyes and looked at him steadily over a distance of some six feet.

'I hope I'd be of some use to you, sir,' she said coldly, a hint of unfamiliar imperiousness in her usually friendly voice. 'I'm not accustomed to allowing anyone ride roughshod over me—smugglers, magistrates, *or* French agents!'

She stared at him uncompromisingly. Her eyes were implacable blue sapphires, her back was straight and her carriage regal. Her bare feet, dirty riding habit and untidy hair did nothing to diminish the force of her personality as she confronted him.

Adam drew in a deep breath.

'My apologies, Lady Angelica,' he said after a moment. 'I did not intend to offend you. I should have known better. Forgive me.' He held out his hand to her.

'Of course.' She took it and shook it briefly. 'I have a quick temper sometimes, particularly when I'm hungry,' she added ruefully. 'I didn't mean to be so overbearing.'

'You're a very unusual woman,' said Adam, looking up at her curiously. 'Did you really follow Ben just because he was wearing a black cravat?'

'Yes.' Angelica laughed a little self-consciously 'He said he was going to visit Sir William but I didn't believe him,' she explained. 'I'd wondered earlier how he disguised his white cravat when he went out smuggling—seeing as how all his other clothes were black—so when I saw him on the stairs and he was wearing a *black* cravat...I acted without thinking.'

'But it was a very acute deduction,' Adam observed, watching her shrewdly. 'My lady, I salute you. Ben's finally met his match! The future will certainly hold some interesting developments, I think.'

He grinned at Angelica's discomfiture, then tensed and turned his head as the door opened, but it was only Thomas.

'It's not what you're used to,' he said, putting a tray down on Angelica's lap, 'but it's the best Joe could produce—and I had to dodge my way up here, so no one saw me. I hope I haven't spilt any.'

'It looks delicious,' said Angelica warmly. 'Besides, I'm so hungry I could eat a hor...goat.' She changed her mind at the last minute as she remembered the groom's occupation. 'Thank you, Thomas.'

She ate the simple meal with relish. She would have been happy to stay and chat to Adam when she'd finished it, but she could see that talking to her was a

considerable effort for him so she left him with
Thomas and went back to her own room.

In her absence someone, possibly Thomas, had
made up the fire and lit some candles. She opened the
bag Martha had sent and found her maid had packed
a warm, practical walking dress and shoes. She put
them on and immediately felt much more comfortable.
There was something very disconcerting about walking
around in bare feet.

She spread out the riding habit before the hearth,
hoping it might dry by the following morning. She
hated the thought of wearing it again, yet she also felt
strangely sentimental about it. She would have to
replace it for Mrs Faulkener.

As she smoothed out the creases she heard the
crackle of paper and frowned in brief confusion. Then
she remembered snatching up James Corbett's letter
the previous morning. She took it out of the pocket
and flattened it out. The letter was even more battered
and stained now than it had been before. The ink had
smudged and run in the damp, but it was still readable.

She put it on the mantelpiece then sat down on the
bed, wondering what to do next. She could hardly go
back to bed so soon, and there was nothing else in the
bare room to occupy her attention. She frowned irritably. After all the excitement of the past few days
this enforced inactivity was almost unbearable.

There was a gentle tap on the door and she recognised Thomas's voice. She went over and opened it
immediately.

'Excuse me, your ladyship,' he said sheepishly, offering her a crumpled newspaper. 'I thought you might
like something to read. An inn's a tedious place if
you're on your own and you've got no taste for
drinking.'

Angelica's smile lit up her face.

'Thank you!' she exclaimed gratefully. 'Is Mr Kennett asleep?'

'Yes, my lady.'

'Would you like to come in?' she offered impulsively. 'I'm sure you must be just as bored with this waiting as I am.'

'Well. . .' He hesitated, then glanced quickly up and down the landing. 'Very well, my lady.'

He came into the room and stood uncomfortably just inside the door.

'How long do you think it will take Mr Faulkener to get to London?' Angelica asked.

'He'll be there by now,' Thomas replied. 'Depends how long his business takes him when he'll be back. He's planning on being here tomorrow.'

'Yes, he said,' said Angelica. She thought of Benoît's business with the Admiralty, and with her father, and wondered which would take longer.

How would the Earl react to Benoît's news? She didn't want to think about that now. She was still basking in the glow of happiness left over from the previous night.

'You must have been with Mr Faulkener a long time,' she said brightly.

'I worked for his father,' Thomas replied, 'but I've known Master Benoît since we were both boys. I would have gone to sea with him, but my mother was a widow, and there were my sisters to think of. . .'

'Yes,' said Angelica abruptly, reminded once more of the Earl. 'There is always someone to think of. I'm sure you took good care of your family.'

'My sisters are married now,' said Thomas cheerfully. 'Ma lives with one of them. I could go with Master Benoît now. But I get seasick—and someone has to take care of Mrs Faulkener's horses.'

'I'm sure no one could do it better,' Angelica said

warmly. 'I still haven't seen the tricks you've taught them. Mr Faulkener says you've taught Billy to count!'

Thomas smiled slowly, clearly gratified by her words.

'Ah, well,' he said. '*I* do the counting, Billy just does what I tell him. Pity I can't say the same for some I could mention!' he added, glowering. Martha's deception clearly still rankled. 'Well, I'd best be getting back to Master Adam,' he continued, before Angelica could think of a suitable reply. 'I'll be there if you need me, my lady, but I don't imagine there'll be any trouble.'

'Thank you, Thomas,' said Angelica.

When she was alone again the room seemed even smaller and more cell-like than it had done before. She had sat reading to her father for endless hours, suppressing her thoughts of the world outside their walls. Now, in an unfortunate parody of those hours, she had to sit in a tiny, empty room with the sound of voices and laughter echoing up from the taproom below—with nothing to do but a paper to read.

She threw the newspaper on the floor. She'd done enough reading to last her a lifetime. And Thomas's comment about his mother had excited her own insidious anxieties about the Earl. She had done everything she could to help him since his accident—but had she done enough? Was there any way she could have found that would have averted his terrible bitterness?

She had loved, admired and obeyed her father all her life; but Lord Ellewood had always been a proud and very private man, not given to sharing his emotions with his daughter. He had never been able to come to terms with his sudden dependence on others, and that made him so hard to deal with.

Her earlier mood of optimism faded, and it was a long time before she fell asleep that night. When she did, her dreams were troubled. Harry, her father, Benoît and even her mother advanced and retreated in a never-ending series of fragmented images. She woke up rigid with anxiety and almost too afraid to move—though she didn't know what had scared her. Surely she wasn't frightened of the people she loved most in the world?

It was a relief to get up the following morning. It was the first time she'd seen daylight for two days and the sight of the sunshine immediately restored her optimism. She couldn't imagine why she'd given way to such foolish worrying the previous night. She ate a hearty breakfast and even deigned to read the despised newspaper. It was nearly a month out of date, but since the news it reported was almost entirely local that hardly mattered to her.

She was engrossed in a story about the peccadilloes of some soldiers garrisoned at Horsham when Thomas knocked on her door.

'My lady!' he whispered urgently, alarm in his voice. *'My lady!'*

'What is it?' She snatched open the door.

'Sir William! He's downstairs, he's going to search the inn!'

'What?' Angelica exclaimed, her heart thumping in sudden alarm. She was remembering Benoît's command that they do nothing to draw attention to themselves.

'They wounded some men on the beach two nights ago,' Thomas said breathlessly. 'And one of his men was killed. Now he's heard there's an injured man here—God knows who informed him—though I can make a guess.' His expression darkened briefly. 'There's no time for that now. Sir William knows Master Adam's in with us. He's been trying to catch him and Master Benoît for years, I've got to hide you both.'

' "In with us"?' Angelica queried quickly.

'The Gentlemen!' Thomas said impatiently.

Angelica suddenly realised that, although Benoît might no longer be actively involved in smuggling, his groom, landlord and a lot of his old friends still were. Even more importantly, Adam had been the one who'd led Sir William on a wild-goose chase all those years ago while Benoît had been confronting her father among the dunes of West Beach. And Adam had come ashore secretly from a smuggling vessel. If the magistrate discovered him wounded at the inn, he might finally have the evidence he needed to apprehend him for smuggling.

'God, what am I going to *do?*' Thomas groaned distractedly. 'You and Master Adam to hide and—'

'*Me!*' Angelica interrupted. 'Why. . .?'

'Your *reputation*, my lady.' Thomas wrung his hands together. 'The master will kill me if anything happens . . .and you can't even climb out of the window, there's a man outside. . .'

Angelica gathered her scattered wits together.

'There's no need to worry about my reputation,' she said firmly. 'Sir William is an old acquaintance. I'm sure I can deal with him.'

'But—'

'You go and take care of Adam. I'll speak to Sir William. Be quick,' she added crisply, as Thomas seemed rooted to the spot. 'Presumably Sir William knows you as well. You wouldn't want to bump into him on the landing!'

Thomas gave her a doubtful look, but he had no ideas of his own, and Angelica spoke with authority. The years spent running her father's household stood her in good stead. Although she didn't know it, she sounded very much like the Earl.

Thomas hurried back to Adam's room as Angelica picked up James Corbett's letter from the mantelpiece. Then she went to stand her ground at the top of the stairs. She could hear Sir William arguing with the innkeeper in the taproom below. The innkeeper was putting up a valiant resistance, but she knew he would soon be overborne. A few seconds later she heard Sir William thrust the old man impatiently aside and mount the stairs.

'Good morning, Sir William,' she said calmly.

At the sound of her voice he stopped dead, halfway up the stairs, looking up at her in blank astonishment.

There was very little light on the landing and he couldn't see her clearly. All he was aware of was a tall, aloof young woman blocking his way. He certainly didn't recognise Angelica.

'Who the devil are you, miss?' he snapped, surprise robbing him of courtesy.

'I beg your pardon, Sir William,' said Angelica coolly. 'I'm sorry you don't know me.'

She moved slightly so that he could see her more clearly in the light from the small casement window.

'*Lady Angelica!*' Sir William gasped in disbelief. 'What the dev—? That is, my apologies, my lady. I had no idea the Earl was staying at this inn.'

'He isn't,' said Angelica imperturbably, although her heart was hammering with nervousness.

She was trying to imagine how her father would have dealt with the situation. She wondered briefly if she'd made a mistake in sticking to her original plan; but if she'd claimed that it *was* Lord Ellewood in Adam's room it would have been too easy to disprove her story.

'He isn't?' Sir William stared at her in confusion and dawning suspicion. 'I have heard no news of your marriage. Surely—'

'Certainly not,' said Angelica austerely, wondering if Sir William thought he'd discovered an elopement. 'No such announcement has been made. I am here on quite other business.'

'What other business?' Sir William demanded bluntly.

Angelica looked past him to his two henchmen staring at her with open curiosity on the stairs.

'It is a family matter, and one I am not prepared to discuss—certainly not in public,' she said repressively.

Sir William flushed angrily, but turned and dismissed his men with a jerk of his head. They retreated reluctantly down the stairs, though Angelica had no doubt they would remain within earshot.

Benoît had wanted to avoid a scandal, and now it seemed she was well on the way to making one—but she couldn't let Sir William discover Adam. Even if they could convince the magistrate he hadn't been involved in smuggling, it would be very awkward for the spy to be seen here. Angelica took her responsibilities seriously.

'Now, miss,' said Sir William grimly. 'Perhaps you will tell me what business brings you so far from home without the Earl's protection.'

'My father has not left home for more than eighteen months,' said Angelica rather bitterly. 'I am surprised you have not heard.'

'I am sorry, Angelica,' said Sir William more gently, startled by the bleakness in her voice. 'I called on him in town several times. I was told he was not at home.'

'I'm sorry. I did not know.' Angelica looked away, momentarily forgetting why she was confronting the magistrate at the top of the stairs.

'I will call on him again,' said Sir William. 'In the meantime,' he added briskly, 'I must warn you that you have chosen a most unsuitable place to conduct your business. I have good reason to believe that there is a wounded smuggler hiding in this inn. Please step aside. I intend to search every room, and I apologise in advance for any inconvenience I may cause you.'

'I regret, I cannot allow you to continue,' said

Angelica resolutely, without moving from the top of the stairs.

Sir William stared at her.

'You won't *allow*—?' he exclaimed explosively. 'My lady, I do not understand you! This is not a matter of personal preference. There is a fugitive from justice hiding here!'

It occurred to Angelica that, if Sir William always wasted so much time making angry announcements about his intentions, it wasn't surprising Toby Faulkener had run rings around him. If Adam hadn't been quite so badly wounded he and Thomas could probably have dealt with the man beneath the window and made good their escape by now. As it was, she was just going to have to make sure Sir William stayed on the right side of the door herself.

'Don't be ridiculous,' she said coolly. 'This is a small inn and I have been staying here for several days. I'm sure I would know if there was a wounded man here.'

'I was told he was brought here late at night. . .' Sir William had been thrown off balance by Angelica's presence and he hadn't quite got his argument together.

'Perhaps you were misinformed,' she said sweetly, well aware of how exasperating the magistrate would find her suggestion. 'I understand it's happened to you before.'

Sir William glared at her.

'Just what is your business here, my lady?' he demanded bluntly. 'I'll not have you make a game of me—or my office.'

Angelica hesitated, staring at him aloofly.

'It's a matter of considerable delicacy,' she said at last, with obvious reluctance. 'I could not confide in you without your promise not to repeat what I tell you.'

'For God's sake!' Sir William exploded. 'You don't

have to coach me on matters of delicacy or honour, miss! What—are—you—doing—here?'

Angelica handed him James Corbett's letter without another word.

Sir William stared at it blankly for a moment, then squinted at it, holding it at arm's length as he tried to read it. The light at the top of the stairs was too poor, and Angelica stepped aside to let him go over to the small window, though she remained standing with her back to Adam's door.

At last sir William lowered the letter and looked at her.

'I had no idea' he exclaimed. 'I had not heard. Poor Harry! But—'

'Please send your men away,' Angelica interrupted. 'You have my word that there are no wounded smugglers in this house, Sir William. Someone had to bring me the letter,' she added softly.

She saw a measure of understanding dawn in his eyes, then he strode downstairs and she heard his strong voice dismissing most of his men.

She gave a deep sigh of relief, then glanced around as she heard Adam's door open a crack.

'My lady?' Thomas murmured questioningly.

'I think we're winning. Stay inside,' she said briefly.

'The master is going to kill me,' said Thomas with feeling. 'Now I really will have to run away to sea!'

He closed the door softly as Sir William came back upstairs.

'What's going on, Angelica?' he said, and from his tone it was clear he was determined to get to the bottom of things. 'Who is in that room? Does the Earl know you are here?'

Angelica hesitated. She had no desire to discuss her affairs on the open landing but, on the other hand, she was afraid to leave Adam's door unguarded in case

someone else decided to investigate. She knew Sir
William hadn't sent all his men away.

'Someone had to bring us the letter,' she repeated, to
gain time. 'You can see it's had a difficult journey.' She
paused. 'Anyone in a position to help Harry might be
in considerable danger if Bonaparte learned their identity,' she said very softly and deliberately. 'I cannot
let you or your men—especially not your men—into
that room, Sir William. Your arrival has certainly
complicated things for us. We were hoping to be as
unobtrusive as possible. Now I dread to think of the
rumours and gossip which will be flying around the
countryside and perhaps coming to the wrong ears!'

'Dammit! My lady!' Sir William flushed angrily. 'I
acted in good faith. If you knew you were conducting
such delicate business in this district you would have
done better to come to me in the first place. I *am* one
of your father's oldest friends even if he is no longer
prepared to receive me. And I hope I can be trusted
to keep a secret!'

'Oh, Sir William, I'm sorry!' Angelica stretched out
an impulsive hand towards him.

The magistrate had clearly been badly hurt by her
father's withdrawal—and now he was aggrieved to
have been excluded from news of Harry's fate.

'I have been so anxious these past few months,
particularly since we learnt about Harry, that I haven't
always been thinking straight,' she said apologetically.
'I didn't mean to offend you—or to be so rude to you
earlier,' she added sincerely. 'But your unexpected
arrival with all your men frightened me half out of my
wits!'

'It wasn't obvious,' said Sir William dryly. 'You
reminded me very much of your father in one of his
more autocratic moments!'

Angelica blushed and bit her lip ruefully.

'I'm sorry,' she apologised again.

'Never mind, m'dear,' said Sir William gruffly. 'You've had a lot to contend with these past two years.' He took her hand and patted it with rough sympathy. 'But if the Earl didn't bring you here who did?' he asked.

There had been no sound to alert Angelica, not even a creak on the wooden stairs, but somehow she knew he was there.

She looked past Sir William straight into Benoît's dark, amused eyes. She had been desperately longing for his support. and now her heart leapt with joyous relief at his unexpected appearance. Despite the hard riding he must have done since they'd last met he was as elegant and assured as ever. His composure contrasted devastatingly with the magistrate's unfocused bluster.

Angelica's hand fluttered in Sir William's, and a brilliant smile lit up her face as she looked at Benoît. All the anxiety and tension were stripped from her eyes and she glowed with bright, happy radiance. Her warmth and pleasure seemed to illuminate the gloomy landing.

Benoît's expression had been watchful as well as amused as he'd mounted the stairs, but for an instant, as he returned her look, his eyes blazed with a passion to match her own. Then the familiar, wolf-wary gleam returned to his eyes, and he turned to face the magistrate.

'*My God!*' said Sir William, staring at Benoît in stunned disbelief. 'Not *you*, Faulkener?'

Benoît grinned. Angelica saw a flash of his white teeth in the poor light.

'Why not?' he asked mockingly. 'Don't you think I'm capable of protecting a lady?'

'Dammit! Faulkener!' Sir William growled. 'That's not what I meant. Although—'

'Although that would, in fact, appear to be the case,'

Benoît interrupted smoothly. 'Forgive me, my lady.'
He took Angelica's hand and kissed it gracefully. 'I
had no idea you were going to have such an unpleasantly exciting time this morning.'

'Not. . .unpleasant,' said Angelica, trying to keep
her voice steady at his touch.

She had spent a lot of time imagining their next
meeting, but it had never occurred to her that it would
take place under the eye of the magistrate. She was
acutely aware that Sir William was staring at them in
open amazement, and she was desperately trying not
to appear self-conscious.

'Sir William is an old friend of my father,' she
continued. 'I could never find it *unpleasant* to talk to
him, but the situation is a little *awkward*.'

'It is indeed,' said Benoît. He smiled faintly and
squeezed her hand reassuringly. Then he turned to Sir
William.

'You should have confided in me, Faulkener,' said
Sir William brusquely, recovering from his initial surprise. 'Then none of this unfortunate business would
have happened. I'd no idea you were acquainted with
Lord Ellewood. But you've always been secretive and
irresponsible!'

'That's not true!' Angelica burst out indignantly
before Benoît could speak. 'He—' She broke off,
biting her lip, as Benoît caught her eye.

'I think,' said Benoît deliberately, 'that we have
spent enough time on this dark and draughty landing.
We might proceed better with a little more illumina-
tion.' And he opened Adam's door.

He did it with so little drama that for a moment
Angelica didn't even realise what he'd done.

'But—' she protested, as it dawned on her he was
inviting Sir William to enter the room.

'After you, my lady,' he said, with unruffled courtesy. 'Sir William.'

'What game are you playing now, Faulkener?' said
Sir William suspiciously, but he went into Adam's
room without further protest.

Angelica felt as if the world had turned upside
down. After all her efforts to protect Adam from the
magistrate, she couldn't believe Benoît was just going
to hand him over to Sir William! He must have some
scheme in mind—but she couldn't imagine what it was.

Sir William took three paces across the room and
stopped dead as he met Adam's strained expression.

'By St George!' the magistrate breathed, completely
stunned. 'I thought you were dead, boy!'

'Just an unfounded rumour, I'm glad to say,' Adam
replied, letting his head fall back against the pillow as
some of the tension ebbed from his eyes. 'Although I
came a bit too close for comfort this time.'

Sir William recovered from his first shock and strode
over to the bed.

'What the *devil* have you been up to?' he demanded
roughly. 'I heard you were going to try your fortunes
in India—and then you took the fever. What did you
mean by disappearing like that without a *word*?'

'Events. . .overtook me,' said Adam. 'I apologise for
my lack of courtesy.'

'Damned improvident, reckless, thoughtless. . .' Sir
William seized Adam's hand and held it very tightly.

Angelica stared at the magistrate in confusion. She
was sure there were tears in his eyes, although he was
doing his best to disguise his emotion beneath his
customary blustering manner. She glanced at Benoît
and saw that he was smiling. Thomas was looking both
unhappy and uncomfortable in the furthest corner of
the room.

'So you're the one who brought Angelica the letter
about Harry!' Sir William exclaimed at last.

Adam hesitated. He looked pale and tired. Sir

William's exuberance had pleased him, but it was also exhausting.

'He has just returned from France,' said Benoît quietly. 'It was a French agent who wounded him. You can understand why we didn't want to draw attention to his presence. I was going to take him to Holly House, but the Manor would be an easier journey for him—you could take the carriage along the sands at low tide.'

Sir William frowned.

'And what will you be doing in the meantime?' he asked bluntly. 'Getting Harry out of France?'

Angelica gasped. She hadn't expected the magistrate to be so acute. He glanced at her sardonically.

'They may have led me on some merry dances over the years, my lady,' he said dryly. 'But I've known both these idle scoundrels since they were in shortcoats. They'd never let a challenge like that go unanswered.'

'Well, we have a number of challenges at the moment,' said Benoît briskly. 'I suggest we start tackling them. Sir William, if you will be kind enough to organise Adam's departure for the Manor, I will take Lady Angelica back to Holly House. Perhaps you would collect whatever you need from your room, my lady.'

Angelica hurried to do Benoît's bidding. She was beginning to feel somewhat indignant that her efforts to protect Adam had apparently been entirely unnecessary, but she wasn't about to argue with Benoît in front of the others. Besides, the sooner they left, the sooner she would be alone with him.

It was another bright, windy March day, with a clear blue sky and a pale, glistening sun.

Benoît had come back to collect Angelica in his

curricle, and she was able to watch the countryside pass by in reasonable, though chilly, comfort.

'Do you mean I did all that for nothing?' she demanded as soon as they were on their way. 'If Sir William is going to take Adam back to the Manor I needn't have tried to hide him at all!'

'I wouldn't say that,' said Benoît, grinning. 'You put up a spectacular defence. I was very impressed.'

'You were?' Angelica looked at him suspiciously, half afraid he was making fun of her. She felt almost shy in his presence, but that was ridiculous.

He glanced at her and smiled, and she felt her heart turn over at the warmth in his eyes.

'Yes,' he said. 'I was proud of you—though I dread to think of the rumours we'll soon have to contend with!'

'But if there was no harm in Sir William knowing, I might have saved myself the trouble,' Angelica protested, although her heart was beating a quick rhythm of happiness at his praise. 'And now I come to think of it—Thomas was terrified of Sir William discovering us! None of it seems to make any sense at all!'

Benoît grinned.

'Thomas's involvement with smuggling is rather more recent than mine,' he explained. 'And he's never had quite the same relationship with Sir William that Adam and I had. It's hard for him to believe that Sir William is not always a threat to our interests. And it would have been unfortunate if Blunderbuss Billy had gone stampeding into Adam's room with half his men gawping behind him. It was just as well you got him to send them away. He *can* be discreet when he wants to be—but it doesn't come naturally to him!'

'It doesn't, does it?' said Angelica, remembering the magistrate's argument with the innkeeper, and then his long debate at the top of the stairs with her. 'If that's how he normally goes about his business, I'm not surprised he hasn't caught many smugglers!'

Benoît laughed.

'He was in a difficult position today,' he said fairly. 'Joe was one of Toby's cronies, so Sir William must have been almost certain, even before he arrived at the inn, that any smuggler it contained wasn't one of the band he fought on the beach two nights ago. That gang is far more vicious and violent than any of Toby's old friends—and Sir William knows it. He may even have guessed that Joe was betrayed by a less scrupulous rival—but he had to be seen to act on the information he received, even if he didn't relish the task. He's usually behaves a little more circumspectly!'

'I should hope so!' said Angelica forcefully. 'Was it always like this, Benoît? I mean, Sir William seems so fond of you and Adam, even though he admits you led him a merry dance—yet we heard pistol shots on the beach that night, and Thomas said one of Sir William's men was killed.'

'Toby always kept violence to a minimum,' said Benoît grimly. 'There have been a lot of unfortunate changes since his death. It may be time to do something about them. Too many men have died, and Sir William is getting too old for pitched battles through the countryside.'

'What do you mean?' said Angelica quickly, suddenly afraid for Benoît. 'What are you going to do?'

He glanced briefly at her, then his rather tense expression relaxed and he drew the horses to a standstill beside the road.

'Nothing at the moment,' he assured her. 'I was thinking aloud. Don't worry.'

'Don't *worry*!' Angelica exclaimed. 'How can I help it when. . .?'

He transferred the reins into one hand and reached up to touch her hair. Her pulse began to race and she caught her breath as she looked into his face. They had spent so long in the dark together that it was almost a shock to meet his eyes in the bright morning sunlight. There was so much warmth and admiration in his expression that she felt light-headed.

'I'm sorry you had such an difficult time in my absence,' he said softly. 'If I'd thought for one moment that you'd be troubled at the inn I wouldn't have left you there. I should have had Thomas take you back to Holly House last night.'

'I wouldn't have gone,' Angelica whispered breathlessly. 'Benoît, it was real, wasn't it? I mean. . .'

He smiled and bent to kiss her.

As his lips met hers she closed her eyes, giddy with relief and happiness. She hadn't imagined any of it. The way he looked at her and the way he made her feel were both quite real. She twisted towards him, responding with her characteristic lack of reserve, and as usual it was Benoît who drew back first.

He laughed softly, stroking her sunshine-bright curls with teasing fingers. She gazed up at him, her wide blue eyes dark with glowing, undisguised emotion.

'Going anywhere with you is about as safe as carrying a live coal in my pocket!' he declared, a wicked gleam in his eyes. 'We *are* on the King's high road, my love. A little more decorum may be in order.'

Angelica blushed. Her lips were still burning from his touch and her body was throbbing with unfulfilled passion.

'Then you shouldn't have kissed me!' she said energetically, secure in the knowledge that he was teasing her.

'The temptation was irresistible.' He grinned, winding a golden curl idly around his finger, and sending a shiver of pleasure down her spine. 'What happened to your protestations of false modesty?' he enquired provocatively. 'Weren't you telling me only two days ago you had no intention of kissing me again?'

'I don't remember saying anything of the kind!' Angelica replied firmly, although a faint smile played on her lips as she spoke.

'What an adaptable memory,' he said admiringly.

'I have a very good memory,' she said placidly. 'What did the Admiralty say?'

'They thanked me for my time and effort,' Benoît replied wryly. 'I've a feeling it was old news to them. They have more than one iron in the fire. But the matter's in their hands now.'

'You mean Adam nearly got killed for *nothing*!' Angelica exclaimed indignantly. 'That's *wicked*!'

'That's war,' Benoît replied dryly. 'We shall have to see what develops.'

'I think it's disgraceful!' Angelica declared forcefully. 'Did they waste any thanks or sympathy for Adam?'

'He didn't do it for a reward,' Benoît said quietly. 'He did it because several of his French relatives died on the guillotine—and they weren't aristocrats. He hates the new regime more than most but I think he's had his fill of spying now. It goes against the grain with him. He's done some good work in the past, more than sufficient to earn him an honourable retirement. I doubt if he'll go back.'

'But you will,' Angelica whispered, feeling a shadow of fear, despite the bright sunlight.

'For Harry? Of course,' Benoît said calmly.

Angelica closed her eyes, finally confronted with the true magnitude of the task she had asked Benoît to perform.

She was bitterly torn by her love for her brother and her love for Benoît. She wanted to tell him not to go—but if she did that she was afraid she was sealing Harry's fate. She knew her brother would never wait patiently in a French prison. At the first opportunity he would make another escape attempt—and next time he might be killed.

She gripped her hands tightly in her lap, unable to speak, because nothing she could say would help. She knew better than to suppose Benoît would break his word because she was afraid for him. He would keep his promise to the Earl, and to her, no matter what it cost him.

She felt him cover her hands with his own, and opened her eyes, looking at him with a strained, tense expression.

'Don't be afraid,' he said softly. 'I will bring Harry safely back to you.'

'I can't help it,' she whispered. 'I am so frightened for both of you. I never saw the danger so clearly before. When I think how I tried to force you—if anything happened to you. . .'

'You didn't force me into this,' said Benoît gently.

He squeezed her hand reassuringly, then reached up to wrap a glowing curl around his finger.

'I made a promise to your father years ago,' he reminded her. 'Even if you hadn't brought the letter to Sussex yourself, I would still have rescued Harry. But I would never have met you.'

'I'm not sorry I came.' Angelica tried to smile. 'I just wish I could go to France with you.'

'I know.' He stroked her cheek. 'Waiting is always the hardest part. I've never relished it myself. But we will come safely home, don't ever doubt it.'

'I won't.' Angelica took a deep breath, trying to banish her anxieties. They served no useful purpose, and they only clouded the time she had with Benoît. They had not discussed the future, but she felt more than ever now that they would share it.

'Did you see Papa?' she asked after a moment.

'Benoît, what is it?' she said sharply, as she saw a flicker in his eyes. 'Is Papa ill?'

'No,' he said instantly, 'far from it! But I didn't speak to the Earl—he'd left London before I arrived.'

'*What?*' Angelica could hardly believe it.

Her father hadn't left his town house since the accident.

'I understand that neither your letter, nor mine, reached him,' said Benoît. 'I don't know what happened to my messenger.' A flicker of concern glowed briefly in his eyes. 'Simpson's an old sailor. He's served with me for the past five years. He's utterly loyal. I hope he hasn't come to harm.'

For a moment Benoît's eyes remained clouded as he thought of his friend and servant, then he focused on Angelica's face. 'The Earl is at Holly House now,' he said quietly.

'*Here?*' Angelica gripped Benoît's hand convulsively. Not for an instant had she considered the possibility that the Earl might follow her. 'Have you spoken to him?'

'Not yet,' Benoît replied. 'I realised he was ahead of me when I was on the road. He probably arrived last night. He's come after you, and I thought the sooner he found you the better—so I didn't delay.'

'Oh, my God!' Angelica felt almost sick with anxiety and guilt.

What fear or anger had driven the Earl to leave the security of his home after being secluded there for more than eighteen months?

'He must be so worried about me,' she whispered. 'I should have gone home straight away. Oh, God! What have I done?'

'He will surely understand you had doubts about me,' said Benoît bracingly. 'As I remember, he is not the kind of man to accept another man's opinion without question. Your actions were entirely natural in the circumstances.'

'I suppose so,' said Angelica doubtfully.

She was still stunned by the fact that the Earl had travelled all the way into Sussex when he had refused point black to go anywhere by carriage since his accident.

'I never thought he'd leave the house again,' she said wonderingly. 'I kept trying to make him go out, but he wouldn't. Perhaps. . .' A smile suddenly lit up her eyes. 'Perhaps his nightmares have receded and he's no longer so afraid of the outside world. Perhaps he didn't realise it until I came into Sussex. He used to like visiting Sir William.'

'I mentioned his arrival to Sir William,' said Benoît. 'I expect he will call later, when he has arranged for Adam's transportation.'

'Yes. Papa would like that,' said Angelica eagerly. 'He's very fond of Sir William. Let's not waste any more time, Benoît. Papa will be so pleased to know you're going to rescue Harry.'

CHAPTER EIGHT

DESPITE her brave words, Angelica felt extremely apprehensive when the curricle drew up outside Holly House. She let Benoît help her down from the curricle, then lifted an instinctive hand to touch her golden curls.

Benoît smiled at her gesture.

'You've obviously been practising your skills,' he said humorously. 'I'm not sure what Martha would say, but to my untutored eye you look charming.'

Angelica blushed self-consciously.

'Thank you,' she said.

Then her smile faded, an expression of elusive sadness flickering over her face.

'I don't know why I'm concerned,' she said quietly. 'Papa won't see.'

She turned her head as Mrs Faulkener came out of the house to meet them. The Frenchwoman's expression was quite calm, but her eyes were strained and worried as she looked at Angelica.

'The Earl is in the library,' she said softly. 'His secretary is with him. They've been here since late last night. He is not. . .very happy.'

Angelica looked sharply at Mrs Faulkener, hearing the undertones of stress in her voice. She had a feeling it would take a great deal to ruffle the Frenchwoman, but the Earl had clearly succeeded.

'He's angry?' said Angelica flatly, needing no further explanation.

Lord Ellewood's displays of temper were never a pleasant experience for anyone.

'Yes,' said Mrs Faulkener simply.

Angelica pressed her lips together in a firm, resolute line, and walked into the house to confront her father.

The Earl turned his head sharply when he heard the library door open. The secretary leapt to his feet.

'Who's there?' Lord Ellewood demanded harshly.

He was a gaunt, ravaged shadow of the man who had once met Benoît on the seashore. He was still tall and rigidly upright, but his fair hair was prematurely white—and the darkened spectacles he wore could not hide the ugly scars on his face. There were deep lines around his mouth, his expression was hard, anxious and angry. His bitterness and frustration at what had happened to him were almost palpable, even submerged as they were by his more immediate fear for Angelica.

If he hadn't known who the Earl was, Benoît wouldn't have recognised him. Despite everything Angelica had said, he was momentarily shocked into silence by his old opponent's altered appearance.

'It's me, Papa,' said Angelica calmly.

'*Angelica!*' Lord Ellewood heaved himself to his feet. His secretary offered him a well-meaning hand and he struck it furiously aside. 'Come here!'

She went to him, stretching out her hands towards him. He groped blindly before him, found her wrist and seized it in a painful, vice-like grasp.

'Are you safe, girl?' he asked fiercely.

He was standing near the window; the scars on his face were livid in the bright sunlight as he turned his empty eyes towards her. He kept hold of her wrist in an almost brutal grip and ran his other hand rapidly up her arm to her shoulder.

'*Are you harmed?*' He shook her roughly back and forth in the ferocity of his anxiety.

'No, Papa!' Angelica cried out sharply, feeling a stab of pain at the bitter fear she had caused him. She reached out instinctively to reassure him. 'I'm quite all right.'

For a single heart-beat the terrible intensity of emotion in the Earl's face relaxed. It was possible to see in the ruins of his once handsome features the man who had chosen not to denounce Benoît—but then his expression darkened.

He released Angelica as violently as he had grabbed her; thrusting her away from him so forcefully that she stumbled back and would have fallen if Benoît hadn't caught her.

'I'm *sorry*—' she began—but the Earl's angry voice overrode her attempted apology.

'How dare you flout my orders?' Lord Ellewood snarled. 'Do you think I'm soft-headed as well as blind? What kind of daughter have I bred? A liar and a coward! Not worthy of the name she bears! By God! I'm glad to be spared the sight of you now!'

His lips were drawn back in an ugly grimace, his tone full of cruel, unmerciful contempt. His words had been intended to wound as deeply as possible—and they found their mark.

'No! *Papa*!' Angelica cried out in horror.

She had seen his rage before, many times, but this was the first time it had ever been directed entirely at her. She had known he would be angry with her, but she hadn't guessed he would be so unforgivingly, corrosively furious.

'Hargreaves!' The Earl turned his grim, sightless head towards his secretary.

'Here, my lord.' The young man leapt forward instantly, almost knocking over the wooden globe in his anxiety to obey.

'You are dismissed,' said Lord Ellewood harshly. 'Now that my daughter has returned—inadequate though she is—I no longer have any need for a secretary who connives behind my back and cannot be trusted to obey a simple order. *Get out!*'

Mr Hargreaves's face was bleached with shock and confusion. He opened his mouth to protest, turned to Angelica in mute appeal, then stumbled out of the room without saying a word.

'You can't do that!' Angelica protested hotly, appalled at her father's injustice. 'It was *my* fault, not his. *I* decided to bring the letter. You *can't* punish him for my fault.'

'He should not have disobeyed me,' the Earl said unrelentingly, his voice grating painfully on Angelica's ears. 'I will not be served by disloyal men.'

'But—'

'Silence!' Lord Ellewood roared savagely. 'I can banish Hargreaves—*your* disloyalty I must live with!'

Angelica stared at the Earl. Her face was drained of all colour, both hands were pressed against her mouth. She knew that her father's vengeful anger stemmed mainly from his fear for her and his overwhelming sense of helplessness—but that didn't make it any easier to bear.

She felt Benoît come to stand beside her and she glanced up at him, recognising the intent, watchful expression in his brown eyes. The wolf in him had been roused.

'My lord,' he said coldly, his quiet, even tones in stark contrast to the Earl's ungovernable ranting. 'I am sorry that you have had such a disturbing few days, but you have no cause to abuse Lady Angelica so. She did not intend to worry you—and her motives were unimpeachable.'

'Who's there?' Lord Ellewood flung up his head, almost like a hound sniffing the wind. 'Who are you?'

'Benoît Faulkener.' He approached the Earl.

The two men were much of a height: tall and broad-

shouldered. But the Earl's body was wasted with pain
and inactivity, his movements clumsy and awkward.

Benoît moved with the lean, controlled grace of a
panther: silent, wary—and potentially dangerous.

The Earl stood listening tensely to Benoît's soft-
footed approach, his hands trembling with furious,
impotent energy.

Angelica caught her breath as she watched the two
men. The difference between them revealed her
father's ruin more brutally than ever. She could
remember when he had been as assured and relaxed
as Benoît.

'Yes, I should have guessed,' said Lord Ellewood
bitterly. 'I remember your voice. An arrogant, insolent
knave. I should have known better than to take you at
your word. *What have you done to my daughter?* Why
wasn't she here when I arrived?'

Angelica gasped. The Earl had been so angry about
her secretive departure from London she'd almost
forgotten she had anything else to explain to him. The
nightmarish situation was getting worse and worse,
and she could think of nothing to say to abate her
father's fury—no excuse for her behaviour.

But she was also growing angry herself, and she
experienced a wild desire not to explain anything to
the Earl. She couldn't believe he had treated Mr
Hargreaves so cruelly, dragging him all the way to
Sussex only to dismiss him at the moment of her
arrival.

'Lady Angelica was quite safe,' said Benoît calmly.

His dark eyes were intent on the Earl's face. He was
standing very still, poised and alert. There was a
coiled, deadly spring of energy within him, but as yet
he had made no attempt to engage the Earl's fury.

'*Where was she?*'

'This morning she was with Sir William Hopwood,'
said Benoît evenly. 'Last night she spent the night at

an inn in Littlehampton. I think the only hardship she had to endure was a certain amount of boredom. She has come to no harm, my lord.'

For a few moments the only sound in the library was the harsh, angry sound of the Earl's breathing. His chest rose and fell as he tried to master his seething fury. Angelica stared at him, white-faced; her hands were clenched together so tightly that her nails dug into her palms.

Even now, she could not imagine what it must be like for her father, unable to see where he was, or how many people confronted him, forced to judge their intentions and sincerity purely by the sound of their voices.

She knew that many blind people found ways of adapting to their handicap, but the Earl was not among their number. His memories of his former prowess were very vivid, and he was too bitter and impatient to learn new skills—yet he was also too young and too active to be content with a life spent confined within four walls. His anger seemed always to be roiling just beneath the surface, ready to scald anyone who inadvertently caused it to erupt.

'Have the carriage prepared,' the Earl ordered tautly. 'We are leaving. I want nothing further to do with this house or the people in it. I am sorry I ever thought of writing to you,' he added savagely.

'I'm sorry my messenger didn't reach you two days ago,' said Benoît equably. 'I replied to your letter immediately. Her ladyship also wrote to you to explain her delay. If you had received those letters, my lord, you would have been spared a great deal of needless anxiety. I have every intention of rescuing Lord Lennard.'

The Earl gave a brief, derisive, insulting laugh.

'Your fine words come too late,' he said scornfully. 'My son does not need the help of a presumptuous jackanapes! And I'll not leave my daughter in this house another minute! Your own actions betray you, cur! I should have had you flogged when I had the chance. Angelica! Order them to put the horses to!'

Benoît's eyes narrowed. He had been keeping a firm grip on his temper, partly for Angelica's sake, and partly because he could imagine the torment the Earl must have been in when he didn't know where his daughter was. But there were limits to his tolerance.

'Whether you wish it or not, I will help Lord Lennard,' he said, an icy, dangerous edge on his soft controlled voice. 'I do not forget my obligations. Nor will I stoop to barter insults with you. You are free to leave when you wish—but Angelica can choose for herself whether she goes with you. I suggest you speak to her more courteously, my lord! Neither her love for you nor her loyalty can be questioned—*but I will not allow anyone to abuse her*!'

Angelica stared, wide-eyed at Benoît, some of her anxiety dissipating in pure astonishment. He was as furious as the Earl. His lean, dark face was rigid with barely-controlled anger, and she could sense the fierce tension in his whipcord body.

'*You* won't allow. . .!' The Earl's scarred face was black with uncontrollable rage. 'A swaggering dunghill cock! I'll destroy you! How dare you interfere! My daughter—'

'May shortly be my wife!' Benoît interrupted curtly. 'Your threats hold no fear for me, my lord. I will not compel Angelica to stay—though it might make it easier for her if I did—but she deserves better than to be forced to share the barren hell you seem to have made of your own life!'

Angelica's heart thudded with amazement, joy and distress. She had wondered if Benoît would ask her to marry him, but in the end there had been no proposal only a flat statement to her father. She was overwhelmed by an almost unbearable maelstrom of conflicting emotions as she glanced from Benoît's rigid face to her father's.

The Earl lifted his head, shocked out of his ranting fury into some deeper, darker emotion by Benoît's words.

'Angelica!'

She didn't immediately answer, and he stretched out a demanding, unforgiving hand in her direction.

'*Come here!*'

Angelica stared at his hand for a few, heart-stopping seconds. His gesture was terrible in its fierce, unmerciful authority. She took two, horrified steps backwards, away from her father, and looked up at Benoît. His expression was intent and uncompromising.

'Is that the life you want to lead?' he asked ruthlessly.

'I. . .' Her voice failed her and she shook her head in a desperate attempt to deny everything that had just happened.

'By God! You'll pay for this!' The Earl raged. 'A smuggling weasel to lay hands on my daughter! *Angelica!*'

He took an unwary step towards her, stumbled into the globe and lost his balance. He struggled wildly for a moment, then crashed to the floor. The globe landed partially on top of him. He cursed viciously and flailed at it, smashing his fist into the object which had betrayed him.

At the sight of her father, fighting with the globe like a madman, Angelica's composure finally broke. She fled out of the library, wrenched open the front door and stumbled out of the house.

The Earl lay on the floor, his energy spent. He was angry, afraid—and humiliated. Above all else he felt humiliated, and his sense of degradation made him vicious. At that moment he was beyond reason. He felt the globe being lifted away from him and he tensed, ready to lash out, but nobody touched him. Benoît set the globe on its feet a safe distance from Lord Ellewood and walked out of the library without a word.

Lord Ellewood heard the door close. He lay still, his anger-crazed mind beginning to clear. He was not even sure if he was alone, but he could hear no sound except his own harsh breathing.

A log collapsed, hissing in the hearth and he turned his head sharply towards the sound.

'Who's there?' he demanded fiercely—but nobody answered.

At last his rigid muscles relaxed and he pushed himself up onto his knees, groping clumsily around him. He was in a strange room. He had no idea where any of the furniture was, or what obstacles lay before him.

His hand encountered a shard of glass, and he snatched it back. He had lost his spectacles in the fall and now they were broken, crushed by the heavy globe. His finger was cut and he sucked it painfully, a bitter, childish wreck of a once proud man.

But his pride would not allow him to remain huddled on the floor. They would come back, and he must be ready. He would get out of here—and then he would destroy the smugglers' whelp-turned-upstart shipowner.

He felt about more cautiously, and crawled across the floor until he bumped into the edge of a chair. He hauled himself up into it and dragged in several rasping breaths. His white hair was dishevelled, but his tragic, livid face was as set and unyielding as a teak mask.

* * *

Angelica ran blindly across the lawn, stumbling over her skirts in her unthinking attempt to get away from her father. She tripped and fell headlong, lying among the broken daffodils beneath an old oak tree. She'd been winded by the fall, and she made no effort to get up again. She rested her head on her arms and drew in deep, shuddering breaths.

Her father's unforgiving, uncontrollable rage had torn her apart. She hated to see him like this—a tragic mockery of his former self. Sometimes she thought it would have been better if he had died when the carriage overturned.

She closed her eyes, trying to calm her churning emotions, and slowly became aware of the sharp smell of broken daffodil stems beneath her arms. She could feel the damp grass beneath her cheek, and there was a robin singing a liquid melody in the branches of the oak tree above her. It all seemed quite unreal to her.

She didn't hear Benoît's footsteps, but she was instantly aware of his presence beside her. She didn't raise her head, but she felt his hand on her shoulder, then he lifted her to her feet.

She looked up at him, her eyes large and hollow in her pale face. He returned her gaze quietly, profound, penetrating concern in his dark eyes. She was dimly aware of the tension in his lean body, but she was too preoccupied by her own feelings to pay much attention to his.

'I keep hoping things will get better,' she said wearily. 'But they won't, will they? The Papa I used to know has gone. You were right. He *was* a fine man. But now. . .' Her voice trailed away into hopelessness.

'Now he's had to endure more than three helpless days of worrying about you,' said Benoît, almost matter-of-factly.

Angelica was jolted out of her gathering despair by his unexpected comment.

'Are you blaming *me* for what happened?' she demanded, in surprised disbelief.

'No,' he said immediately. 'Come and sit down.'

Angelica resisted his guiding hand. She was staring at him with doubt, and a hint of rebellion, in her blue eyes.

'I wasn't criticising you,' he said quietly. 'I don't believe you have anything to reproach yourself with.'

'How generous of you!' Angelica snapped, swinging away from him, her latent anger with her father finding a ready outlet. '*You* are not the arbiter of my conduct. You have no *idea*—' She broke off abruptly, biting her lip.

She hadn't cried earlier, but now she felt close to tears.

Benoît looked at her searchingly.

'No, I don't,' he replied, more curtly than he usually spoke. 'Despite what you'd said, I wasn't prepared for such a profound change in the Earl. Are such episodes commonplace?'

'Not...exactly,' said Angelica unsteadily, turning slightly away from Benoît.

She reached out and touched the rough bark of the tree trunk, almost as if she was seeking comfort from its solidity.

After a moment Benoît covered her hand with his. She felt the warm pressure of his fingers and looked up, blinking back her tears.

'He *hates* his blindness,' she said, her words tumbling over each other as she finally voiced her anguish. 'He *hates* his helplessness, and he *loathes* being dependent on others. He has become cruel and vengeful. He lashes out at the slightest provocation. He's had more than a dozen valets since his accident! Poor Mr Hargreaves—' She broke off, her voice strangled by a sob.

'We'll worry about poor Mr Hargreaves later,' said Benoît firmly. 'Does he lash out at you?'

'Sometimes. Never like today.' Her voice caught on a sob as she struggled not to burst into tears. 'Perhaps he's right. I *was* a coward when I didn't tell him myself I was coming—but I couldn't face an argument with him.'

'Harry's safety was your priority,' said Benoît reasonably. 'You can't blame yourself for putting his interests first. You've put your father first for a long time.'

'He *needed* me,' she said brokenly.

She looked up at Benoît, her pain and sense of betrayal nakedly exposed in her blue, tearfilled eyes.

She had tried so hard to take care of the Earl since his accident. She had turned her back on her own life and friends when he'd made it plain he didn't want strangers around him. She had endured his impatience and lack of gratitude without complaint and in the end she had been desperate for Harry to return home to them.

Harry was always jolly and lively. Harry could cheer anyone up. She had pinned her hopes on the possibility that he might be able to conjure Lord Ellewood out of his black, despairing moods. She was miserably aware of her own failure to do so.

But now her love and devotion had been rewarded by anger and cruel recriminations. Her father's rage had been out of all proportion with her offence. How could he have accused her of such dreadful things? He'd even said he was *glad* he could no longer see her!

She could hear still hear his grating voice as he heaped reproaches on her stricken head.

Liar. . . Coward. . . Not worthy of the name you bear.
Was that what he really *believed*?

'How *can* he not know I did it for his sake, as well

as Harry's?' she whispered bitterly. 'I've never been disloyal to him. *Never*! I thought—if only Harry came home...I knew it couldn't go on. It's been so... *killing*!'

'Yes, I see,' said Benoît slowly. 'What are you going to do now?'

'What do you mean?' Angelica swung round to face him, a startled question in her eyes as she wondered if he was retracting his earlier words in the library. 'You said...'

'And I meant it,' Benoît assured her softly. 'Although I hadn't intended to raise the subject in such a blunt way.' He paused, looking down at her with quiet intensity and she felt her heart skip a beat. 'Will you marry me, Angelica?' he asked, his voice very deep.

She gazed up into his warm brown eyes, seeing in them the love and support which she needed so much. She had never dreamt that he would propose to her under such circumstances. The joy and excitement she had anticipated feeling at this moment were inevitably muted by the situation—but not her love for Benoît. The burden of anxiety she had been carrying for so long seemed to grow lighter as she realised how willing he was to share it with her. She sighed with deeply felt happiness.

'Yes,' she said simply. 'Oh, yes. I will.'

Benoît smiled, his usually guarded eyes blazing with triumphant love. He reached out to take her in his arms and she felt the tension leave his lean body. She suddenly realised how difficult he must have found the scene in the library. His debt to the Earl and his desire to protect her from Lord Ellewood's anger must have torn him in two different directions—just as Lord Ellewood's black moods had been tearing her apart for so long.

She put her arms around him and hugged him

fiercely, thanking him wordlessly for his understanding, his love and his support. His hold on her tightened, and for a moment she was content to stand within the circle of his embrace—but she could not forget her father, still waiting in the house. Until she had achieved some kind of reconciliation with Lord Ellewood she could not truly contemplate the future.

'What do you want to do?' Benoît asked at last.

'I don't know.' Angelica lifted her head and looked at him, seeing from his expression how well he understood her conflicting emotions. 'I'm not sure if I can face talking to Papa again right now,' she admitted with bleak honesty.

'He travelled all the way from London to find you,' Benoît reminded her gently. 'You said yourself he'd never left the house before—'

'Because he was *angry* with me!' Angelica interrupted bitterly. 'I'd hoped it wasn't so, but—'

'He was also afraid for you,' Benoît reminded her. 'His first words were to ask if you were safe. He's had no choice but confront his handicap these past few days, *mon aimée*, and that can't have been easy for him. I don't imagine he's had much sleep since you left either. When he's had time to calm down, you may find he's much more rational.'

'Perhaps.' Angelica bit her lip irresolutely.

She knew that there was probably a great deal of truth in what Benoît said; but she still felt hurt, betrayed and disappointed. There had been too many times when Lord Ellewood had spoken crossly to her when she'd only been trying to help. Too many times when he'd taken his frustration out on those around him, and she'd been helpless to intervene. Mr Hargreaves was only the last of a long line of people who'd suffered from the Earl's lack of tolerance.

All the small, daily frustrations and disillusionments of the past eighteen months melded together to create

a core of revolt in her heart. She didn't want to go
back to her father—to apologise, explain and try to
make amends. She was tired of trying. It was his turn
now.

She looked back at Benoît and he read her thoughts
in her unguarded, almost defiant blue eyes.

She didn't have to go back to see the Earl if she
didn't want to. She no longer had to explain anything
to her father—and she could be as stubborn as Lord
Ellewood when she chose.

Benoît smiled faintly.

'I've noticed a distinct family resemblance between
you before,' he remarked dryly. 'If I were in your
shoes, *mon amour*, I would feel angry and resentful—
and very hurt. But it may still be worth trying to talk
to him.'

Angelica sighed, glancing towards the house, wondering what her father was doing now. She knew
Benoît was right. She had to try to make peace with
the Earl. If she didn't, she would never forgive herself.

'Yes, I know,' she said. 'I'll talk to him.' There'd
never really been any question that she would do so,
but she'd needed a few minutes to collect her courage
and her resolution. 'I was so surprised and pleased
when you told me he'd left London,' she added, with
resolute optimisim. 'Perhaps things *will* be different
now.'

The Earl didn't know how long he'd been sitting in
the library when he heard low voices in the hall. He
had experienced a frightening kaleidoscope of
emotions during his long, dark isolation, but now he
was bored and impatient. He was used to being obeyed
instantly—being ignored was a new experience.

He couldn't leave the library because he wasn't
prepared to go stumbling around a strange house, his
helplessness plain for everyone to see—but he hated

not knowing what was going on. He didn't know where Angelica was. He didn't know what Benoît was doing and his volatile temper had begun to stir again.

He turned his head as the door opened.

'Who's there?' he demanded fiercely.

'Henry! *Old friend!*' Sir William strode across the room and seized the Earl's hand before Lord Ellewood could react. 'I'm so glad I haven't missed you. I came as soon as I heard you were here!'

He shook the Earl's hand warmly between both of his. The pleasure in his voice was unmistakable. If he was shocked by his old friend's appearance his cordial tones didn't betray it.

'William?' said Lord Ellewood, almost tentatively. He had forgotten Benoît's reference to the magistrate and he was taken completely by surprise by Sir William's arrival.

'"Blunderbuss Billy", more like!' Sir William gave a crack of self-deprecating laughter. 'Dammit! I was sorry to hear about Harry—though it sounds as if he's more than a chip off the old block. Gave the Frogs a good run for their money by all accounts!'

He pulled up a chair beside the Earl and sat down.

'How do you know about Harry?' Lord Ellewood demanded, frowning.

'Angelica told me. By George she's turned into a fine young woman,' said Sir William enthusiastically. ' Gave me a rare dressing-down for trying to discuss family business in public. I had no idea you knew young Faulkener. If anyone can get Harry out of France, he can!'

The Earl bit back a hasty retort. He wanted to deny all knowledge of Benoît, but he had sufficient control of his temper to realise that it wouldn't be wise. Whatever Angelica had been doing in Sussex over the past three days, she had been with Benoît Faulkener.

It would not do her reputation any good if her father publicly denounced him.

'I met him several years ago,' he said shortly. 'Where did you see Angelica?'

'At the inn, in Littlehampton,' Sir William replied, sounding surprised. 'It's a pity you didn't send her to me, she would have been much more comfortable waiting for Adam at the Manor. *That* was a surprise, by God! I thought the boy was dead! You needn't worry about him though. I've got him safe at the Manor—and no Froggie agents will have a chance to pig-stick him there.'

'*Adam?*' A variety of unreadable expressions chased each other across the Earl's ravaged face.

'Young Kennett.' Sir William nodded vigorously. 'An excellent choice to bring you that letter. I take it you know its contents by now? Of course, Angelica wouldn't delay in telling you. But Adam's led me some fine dances over the years,' he continued almost indulgently. 'Do you remember that night we went hunting for smugglers? Adam told me in the carriage only today that he'd been the fox who led me so far astray. And you came back without your horse that morning. You never did explain how that happened! What days those were!'

'Yes.' Despite himself, the Earl sighed.

'Well, now that you're in Sussex, I'll be offended if you don't come to stay with me at the Manor,' said Sir William gruffly. 'Been trying to get you down here again for years!'

'You are very kind,' said the Earl, his tone unintentionally cold. 'But I'm afraid I must disappoint you. Angelica and I are returning to town immediately.'

'Nonsense!' Sir William exclaimed forcefully. 'You've only just arrived. Besides, I'm sure you'll want to talk to Adam. Get the news straight from the horse's mouth as it were! I wonder what Faulkener's got in mind? It's a pity Adam's so badly knocked up or they could have tackled it together.'

The Earl hesitated. He still felt extremely hostile to Benoît, and he was fiercely anxious to return to the security and familiarity of his own home. On the other hand, there was something unaccountably pleasant about the magistrate's explosive company. Apart from anything else, he still retained his remarkable ability to supply both sides of the conversation.

Besides, it was becoming glaringly apparent to the Earl that Sir William was almost as much in the dark about recent events as he was.

The magistrate believed that Adam Kennett— whoever the devil he was—had brought James Corbett's letter to England. Whereas Lord Ellewood knew for a fact that that was not the case—so who was Kennett? And why had he apparently been injured by the French?

The Earl's hunting instincts were aroused. If Angelica wouldn't tell him the truth—he blocked out the thought that he hadn't given her much opportunity to do so—he would find it out for himself. They would see there was life in the blind old dog yet.

'I'd hate to disappoint an old friend,' he said, tacitly accepting Sir William's invitation.

'Good man!' Sir William bounded to his feet, landing an exuberant buffet on the Earl's shoulder.

'I'll have them prepare your gear at once. By heaven! This will be a day to remember!'

'I believe it will,' Lord Ellewood said, smiling for the first time in several days.

For the past eighteen months everyone he'd met had treated him as if he was not only blind, but also extremely frail. Sir William's thoughtless ebullience was oddly gratifying.

* * *

'Papa! How could you?' Angelica burst into the library.

Her cheeks were burning with colour, her eyes blazing with fierce, uncompromising anger.

'Angelica?' Lord Ellewood hauled himself instinctively to his feet.

'How *could* you dismiss Martha?' she demanded, her voice throbbing with furious indignation. 'How *could* you stoop to such a thing? To punish her for her *loyalty*! This morning you dismissed Mr Hargreaves for his *disloyalty*!'

'She has shown no loyalty to me,' said Lord Ellewood gratingly.

'She's *my* maid!' Angelica exclaimed passionately. 'Would you have had any respect for her if she'd betrayed *my* trust?'

'Respect?' the Earl snarled. 'She's a damned servant! As long as I pay her wages she'll obey my will! I will not tolerate defiance in *any* member of my household.'

Angelica stared at him, her chest rising and falling in quick, angry breaths. She could sense her father's volcanic temper was about to erupt, but she no longer cared. His treatment of Martha had goaded her beyond caution. The small spark of revolt she had suppressed earlier had now been fanned into blazing flames of rebellion by what she'd just discovered.

She and Benoît had returned to the house to find that Sir William was sitting with the Earl. Angelica had immediately decided to delay speaking to her father until he was alone. Benoît had agreed, and she'd seized the opportunity to go up to her bedchamber for a few moments of quiet reflection.

But Martha had been waiting for her, and one glance at her maid's face had been enough to tell Angelica that things were badly wrong.

Lord Ellewood had arrived at Holly House in the

early hours of the morning, and he'd instantly had Martha hauled out of bed and dragged before him. He'd subjected her to an even worse ordeal than Angelica had suffered later—and it had culminated in the maid's dismissal.

As far as Angelica could tell, Martha had remained stoically loyal to her mistress throughout, refusing to reveal more than the barest minimum of information. Angelica was bitterly aware of how much anxiety she had caused Martha, and she couldn't forgive herself for putting the maid in such an impossible situation.

But nor could she forgive the Earl for venting his fury on such a powerless victim.

'Then you may soon have no household left,' she said bleakly, the white heat of her anger dying as she confronted her father across the library floor. 'I understand you dismissed your valet before you left London. Today you have discharged Mr Hargreaves and Martha. You told me once I should judge a man's character on the way he is viewed by his servants not his peers.'

She paused.

There was no sound in the room except Lord Ellewood's rasping breath and the soft, measured tick of the clock. His head was flung up, his sightless eyes turned towards Angelica, but he did not speak. Though she did not know it, her words had struck a wounding blow. The Earl was already ashamed of his treatment of Martha, but he was far too angry to admit it.

Lord Ellewood had been alone when Angelica had thrown open the library door, but now she was dimly aware that there were people standing behind her. She ignored them. All her attention was concentrated on her father.

'I'm sorry I left London without telling you,' she said steadily. 'I'm sorry I exposed Mr Hargreaves and

Martha to your wrath. I won't forgive myself for that. But, Papa, if I'd thought you would listen or understand, I would have *told* you why I had to deliver your letter myself—and if you'd told me what you must have known about Benoît I wouldn't have needed to.'

'*Told* me?' the Earl said harshly. 'Who the *devil* do you think you're talking to, girl?'

'I don't know,' said Angelica flatly. 'Certainly not the father I remember. Goodbye, Papa.'

'What do you mean?' Lord Ellewood's expression darkened. He was breathing heavily.

'I mean I will not be returning to London with you,' she said, with wintry finality. 'You will have to find someone else to sit in the dark and read to you while the rest of the world goes dancing by.'

She turned on her heel and walked out of the library without waiting for his reply. Benoît stepped crisply aside to let her pass. Sir William simply stared at her in open-mouthed astonishment.

'*Angelica!*' Lord Ellewood roared.

She put her foot on the first tread of the stairs and began to walk slowly upwards.

'*Angelica!*'

She didn't pause, or even look around. There was no colour left in her cheeks, but her lips were pressed resolutely together. She had made her decision and she would not be swayed—certainly not by Lord Ellewood's unreasoning anger.

'She will not come for such a summons,' said Benoît quietly.

He closed the library door and turned to study the Earl thoughtfully. Sir William was still standing silently, staring from one to the other with a mixture of bewilderment and appalled disbelief on his face.

'This is your doing!' Lord Ellewood accused Benoît savagely. 'You've polluted her mind with your insidious—'

'I've never been called insidious before,' Benoît interrupted coldly. 'If you believe I've turned Angelica against you, then you are mistaken. You seem to be doing very well without my help!'

'I'll *never* consent to her marrying you!' Lord Ellewood ground out.

He was shaking with fury, his hands clenched convulsively, but he had himself rigidly under control. He had no intention of humiliating himself again. He didn't risk taking even a single step towards Benoît.

'We don't need your consent,' said Benoît equably. 'Angelica is twenty-three years old. She can make up her own mind.'

'I'll disown her!' said Lord Ellewood wildly. 'She'll get nothing from me. Not a single penny.'

'She doesn't need your money,' said Benoît coldly. 'I am quite capable of supporting a wife. Your respect is much more important to her. Whatever she's done, she did out of love for you and Lord Lennard—but you've treated her worse than you did an insolent smugglers' whelp who held you at gunpoint!'

'Don't lecture me, sir!' the Earl blared. 'I will not leave Angelica in this house with you. Where's Hopwood?'

'H-here.' Sir William stumbled over his answer, too shocked to be coherent.

Lord Ellewood dragged in a deep, searing breath and then he hesitated. The library was filled with his fierce tension as he stood stock-still, battling with his powerful emotions.

He'd intended to order the magistrate to fetch Angelica back. He'd intended to drag her, kicking and screaming if need be, away from Holly House.

But he didn't.

He lifted his ravaged, scarred head like a proud old lion, and said with frozen dignity, 'It seems that my daughter will not be accompanying us to the Manor,

William. I believe there is no longer any need to delay our departure.'

Sir William swallowed. He was still trying to catch up with events. He looked desperately from Lord Ellewood's rigid face to Benoît's wolf-wary, watchful expression.

'I'll see if the carriage is ready,' he said hastily. For once in his life he had no stomach for taking part in a melodramatic scene.

'You're still there,' Lord Ellewood stated flatly, as the door closed behind the magistrate.

'Yes, my lord.'

'Yes,' the Earl repeated, the single word dropping into the silence of the library like a stone.

Lord Ellewood listened with all his might, but even so he could hear no indication of Benoît's presence—not even his breathing. He might have been talking to a shadow—or fighting a shadow. No man could defeat a shadow.

'If I could still see, you would never get away with this!' he said savagely.

'If you could still see, you would *nevertheless* have asked for my help to rescue Lord Lennard,' said Benoît coolly, 'because I have connections which are not available to most men. But, if you could still see, you would not be so eaten up with frustration and envy that you're blind to the practical good sense of what you've done. Harry will be safe with me, my lord. So will Angelica—and you know it.'

'I have the promise of a smuggling cur for that?' the Earl jeered sarcastically.

'You have *my* promise,' Benoît said, a note of steely assurance underpinning his unemphatic reply.

'I believe your carriage is waiting. *Au revoir*, my lord. I am sure we will meet again.'

CHAPTER NINE

ANGELICA and Benoît were married the following afternoon by Special Licence. Angelica wore the same ivory satin gown she had worn to dinner at Holly House three nights before. She stood in a shaft of sunlight from the alter window of a small London church, her golden hair framing her face like a halo, and made her vows in a firm, confident voice.

There were no friends or relatives in attendance. But it didn't matter because, as Martha pointed out when she was dressing Angelica, the only person a bride really needs to be present at her wedding is the groom.

'You followed me all the way from London to deliver these letters?' the Earl demanded gratingly.

'Yes, my lord.' Benoît's messenger stood tiredly in front of Lord Ellewood. 'Captain Faulkener bade me deliver them directly into your own hand—but I was waylaid near Epsom.'

'Attacked?' said Lord Ellewood sharply.

'Yes, my lord.'

Simpson held his right arm stiffly, and there was a rough bandage around his head. The Earl could not see the man's hurts, but he could hear the cracked strain in his voice.

'What happened?'

'They knocked me cold and took my horse. I don't remember much, but I was told they were searching me when they were frightened off. Otherwise I expect they would have taken the letters.'

Simpson fell silent. He was bone-weary and ached

in every fibre of his being. He had discharged his duty, and now he longed for nothing more than a chance to lie down and sleep.

'And when you were fit to ride you carried on to London,' said Sir William, involving himself in the conversation for the first time, 'and when Lord Ellewood wasn't there you followed him back to Sussex, and then from Holly House to here. When you discovered his destination, didn't it occur to you that there was no longer any need to deliver the letters?'

'No, sir.' Simpson straightened his shoulders. 'The Captain gave me strict instructions. He would not expect me to fail in carrying out his orders.'

'Thank you,' said Lord Ellewood distantly. 'Your dedication to duty is commendable.'

He held the two letters between his fingers. They were creased and dirty, but the seals were still unbroken. He wondered if he had the courage to ask Sir William to read them to him. He put them in his pocket, fumbling a little as he did so.

'You poor fellow! You must be exhausted!' Sir William sprang to his feet as Simpson's shoulders slumped lower. 'Come with me.' He clapped the seaman on the back, making him stagger. 'You must have a good meal and a long rest before you go back to Holly House. Your master's not there at present, so there's no hurry. Your devotion deserves a fat reward. Be sure I'll tell him so when I see him.'

'Oh, no,' said Simpson, his speech a trifle slurred. 'The Captain knows I don't serve him for reward. We've been halfway round the world together. I'd never—'

His legs buckled under him, and he would have fallen if Sir William hadn't seized him.

Lord Ellewood sat quietly, listening to the magistrate bellow for his servants to bustle about and take care of Benoît's exhausted messenger. He was thinking of Angelica's bitter reminder that he had once told her the truest judge of a man's character was his own servant.

Angelica spent her wedding night at a coaching inn just south of London. Benoit normally stayed with his partner, Josiah Crabtree, when he visited the City, but he had too much tact to suggest such an arrangement on this occasion.

The busy inn suited Angelica perfectly. She was fascinated by the teeming life all around them. She stood at the window of their bedchamber, watching the lamplit arrival of a private coach in the yard below, delighted to be at the heart of so much activity.

She felt Benoît come up behind her. He slipped one arm around her waist and pulled the curtain closed with his other hand.

'Ma chère femme—' he kissed the graceful curve of her neck and shoulder '—you are supposed to save your attention for your husband on your wedding night—not a crowd of noisy strangers!' There was an unmistakable note of amusement in his deep voice.

Angelica caught her breath, relief as well as sensuous pleasure filling her at the touch of his lips on her soft skin. He had escorted her to London with such formal correctness she'd been afraid he'd been annoyed with her for forcing him into such a hasty marriage.

That hadn't been her intention when she'd walked out of the library the previous day. She hadn't thought any further than the fact that she could no longer allow her father to dominate her life. Lord Ellewood's cruelty to Martha had been the last straw.

It had been Benoît who had insisted they be married immediately. Angelica was aware that his decision had been prompted by a desire to protect her from scandal, but they had barely discussed the matter. She had been a preoccupied travelling companion, and he had been scrupulously punctilious in his dealings with her since they'd left Holly House.

She leant back against him, grateful to be enfolded once more in his embrace.

'Are you thinking about Lord Ellewood?' he asked softly, brushing her hair with his lips.

'Yes,' she admitted.

Her sentiments towards her father were confused. She felt angry, resentful, betrayed, sad, guilty—and liberated.

'When we go back to Sussex we'll call upon him at the Manor,' Benoît promised. 'I'm sure the breach between you is not irreparable.'

'No,' said Angelica flatly.

'Angelica—!'

'No,' she repeated uncompromisingly, slipping out of his arms and turning to look at him.

He returned her gaze, a hint of a frown in his dark eyes.

'What do you mean?' he asked quietly.

'I mean I will not go crawling back to him, begging his forgiveness, when it is he who should be apologising for his behaviour,' Angelica said stonily.

'I'm not in the habit of crawling anywhere,' Benoît replied dryly, 'and I certainly wasn't suggesting my wife should do so, but—'

'But what?' Angelica snapped. She hadn't realised how sensitive she was about the situation with her father until Benoît had broached the subject. 'Nothing's changed except we're married. If Papa was prepared to disown me rather than let me marry you, do you think he's going to be any more forgiving now I'm your *wife*?'

'I think that now he's had time for reflection, he may be more reasonable,' Benoît replied. He spoke mildly, although there was an underlying tension in his tone. 'I doubt—'

'That's what you said yesterday!' Angelica interrupted forcefully. 'And then it turned out that he'd dismissed Martha. He's not going to get any more reasonable—he's *not*!' Her voice cracked and she turned away to rest an unsteady hand on the mantelpiece, staring down into the fireplace with unseeing eyes.

The rift with Lord Ellewood was more painful for her than she was prepared to admit, even to herself.

'Lord Ellewood dismissed Martha in the middle of the night—before you'd returned to Holly House,' Benoît reminded her sharply. 'You only found out about it *after* you'd already had one argument with him—and then you used it as a pretext to leave him.'

Angelica spun round to face Benoît, consternation in her fine blue eyes.

'Are you *blaming* me for what I did?' she demanded fiercely.

'No, *mon aimée*,' Benoît said equably. 'But I do want you to see things clearly—and I don't want this temporary estrangement between you and your father to become permanent.

'Lord Ellewood may already have been regretting his treatment of Martha, or he may not have been. We don't know, because when you confronted him in such a rage you forced his hand—just as he had forced yours earlier. You are both proud people. But I won't let you become locked in a spiral of anger which can only lead to increasing bitterness and pain for everyone. We will go back and see him.'

Angelica stared at him, doubt and disbelief in her wide blue eyes. She could hear the undercurrent of steel in Benoît's cool voice, and she knew he meant every word he said. She was far too overwrought by all the emotional upheavals of the past few days to

give any rational consideration to his motives for
saying it.

Her first, horrified reaction was that he was taking
the Earl's side against her. Why was he so determined
not to lose Lord Ellewood's favour?

'Why are you so anxious I make peace with Papa?'
she demanded wildly, fear and suspicion in her eyes.
'Are you afraid he will indeed disown me? A penniless, disinherited wife would be a dreadful burden for
an ambitious, but nameless, man—wouldn't she?'

The moment the words left her mouth she regretted
them. She pressed her hands against her face, appalled
at what she'd just said, her huge eyes locked on
Benoît's rigid expression.

His jaw was set like a rock; a muscle twitched in his
cheek and his eyes were narrow and dangerous.

'I should have left you with the Earl,' he said
harshly. 'You clearly deserve each other. You could
have traded insults to your hearts' content.'

'I'm *s-sorry!*' Angelica whispered, a stricken
expression in her eyes as she reached out to him
imploringly.

'Why did you marry me?' Benoît asked implacably,
his eyes granite-hard as they locked with hers. He
ignored both her outstretched hands and her pleading
look. 'Why did you stay in Sussex an extra day?'

'What?' Angelica stared at him uncomprehendingly.
She felt dazed and bruised. 'You know why.'

'Because you didn't *trust* me!' Benoît flung at her,
with brutal irony. 'No, *ma douce amie*, that isn't good
enough! You must have known you could trust me or
you wouldn't have gone jaunting unchaperoned
around the countryside with me. *Why did you stay
after you'd delivered the letter?*'

He took two strides towards her as he spoke and
seized her by the shoulders.

'*Why?*' He shook her, the strength of his grip

making her wince, although she was not aware of
feeling any pain.

'Because I c-couldn't bear to go back to London!'
Angelica stammered, dismayed by the blazing anger
and suspicion she could see in his eyes.

She could feel the fierce, ruthlessly controlled rage
which coursed through his whipcord body. He'd
relaxed his grasp on her shoulders the moment she'd
flinched, but his fury was no less disturbing because
she knew he hadn't deliberately hurt her.

'That's it, isn't it?' He released her suddenly, as if
she'd burnt him.

He turned on his heel and took a couple of hasty
strides across the room, his hands clenched into fists.
Angelica watched him, numb with shock.

'*Ma douce séductrice* indeed!' he snarled savagely
over his shoulder. 'You knew the impact you'd made
on me from the first and you decided to take advantage of it. I dare say it would have suited you better if
I'd been a gentleman born and bred—but you were so
desperate to escape an unbearable life that any halfway respectable man would have done!'

'No!' Angelica protested.

'No?' he taunted her bitterly. 'I've known experienced harlots pursue their quarry with more...
hesitation...than you've used to entrap me. *My God!*
What a fool I've been!'

He was still standing with his back to Angelica. He
lifted an unsteady hand to run his fingers through his
black hair. Then he leant his forearm against the
bedpost and rested his forehead against it. His other
arm hung by his side, his hand clenched into a fist. It
was the first time Angelica had ever see him lose his
composure so completely.

Her own hasty temper had been thoroughly roused
by his unfair accusations. Her blue eyes blazed with

indignation. She opened her mouth to hurl a scalding rejoinder at him. But the bitter words died on her lips.

Her eyes were riveted on Benoît's rigid shoulders. Her anger drained away, to be replaced by a cold, hollow fear. She drew in a deep, shaky breath. They had been married only a few hours, yet already they were locked in a bitter dispute. Was this marriage a dreadful mistake?

For a few seconds she was overwhelmed by a desperate desire to escape: but then her shocked mind began to function again.

Benoît loved her.

She knew that with deep, wordless, instinctive certainty. The ferocity of his anger was a measure of how much he cared for her—and how much her cruel suggestion had hurt him.

In her own pain and confusion she had accused him of being a social-climbing fortune-hunter; and then she had inadvertently confirmed his apprehension that she'd simply used him to get away from the Earl. Perhaps he even suspected that her decision to marry the brickmaker's grandson was part of her revenge on the autocratic Lord Ellewood.

Benoît didn't lack self-confidence, but even he wasn't armoured against such a wounding slight from the woman he loved.

And he did love her. Angelica had never been so sure of it as she was when she gazed at his rigidly held shoulders and listened to his harshly controlled breathing. He was a guarded, cautious man, who had revealed more of his feelings to her than she suspected he had ever revealed to anyone before. She could not betray his trust.

'I stayed because I could not bear to leave *you*,' she said clearly, her heart pounding with quick anxiety as she tried to make amends for her unthinking, damaging accusation.

She walked over to him and reached out almost tentatively to touch his unresponsive back.

'I didn't know that—I didn't admit it to myself,' she continued, trying to speak steadily, although a pulse beating in her throat threatened to rob her of her voice. 'I told myself I was doing it for Harry's sake, because I didn't know if a smuggler could be trusted to rescue him. But it was for my sake I stayed, because I'd found. . .' She faltered and paused, trying to compose herself.

Beneath her hand she felt Benoît's tense muscles slowly relax, but he did not alter his position.

'I remember my first Season,' she said softly, gaining confidence. 'I had such high hopes, Ben. I thought I was going to find love and life—and perhaps even adventure—in the fashionable drawing-rooms and ballrooms of London.' She sighed, lost briefly in the past.

'It *was* exciting at first,' she continued wryly, 'but then I saw my friends get married. Sometime they found love, but mostly they didn't, and I thought—is this all there is? Will I have to chose between being a lonely spinster or a lonely wife? So I decided years ago I'd never get married unless I found a man I could love—and who loved me. I didn't care whether he was a prince or. . .or a *smuggler*.'

She slipped her hand through Benoît's arm and leant her cheek against his sleeve. His muscles were no longer rigid with tension and she felt a wave of relief wash over her as she realised he wasn't angry with her any more.

'I didn't have to marry you to get away from Papa,' she murmured, almost provocatively. 'Aunt Sarah in Bath has been sending me increasingly urgent invitations to visit her for nearly a year. She's a very high-spirited old lady, Harry's devoted to her. It was a difficult decision to make, but. . .'

Benoît turned round and slipped his arms around her waist. She looked up at him a little diffidently and saw a gleam of wry amusement in his dark, still shadowed eyes.

'That has to be the most long-winded, roundabout apology I have ever received, *mon aimée*,' he said, a hint of familiar humour in his voice.

Angelica was overwhelmed by a strange mixture of relief and nervousness; but she was too shy to reveal her feelings. She tried to hide them behind mock indignation.

'You *knew*, and you let me keep talking—!' she exclaimed.

'I was waiting to see if you'd ever manage to come straight out with the words, "I'm sorry. I love you",' he said softly. 'They stick a bit in that graceful throat, don't they, *ma chérie*?' He stroked it gently with sensitive fingers. 'I can't remember ever hearing you say them.'

Tears sparkled in Angelica's eyes.

'I do love you,' she said breathlessly. 'I love you with all my heart and soul, and nothing will ever change that. I'm sorry I said such a horrible thing to you. I know—'

His arms tightened around her and he stifled the rest of her apology with a kiss. She clung to him, trying to show him in her response to him how truly she meant what she'd said.

'I'm sorry too, *mon amour*,' he murmured a few moments later, his cheek resting against her hair as he held her against him. 'I know you didn't set out to trick me into marriage—I knew it even when I said it. It was just. . .'

Angelica lifted her head to meet his eyes and laid her fingers gently on his lips. Tears dampened her cheeks, but she didn't try to hide them. She smiled a little unsteadily.

'I gave you good reason to be angry,' she said softly, distress in her eyes. 'I've been so cross with Papa—yet the moment *I* felt hurt and confused I acted in exactly the same way. I lashed out at someone who loves me and wanted to help me.'

A sob caught in her throat and she swallowed, trying to suppress her tears.

'I'm not really as brazen as a h-harlot, am I?' she whispered anxiously, unable to conceal her own pain at the things he'd said to her.

'No!' Benoît exclaimed. 'No. I'm sorry, *mon aimée!* It was a cruel, unkind thing to suggest. Don't ever worry about it again.'

He smiled crookedly and stroked her cheek, brushing away her tears with infinitely tender fingers.

'Almost the first thing I noticed about you was the way your actions are guided by your heart,' he said softly. 'I think perhaps I am a little daunted, as well as captivated, by your openness. By nature I'm far more cautious and secretive. You will have to teach me to be less guarded, *mon amour.*'

Angelica gazed up at him, seeing his lean, dark face through a haze of tears.

She was remembering the inherent honesty with which Benoît had always treated her. Occasionally he had obscured facts, but only once had he deliberately misled her—and that had been about Adam's arrival. She didn't deserve his praise.

She bit her lip, struggling to control her overtaxed emotions.

Benoît smiled faintly, a quietly understanding expression in his brown eyes. He stroked the nape of her neck with gentle fingers.

'Ever since we left Sussex you have been so determined not to admit to any doubts—or reveal how upset you are,' he murmured. 'I do know, *ma chérie*, however insensitive I may have seemed. You won't have to face Lord Ellewood alone, I promise. I'll be with you. And we won't go to him until you're ready.'

Angelica gave a little gasp, and then the pent-up feelings of the past few days finally found release in a flood of tears.

Benoît held her comfortingly, stroking her hair and speaking softly to her until the first storm of emotion had passed.

Angelica let him support her, profoundly reassured and moved by his response to her. She could feel the firm texture of his coat beneath her cheek, and the relaxed vigour of his strong body against hers. His arms provided her with a haven and a source of strength. She knew with absolute conviction that from now on home was not a place, it was a person. Benoît was the only home she needed.

When the worst paroxysm of tears had passed, he guided her over to the bed and sat down beside her, one arm supporting her as she rested her head on his broad shoulder. She felt drained and exhausted, but so much better than she had done earlier. A crushing burden had finally become lighter.

She sighed, and accepted the handkerchief he offered her.

'Thank you,' she whispered, blowing her nose. 'I'm sorry,' she added a moment later with the first hint of humour she'd shown all day. 'A damp and over-wrought bride is probably not what a man hopes for on his wedding night!'

Benoît chuckled and brushed her curls with his lips.

'I can think of worse things,' he said reflectively. 'And you are safely in my arms, *mon aimée*, even if you have just wept all over my best coat!'

Angelica smiled with weary contentment as she nestled within the circle of his arm. The nervous energy which had propelled her through the past twenty-four hours had finally burnt itself out. She was grateful for the interlude of quiet, gentle good humour.

'Adam's right,' she teased Benoît softly. 'You are a dandy! I thought so the first time we met. All you need is a gold ear-ring. . .!'

'You had me cast in the role of pirate from the first!' Benoît retorted. 'I've told you before—I'm a respectable businessman.'

'Who gets woken up by smugglers in the middle of the night,' Angelica reminded him, lifting her head to look at him. 'Where *did* you go that first night I stayed at Holly House?'

'What a long memory you have!' Benoît remarked, grinning. 'One of Tody's old friends broke his arm escaping from Sir William,' he continued matter-of-factly. 'I learnt a lot from my father before I went to sea. They wanted me to set the bone for him. Being the trustworthy fellow that I am, you understand!'

'Respectable. . .trustworthy. . .I've married a paragon of virtue,' Angelica mused, a twinkle in her tired blue eyes.

Benoît smiled, but didn't rise to the bait.

'You look worn out, and pale as a ghost,' he said softly, stroking her dishevelled curls. 'Did you sleep much last night?'

'No,' Angelica confessed ruefully.

'I thought not. You must rest tonight.' Benoît kissed her lightly and stood up. 'I'll send Martha to you.'

'Benoît. . .Ben.' Angelica paused, gazing up at him with wide, dark-circled eyes.

He reached down to take her hand in his, lifting it to his lips.

'We've the rest of our lives together,' he said quietly. 'I know you're my wife, Angelica. I don't have to prove it at the first opportunity. Besides,' he added wickedly, 'as I recall, you find being jolted about in a carriage extremely traumatic. That was the reason you gave for staying at Holly House an extra day, wasn't it? I'm sure you need a good night's sleep just to recover from the journey up to London!'

Angelica woke slowly in the early hours of the morning. The room was shrouded in silky darkness, and at first she could see nothing when she opened her eyes. For a moment she felt confused, but then she heard Benoît's unhurried breathing and remembered they were married.

She hardly dared to move for fear of waking him, but she eased carefully over until she could look at him. He had opened the curtains before getting into bed—she thought perhaps he disliked being cocooned away from the sky—and she studied him in the dim light.

She could see his firm, slightly aquiline profile, and hear his slow, steady breathing. He had always been so alert and so forceful. It was strange to see him exposed and vulnerable in sleep. She could hardly believe that all she had to do was reach out to touch him. And he wouldn't even know.

She sighed soundlessly, and cautiously propped herself up on her elbow, scarcely daring to breath in case she woke him. He was brother to the wolf; she could not imagine her actions wouldn't disturb him, but his breathing continued slow and sure.

She couldn't help herself. She stretched out a single, tentative finger to touch the curve of his shoulder. He wasn't wearing a nightshirt, and she suddenly wondered if he was completely naked beneath the sheets. A tiny thrill of excitement tingled through her body.

His flesh was warm and firm beneath her delicate, questing fingers. She couldn't resist letting her hand glide gently over his collarbone. Her heart began to beat faster. She felt guiltily that she was stealing an illicit pleasure, but the temptation was irresistible.

A sunburst glow of joy flooded through her as she finally realised that she was, irretrievably, Benoît's wife. He was her husband, and she had a perfect right to reach out to him in the night.

Her touch was no less imperceptible, but considerably more confident, as she began to trace the contour of his muscular chest. She was so absorbed in her task that she was completely taken by surprise when he caught her hand in his.

'*Ma douce séductrice*,' he murmured softly, without opening his eyes.

'I thought you were asleep!' Angelica exclaimed, disconcerted. She tried to withdraw her hand, but he tightened his hold on it.

'I was. But you could rouse a carved stone knight from his tomb!' he retorted, a smile in his voice as he turned his head to look at her.

'Oh.' Angelica blushed in the darkness.

'Oh?' Benoît slipped an arm beneath her waist and drew her to lie alongside him. 'Were you hoping I wouldn't wake up?' he enquired teasingly.

'Yes…No!' Angelica replied, feeling flustered. 'I mean—'

She was acutely conscious of the feel of Benoît's lean, vigorous body through her thin nightgown. Her weariness of the previous evening had vanished. A warm, anticipatory excitement began to flow through her veins.

Benoît chuckled and lifted his hand to slip it beneath her heavy golden hair as she looked down at him. His fingers gently caressed the nape of her neck, and a quiver of pleasure rippled through her.

'I thought it was usually the Prince who was supposed to wake the Princess,' he murmured provocatively, 'and you haven't completed the spell, *mon amour*. If you really want to be sure…'

Angelica hesitated for a fraction of a second.

'You've tricked me like that before,' she reminded him huskily.

'The circumstances are not entirely similar,' Benoît said softly. 'You weren't my wife then.'

'And you never intended to tell me how you're going to rescue Harry, whether I kissed you or not!' Angelica exclaimed, with remembered indignation. 'It was an underhand, dastardly. . .!'

Her protests faded as Benoît allowed his hand to trace the curve of her back. She was still propped up on her elbow, half leaning, half lying against him, and she could feel the play of muscles in his arms and chest as he explored her warm, vibrant body.

'I thought the action provided its own reward,' Benoît teased her gently. 'I certainly found it more satisfying to kiss you than to discuss tedious rescue plans.'

'Because you have a. . .secretive nature,' Angelica gasped, as his fingers investigated the soft, sensitive skin of her throat, just below the neckline of her nightgown. She was finding it increasingly difficult to think coherently.

Benoît chuckled softly.

'I don't think that's why,' he murmured, and drew her head down until her lips met his.

She melted against him, her hair falling around them like a curtain in the darkness. She was lost in a world of delicious sensations. Her hand still rested against his chest and she could feel the firm, rapid beat of his heart. His mouth was warm and almost languid against hers. She realised they had all the time in the world.

When at last she lifted her head, her lips were swollen with tender passion and her whole body glowed with fiery anticipation. She could hear his quickened breathing, and feel the rise and fall of his chest beneath her hand. The desire to touch him more intimately was irresistible, and she let her hand drift inquisitively across his torso. She was in no doubt now about the lean strength in his virile body. She bent and pressed a kiss against his chest.

Benoît caught his breath, uttering a soft, wordless exclamation, and rolled her onto her back.

Her heart leapt in sudden surprise, but then she was overwhelmed by new sensations of pleasure. She slipped her arms around his neck and lost herself in another long, deep, infinitely satisfying kiss.

There were dark shadows all around them. She was excitingly aware of the gentle weight of Benoît's upper body pressing her firmly into the bed. She ran her hand down his arm, feeling his biceps tense at her touch. She felt utterly secure in his embrace.

He kissed her throat and she let her head fall back against the pillow, arching her body towards him. His hand rested lightly on her waist, burning through the fabric of her nightgown as his lips explored the hollow at the base of her throat.

Then he reached down and began to ease up the hem of her nightdress.

A wave of intense, almost heart-stopping expectation swept over her. She gasped, hardly daring to breath at the first, electrifying touch of his hand on her naked leg. He let his fingers slip sensuously across the tingling flesh of her outer thigh; trailing them over her hip until his hand came to rest lightly on her stomach.

Her heart raced. Her world had shrunk until it was contained within the murmuring shadows of the sturdy fourposter bed; yet at the same time she felt as if she were soaring in a lofty, star-filled sky.

She murmured incoherently. She was full of wonder at the glorious sensations which consumed her, yet she was hungry for even greater fulfilment.

She rolled slightly towards him, her fingers pressing convulsively into the muscles of his shoulders. She felt his hand move against her burning, excited flesh, curving around her side as he continued his upward exploration. The soft material of her nightgown seemed almost harsh when it brushed against her sensitised skin as Benoît pushed it aside.

She lifted her hips instinctively to make it easier for him, then caught her breath as his hand cupped her throbbing breast. She closed her eyes, surrendering entirely to the glorious sensations he was arousing within her.

His strong fingers teased her taut nipple gently, stimulating currents of desire which seemed to spring from deep within the centre of her body. She breathed in quick, erratic gasps, conscious only of Benoît.

He moved against her, gently nudging her legs apart with his knee. The pressure of anticipation within Angelica became almost unbearable in its intensity. She hesitated, a brief, last-minute nervousness tightening her muscles. She could sense the wild, fierce energy in his lean body, and it half frightened her, half exhilarated her.

'Je t'aime,' he murmured and waited, softly kissing the corner of her swollen mouth and stroking her breast almost soothingly.

She realised he was holding his desire in check with ruthless self-control and she was overcome with a rush of tenderness as well as love towards him.

She relaxed, no longer resisting him. He lifted himself until he was poised above her, his elbows braced on either side of her body. Her heart pounded with excitement. She was intimately conscious of the arousal in his lean, taut body. She wrapped her arms around him, delighting in the play of muscles in his strong back.

She felt a few moments of gentle questing, and then a sharp pain which almost made her cry out. She clung to Benoît, digging her fingers into his shoulders, turning her head briefly aside. He kissed her cheek softly, almost reassuringly. She sighed as an entirely new and seductive warmth began to radiate through her body, and turned her head to meet his kiss with eager, responsive lips.

Her whole world was filled with the feel, taste and scent of her husband. She was aware of nothing but her love for him, and the infinite joy and pleasure it gave her to be in his arms, completely united with him.

The tempo of his movements began to quicken. She was borne away on a rhythm of almost primal intensity. Golden fire pulsated through her body, exploding the shadows around them with glorious flashes of light. She seemed to hover breathtakingly on the edge of a precipice, gazing up at the bright stars in the dark void above, not knowing what lay beyond—and then the morning sun rose, enveloping her in swirling, glowing colours and warm, vivid, deep satisfaction.

It seemed a long time later when she sighed contentedly and stirred in Benoît's arms.

'*Mon aimée?*' he murmured softly.

'Mm.' She pulled herself up to press a kiss against his cheek.

Then she relaxed to lie half across him, her fingers laced together so that she could rest her chin on the backs of her hands as she looked at him. The first pale light of dawn was creeping in through the uncurtained window, and she could see him quite clearly.

His black hair was dishevelled, but his lean, hawk-like face was more relaxed and contented than she had ever seen it. He was watching her quietly as he stroked her hair. There was a hint of humour, as well as a question in his brown eyes, but the wolf-wariness she was so used to was completely absent from his expression.

She smiled, luminous happiness and profound satisfaction glowing in her blue eyes.

'So this is married life,' she said musingly.

'Does it meet with your approval, *ma chérie*?' Benoît enquired softly, winding a lock of her hair around his finger.

Angelica hesitated, a teasing reply on her lips. Then her expression sobered as she realised her answer was more important to Benoît than his light-hearted manner made it seem.

'Oh, yes,' she replied, with heartfelt sincerity. 'Yes, my love, you know it does.'

She drew herself up so that she could kiss his lips, her hair falling around them like a cascade of gold in the morning light.

'And I thought you would be too tired after all your exertions of the past few days,' said Benoît, a few minutes later. 'That will teach me to underestimate you, won't it?'

Angelica laughed and propped herself up on her elbow. Benoît blew at an errant tendril of golden hair which was tickling his nose.

'I could never be too tired for you,' she declared, a reprehensible twinkle in her eyes. 'What are we going to do now?'

'Within the next hour or so, or within the next few days?' Benoît enquired, raising one black eyebrow humorously.

'The next few days,' Angelica clarified her question. She had a very good idea of what was likely to happen within the next few hours.

'Go back to Sussex.' Benoît caressed her shoulder absentmindedly, but he was looking past her, up into the shadows of the bed canopy.

'To see Papa?' Angelica asked.

'Partly.' He turned his head to meet her quiet eyes. 'I must also see Adam and do something about that gang of smugglers which is causing Sir William so many problems.'

Cold ripples of fear crawled down Angelica's spine at his words, but she remained completely still, determined not to let him sense her anxiety. She knew he would do whatever he believed he had to do. It wouldn't help him if he also had to worry about her reaction to his plans.

'How will you go about it?' she asked, trying to sound matter-of-fact.

Benoît smiled lopsidedly.

'No words of warning or disapproval?' he asked quizzically.

'It wouldn't make any difference, would it?' Angelica said breathlessly. 'Besides, I tried so hard to persuade you to rescue Harry. I'm hardly in a position to complain now.'

'But you are worried.'

'I'm trying not to be,' she assured him. 'How could you tell?'

'When you're lying so close to me? It wasn't difficult.'

'Oh.' Angelica lowered her eyes, biting her lip ruefully. 'What are you going to do?' she asked.

'I'm not sure,' he said slowly. 'The role of poacher-turned-gamekeeper is new to me. It sticks in my throat a little to hand them over to be hung and gibbeted — killers though they are. We shall have to see.'

Then he turned his head and smiled at her.

'I won't come to any harm,' he said confidently. 'And think of all the adventures we'll have when Harry is safely home and you sail with me.'

Angelica's face lit up.

'You'll really take me with you?' she exclaimed joyfully.

'I'm not leaving you behind!' said Benoît firmly. 'I'm a very generous man. If I'm soaked to the skin in a torrential rain storm I shall expect my wife to be likewise cold and wet. No more living in idle luxury for you, my lady! You are going to learn at first hand the tedium of being becalmed in mid-ocean, the inestimable frustration of—!'

He caught his breath and rolled away from her as Angelica moved her hand purposefully across his lean stomach.

She blinked in surprise at his emphatic response to her action. She had simply intended to distract him from his mock-solemn list of the discomforts awaiting her. But then she guessed the explanation for his reaction.

'You're ticklish!' she exclaimed in delight, reaching towards him again.

'It's a base lie!' He grabbed for her wrist, missed, then gasped, his body jackknifing, as she ran her fingers provocatively below his ribs.

'No! It's true!' She started to laugh as he seized her hands and rolled her neatly onto her back. 'Now what?' She looked up at him challengingly as he held both her wrists in a firm grip.

'I'm not sure.' He grinned down at her, sunlight warm on his cheek. 'We could call a truce.'

'Oh, no!' She shook her head gleefully, her hair spread out wantonly across the pillow. 'After all the times you've made fun of me, all the times you've seemed so cool and sophisticated and in control—and all I had to do to get my own back. . .'

She tried to pull her arms out of his grasp, a wicked expression in her blue eyes. He resisted her attempt to escape without difficulty.

'Don't worry, *mon amour*. . .' he transferred both her wrists into one hand, a hint of laughter in his voice '. . .you have always had far more subtle methods of wreaking your revenge on me.'

'So you've said before,' Angelica murmured, as he bent towards her, his lips brushing hers. 'But I'm sure none of them are quite so satisfying. . .'

'Positive?'

'Mmm.'

'*Angelica!*' The only reason Benoît didn't leap completely out of bed was because he was too tangled in the bedclothes.

She laughed uninhibitedly, feeling deliriously happy and unbelievably lucky.

'You're not safe to be near,' Benoît growled, keeping a wary distance, although there was an answering gleam of humour in his brown eyes. 'Very well, my lady, two can play at that game.'

He dragged back the bedclothes in one swift gesture and it was Angelica's turn to gasp. She reached out to pull down her nightgown, but he caught her hand.

'It's only getting in the way,' he said softly, the laughter in his eyes replaced by a far more intense emotion. 'Sit up.'

Angelica did so, feeling shy as she allowed him to draw it over her head and toss it away.

'*Ma belle,*' he murmured huskily, and kissed her shoulder.

'I'm going to have to practise my French,' she said unsteadily, as they sank back onto the bed.

She was truly naked in his arms now, and in the morning light there were no comforting shadows to hide them. But she didn't need to hide from Benoît. He was her husband and he loved her. Her brief moment of shyness passed.

'I shall take pleasure in teaching you, *mon aimée,*' he replied lightly, and then stiffened as she laid her hand on his ribs.

'Don't you trust me?' she whispered, meeting his eyes.

'No!' But he didn't try to stop her as she slipped her hand delicately over his side towards the flat plane of his stomach.

'I trusted you.' Their eyes were locked together and

a smiled tugged at the corners of Angelica's mouth as
she continued her deliberate caress.

'I know,' Benoît half groaned.

She could feel the tension in his body as he exerted
all his self-control not to jerk away from her hand.

'It can't be that bad,' she teased him, exhilarated by
the power he was allowing her to have over him. 'I
haven't done anything to make you jump.'

'It's not what you've done—it's what you might do!'
he retorted. 'I didn't expect my wife to startle me half
out of bed on our wedding night.'

Angelica giggled.

'And you don't want me to do it again?' she said
provocatively.

'I can think of more rewarding ways to pass our
time,' he replied softly.

Angelica hesitated. Her hand still rested gently
beneath his ribs. She had no real intention of torment-
ing him, but she couldn't help relishing the fact that
she had finally found a way of turning the tables on
him.

He chuckled.

'Make up your mind quickly, *mon ange*,' he recommended. 'We've a lot to do today. But before we
begin. . .'

She moved her hand carefully around his body to
his back and he exhaled with relief.

'I thought we'd already begun,' she murmured, her
eyes gleaming wickedly as she rubbed his back in slow,
sensuous circles.

'My error,' said Benoît hoarsely. 'You're quite right,
mon amour, we have!'

EPILOGUE

June 1809

THE tide was coming in. Lord Ellewood could hear it. He stood on the beach and listened to the waves rolling up the sand. He could hear the seabirds screeching overhead, and feel the hot June sun scorching his scarred cheek—but he could only imagine the glitter of sunlight on the sea.

The Earl had remained at the Manor House for more than three months, a difficult and uncomfortable guest for both Sir William and his household. He had shown no inclination to go back to London, yet he had refused point-blank to receive Angelica on the two occasions she had attempted to see him. The first time she had come with Benoît; the second time she had come alone. That had been more than two months ago.

The relentless passing of the lonely days gnawed at Lord Ellewood's soul. He had hoped that Angelica would make one more attempt to see him, but she had not—and he was too proud to go to her. The days passed, but time seemed to stand still. Until Benoît and Harry returned from France, life could not begin again for any of them.

Lord Ellewood lifted his head to taste the sea breeze. He didn't know what he was doing on the beach; he only knew he had been driven by a deep, compelling need to come back to the sea. He had ordered a frightened servant to bring him—but he had forbidden the man to follow him down over the pebbles to the sands.

Now he stood by himself, a stiff-backed, solitary figure, braced against a gale which did not blow; and wondered bleakly if the waiting was as agonising for Angelica as it was for him—and if his son would ever return home.

He clenched his fists together in anger, frustration, and shame. He was bitterly ashamed of his behaviour over the past two years—but it was hard to bow his head and make amends. The harsh, discordant cries of the seagulls suited his mood. The hot summer sunshine on his cheek seemed incongruous. There was no harmony left in his life.

He heard boots crunching on the pebbles behind him and swung round furiously on the approaching servant. Dear God! Did he no longer have any authority even over a groom?

'I told you to stay away from me,' he snarled viciously. 'I'll summon you when I want you!'

'You already did,' came Benoît's cool, soft voice. 'Four months ago. Good afternoon, my lord.'

Lord Ellewood was shocked into silence: plunged back sixteen years to the last time Benoît's voice had come to him out of the darkness on these beaches.

The Earl had not been able to see his opponent then, and he could not do so now—but this time no dawn light would reveal Benoît's features to him. It was the final, damning confirmation of all he had lost, and everything he would never be again.

He held his body rigid, tense with conflicting emotions, as he struggled to master himself.

'Harry?' he grated at last, his anxiety for his son finally overriding every other concern.

'Is safely home,' said Benoît calmly. 'He's a brave, resourceful lad. I'm sure he'd have managed without my help—but it didn't hurt to expedite things a little.'

The knots of fear slowly eased from Lord

Ellewood's muscles and he sighed, his square shoulders slumping slightly in pure relief.

'Where is he?' he demanded. 'Why hasn't he come to me?' A new spark of fear ignited within him. 'Is he injured?'

'No. He's with Angelica,' said Benoît equably.

Lord Ellewood's expression darkened.

'Have you turned my son against me—as well as my daughter?' he asked acidly.

'I've turned no one against you,' Benoît replied coldly. 'Certainly not Angelica. How many times do you intend to rebuff her before your pride is assuaged, my lord? Or have you indeed disowned her?'

'Damn your—'

'*No!*' Benoît's icy voice sliced across the first rumblings of Lord Ellewood's anger like a knife. 'Save your curses. They earn my contempt—not my respect. Did you lose your backbone as well as your eyes when the coach overturned?'

The scorn in Benoît's tone, even more than his words, stabbed straight to the Earl's heart, striking with the freezing, bitter intensity of a winter frost, completing the work Lord Ellewood's self-disgust had already begun.

The Earl dragged in several painful, sobbing breaths. He no longer felt the hot summer sun blazing down on his body. He was lost in a black, barren world of his own. His darkest, innermost fear had been hurled in his face with uncompromising directness by a man he could not help but respect.

For two years he had been driven by rage; but now he had worn out his anger, and he had nothing left with which to replace it. For a moment he felt utterly desolate.

But Benoît's words had had the force of a challenge. And Lord Ellewood suddenly realised that the cost of refusing to meet it was more than he was prepared to pay. He released his breath in a long sigh. His inner battle had left him empty and drained of emotion.

'You must despise me,' he said tonelessly.

'No,' said Benoît quietly. 'I pray to God I will never be set the same challenge.'

'Are you not the one who told me—on this very beach—that you'd rather try, and fail, than live knowing you'd never had the courage to try at all?' Lord Ellewood asked sharply. 'No wonder I've earned your contempt.'

'I was young and arrogant,' said Benoît, a hint of apology in his tone. 'I wouldn't have the gall to repeat those words now. Will you walk with me?'

'Do I have a choice?' Lord Ellewood enquired, with a flicker of resigned humour. 'The field is yours, sir. It's time I attempted to preserve my dignity at least.'

He allowed Benoît to take his hand and tuck it through his arm, and they began to stroll along the tideline. They were much of a height and their strides were of similar length. The Earl found it surprisingly easy to keep pace with his companion.

'I think you'll find you've retained more than that,' said Benoît quietly. 'It wasn't for your swordsmanship I respected you sixteen years ago.'

Lord Ellewood drew in a sharp breath.

'Angelica must hate me,' he said bleakly, with uncharacteristic openness. The events of the past few minutes had shaken him out of his usual reserve.

'No. She never even came close to doing so,' Benoît replied, without hesitation.

'I thought she would come again, but she didn't,' said the Earl, following his own train of thought. 'I thought she would come again...and next time I would have—' He broke off. 'Next time isn't good enough in this uncertain world,' he said bitterly. 'I should know that by now—if you delay, next time may never come.'

'It will come,' said Benoît, with the quiet assurance Lord Ellewood remembered from sixteen years before.

They paced on in silence for a few moments, then the Earl roused himself from his introspection.

'Harry's safe, you say?' he said gruffly, although he didn't doubt Benoît had told him the truth.

'Angelica says he's thinner than he was, but otherwise he's completely irrepressible,' Benoît replied humorously.

'But he didn't come to find me,' said Lord Ellewood flatly. He had been hurt by that omission. 'Does he also despise me for what I've done? If I were in his shoes—'

'I asked him to wait,' Benoît interrupted equably. 'I had an axe of my own to grind first, my lord. But have no doubt—Harry is as eager to see you as Angelica.'

They took several more steps in silence.

'What do you want of me?' the Earl asked discordantly.

He felt raw, and painfully exposed to the contempt he was sure Benoît felt towards him. It was a measure of his real courage that he had accepted the need to have this conversation at all.

'I want nothing,' said Benoît quietly. 'Angelica would like to have her father back, I think.'

The Earl stopped walking abruptly. He turned his ravaged face towards the sea, away from Benoît.

'I've re-employed Hargreaves,' he said harshly, after a very long silence.

'I know,' said Benoît. 'So does Angelica. She's very happy.'

'*Stupid!*' Lord Ellewood exclaimed suddenly, referring to the absent secretary. 'He should *never* have let her outmanoeuvre him! But he never failed me before, and I can't hold him entirely to blame. She's as stubborn as a mule!'

'It's a family characteristic,' said Benoît mildly. 'Do you still blame Angelica for what *she* did?'

'She disobeyed me!' said Lord Ellewood gratingly.

'You prize obedience above all other virtues?' Benoît enquired softly.

'*No!* Damn you!' Lord Ellewood snapped. 'But in my daughter. . .'

'You left her with the impression that I was a disreputable smuggler,' Benoît pointed out. 'You must have known it wasn't true. Angelica had no difficulty finding me, and I've only owned Holly House for the past three years! In the circumstances—knowing as little about me as she did—it was inevitable she would want to confirm my integrity. You'd have done exactly the same thing in her position.'

Lord Ellewood swallowed a hasty retort.

'I didn't want her to get foolishly romantic notions about you,' he said grittily, almost as if he were speaking against his will. 'A rich, handsome, adventurous shipowner—she's been desperate to travel for years—and far more restless over the past few months.' He grunted sardonically. 'My petty-mindedness backfired on me, didn't it?'

'She was certainly very suspicious of me when she arrived,' said Benoît reflectively. 'Practically the first thing she asked me was whether the brandy I was offering her was smuggled.'

The Earl gave a crack of unexpected laughter.

'She must have inherited her tact from me,' he observed dryly.

He hesitated, then reached into his pocket and drew out two letters which he held out towards Benoît.

'My lord?'

'You recognise them, I'm sure,' said the Earl ironically. 'Your messenger delivered them to me on the day you were married. Poor fellow rode himself into the ground to get them to me. Take them.'

Benoît did so, noticing that the seals were still unbroken.

'I couldn't bring myself to ask William to read them to me, and there was no one else,' said Lord Ellewood distantly. 'I want to know what Angelica said.'

'You could ask her.'

'No! I want to hear what she wrote to me then,' said the Earl harshly.

'Very well.' Benoît glanced shrewdly at Lord Ellewood, then broke the seal and quickly scanned the letter. He smiled faintly, and began to read aloud.

'Dear Papa, you will be glad to learn that I have safely delivered your letter to Mr Faulkener. I arrived yesterday afternoon, when he was away from home, but his mother made me very comfortable while I waited for him. She remembered you from your previous visits to Sussex—'

'Determined to make it sound like an ordinary social call!' the Earl interrupted scornfully. 'As though that could make it any better.'

Benoît grinned and carried on reading.

'When I met Mr Faulkener I was relieved to discover that, to all appearances, he is a very respectable gentleman—'

'Ha!' the Earl exclaimed.

'I am sure he has both the ability and the means to rescue Harry. He has indeed agreed to do so. Unfortunately, he will not tell me when or how he intends to set about it. I confess I am a trifle disturbed by his reticence because we do know so little about him—'

'Hoist by my own petard,' said Lord Ellewood fatalistically.

'However, I did have the great good fortune to see your old friend Sir William Hopwood this morning, and he appears to be well acquainted with Mr Faulkener. It seems a pity to leave before I have taken this opportunity to discover more about him, so I will return to London tomorrow. I am sorry that I left without discussing my plans with you, but we had an uneventful journey yesterday and Martha and John Coachman have taken good care of me. With all my love, Angelica.'

Benoit folded the letter and put it back into Lord Ellewood's hand.

'Thank you.' The Earl weighed it for a few seconds in his fingers. 'I would have been infuriated by her impertinence if I'd received this in London,' he remarked.

'I don't think that was her intention,' Benoît replied quietly.

'No. I know.' Lord Ellewood returned the letter to his pocket. 'William hasn't said anything about meeting her at Holly House before their encounter in Littlehampton,' he said curiously.

'They didn't meet face to face,' Benoît explained, smiling faintly. 'She overheard Sir William accusing me of being a dastardly smuggler and a traitor to England into the bargain. That's why she stayed in Sussex. She thought I might sell Harry back to the French. And why she followed me when I went to meet Adam.'

There was a further silence while Lord Ellewood absorbed that information.

He could hear the waves lapping gently on the sands beside them, and he could remember the glittering expanse of the beach that stretched out before them. There was a little less pain in that memory now than there had been.

'No, that's not why,' he said at last. 'I know my daughter better than that, and I believe I know you better than that. She didn't think you were a traitor. But it doesn't matter now, she's your wife.'

'Yes, she is,' said Benoît.

'You'll take better care of her than I can,' said Lord Ellewood harshly.

'I'll take care of her,' said Benoît quietly.

'Where is she?' Lord Ellewood demanded.

'About a hundred yards away.'

'What?' The Earl was very shaken.

'You don't think she'd have let me come alone, do you?' Benoît asked quizzically. 'She and Harry both. We followed you from the Manor, but I wanted to talk to you first. They've been waiting with the horses.'

'My God!' Lord Ellewood drew in a deep, unsteady breath. 'I didn't expect that. Harry as well, you say? My God!'

'They'll come when I signal to them,' said Benoît. 'And I'll do that when you give me the word.'

'No more ambushes, hey?' Lord Ellewood tried to inject a note of liveliness into his voice. 'That seems to be my destiny on these beaches, doesn't it? To walk in darkness and run blindly on my fate.'

'Not necessarily,' said Benoît calmly.

'My God! I hope if you and Angelica have children they inherit *your* tact!' Lord Ellewood exclaimed forcefully. 'Why don't you just tell me I've made my own darkness these past two years?'

Benoît chuckled.

'That *would* be impertinent, wouldn't it?' he observed. 'I think your own children are getting rather impatient, my lord. May I. . .?'

'Yes, yes,' said Lord Ellewood hastily.

They began to walk back along the beach. The Earl listened intently for sounds of Angelica and Harry's approach. Then he heard quickly running feet.

'Angelica?'

'Papa.' She flung her arms around him.

Lord Ellewood hesitated fractionally, then embraced his daughter stiffly. It was still so hard to unbend.

But it was even harder not to respond to her. He felt her sunny curls beneath his harsh cheek, and suddenly he was hugging her so tightly she thought her ribs might crack. He had been afraid he might never hold her in his arms again.

'Harry's home, Papa.' She lifted her head to look at him.

The Earl grunted, not trusting himself to speak. He lifted his hand almost tentatively, and felt the tears which stained her cheeks.

'Of course he is,' he said gruffly. 'Do you really think I'd entrust my son's life to an incompetent jackass? Well, where's Harry, by God?'

'Here, sir.' Lord Lennard came forward, grinning broadly.

His likeness to Angelica was unmistakable. His unruly curls were almost angelic in their golden fairness, and his blue eyes were as clear and lucid as hers. But his debt to his father was also clearly apparent. He was thin-faced and sallow from months of hardship, but there was no doubting the determination in his firm jaw, or the vigour in his long-limbed body.

Lord Ellewood gripped his son's shoulder fiercely.

'Good lad,' he said roughly. 'You've seen some sport since you were last home, I'll be bound. You must tell me all about it.'

'Yes, sir!' said Harry enthusiastically.

'I look forward to it.' The Earl shook Harry back and forwards a couple of times to emphasise his words. Then he turned his attention back to Angelica.

'No more books for you,' he said abruptly. 'No more books for me, either. I've been talking to Adam

Kennett. He plays a damned good game of chess! He won't tell me how he managed to get himself wounded, but he *has* told me about the tricks Faulkener's groom teaches his horses. So I was thinking—how hard can it be to ride along an empty beach?'

Angelica stared at her father in amazement, then turned to look at Benoît. He grinned.

'I'll talk to Thomas immediately, my lord,' he promised.

'Good! We've wasted enough time,' said Lord Ellewood briskly. He hesitated. 'I've been following your husband's career for years,' he said gruffly to Angelica. 'You've made an excellent choice, girl. I'm proud of you! Harry!' he continued before Angelica could respond.

'Yes, sir.'

'Walk me down the beach,' the Earl commanded. 'I want to hear all about *your* adventures now!'

Angelica turned to Benoît as her father and brother strode away. Tears of happiness and relief sparkled in her eyes as he took her in his arms.

'I'm so happy,' she whispered. 'After all these months of waiting, you've come home—and Papa. . .' her voice was temporarily suspended. 'I didn't mean to cry,' she murmured, leaning her head against his broad shoulder.

Benoît smiled, stroking her golden curls gently.

'I'm not complaining, *mon aimée*,' he said softly. 'I think my impatience to get home was greater than Harry's! I've never left a wife behind before. It's an experience I intend to avoid in the future!'

Angelica gave a watery chuckle.

'I'll hold you to that,' she assured him, and sighed contentedly, happy simply to be in his arms.

The past few months had been very hard. She had

done her best not to worry about Benoît and Harry, but it hadn't been easy.

And all the time she had known her father was only a few miles away, enduring exactly the same anxiety, but refusing even to speak to her. There had been so many occasions when she'd longed to talk to him; but she hadn't visited him a third time because she hadn't been able to bear the possibility that he might reject her yet again.

But now she was here on the sunlit beach with her husband, and the Earl had said he was proud of her.

She lifted her head and looked at Benoît. His brown eyes gleamed with the familiar half-teasing, wholly loving expression as they smiled into hers. His black hair glinted in the sunshine, but his lean, watchful face was relaxed and unguarded. The wolf within him slept.

She touched his cheek with gentle fingers, then slipped her arms around his neck, drawing his head down to hers.

'I am so glad you're home,' she murmured. 'I missed you so much.'

He kissed her gently, and then with growing passion. The blue sky arched above them, and only the lightest of summer breezes tugged at Angelica's skirt. It was hard to remember how bleak and desolate the sea-shore could be—and the pitched battles which had been fought here.

'Hmm,' said Benoît rather hoarsely, some time later. 'I think I've mentioned before the hazards of going out in public with you, my lady!'

Angelica started to laugh from pure joy, and a second later he was laughing with her. He picked her up and swung her exuberantly round on the shining sands, while seabirds rose, protesting, above them.

'Faulkener!'

Benoît set Angelica down on her feet again and they turned to see Lord Ellewood striding towards them. Angelica tensed instinctively. It was a long time since she had seen her father move so purposefully, but then she saw Harry was grinning and she relaxed.

'Faulkener!'

'Yes, my lord,' Benoît responded, his hand still on Angelica's waist.

'William's been telling me tales about a villainous gang of smugglers that were terrorising the country-side a few months ago,' said the Earl energetically. 'He said he found it impossible to obtain any solid evidence against them. Everyone was too frightened to talk. Then one day the three ringleaders vanished and the whole thing fell apart.'

'Really, my lord?' Benoît said politely.

He drew Angelica back to lean against him, slipping his arms loosely around her waist from behind, and looked at the Earl over the top of her head.

'So I understand,' said Lord Ellewood briskly. 'Hopwood's been going around in a state of thwarted curiosity for the past three months. He almost came to blows with Kennett the other day when Adam swore he didn't know anything about it!'

'Dear me,' said Benoît mildly. 'Why should he suppose Adam knows anything about it?'

'Because you're as thick as thieves?' Lord Ellewood suggested dryly.

He laughed suddenly, startling and delighting Angelica because it was so long since she'd seen her father in such a good humour.

'Now you're back, you can indulge *my* curiosity,' he said pleasantly. 'In lieu of asking for permission to marry my daughter. What the devil *did* you do with those murderous brutes, Faulkener?'

Angelica twisted in Benoît's arms to glance up at him. A twinkle of shared amusement passed between them, then Benoît glanced from Harry to Lord Ellewood and grinned.

'They suffered the same fate you once suggested for me, my lord,' he said matter-of-factly, but with a hint of amusement in his voice. 'I had them pressed into the navy.'

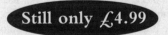
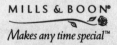